D1395374

HERMIT

HERMIT

S. R. WHITE

First published in 2020 by
HEADLINE PUBLISHING GROUP

1

Cataloguing in Publication Data is available from the British Library

Hardback ISBN 978 1 4722 6841 9
Trade paperback ISBN 978 1 4722 6844 0

Typeset in 11/15.25 pt Adobe Garamond Pro by Jouve (UK), Milton Keynes

Printed and bound in Great Britain by Clays Ltd, Elcograf S.p.A.

Headline's policy is to use papers that are natural, renewable and recyclable products and made from wood grown in well-managed forests and other controlled sources. The logging and manufacturing processes are expected to conform to the environmental regulations of the country of origin.

HEADLINE PUBLISHING GROUP
An Hachette UK Company
Carmelite House
50 Victoria Embankment
London EC4Y 0DZ

www.headline.co.uk
www.hachette.co.uk

This book is dedicated to my mother,
Patricia, a woman of letters and
language her whole life

Chapter 1

In the purple pre-dawn: the ink-black pools and white spray of Pulpit Falls. Dana Russo was here on this morning each year, and it always seemed the same. Never rained, never snowed. Bruised and sullen, every time.

She could easily climb over this flimsy fence. Two strands of wire threaded between rudimentary wooden posts. It was nothing, would only take a second. She wouldn't have to jump, really. She could just fall.

Maybe that would be better. Dana knew about trajectories: it was part of her job. If she landed on the middle rock – the one splitting two churning arcs of swift water – they'd understand it was deliberate. She'd have died in a manner that would demand close scrutiny. It would oblige them to sift through her life, looking for the explanation. Her emails and private documents, the contents of her safe, her diary. Everything would be exposed and picked over. She'd be dead, and then sliced open. Dana knew how far investigations could burrow; the kind of stones they turned over.

Whereas if her head struck the nearside bank, cleaving open her skull in a single strike, it might be considered an accident. There had been a lot of rain recently, and then this icy spell, so the edge was brittle. They might think her stupid or foolhardy, but they couldn't prove she'd meant it. Perhaps then, they'd have less reason to pilfer the remains of her life and hold them up to the light.

A cold breeze slapped her face. Below her, a hawk skimmed the surface of the calmer water downstream. She watched its careless, immaculate wheeling and heard a keening cry through the misty air. Eucalypts on the far shore hissed; the blustery chill made her eyes water.

This was her Day. The day Dana granted herself full permission to think about all this; to examine it and ask if she found herself wanting. Each day through the year she kept it as locked down and hidden away as she could. Often, she failed. She failed because while the threat and the shame kept its strength, she waxed and waned: she was the variable. It was her reaction that stumbled frequently – she drifted with good days and bad, triumphs and disappointments, strong and weak. She tried to contain it adequately by allowing it one day of total freedom. For this Day alone, she deliberately and overtly questioned from every angle if she wished to live another year. If she was still asking at midnight, the contract was made: she would try to carry on until the next Day.

Last year she'd sat with the engine ticking over, safety belt unbuckled, staring at a large tree near her house. She'd fretted that the road wasn't straight enough to gather a killer speed: she could ram into it, but she might still be alive afterwards.

Now she was shivering in an empty car park. She stepped back from the edge and squatted, hidden from any dog-walkers or joggers, her back uncomfortable against the car's radiator grille.

This place – already a wound in her mind. Her memory reeled and spun, back to an identical day that changed her life. Being found at the foot of the falls would invite comparisons, make people reach for connections.

So she couldn't jump. But she knew how to shoot.

Dana closed her eyes and counted to five. She held her revolver in both hands; it juddered as she struggled for breath. The barrel felt sharp on the roof of her mouth. It grazed and nuzzled, begging for the chance to release her. The trigger pressure on this weapon was hefty, but her thumbs squeezed consistently. Saliva oozed silently down to the grip.

Up: she must point up. She knew this. Shifting herself a little against the car, adjusting her posture, the memories skidded past her. Even though she fought to rein them in, they started to pulse faster, became subliminal. She closed her eyes again, squeezed a little more, feeling the trigger mould a groove in her thumbs. A silent tear caressed her cheek.

All Dana had to do was move her thumb a centimetre. Then it would be over. She'd never have to think about it again. There would be no more recriminations; no more hours glaring at her reflection, daring herself to own what she'd done. She'd never have to wake up again with a feeling of dread already drenching her. There must be something better, beyond this. If only she could do it. If only she had the courage. If only—

She could feel the phone vibrate despite her thick jacket. She hesitated, blinked hard and swallowed. The ringtone wouldn't go away.

Dana hid when she could from loud noises, from bright lights, from squealing children and yapping dogs; from sentiment and kindness, from impatience and arrogance. She needed the flat line of quiet consistency. Usually she struggled through much of it beyond the gaze of others. Especially on this Day, she had nothing to give, and every moment since midnight she'd been a beat away from snapping. The pressure it created was volcanic, irresistible.

The ringtone still wouldn't go away.

The gun bumped against her lip, numbing it on contact. Dana glanced at it, put the safety on and holstered. On her forehead was a cooling sheen of sweat; she felt clammy and nauseous under her coat.

She stood uneasily and leaned against the car. In the windscreen's reflection she loomed across the convex glass, pallid and desperate. Swearing, she fished out the phone and swiped.

'Yes?'

'Dana?'

Neither of them could hear above the roar of the waterfall. 'Hold on,' she shouted, and climbed into the car. Closing the door silenced the siren call of her pain. All she could make out now was her own stuttering breath. 'Yes?'

'Dana, glad I got you.' Bill Meeks, her boss. 'We have a dead body. Sending you the route. It's kinda hard to find if you've never been there . . . Dana?'

She wasn't ready. Wasn't up to doing that. Her hand was shaking; she dropped her keys. 'Isn't Mikey on call?'

There was a pause. Did she come across as irritable, unprofessional? Why should she care either way? She wasn't first on call today.

'Yeah, he's had to go to Earlville Mercy. His kid: stomach pains. You're next cab off the rank. See you in twenty.'

He was gone before she could grunt any kind of reply. She looked back at the fence, and the void.

Someone just kept her alive, by dying.

Something didn't want her gone. Not yet.

Chapter 2

Jensen's Store was down a rutted track about two hundred metres off the Old Derby Road, between Carlton and Earlville. Surrounded by tall pines, its solitude and serenity meant it made little sense as a commercial venture – there was no road frontage; the sign for it was half obscured by undergrowth and unlit. If Dana hadn't been following instructions on the phone, she'd have overshot. Behind the building, forest stretched away gauzily.

The building itself was a lazily designed flatroof; wilfully utilitarian, it had a short overhang on a frontage that was mainly glass, speckled with fluoro-coloured posters of special offers. The parking area to the side was simply gravel and mud, mixed by spinning wheels and crunching boots. It was rutted and slippery in the despondent winter.

The emergency vehicles were parked herringbone along the approach lane: the area around the store was being tracked by a single-file line of uniforms, treading slowly as they scoured the frozen soil. The sun was above the horizon, but obscured below lingering mist which billowed lazily through the trees and gave everything a grey, ethereal wash. The occasional ghost gum stood out, a sharp vertical sliver like pristine flesh. Ferns glinted silently with crystalline frost.

To one side, two paramedics gazed at the gloom and drew testily on cigarettes. Their green smocked uniform had short sleeves; one seemed oblivious to the damp chill, the other yanked on the zip of a red puffa jacket. The hardier of them gave a raised-head acknowledgement as Dana passed; she couldn't place him but nodded back in any case. Aside from the search team, she and Bill were the only cops available for now.

She snapped on some gloves at the entrance, where a wire basket offered two-for-one on rubber-soled deck shoes. When she started as a police officer, putting on latex gloves was a cop or a medical thing: now everyone did it, even if they were only heating a pastry. She checked her boots, tapping off some mud from her waterfall visit, and covered them with plastic booties that swished as she crossed the aisle. Reflexively, she looked for cameras: one over the checkout counter, and that seemed it for the interior. Maybe there were others hidden.

The police incident code had been 'response to silent alarm', so she knew that much. Little else. The alarm was one of those that covered the perimeter of the building, not internal movement. By the first aisle was a pinboard of local notices – grass-cutting services, a wooden aviary free to a good home and a ratty-looking old Ford Falcon to be gutted for spares. Above this, a gallery of the regular staff, who were all 'looking forward to helping you'.

As she reached the third aisle, staff from the medical examiner's office came into view, holding the stretcher. The two bearers had the same red hair and freckled faces, similar bloodless lips and consumptive countenance. She thought they might be twins and considered this an odd kind of family occupation. They paused automatically when they reached her, looking stoically up and forward to nowhere while she peeled back the zip on the body bag.

The victim's face was puffy but looked oddly contented. The serenity of dead people never ceased to amaze Dana. Even those who'd suffered violent, lingering or painful demises: they all took on a repose of quiet satisfaction, as if a job well done. Somehow, in a small way, it gave her hope. They usually looked . . . pleasantly asleep.

The victim was maybe late thirties, and shaven-headed. His skull was broad at the forehead, giving him a massive and tipped-forward look even when horizontal. He was absurdly tall, with a large, bear-like jaw, and the collar of his T-shirt was ripped on one shoulder. With the body bag zip further back, Dana could see the entry wound. Just one, it looked like. No hesitation marks she could see, no splatter. The bleeding would all be internal. A smallish rose of dried blood on the T-shirt surrounding it and some smeared and bloody finger marks. Maybe a palm, too.

She guessed a blade of fifteen centimetres – it would need to be that long to pass the ribs and enter a major organ. Sometimes, only one wound spoke to expertise but frequently it was blind luck. In a melee of two people grappling for their lives there was little time or space to be forensic. The attacker might have stabbed purely to get the victim off them, or get away, or make them stop. Few people wielded a knife accurately – their efforts were often wild and desperate.

She zipped up carefully. 'Thank you,' she said quietly. The 'twins' headed for the door in lockstep.

Around the corner, Bill crouched by some blood droplets. There were several packets of rice behind him which had dropped from a shelf without breaking open. That appeared to be the extent of the physical evidence. A minor clean-up in aisle three: on a par with a kid spilling some chocolate milk. Even one pint of blood looked like a serial-killer rampage if it was sprayed around in a struggle; this was maybe ten drops.

Because of the solitary stab wound, Dana had expected the knife to be on the floor. A single stab in panic, in the midst of a scuffle, usually prompted the stabber to drop the blade and flee. At the very least, they let go in shock at what they'd done, or in disbelief that the person in front of them was dying. That didn't seem to have happened here.

Bill glanced up. He would have been handsome when younger. In fact, she'd seen pictures of him up to his forties when he was exactly that. It was as if he'd signed a Faustian pact: breath-taking until mid-life, then your face will collapse. He looked almost a travesty of what he once was and she sometimes wondered – as someone who'd never experienced one – what it was like to have a definable golden era behind you, a period when your whole life glowed and others basked in it. Perhaps the juxtaposition was painful, or maybe it was comforting to have been something significant, once.

'Hey, Dana. Sorry to take your day off you.'

She nodded non-committally, unsure exactly how much Bill knew about her motivation for taking this day off work each year. He knew it was an important date – half the station knew that much – but she didn't know if his knowledge went beyond that.

Best not to ask. Best to avoid.

'One stab wound,' she noted.

'Suspect is headed to the station. Knife is still someplace unknown – we'll need a detailed finger search of the store, and maybe the undergrowth within throwing range. Unless the killer departed and took it with them. Patrol responded to a silent alarm linked to the station.'

'A professional?'

Bill hefted himself up and rubbed the base of his spine. 'I only saw our suspect briefly. No ID, nothing obviously incriminating. Couldn't get a word out of him except his name. Nathan Whittler? Ring any bells for you? Nah, me neither. But, uh, dishevelled and disorganised at best. Could be a serial killer, for all we know. But no, I doubt he's a hitman.'

'Hmmm.' Having nailed one last year, she didn't believe *professional killer* meant anything beyond financial payment. That hitman had been an idiot, in a dozen different ways. But he'd been paid to do it.

Bill stretched out a kink in his back. 'Dead man is Lou Cassavette, the store owner. There's a sleeping bag, a home-electronics mag and some Chiko Rolls in the storeroom by the freezer section. Looks like he was waiting up for someone.'

'Hmmm, breakfast of champions. CCTV? I saw the camera by the checkout, but' – she glanced up and down the aisle – 'I'm guessing we're out of luck here.'

'Yeah, only one other camera, in the storeroom. Overlooks the food-prep area out the back.' Bill schlepped off a glove and scratched his forehead.

Dana took out a torch to see the blood drops more clearly. There was no way her kneecap would let her crouch down. 'Mr Cassavette didn't trust his own staff. He watched if they were dipping the till; he watched if they were spitting in the food. So maybe the suspect is an employee, or ex-employee?'

Bill nodded. 'Way ahead of ya. I've got Luce checking for employment records as we speak. See these?' He pointed at the bloodspot trail and she swung the torchlight back on them.

She followed the pathway with a silver beam. 'Half of them in one place – where he was stabbed? Then he fell, or staggered, back a couple of paces, then they stop.'

'That's how I see it,' Bill replied. 'Stabbed here . . . fell back to here . . . and either he or someone else clamped something on the wound to stop the flow.'

'Does our suspect have any blood on him?'

Bill stood again and smiled. 'Oh, yeah. He has blood on his hands. Bent over the guy, hand pushed against the wound.'

'Burglary gone wrong?'

Bill waved at a corner of the store. 'Looks like he climbed in through that window over there. Professional, too. Put a bag on the windowsill so there'd be no marks, and bags on his shoes, too. He had a rucksack full of loot, but . . .'

Dana had reached the end of the aisle and could see the entry point.

She scanned the floor less for prints, more for detritus like leaves or burrs; but there was nothing. The guy had entered smoothly and professionally, like he'd done it a hundred times before.

She turned back. 'But?'

'See for yourself. Weird.' Bill pointed at a red rucksack to her left. It was well worn but still in good shape – in the gathering daylight she noted fresh dubbin recently applied to the seams. Through the open top she could see several paperbacks and two packs of mosquito repellent. Prising past these with a pen, she saw cans of beans and some chocolate bars. The rest was lost in the bowels of the rucksack. She'd get a full inventory later.

She ducked her head around the corner as Bill took out his phone. 'Why was he stealing this? He could buy all this for next to nothing.'

'Exactly. Why kill for that? Why *be killed* for that?' Bill shrugged his shoulders and turned away to dial.

Dana took a glance back towards the exit and the preceding aisles. A couple of mountain bikes would be worth several thousand; she imagined fishing rods weren't cheap. There were cigarettes for sale behind the counter, but they were secured by a roller door as per the law: she hadn't seen any in the rucksack. The burglar seemed professional enough to enter seamlessly but amateur enough to steal cheap, largely unsellable items. The owner appeared ready to die for a minor point of principle – for stuff that wouldn't even register on his insurance premium.

Halfway down the next aisle, splayed across the tiles, a packet of kitchen knives lay at an angle. The plastic lid had been ripped and one knife was missing. It seemed, from the indentation in the packaging, about the right size. She heard a murmur of Bill's conversation, then his farewell to whoever.

'Hey, Bill,' she called over the top of the shelving. 'Killer didn't bring his own weapon?'

Bill leaned around the corner. 'Yeah, looks pretty ad hoc, doesn't it? Assuming that gap in the packaging turns out to be the weapon.'

She looked more carefully at the way the lid was ripped. It was still creased from the guy's grip: rushed, but not frenzied. She wondered briefly why whoever did it had taken the third-longest knife and not the biggest one. Surely he would have wanted the best weapon he could get if the attack was spontaneous? And what had Cassavette done to make him feel he had to attack?

'Did Cassavette have a weapon?'

Bill rocked his hand. 'Maybe. Haven't found one for him either. When Forensics get here they'll search the whole place. But nothing yet.'

She realised she was wasting battery and switched off the torch. Golden light was now spearing in through the skylights on the eastern side of the building, glittering off the visible silver insulation in the ceiling. She could see cobwebs in the corners. Refrigerators hummed. The whole tone of the place was upbeat and direct – buy now, try this, grab one of these, limited time offer. All the colours on the walls, the packaging, the posters and special offers; they were lurid candy and cartoonish. Lonely, desperate homicide was a counterpoint.

'So . . .' Dana scuffed a foot against a kick plate below the shelving. 'Guy comes in, ready to steal some beans, apparently. Gets halfway through; Cassavette makes himself known.' She turned and went to the end of the aisle, pointing with the torch. 'That's our man's escape route. I'm guessing all the doors were locked.'

'Yup, and the lights were off. Someone opened the mains box and shut the power off before they came in.' Bill joined her near a display of toys for kids of all ages. 'Patrol switched it back on after they found the suspect and the body.'

'This place doesn't have back-up generators?' Most did these days; the cost of replacing stock after an outage was horrendous.

'They do, but they're only wired to the freezers and refrigeration.'

Dana nodded. 'So it's totally dark. Cassavette comes out of his hidey-hole over there; the burglar's only way out is back through the window he used. You have to assume Cassavette – either deliberately or accidentally – blocked the escape.'

'Logical. He's clearly been waiting up nights expecting a burglary; he figures help's on its way because the silent alarm was activated when the window opened. All he has to do is contain the guy until the cavalry arrives.' Bill went to the window and looked out at the parked vehicles. The uniforms were trooping back to three marked Commodores, disconsolate.

'Yes. So why would the burglar go crazy? I mean, he looks like a pro – the forensic awareness, the very particular choice of what to steal. That isn't random, it's planned. So if he's a pro and it's all gone a little wrong, why fight your way out? Why so desperate?'

'Maybe he's on two strikes and this will send him away for a while?' Bill turned back to face her and held his palms open. 'I dunno. First sweep of the databases might tell us.' There was a crunching of gravel outside. 'Ah, proper search team.'

'He was completely silent about what happened?' asked Dana as they headed for the door.

'He hasn't said a word, as far as I know.' Bill waved to Stuart Risdale, the head of the search team, who gave the thumbs-up as two others disgorged themselves from a darkened SUV. 'Check that. The guy repeated one word.'

Bill turned to face Dana as the freezing air hit them from the doorway.

'Guy said, "Sorry." Several times.'

Chapter 3

It was fourteen minutes' gentle drive from Jensen's Store, down a series of backroads, to the Cassavette house on the outskirts of Earlville. Dana had time to find a classical-music station on the way.

Earlville was considered the less prosperous of the 'twin towns'. It had a sneering, fractious relationship with Carlton; a kind of sibling rivalry between orphans. Marooned in a region of forests, swamps and lakes, the two towns were merely background noise for city dwellers three hours away. Earlville thought Carlton was full of snobs and the wasting of public money; Carlton thought Earlville should give up its nostalgia for low-paid sweat jobs and join the modern world.

Most of the properties along the route were large 'lifestyle blocks': homes set back among the gums and myrtle, surrounded by pony paddocks. Faux-hacienda, with terracotta tiles replacing Colourbond, seemed the look *du jour*. Well-tended horses chewed thoughtfully near the road, steam rising gently from blanketed flanks. Twice she saw puffing teenagers hoisting tack on to a shoulder. Maybe the first thing in their adolescent lives they'd shown consistent sacrifice for; perhaps that was why their parents indulged it.

Many homes on this road had ostentatious stone entrances; Dana could tell which ones had electric gates, too. She'd noticed a while ago that shuttering off the outside world – and thus implying that everyone was a threat – was something that had seeped gradually from the city to Carlton. Score minus one for the famous Aussie egalitarianism, she thought: now, just like in so many other places, 'others' were a potential risk to be managed.

Bill was now at the station, debriefing the first-on-scene officers and prepping the suspect for interview. Lucy was driving in from home. Mike was on his way back from Earlville Mercy hospital and would ride as first assist to her investigation. Mike was a completer-finisher. Thank God: Dana had proper back-up.

Too early for commuting SUVs, she had the road largely to herself. Her pre-dawn excursion to Pulpit Falls kept pushing itself to the front of her mind. She had enough strength to shove it back temporarily, but she knew it couldn't be contained.

Even *murder* was just a displacement activity. Investigating a killing staved off the force and resonance of memory, the crippling panic and catastrophic damage it caused. She'd granted her blind-siding depression one Day of freedom, and now she was compromising that. It would exact a price for the betrayal.

Her mind drifted a little: the Day seeped in. Slivers of a scalding blue sky long ago, scarlet blossom on cool grass, filigreed shadow and soap bubbles: she could almost feel the light that had sparkled in front of her. She shook her head. If there ever was a right time to consider that – and she didn't feel there was – now was not it. She held the steering wheel tight and in her head she screamed, *Focus*. Work: work would surely drive out everything else. It always had.

The crime scene had been a series of pieces, not a coherent whole. If the killer was the burglar, it didn't make sense – the burglary seemed like a professional job, and a professional would surely simply hold up their hands to the break-in and take the consequences. There would be no need to do anything more. Maybe Cassavette was the type to fly off the handle: *How dare you steal from me?*, and so on. But even then . . . the knife packaging. If the burglar had punched or kicked Cassavette and he'd hit something fatal on the way down: that would have been an understandable death. But when someone reached on to a shelf, tore open a pack of knives – selected the third smallest; that bothered her, too – and then stabbed: it was a degree, however small, of forethought that seemed at odds with an ad hoc altercation. There was something big beyond the obvious.

If it hadn't been the burglar, the options would fan outwards from the life of Lou Cassavette. Family, business partners, friends, disgruntled former friends, people he owed, people who owed him, former lovers, spurned would-be lovers. She mulled over a list of possibles and how they might be narrowed down. She'd put Mike on to it. Dana was the primary and would pursue the prime suspect. Mike would look at other options and play devil's advocate to whatever she was thinking.

As she got nearer the Cassavettes' home the landscape changed. Lush gardens and majestic trees disappeared, replaced by scrubby lots and small industrial units. Roofs turned to scrappy and rust-flecked old Colourbond, neat verges dissolved, spangled concrete prevailed. The luxury of space disappeared and the average wage spiralled down to . . . *mean*. Next to a small strip of stores, high-set floodlights still illuminated the mist-draped parking area, where hooded skateboarders regularly outnumbered cars. A barricaded store in the middle of the strip promised to buy your gold for cash. To one side, a mini-mart offered to unlock any SIM card; on the other, an office window claimed that no cash was kept on the premises overnight.

She turned past a faux-stone entryway on to a new estate. It had been built to exploit the new freeway junction ten minutes away but had turned into a money-laundering opportunity for international crime. The banks now owned half the houses, and most of the rest were held by the courts and tax authorities: shells where it was foolish to fit copper pipes, or wiring. Earlville's now-shunned mayor had opened the estate in a flurry of ribbons, flashbulbs and gurning optimism. He had been indicted but was still awaiting his chance 'to put the record straight'. Actual owners were thin on the ground and either full of regrets or blessed by their endless and ignorant patience.

Low homes, more roof than brick, hunched on curved streets that must have looked lovely in the artist's rendering. In the publicity the streets would have shimmered under blue summer skies, casually populated by hand-holding couples smiling as their offspring launched a toy yacht in the ornamental lake. In the chilly early morning of a weekday the streetscape was silent and bleak: kerbside holes awaiting 'heritage street lighting', front-yard saplings shivering and inconsequential. Roads finished abruptly, with vandal-proof fencing shielding vacant blocks. The developer hadn't finished the street signs yet: it took three attempts down identikit cul-de-sacs to find the place.

Dana parked outside the Cassavette home as a grey BMW swept towards the main road, xenon headlights slicing the gloom. The driver held his phone to his ear, barking silently as he passed her. She took a deep breath. The Cassavette house was identical to the one each side; a series of three joined at the garage. A way of shoving smaller blocks on to each development. A country the size of a continent, she thought, and we're ramming people together. The homes would each have the same floorplan, and neighbours would feel a bizarre sense of familiarity when they entered the house next door. The Cassavettes had forgotten to bring in the rubbish bin – it sat forlorn at the beginning of their path.

Uniform patrol hadn't spoken to anyone yet; she would have to do The Knock. Some officers ran from that responsibility: she had an autopilot mode she could use. Telling the nearest or dearest had a rhythm, structure and etiquette she could understand, which both reassured and rescued her. Dana had done it twice before. Those hadn't felt as difficult as they should have: she'd been cocooned by the recipient's shock. Their emotional concussion allowed her to get away with her own reticence. They seemed to want to make tea or coffee or offer cakes; they rarely asked tricky questions.

She skirted around empathy because, primarily, it wasn't helpful to the investigation. Close family were close enough to do more harm than good, to harbour grudges and nurture fears: they knew weak spots and moments to strike. Dana knew that well enough. Close family were therefore suspects until proven otherwise, and it hindered clear thinking to have already been sympathetic. Dana tried to strike a balance between humane and professional – if push came to shove, she'd always take the latter.

The door knocker was a metal lion's head. When she used it, the door – being cheaper than the knocker it held – clattered in the frame. They threw these places up, she thought. Above the door, the soffit was already peeling paint.

The woman who answered was small, neat and oozed rapid capability. Dana made instant calculations. The woman would have fast-twitch muscles, she would eat and walk quickly, she would glance around like a bird, and she would struggle to relax. People would call her a dynamo, sparky, busy. Megan Cassavette was around one metre sixty, dark hair pulled back from a scrubbed, pretty and slightly freckled face. No-nonsense, she would be slightly unaware of her own attractiveness and as a result underestimate who she could attract. She wore a black business suit over an electric-blue blouse. Dana never noticed shoes.

'Yes?'

Dana offered her ID palm up, as if inviting the woman to pick a card, any card. 'Good morning. I'm Detective Dana Russo. Are you Megan Cassavette?'

Megan took a half-step back. Her hand rose to her throat, where it touched a thin gold necklace over a slight skin-blush. 'Yeah, I am. What is it? Lou? Is Lou okay?'

'Maybe better inside, Mrs Cassavette?'

Dana waited at the threshold until Megan had retreated almost behind the door. The walk into the living room was too long for both of them: Dana wanted to blurt it out and Megan had already guessed. It seemed a charade to say it out loud. Megan perched on the edge of an armchair and reached into her sleeve for a handkerchief, while Dana set the recorder going.

Dana started speaking as she sat. 'Your husband was at Jensen's Store last night?'

Megan nodded, and her breath caught for a second. She flashed a look to a framed photograph next to a large-screen TV: the couple waving kayak paddles triumphantly in crisp New Zealand air, bookended by snow-capped peaks. He was a head and neck taller than her. Wet hair suited Megan; a damp T-shirt accentuated Lou's gut. It struck Dana that Megan was a fair bit younger than her husband – perhaps ten years. Or maybe, simply much better looking.

'Uh, yeah, we own it. Lou thought someone was stealing, so he camped out there sometimes. I told him . . . oh, God. What happened? Is he hurt? Tell me.'

Dana focused her effort on keeping eye contact. Megan Cassavette had grey eyes; she'd rushed the mascara. 'We don't know all the details. Mr Cassavette was stabbed this morning, at around five thirty. He died at the scene, before officers could reach him.'

Sometimes they crumbled, but often they didn't. Megan opened her mouth to speak, then closed it. Dana didn't want to stare obtrusively, didn't want to look away. She re-set her position on the couch purely for something to do. Raw emotion was heading her way; it prompted her flight response.

'Mrs Cassavette? Is there someone I can call for you? People usually don't like to be alone—'

'Usually?' It was snapped, and there was a moment when Megan seemed on the point of attack. Then it faded. 'Oh, of course. You must do this all the time. God, how horrible for you. Uh, no, thanks. I'll call my mother soon. Yeah. No. Thanks.' She swallowed hard to keep the tears back – Dana saw a shard of stubborn pride in it.

Dana nodded. 'I understand this is the last thing you want to do, but it would really help our investigation if you could answer a few questions. Are you up to that, Mrs Cassavette?'

Megan glanced to the fireplace then drifted slowly back to Dana, as though she were spinning through the air and couldn't tell which way was up. 'Uh, sure. Ask away.'

'Thank you. Have the two of you lived here long?'

Megan was looking straight at her, but Dana understood that she wasn't really seeing anything. Megan coughed and tried to focus. 'Mm, nearly a year. Yeah. A year next month. Moved out here when we bought the store. Country scenery, you know?' She waved vaguely at the kitchen, which lay at the far end of the living room. Through its window was a framed view of a metal fence, a water butt and a Hills Hoist that hugged itself in the chilly gloom. 'Fresh air, fresh start. That sort of thing.' Her reply held a trail of bitterness. 'Who did it? Have you caught him?'

Dana took a second. 'It's very early in the investigation, Mrs Cassavette. Very early. There's a lot of ground to cover.'

Megan's eyes narrowed slightly, as though she were calculating.

Dana tried to ease her back to the moment. 'Moving out here from the city. Was it a success?'

Megan shook her head and a small tear escaped. 'No, not really. Lou and I were running.' She stopped to wipe her nose. 'From each other, from ourselves. This was supposed to turn it all around.' She squeezed her handkerchief tight. Her voice faded to a whisper. 'Jesus.'

Dana didn't know what to say. She tilted her head slightly, hoping that would imply a thousand words of sympathetic consolation. 'You said your husband thought someone was stealing?' she resumed.

Megan had stopped moving, looking, feeling – breathing.

'Mrs Cassavette? Stealing from the store?'

'Hmm? Oh, yeah. Well, *after* he'd pocketed the cash from the sale, the old owner said he thought someone was stealing. Little bits of stock kept going missing, but he couldn't work out how. We thought maybe shoplifters, or more likely some of the staff.' Megan stopped long enough to draw the back of her hand across her eyes; the make-up smeared a little. 'The old guy was a soft touch, employed stoners and losers. Lou put a couple of cameras in and changed some of the staff. There was nothing wrong at first. He thought the last guy didn't manage the place properly.'

Talking about something peripheral had helped Megan get some control. Her voice quivered less. 'But then, about three months in, stuff definitely went. Stupid stuff – low grade, nothing, really. But it annoyed Lou. He hates – *hated* – things like that. It was the principle, not the money. So every few nights he was sleeping in there. Christ knows what he thought he'd do if he . . .' She glanced up. 'That's what happened, isn't it?'

Dana felt skewered by the look, and by the obvious but reasonable question. 'We don't know many details yet, Mrs Cassavette.'

'For God's sake, will you call me Megan? Mrs Cassavette is a stupid mouthful. Stop being so polite.'

But, Dana wanted to say, *polite is my default. I need it.*

'I'm sorry, Megan. All we know at the moment is that your husband died in the store, possibly from a single stab wound. Do you know of anyone who'd wish him harm?'

'Lou? Christ, no.' Megan snorted and stood up. She smoothed down her blouse – Dana had noticed it was creased – and re-tucked a stray hair. 'We hadn't been here long enough to annoy anyone but each other.' Megan examined her hands: flawless but unpainted nails. 'He'd had a couple of arguments with suppliers, but nothing that would explain . . . no.' She walked over to a sideboard and straightened a pile of magazines, talking to the wall. 'He was getting fed up with the old "That's how we do things out this way" mentality. Like the internet never happened, you know?'

She turned back, as though Dana were some retail consultant. 'Like Lou couldn't get his stock trucked in overnight from all over. He was trying to be nice. He was trying to bring some locals along with him. That Earlville mentality – they warned us, but we didn't realise. They wouldn't play ball.' She looked to the window and the grey sky. 'But that was nonsense. No one would do this . . . for that.'

She regathered. 'I can't think of anyone else here who'd hurt him. No.'

'What about from your old life in the city? Any grudges, enemies made – things like that?'

Megan sniffed and looked away, like she'd heard a shot in a forest. 'Coffee?' She was already on the move, with the bustling style Dana had predicted. Sudden switchbacks weren't unusual after this kind of news – Dana rode it. 'Thanks. Flat white with one, please.'

Megan waved an arm in acknowledgement but didn't turn around. She began to navigate the process in a series of accurate, snappy movements. Dana left her to it, glancing over occasionally for signs of heaving shoulders or a clutch of the countertop. Between sidelong looks, she examined the happy snaps above a collection of paperbacks. Photos of the loving couple; judging by Megan's hair, all taken in the last few years. Only three of the photos showed them wearing rings. Dana reckoned they had been together for three or four years, married for perhaps two; the initial romance a little whirlwindy. Megan maybe settling because Lou seemed rock solid and established: a man, when she'd dated tall adolescents for too long.

'I'm old-fashioned enough to have them printed out and framed.' Megan's voice was unexpectedly close. 'Just having them on your phone, it's like it doesn't really count. Like you don't want them enough.'

Dana took the coffee. Both mugs had the same company logo. 'Thanks. I can't even operate the camera on mine. I guess it has one.' She nodded at the mug. 'You work for City Mutual?'

'Yeah, claims adjuster, in Earlville.' She eye-rolled. 'It's as riveting as you imagine it would be. Spent part of yesterday checking the price of table lamps.' She drifted for a moment. 'We needed a solid income while the store got on its feet.'

They sat again. 'Tough times, huh?'

Megan took a sip. Making coffee had given her time to gather herself a little. 'Retail's always tough. Lou had big plans for the place, but it was going to take a while. He turned one corner of it into a little café. We're a nation that can't do anything without sipping a latte first, he reckoned. Wanted to add an antiques place on the side. Make it a "destination".' She air-quoted, then spoke to the ceiling. 'Dreams outside his reach, every time.'

Except, thought Dana, *for you*. Lou married up: he got that one right.

Megan shook her head, suddenly wearied. Shock like this didn't come through consistently; it bit in nasty little spasms, asymmetric steps down to despair. 'We used to run a little supermarket. Updated milk bar, really, in the 'burbs. You know the kind of thing – you forgot something basic, couldn't be bothered to cook? Overpriced, but you paid it, coz it was just around the corner? That was us.'

And, suspected Dana, Megan had been pretty happy with it. Probably kept her friends from college, had enough money. In retrospect, that life had been sweet, even if they'd both talked at the time about trying for something better. Maybe only Lou actually believed the vision, and Megan didn't hate it enough to draw a line in the sand.

Dana was conscious that Megan's coffee-making had dodged a previous question.

'From your former life in the city, Megan: any grudges, enemies, problems that might have followed you here?'

There was a short pause. Possibly, thought Dana, Megan was reaching back to past events and scanning them. Or maybe she was judging what should be revealed and what should be left for the police to discover themselves. Dana tended to veer towards the latter in such situations, unless she had good reason not to do so.

'No, I . . . no. Just an ordinary couple. We ran a corner shop, not a crime syndicate, Detective. We sold milk, pre-cooked chook, cigarettes in large cartons, DVDs for the terminally bored.'

Dana nodded, but it slid into her mind to ask Mike to be exact with the follow-up. Megan was quick to paint a certain type of picture, and Dana felt it was a little too quick.

'Megan, one of the things we have to do is establish exactly where everyone was within a certain timeframe.' Dana glanced at her face for signs of opposition, but Megan was semi-zoned out. Her coffee was tilting forward. Dana reached out silently and carefully nudged it back to level: Megan didn't notice.

'Megan?'

'Hmm?'

'Just a couple of questions. Can you tell me where you were from midnight last night until I arrived at the door?'

'Oh, yeah. I was here. All night. Uh, watched the end of the footy, texted Lou goodnight – he texted back – and then bed.' She put down the coffee and puffed her cheeks. 'Got up usual time for work. I was about to brush my teeth and head out when you arrived.'

Dana nodded. Most people don't put their jacket on *before* they clean their teeth, she thought. 'I have to ask: is there anything to verify that? Beyond texts, I mean. Wave to any neighbours? Go online at all?'

'I'd had a couple of glasses, so I hit the pillow. I wasn't expecting Lou back before I went off today. When he does these little vigils he normally pops back after the store's opened, for a shower and clean clothes. We don't usually see each other till dinnertime.'

In the modern world most alibis came from devices. Mobile phones could be cross-referenced with triangulation of transmission masts to give a location and time; cars sometimes had black boxes and satnav.

'Did you use any technology last night? That sometimes helps us to place people.'

Megan frowned. It seemed to cross her mind to be indignant about having to disprove a negative, in the midst of grief. Then, she thought for a second.

'No, I don't believe I . . . uh, Big Brother.'

'Excuse me?'

'We have an electric meter that logs each socket, apparently. Lou used to call it Big Brother whenever he was railing against government generally. I usually tuned him out when he did that. But maybe it can tell you when I was home, at least?'

Dana nodded, unconvinced. 'We'll look into it.' Lucy would do that.

Alongside alibi was motive.

'Final question for now, I promise. Does anyone stand to gain if something happens to Lou? That you know of?'

Megan opened her mouth, closed it, then smirked. She drew back slightly. 'You can't seriously . . . oh, wait, you'd have to check stuff like that.' She rested her elbows on her knees and leaned in close: confidential girl-talk as she rubbed her wedding band absent-mindedly. 'Detective, this house is rented. All the money's in the store, which has debts the size of Brazil. So I'll probably end up with nothing but bills. Assuming I can sell that damn store to anyone.'

Megan eased back. 'Anyone else? Nah. We're not big enough competition for the big guys; there's no one itching to see the back of us. We were just small fry trying to swim, that's all.'

Dana nodded warily. Something in her back-of-mind radar went *ping*, but she wasn't sure what. 'Does your mother live nearby?'

'Uh, yeah. Ten minutes. Can I ring her now?' Megan was up and pecking at the phone before Dana could answer. Dana stood and mouthed, 'I'll be in the kitchen.' Megan nodded distractedly as her mother picked up.

It seemed strange to Dana for someone to immediately reach for their mother at a time of crisis; to see her as a sanctuary, an emotional harbour. Logically, Dana understood it: but it was the difference between comprehension and empathy. Just like she could comprehend the adrenaline rush of a parachute jump but would never set foot on the runway.

Dana made some phone calls: summoning a search team for the Cassavette house and letting Dennis the Tech know that Lou's computer, and Megan's laptop, would be coming his way shortly. He reminded her about the potential for memory sticks and external drives – his pet hate when cops thought providing the computer was all there was to it. Dana wanted to see Megan's mother and Megan's reaction to her, to see what that kind of intimate support looked like. She rationalised it to herself by imagining she was 'sort of with' Megan until family help arrived. Besides, she needed islands of solitude when she dealt with people, especially when they were emotional.

She asked Megan for a copy of the will and life insurance. Megan, as Dana had expected, knew where they were and had an efficient filing system. She handed them over wordlessly and padded away to the fireplace.

Dana looked closely at the calendar on the kitchen wall in case there was something useful – medical appointments, that sort of thing. Nothing but birthdays and anniversaries. She speed-dialled Mike.

Mike Francis picked up on the second ring. 'Ahoyhoy.'

'I've said before, Mikey, it'll never catch on.' There was a smile in her voice. 'That's why Edison invented "hello".'

'If it's good enough for the man who invented the telephone, it's good enough to use *on* the telephone . . . Sorry you caught a live one on your day off.'

'Maybe better to be busy today, anyway.' Dana paused. 'You're first assist, is that right?'

She could hear Mike trying to move a mint around in his mouth. 'Uh-huh. What do you need?'

'Okay, several random things, no particular order.' Dana poked her head around the corner: Megan was staring expectantly at the driveway and clutching her elbows. 'Please check the ages and marriage certificate on the Cassavettes – I want a read on their relationship and I only have her to go on. Find out what day and when the rubbish is emptied around here – she doesn't have an alibi except herself and she kind of ducked the question. We'll need reliable uniforms to do some door-to-door with her neighbours. Just background – the usual bull about "Someone might have noticed strangers," etcetera. I imagine someone will be a right old gossip. I have the will and life insurance here, but check the Cassavettes' financials and phone records. Thank you.'

There was a short pause as Mike finished noting the instructions – it would be small, round, formidably neat good-boy-at-school handwriting. '. . . financials . . . phones. Got it. Not happy with the burglar we got?'

'Covering all the bases is all. Oh, and any intelligence from the

Cassavettes' past in the city. I know you're already on it, but her answers on that were a little pat for my liking. Thanks, Mikey.'

As she finished speaking a burgundy Honda squealed to a halt outside. A salt-and-pepper, post-hip-operation version of Megan got out and hustled across the lawn. Her obvious anxiety for her daughter made Dana's eyes prickle. Megan opened the door and, as it tilted shut, Dana saw her fall against her mother's shoulder and convulse.

Chapter 4

Carlton was the police headquarters for the region, but this was an accident of history rather than by intent. Earlville had the busiest facilities and most officers, but the regional politicians lived in Carlton and wanted senior officers available for a conspicuous chat.

The town's founding fathers had envisaged a grandiose civic plaza, with the impressive facades of state grouped around an open square to imply democracy and accountability. But behind the Grecian columns of city hall and the court, thick walnut doors shielded the elected from the gaze of the plebs and all the actual work went on out the back. It was the equivalent of a conjuring trick: the visible architecture was the shiny baubles and slick chatter; the prosaic buildings beyond were the flaps, trapdoors and false walls that made it work.

The police station was literally an adjunct to the court: there was a Corridor of Doom to take prisoners straight from the custody suite into Courtroom One. The building itself was a shallow-roofed, three-storey affair, draped in an awful butterscotch render that was constantly 'too expensive' to replace. It sat across from a small open green, below which was a staff car park that stretched under the station itself. The station's official entrance was artfully hidden at the moment, behind a Mobile Incident Room that was parked there near-permanently. Carlton's police station was a building for police to work in, not a public building.

The public remit ran only to a reception with two tiny interview rooms off it. Hard-working vinyl floors and wipe-down emulsion spoke of the attitude towards visitors: they would be careless, annoying, intrusive and require effort. Bill Meeks was trying to coax some pot plants and piped music into the scene, but the Police Board had scoffed at it. In their view, the type of people who were required to come to a police station didn't deserve the niceties: either they were a victim and simply needed help, or they were a suspect and deserved stony-faced indifference.

Whenever Dana stepped through the reception door into the main part of the building a little piece of her felt like she was home. Only at Carlton for eighteen months all told, she was familiar now with the carpet-cleaner smell, the staleness of the air, the background hum of air conditioning and sub-par typing. Dana liked order, and the place had a hierarchy for everything – rank, of course, but also furniture and location. Bill was upstairs in a corner office with a leafy view and a conference table. The best chairs went to the operations room, which operated 24/7 in a twilight, non-glare world of headsets, weary routine and occasional adrenaline. Detectives were downstairs in a corner with few windows, but they got a slightly better form of elderly desk: a little less tape holding it together and marginally more chance that the drawers were lockable. Uniform were the ultimate hand-me-down youngest child: partially in the basement, watching the oldest computers in the building whirr and wheel to a halt.

Dana emailed the recording of her discussion with Megan so that Lucy could type it up and précis for the briefing later. The investigation already had its place on the station's shared drive: all documents would be simultaneously available to the whole team, with Lucy compiling the log and tracking file updates. They'd started this system only months ago, and they still had to chase many to add their contribution online. Forensics were always late to the party, and the autopsy was still typed and couriered over. Normally, Dana was relentlessly old-school and would have relished a pile of folders to neaten. But in a murder investigation she recognised the time saved by being able to search individual words and cross-reference data quickly.

Interview preparation was one of Dana's favourite tasks. While it held urgency and importance, it couldn't be rushed. She was allowed to take her time – delve, think, plan. She got a magic pass from the hurly-burly of instantaneous decisions, by-the-kettle socialising and reflex thinking.

There was footage from the custody suite as Nathan Whittler was brought in: her first look at his body language, and the first time she heard his voice. He stared at his feet, shuffling forward as if he were on a chain gang. It was unusual, but not unexpected – people often had little idea of the correct behaviour. Dana noted the officers' mild shove in the back when Nathan was too far from the custody bench: he accepted it without acknowledgement, as if it were his due.

He was, in Dana's own phrase, 'becoming Zimbardoed'. She was fascinated by a psychology experiment from the 1970s, where student volunteers in a fake prison took on the role, language and gestures of supplicant prisoner and overbearing guard. Zimbardo had speculated that certain pre-conditions created certain behaviour, regardless of previous personality. Nathan was acting out the role he thought he was there for: someone who'd been caught. It was either naïve or coldly calculating; the optics would be the same. His apparent meekness could be a great piece of acting, or a prelude to tortuous and brittle interviewing.

The next logical question, she mused, was what would open him up. Assuming he was intimidated by what had happened and what was occurring now, what would set him loose? He answered the standard custody questions with a hoarse whisper or slight head movements. Dana couldn't gauge accent, or dialect, or any hint of where he might have been in the recent past. His responses were soft, arrived at after due thought, and cursory. Nothing more than the minimum.

Simpson, the custody officer, peered over the top of the monitor.

'Do you agree that the doctor may examine you to ascertain your fitness for detention and interview?'

A nod at the floor.

Simpson was, she knew, patient and respectful – it made him a safe pair of hands. But even he was becoming exasperated; hemmed in by four walls for an entire shift, the least he expected was to be acknowledged.

'Don't talk to the floor, Mr Whittler, talk to me. Look up.'

It seemed Nathan tried, but failed on both occasions. A sigh from Simpson, who tapped on the keyboard again.

'On any medications, medical treatment?'

A shake of the head, a glance to his left.

'The power of speech, Mr Whittler. Use it.'

'No, nothing.'

Dana strained to pick out some remnant of where Nathan might have come from: zero. His language was a flat bat; he was stripping out nuance, clues and emotion.

'What happened out there, Mr Whittler? In Jensen's Store?'

The mention of the location made Nathan flinch, as if slapped. Not only did he turn his face, but his hands came up reflexively, as though warding off future attacks. Simpson looked bemused.

'What?' Simpson turned to the two uniforms. 'He always like this? What happened?'

Nathan slowly took his arms down, seemingly wary.

'Yeah, he is,' replied one officer. 'One guy dead in the store, stabbed. This one, over the dead body.'

Simpson typed briefly then pointed to Nathan's hands.

'Hence, the blood. Yeah. We'll put him in the suite and get forensics done first.'

Nathan looked down at his hands, apparently alien to him. As if they'd acted against his wishes, or without him knowing at all.

'Anything to say at this juncture, Mr Whittler?'

A vehement shake of the head – his most definite action so far. Something juvenile about it, Dana felt, something unformed. Another shove in the back, more shuffling from Nathan, and he disappeared from sight to the forensics suite. They would take blood, fingerprints, DNA and change his clothes. She saw the doctor walk past, on his way to observe the process.

In the forensics suite Nathan reacted to being touched as if he were being scalded by acid. He screwed up his eyes when a mouth swab was taken with a cotton bud. Doc Butler suggested that, after trace samples had been taken, Nathan should clean himself up rather than have his hands washed by a tech. The flood of relief on Nathan's face was palpable and, she judged, difficult to fake.

Doc Butler was used to people in shock – usually victims – but she could see even he was struggling with Nathan Whittler. He got minimal replies to the stock questions that rooted Nathan in the present day, aware and cognisant. But anything beyond that – nothing.

'You from around here, Mr Whittler?'

'What is it you do for a living?'

'If you could tell me your doctor, I could follow up on any medical history.'

All met by silence, and a thousand-yard stare at the wall in front of him. Nathan Whittler had clearly decided on a strategy whenever anyone broached anything personal or to do with the murder. He simply shut off and refused to play.

'Were you hurt out there, at Jensen's?'

Nathan's hands moved quickly up to his face, like a boxer on the ropes. He shuddered slightly and refused to uncoil. When Doc Butler touched Nathan's forearm, trying to get him to relax, Nathan pulled away sharply.

'Okay, okay. All a bit too difficult for now, I get it. Well, Mr Whittler, you're fit to be detained and fit to be interviewed. I'll keep that under review.'

When he had concluded the examination Doc Butler gave a sardonic glance to the CCTV camera, as if to say, *Well, I'm all out of ideas. You try.*

Dana sat back. The need to uncover the basics was stronger now. Usually, interviewees yielded enough to give the police a start and one thing led to another – home address to work record, to tax number, to car, to telephone . . . but if someone didn't fire the starting gun, the investigation stalled. It was always tougher, and slower, when the team had to do it all themselves.

On the face of it, Nathan was a restrained, tightly wound and slightly shambolic enigma: it was as though he'd always thought he would end up here, but was still disappointed he had. Although, she thought as she scratched some notes, if he wanted to slide out of a murder charge, all this submission might be a way to go about it.

His reaction to the store's name troubled her. He'd recoiled twice and said nothing. No denial, no explanation; no information at all. Yet it didn't feel to her like he had a guilty conscience; more that he had deliberately shut down about the whole thing and couldn't be reached. Wouldn't let himself be reached. Maybe Bill Meeks could coax some words from him. If not, they were flying blind.

Suspects who didn't talk gave themselves – whether they realised it, or not – the best possible chance of being convicted for something they didn't do.

But also, she reflected, the best possible chance of getting away with something they did.

He was seated bolt upright in Interview One, palms clasped between his knees, incongruous in the paper jumpsuit. Shadows half obscured a large, impressive brow, like a Lincoln statue. His face had heft and gravitas, but it jolted with anxiety.

One heavy, stark ceiling light swayed slightly in the draught from the ventilation; it resembled a slowly spinning vortex. Under it he seemed patient but cowed, ridiculous in the spotlight. There was so little stimulus in the room that most people looked up and around, into every corner, under the table – anywhere. Sometimes they wandered around, stretched, tapped at the glass. But Whittler stared evenly at the other chair, as if someone was going to magically materialise.

'That's him, then.' Dana saw pale skin and slightly hunched shoulders, perhaps two days' growth around the jowls. The man rolled his neck briefly, working out some kinks.

Bill nodded. 'The one and only Nathan Whittler.'

She knew he'd come from the suicide-watch cell: a glass-fronted cell visible from the main custody desk, with a written command to sign for the prisoner's safety every ten minutes.

'He's been kept in the Lecter Theatre, yes?' she asked.

'Oh, yeah, he has. Doc's orders, and I can't blame him. This guy behaved like a scalded cat whenever anyone spoke. Even asking his name made him jump. Doc only got grunts, nods and headshakes. No conversation at all.'

They stared back through the glass. It reminded Dana of a zoo; peering intently into the semi-darkness of the reptile house, convinced there was something there to observe. Here, she was watching a man do nothing. But that in itself felt significant.

Bill re-hefted a slab of files in the crook of his arm. 'Something about him makes me think he's going to be big news. Good luck with him.'

'What?' Dana wasn't used to having her competence, or chances of success, second-guessed by Bill.

'I mean,' said Bill, scratching his chin, 'that it might be impossible to tell if he's lying. When he's lying.'

'Because?'

'Well, look at him. Either the worst or best poker player I've ever seen. All the rules about body language go out the window. I spoke to him about his rights when he came in: when you start talking, he's all over the place. You can't tell his mood or direction from posture, eye contact, tics, impulses, gestures – nothing. He might be up, down or sideways: you've got no basis for working it out. And as for chat: forget it. I got five words in ten minutes of asking. Blood from a stone. Never seen anyone so addicted to shutting up.'

Dana nodded thoughtfully. The two officers who'd brought Nathan into the station reported he'd stared at the ground the entire trip, said nothing but his name, offered no resistance or reasons. But Dana was used to some people being crushed by the fact of arrest, by the reality of it. They became swamped by a sense of their life tumbling away from them. So she took that kind of reaction with a pinch of salt.

All the same, Bill's observation seemed to fit. Nathan Whittler was not their usual kind of suspect. It wasn't, she guessed as she watched him now, simply that he was scared of being in a police station. He wasn't unnerved only by having been arrested next to a dead body. It went deeper than that.

Nathan Whittler seemed terrified of people. Any people.

'Why me, Bill? For this one?'

Bill turned to her. 'Okay. Officially, it's because Mike was first lead, but he's worked four nights in a row and he's beat. Plus, he had to take his kid to Earlville Mercy in the early hours. Don't forget to ask him how the little ankle-biter is either. I know you.'

It was true. To remember that kind of nicety, she needed it written down.

'And unofficially?'

'Well, now. This guy's going to be a hard nut to crack, and I need it cracked. It's possible we'll have nothing definitive, except what he gives up. I suspect all the evidence we find will eventually point to Whittler being responsible. But if there's no witnesses, and no apparent motive, he'd be hard to pin for murder. He can probably get away with a lesser charge, unless he gives us enough ammo. That being the case, I want someone who can empathise, make him open up.'

'Mikey can empathise. I've seen him do it.' Dana remained in awe of Mike's ability to appear less like a detective, more like the guy on the next bar stool, listening to a yarn to while away the time. It was a skill, and one she didn't feel she had.

'Yes, he can. For certain crimes, and certain suspects, he's the best of all of us. But not in this case. Trust me, Dana. You're perfect for this one.'

She looked back at Nathan Whittler, who remained focused on the empty chair, muttering some kind of mantra. 'He's still judged fit to proceed?'

'Oh, yeah. Doc Butler took a look at him twice. Yeah, he's fit to be detained and fit to be interviewed. He knows where he is, who he is; he can count backwards from a hundred. He's aware of which side of the road we drive, and so on. So yeah, he passed . . .'

Dana took a sidelong glance; Bill was frowning. 'Except what?'

'Except,' Bill paused, as though unsure whether to tell her or not. 'Doc told me he was fragile. Incredibly fragile. Doc called him "a frightened deer". A frightened deer with one-word replies to everything. You'll need to prise him open gradually.'

Dana chewed her lip. Prising gently was the most difficult of all. Fragile tended to go one of two ways – they either opened up like a shucked oyster or became impossible. Most people could be goaded or threatened into jabbering, but she got a sense that Nathan Whittler would be someone capable of deep and abiding silence.

'Hmmm. I guess. I've done the prep, so I'm ready to go at him. Has he got a lawyer yet?'

'Nah, refused one.'

Dana faced her boss with a slight crinkle in the middle of her forehead. The one usually reserved for recalcitrant machines, cryptic puzzles and people who didn't mean what they'd just said.

'Oh, c'mon, Bill. He refused?'

Bill raised one unhindered, apologetic hand. 'I swear. Asked him twice, got it on tape – that's the five-word prize he gave me – and got it in writing.' He tapped the files in his arms. After a pause and a slight smile he added, 'He's probably one of those, uh, "Nothing to hide so nothing to fear" types.'

'So we're on the twenty-four-hour clock? Damn.'

'Yes, we are. The court will force legal counsel on him tomorrow morning, regardless. Clock started at Jensen's store at 0603, officially. Take off the required eight hours of sleep, then we have to stop questioning at . . . 2203 today. Allowing for breaks and everything, we can actually sit in a room with him for maybe five hours today. Tomorrow morning, his new lawyer will ensure he shuts up until he's in court. The good news is, he's been told all that, and he's still sure he doesn't want a lawyer.'

'He's a homicide suspect. Blood, literally, on his hands. And he doesn't want a lawyer. Does he really know what's going on here?'

Bill smirked and looked through the two-way mirror.

'Now that, Dana, is the sixty-four-thousand-dollar question.'

Chapter 5

'Mr Whittler?'

Nathan shuffled in his chair and nodded slightly at his foot. Dana placed her files and a legal pad on the table. The topmost folder held some data collected at the crime scene and some internet searching and database mining. The three unmarked files below it were expense forms from five years ago, there only to imply depth of evidence.

She held out her hand. 'I'm Detective Dana Russo.'

Nathan squirmed a little, before offering a quick, lukewarm handshake. His hand was damp, he was distracted; he gazed at the corner of the room and withdrew his hand as if she were toxic. Various ideas flipped through her mind. Scared? Misogynist? Autistic?

'May I sit down, Mr Whittler?'

She nearly always made a point of asking. Some suspects took it to mean they had control of the room – it made them complacent and sloppy. Some suspects assumed she was weak – it made them underestimate her. This time, she simply wanted Nathan to know she was polite and courteous. She sensed this might matter to him. Dana believed she always had control of the room: she was allowed to walk out of it, after all. Once again, Nathan nodded at his foot.

'I'll be conducting an investigation concerning the events that happened this morning. Would you like something to drink?'

Nathan scratched his arm without responding, as if everything she'd said were birdsong. Just when she thought he maybe hadn't heard, and she felt she needed to ask if he had hearing problems, he mumbled, 'Some water, please.'

Dana flicked a hand towards the mirror and turned back to Nathan. She saw now what Bill had meant. His gestures – those that existed – seemed separate from his thoughts. There was no eye contact at all. In retrospect, they should have set up the room differently; chairs at near right angles, rather than facing each other. Like a counselling session. What was that old saying? *Women talk face to face, men talk shoulder to shoulder.* But if she moved the chair now it would seem intimidating and obvious.

'Mr Whittler, there are a couple of items we need to cover before the interview begins.' She could feel herself slowing down, focusing on syntax and manners. 'Would you please confirm that your name is Nathan Whittler and your date of birth is November 25, 1980?'

Again, a nod at the floor. He now seemed fixated on an ingrained stain halfway between him and the mirror. The stain was raspberry cordial, but it looked like dried and faded blood: it was left there as subtle insinuation. If he moved his eyes at all, it was a quick flick at his reflection. Perhaps wondering who was on the other side of the mirror; or possibly, fascination with his own image.

'I'm switching on the tape now, Mr Whittler.'

She held her finger on the button and waited until he glanced at it. The agreement would have been unnoticeable if she hadn't been searching for it. Small movements with no social graces: Dana was already filing and calibrating.

Two recorders: one digital, one old-school. The tape made its familiar grating sound in the first few seconds then settled down to a hum.

Nathan returned to a hunched, slightly foetal position. If he'd been allowed to turn his back, she sensed he would do so.

'Please confirm to the tape that you have, at this time, decided not to have a lawyer present. You can at any time request a lawyer and one will be provided for you.'

Another slight nod to himself.

'Please state this out loud, Mr Whittler. It relates to your rights.'

Nathan leaned forward, arching slowly towards the tape machine and away from Dana. When his face was centimetres from the tape, he spoke.

'I confirm that, Detective Russo.' There was no trace of a regional accent, distinctive pattern or clear intonation – his voice could have been ordering a burger or recounting a car accident. His speech was slightly testy, precise and, she sensed, fussy. He sat back and resumed his coiled vigil.

'Thank you, Mr Whittler. When you speak, you don't need to—'

There was a sharp knock and an officer brought in a bottle of water. Dana watched Nathan frown.

'Mike, I think Mr Whittler will need a cup for drinking that. A cup with a handle, in fact.'

Mike snorted, until he realised from her face that she was serious. He sighed and left the room.

Dana turned back to Nathan, who was thumbing a chipped edge of the table. 'I'm sorry about that, Mr Whittler. I'm afraid we've raised a generation with no etiquette.'

Nathan smiled at the table for a second, then stared at his shoe. Mike returned with a cup and plonked it down noisily.

'We won't need you again, thank you, Mike,' she called to his departing back. The door closed with a solid thump.

Dana took the chance to pause. The room was heavily insulated; there was a busy plaza nearby and police vehicles came and went below them, but noises rarely filtered into this space. She wrote slowly on the pad, watching him from the corner of her eye. Eventually, he opened the water bottle and poured. His motor skills were slow and measured; he tilted the cup as if he were pouring a beer. The glugging sound was incongruously loud. She watched him scrape the cup's rim along the side of the bottle to catch a drip. He didn't take a drink; instead, he turned the water bottle so that the label faced him.

Dana let the silence linger, openly studying him, watching the reaction it produced. As she'd expected, he turned away, as though she'd bullied him in a schoolyard.

'You're finding the number of people around you disturbing, Mr Whittler.'

She didn't ask; she stated. He didn't reply.

'I thought about this as you were brought in. I can't necessarily reduce the number of people around you, but perhaps some explanation will give you a little context.'

No response. Although he shivered: seemingly involuntarily, judging by his slight grimace. Any body language, any inflection – let alone any comment – appeared to him an unconscionable degree of exposure on his part. Perhaps he would prefer total darkness, or to be a disembodied voice: being visible and tangible was apparently unfamiliar, worrying. She sensed that dealing with Nathan Whittler would be like walking on coral – sharp, unsteady, desperately fragile; wanting to explore but fearing that, with every step, she would be destroying what she sought to understand.

'You're being held in a glass-fronted cell, for now. I apologise for that, but we're guided by the advice of our specialist doctor. He's concerned – as we all are – that you're finding this situation difficult, and this makes you . . . vulnerable. We'll play that by ear, Mr Whittler, but the current situation is medically guided, and for your own welfare.'

Nathan scratched his ear with a shaking hand, which he then enclosed with the other. Dana looked for a sign of some kind that she was helping. She found nothing.

'My aim in speaking to you, Mr Whittler, is to restrict ourselves to short stretches of conversation so that you're not tired out.'

While Dana was talking he gazed around the room, as if this were the first time he was truly cognisant of it. She followed his gaze. Blank blue walls drew the eye to the mirror. She wondered if he'd seen enough television to know there were people beyond.

'I sense that your unease goes beyond being in a police station and being interviewed. So allow me to clarify. I'll be the only person you need to speak to, unless you choose to talk to anyone else. So you needn't try to work out, or work on, dealing with anyone else. It's only you and I, Mr Whittler.'

The silence seemed to shift in some intangible way: a little more amiable.

'We often have wilfully gabby people in here,' she continued. 'They talk and talk but say nothing. Frankly, it'll be nice to speak to someone who measures and values words.'

His features softened and his lips twitched. Dana felt her skin flush slightly at the realisation that she had her technique for the coming interviews. This time, he knew the microphone would pick him up without leaning forward.

'I think that I will speak to you, Detective, but not to anyone else. That is my preference.'

It was soft and sharp at the same time: it made Dana stop for a moment. Responsibility, opportunity. Pressure.

'Mr Whittler, we haven't found an address for you as yet. Could you tell me your current address, please?'

'I cannot, Detective Russo.'

She paused, waiting for him to fill the space. The tape spooled on.

'I see. Are you currently homeless, Mr Whittler?'

He shook his head. 'No, I'm not. I have a home, but not an address.'

Riddles. Unlike most detectives, she liked suspects who talked elliptically, who danced around and made the police do the work. In her experience, the suspect gave her credit when she worked it out – it took their communication to a different level.

'The logical inference' – she glanced at him and thought she spotted a gold star for using the word – 'would be some form of mobile home – a caravan, or a motorhome, or a boat.' She watched him carefully. Not a flicker. 'But I don't sense that's correct.'

Just a small shift in his chair, maybe ten centimetres. He hid it with another scratch at his arm, which she could see held five or six insect bites. But he did move.

'Would you like some calamine for those bites, Mr Whittler? I'm sure we could find some.'

'No, thank you, Detective. I'm quite used to them.'

She made sure he noticed her scribble on the pad. She was certain he couldn't read her scrawl upside down – few could read it at all – but he watched her take note of something significant.

Dana needed to see that he wanted to know.

'So, your accommodation. We'll come back to that, if we may. I'll write "undefined" for now.'

His stony expression affected disdain for whatever she was recording, but again she saw him inching towards her.

She changed tack. 'I'm sorry about the jumpsuit, by the way. It's standard issue. We needed your clothing for forensic analysis.'

He shook his head a little sadly.

'Mr Whittler? Something about the jumpsuit?'

He risked – and it felt like a risk to her – a quick glance at her face. Then he shied away, as if he'd stared at the sun. He recomposed himself with some deep breaths: she recognised the technique as a stomach-settling, centring exercise from her youth. It took her inside herself: deep down, away from whatever she was facing.

'The jumpsuit is not problematic, Detective. I think the process, however, was unnecessary.' He was talking to the table leg.

'The process? Please explain, Mr Whittler.'

He folded his arms and for a second Dana thought he'd clam up entirely. Her heart yelped as she thought she'd blown it, and blown it early. In the split-second that followed she realised how much she had already been drawn into him.

'To wear this jumpsuit, Detective, I had to take off my own clothes. As you say, they're needed for forensics, and I understand that. But it meant I had to undress . . . well . . . in front of other people. I assume you make everyone do that; but still . . . I found it . . . uncomfortable.'

He sat back a little. She paused before replying. His fear of people seemed deep, defining. She needed to understand more about where it came from and what it implied – it suffused everything he did.

'Yes. Yes, Mr Whittler, I can understand that. I apologise. Unfortunately, we have a standard procedure we have to follow with everyone, regardless of circumstance. The courts demand that we do it the same way each time.'

'Hmm. You're someone who values her privacy, Detective. Yes?'

People had accused her of projecting that. She had been charged with being introspective, a deep thinker; a non-sharer. And it had come with that pejorative tone.

'Yes, very much so. It's a dying art, don't you think?'

He seemed unable to actually smile, but capable of a smirk.

She paused again, sizing up what she needed to do at this point.

'The court's demand: it's intended to protect your rights, in part. But I can see how it would . . . affect your privacy. I'll try to ensure it's done more respectfully if it's needed again.'

He nodded sagely at the floor and his reply was almost a whisper.

'Thank you, Detective Russo.' He sipped at the water; his hand shook a little. He reached with one finger and lightly touched the bottle cap.

'May I ask you about your early life, Mr Whittler?'

He scratched at his bites again, but absent-mindedly, as though he did this so often it was subconscious. She took his silence as not quite assent, not quite dissent: she edged across the highwire in between.

'You were born near here?'

He looked up towards the ceiling momentarily; the information appeared to be a reach, and she wondered why. Again, she thought of Bill and his view that Nathan would be hard to catch in a lie. But this information could be – was being – checked.

'Yes, in Earlville. Or rather, in the ambulance on the way to Earlville. So I'm told.' This last was added as if the source were unreliable and he couldn't be held responsible for it. She took it as an indication that he didn't want to spill anything that was untrue.

'Are your family still in the area?'

'I don't know. They were.'

Dana stared evenly at him.

'I'm sorry, Detective Russo. I didn't mean to sound short. I simply don't know if they're still there. They were the last time I looked. But that, as I'm sure you'll discover, was a while ago.'

Something thrummed in Dana's blood: her sixth sense that she was close to something that mattered. 'How long ago would you classify as "a while"?'

Nathan looked at his fingers; it made her look at them, too. Elegant, long, neat; they lacked callouses or any other signs of heavy manual work. If Dana had seen a photo of them, she would have assumed he was an office worker – it fitted with his pale skin. He looked the indoors type.

'It's 2019 now, isn't it?' he asked. Dana nodded in reply; he would have seen only the edge of her shadow moving. He drew a deep breath.

'Well, then, the last I heard from my family was fifteen years ago. Yes, fifteen.' He tilted his head to one side, as if history could slosh into it.

Dana was finding her way towards something here, but it was groping rather than striding.

'So you lost contact in 2004, is that correct?'

'That autumn, yes. We had a farm, about halfway between Carlton and Earlville. I was living with my parents, Martin and Pamela, and my brother. Jeb.'

His voice quivered towards the end. He flicked a look at the mirror. Perhaps, thought Dana, he's shut them out of his mind for so long, and now they're creeping back. Maybe he knows exactly what information he's giving out and what the consequences are. He'd know he'll be traced through that, and surely they'd have a fix on who he is and where he's been in the last fifteen years. She wondered why he was so confident in giving the information: it jarred with his reticence and seemingly acute need for privacy.

'Would you like us to contact any of your family?'

Nathan puffed his cheeks and sat back. His skin flushed and she saw his neck muscles tighten. He took thirty seconds to recover his poise. She saw how much he'd been rattled. Dana let the moment stretch. She had the feeling that any silence from Nathan was not a signal that nothing was happening. It resonated for him in a different way: it was a period of noiseless reflection, not an absence of thought.

After a minute or so, he replied. 'No . . . no, I don't think so, thank you, Detective. I can't imagine they'll want to . . . no doubt they'll find out that I'm here, but I don't think I need to waste anyone's time actively telling them so. I'm sure you're very busy.'

Each sentence rolled off the last; by his previous standards, it felt very deliberate – almost tactical. Dana often interviewed people who had family problems, but it rarely slid through her own skin. Nathan's flustered reaction somehow seemed to chime with what she might say, given the same quandary.

'So, fifteen years ago you lost contact with your family. Was there some kind of falling-out?'

Again there was a stiffening, one he tried to hide by coughing unnecessarily. She mentally closed off a box in her strategy and knew to keep away from the subject – pushing it again at this stage would, she felt, prompt only resistance or shutdown.

'Not really a falling-out, no. I mean, not one incident. It was me that left the family home. Families don't always work out, do they, Detective?'

She wrote slowly, unsure if Nathan was merely fishing randomly or if he'd seen in her features something he recognised – some form of alignment. The direction of the conversation was beginning to bother her, starting to veer off on to swampy ground.

Nathan scratched at his palm, where the blood had pooled before. Seeming to believe that some was still there, he ran a fingernail along his fate line and studied it, looking for detritus.

'No, not always. When we bumped into you, Mr Whittler, you were in Jensen's Store, on the Old Derby Road. Had you been there before for any reason?'

Nathan shifted his weight, leaning forward slightly and resting his elbows on his knees. Now his face was level with the edge of the table, though his focus remained on his bloodless palm.

'Yes, every now and then. For supplies, you know. They have a lot of useful things in that store.'

Dana noticed that he had slipped into adding irrelevant details; almost as if he thought this was what a conversation would sound like. She sensed that if she waited . . .

The silence unravelled and stretched.

One minute became two. Became three.

Inside her head was a roaring rush, a desperation to start asking further questions. Dana made herself be still. She looked evenly at the top of his head, focusing on her breathing and the widow's peak in his hair. His shoulders rose and fell: she noted the moment at which a slight judder infected the movement. The shudder became stronger, until he leaned back with tear-rimmed eyes. Still he wouldn't look at her; his vision slid to the wall with the mirror and appeared distraught at what it found. She could see tears sliding down his cheeks, snot appearing at one nostril. His voice trembled when he finally gave way.

'I've . . . done terrible things, Detective. I'm so ashamed. So . . . ashamed. I knew it wasn't right, but I kept going, I kept on . . . terrible. I had no right, no right at all.'

He ran a forearm across his mouth and forced himself to gaze blearily at her shadow. 'At the store . . . is he . . . ?'

'He's dead, Mr Whittler. He's dead.'

Chapter 6

Dana took a deep breath when she closed the door on Nathan. It had taken five minutes for the silent crying to stop. He now had a sandwich, some tissues and a paperback she'd commandeered for him. They both wanted a break, but he didn't wish to go back to his cell. Bill was eager for feedback but realised she needed a moment.

She felt in her pocket for a second, shook her head and took a deep breath.

'Told you so,' Bill called to her as he approached. 'That's why you've got this and Mike hasn't: Whittler's a nightmare to open up. Could take days, and we only have a few hours.'

She nodded, exhausted already. Some of it was holding the Day at bay, but much of it was Nathan Whittler. He required total concentration; she believed the devil would be in the detail: where his fingers were touching, a quiver in his voice on a key word, what went unsaid.

The corridor had a series of skylights – illumination without compromising security – and they walked through cylinders of muted daylight. The main custody suite was quiet now: two overnight drunks and a burglary suspect had been kicked out after an early breakfast. Simpson, the custody officer, smiled at Dana as she passed. He liked her – she never asked him to bend the rules, was scrupulous about paperwork and gave him plenty of notice when she wanted to speak to a prisoner. He worked eleven-hour shifts without daylight: anyone who played the game properly was okay in his book.

They made their way to the drinks machine. The ceiling light was overly white and antiseptic, like in a dental surgery. She caught a half-reflection in the glass front of the machine. She looked shattered, her hair thin and strained, her skin sallow. It wasn't all down to a sunrise swallowing a revolver. Nathan had, in a short time, taken a toll.

Bill pretended his glasses needed cleaning. Patience was one of his virtues, alongside a purity of faith. In her. He pointed at the button for bottled water, because she was standing there, looking vacant.

'D'oh, sorry, Bill. First impressions? Okay. You were right, he's way off beam with almost anything. All our rules and training are pretty much useless.' The bottle slid reluctantly until it toppled into the drawer below.

Bill nodded. 'Told you. He reminds me of someone, or something, very strongly. But I can't quite place it. Like it keeps sliding away when I focus.'

Dana smiled. 'Yes, he has that kind of quality about him: not exactly slippery, more . . . hard to define. I don't even think it's deliberate. There's something inside that makes him that way, something about his past.'

They walked slowly down the corridor. On each side were open doors and slivers of chatter; the clicks of typing and mouse-manoeuvre, low-muttering telephone conversations and the poppy chirp of personalised ringtones. Uniforms mingled with admin; whiteboards were crude mixes of handwriting and extravagant arrows. Too many shards of too many stories she didn't know about. She needed her space. She needed to think.

'Yeah,' Bill said. 'His past. About that. We're having trouble finding anything after 2004. When I say "having trouble", I mean of course we have nothing. Absolutely nothing.'

'Maybe he went travelling or something.' Dana entered her office and switched on the light. Recent emails from Central made it clear they were to become a low-carbon organisation. 'I think he took off for a big reason. He denied it, but it felt like there was some kind of family problem; a dispute, maybe.' She stood next to her desk and slipped off her shoes.

'We've had officers check out the Whittler family home. But it's not in the family any more: it's an equestrian centre now. His parents died in 2007 – ravine versus car, ravine wins. Whittler may not know about that, I suppose.' Bill sank into a chair and played with a stray thread on his trouser hem. 'That only leaves the brother, Jeb. He's travelling back from some business meeting or other, apparently. He's . . .' Bill glanced at his watch, 'hopefully two hours away.'

He glanced beyond her shoulder to the wall. Most detectives – those who had their own office – used that as the Ego Wall. The venue for family photos, certificates, plaques swapped at inter-agency gatherings; a framed snap of the detective glad-handing or yukking it up with some minor celebrity. This wall had a fire-evacuation notice, a defunct taxi company's business card and a stain of undetermined origin.

Dana defaulted to a fingertip-to-thumb tapping. Nathan's talk about families prompted that particular reflex – a habit she couldn't shake, from a time when that was the only thing she could do.

'Okay, we'll need to tread carefully about his parents. Some dark history there, I sense. So where the hell has Whittler been for fifteen years?'

'All the usual channels are blocked. Lucy found no tax or credit trail, no phone records of any kind. His bank account has the same amount it had back then – never been touched. We can't find any employment records, or social security. It's like he's been living off thin air, in thin air.'

Reaching for a drawer, Dana checked for her inhaler. There were seven, lined up like sentries. There should be six, because she should have one on her. It bothered her that she'd forgotten and simply gone into the interview room *unarmed*. She pocketed one, tapped each of the rest with her index finger and closed the drawer.

'I got close, with those guesses about where he's been living. Not quite, but close.'

Bill finally snapped the thread and rolled it into a ball. 'My guess, if I hadn't met him, would have been living wild. Not for fifteen years, obviously; just off and on. But hell, if you do that for even a few weeks, it's blindingly obvious, you know? He'd smell; he'd be slightly dirty; his hair would be a wreck. And he'd have that leathery tan you see with winos and down-and-outs. He has none of that.'

Dana sat and clicked her emails. The most recent said Lucy would be arriving soon. 'I know, I know. Especially in this weather, too, he'd want to be indoors. And yet, that's the only kind of thing that fits, isn't it?'

Bill nodded.

Dana stood to ease her knee and resumed her fingertip tapping. 'Unless he's been living a long way away, or under a different name, he has to have been basically off grid. Maybe he got paid in cash and lived in someone's caravan, or above a garage; perhaps he was living rough for a while but he's been crashing with someone and got himself cleaned up. There are a couple of trailer parks towards the refinery, for example.'

'That's possible,' Bill admitted, then fell silent.

'But?'

'Look, it's always possible that he's a statistical outlier – a loner who's in the wrong place at the wrong time, or whatever. We know murder's sometimes like that. But I want to put it out there early, Dana: he could be something else entirely. He looks to have done all this deliberately. Assuming it's the case, then, the isolation? It takes a whole raft of intent to keep hidden in the modern world. You have to stay away from mobile phones, from cars, from CCTV cameras, from people. You have to organise your life to be either very transitory or purposely kept from view. Cash in hand, never putting down roots, keeping on the move: however he organised it, he did it. And he did it consciously. There has to be a mighty powerful reason to make that decision and follow it up for that length of time.'

Dana's gut reaction so far was that Nathan Whittler was too far off society's radar to be a threat to that society. But then, the Unabomber had lived off grid. And gone undetected for decades.

'Yes, I see that, Bill. Although, there might be many reasons behind it – not necessarily criminal ones. He could be hiding from someone, for example. We have witness protection for precisely that kind of reason – they're often good people in a bad situation.'

'Granted. But let's keep the darker options in mind for now. I mean, he said himself – "terrible things . . . I kept going . . . had no right" . . . Let's allow Whittler – or the evidence we uncover – to prove that it's benign. If it is. I mean, if someone is ghosting around the region, they can do anything. We have six undetected homicides in this region over the past five years alone. Throw in the whole state, let alone across the borders, and the numbers multiply. He could be anything at this point in the game. It's possible he killed Lou Cassavette for a trivial reason, or because capture by Lou might expose what he's done in the past. As far as we can tell right now, no person in the state has fewer alibis than Nathan Whittler. No life is empty, Dana: he filled it up with something. Maybe something he doesn't want anyone to know about.'

Bill didn't say such things for effect. He was right, she thought, about what should underpin the investigation at this stage. She needed to avoid being drawn in too tight, too quickly.

Dana stared when Lucy came in; Dana thought it wasn't obvious. She noticed that Lucy had her hair pulled back today: usually it swept down to her collarbone.

'Hey, Dana,' she smiled. 'Stop your silly habit.'

Dana glanced down at her hand. Thumb and index finger were touching. A small thing to the others but for Dana a stepping stone from the past. That was why she'd asked Lucy to nag her about stopping it.

'Uurrgghh, I was doing so well. Three weeks, I managed?' It was also shameful, Dana felt: childish, like thumb-sucking. Thank God no one knew its true significance and saw only a nervous tic.

Lucy stepped back a shade. 'I make it maybe four days, but who's counting? I called in on Forensics.'

She thumped a set of papers down on the desk. So much for the shared drive, Dana thought. Bill leaned forward to see but everything was upside down and in an absurdly small font. Although all three knew that everything seemed to be in an absurdly small font to Bill these days: vanity prevented glasses, and squeamishness about eyeballs prevented contacts.

'The headlines,' began Lucy. 'No sign of the weapon yet, but they're starting the fingertip search now they've done the big stuff. Your guy in custody? Well, he was wearing plastic bags on his shoes and he had gloves. So don't expect much from footprints, fingerprints, or anything in the DNA.'

Dana flitted between the paper and Lucy's eyes. 'He had blood on his hands, though?'

'Through the gloves. We haven't found any bloody fingerprints on shelves yet. The store wasn't heated, so I suppose he never got too warm and prickly. But there will be fingerprints generally – dozens of people. Might take a while to sift through and find the relevant ones.'

'Great.' Dana eye-rolled. Any store would have heaps of people prodding, testing, picking up, discarding: it was a forensic free-for-all that would hinder the investigation. 'We can pretty much assume that he was the one who climbed in the window, though. It's not like we need that.'

'Assume, not necessarily prove. But yeah, he can't deny being there, and he can't deny he has no permission to be there. However' – Lucy reached down and turned the page, tapping with a purple talon at the second paragraph – 'the blood on him matches the victim's type. DNA, as you know, takes longer. There's no spread on the victim because there's only one wound, so no arterial spray or anything.'

Dana sighed. 'Okay, but he sort of knows that already. Must know that. He doesn't seem particularly bothered.'

Lucy frowned. 'Not bothered?'

'Not at all,' replied Dana, sliding herself into the chair. 'I mean, most people in that situation – even those dumb enough not to have a lawyer by now – most of them would be calculating the odds. They'd weigh up what they think we have: motive, forensics, any witnesses, and so on. Then' – she looked at Bill – 'they'd try to get ahead of the game. Explain being in the store; why it wasn't them; how the blood came to be on them, and so on. They'd get their retaliation in first.'

'But he's not?' Lucy directed the question at Bill.

'No, Luce, he isn't,' replied Bill. 'As Dana says, he seems unaware of the repercussions. Maybe he knows that, by this time tomorrow, we'll be struggling to get anything out of him. I mean, he could pretend to play ball today and misdirect us. Then his lawyer tells him to shut it. He looks like he co-operated, and we came up with nothing. Could be a strategy with a jury in mind.'

'Or,' interjected Dana, 'he has other things on his mind that he thinks are more important. Might be more important.'

They all chewed on that for a moment. The notion that something could be more pressing to Nathan than being a murder suspect felt strange. He appeared to have other priorities, and his interrogation seemed a distraction. He behaved as if, at any moment, someone would see that suspecting him was laughable and would simply let him leave. It struck Dana that, if Nathan had committed other or greater crimes, that might be his reaction to arrest for this one.

Dana broke the silence. 'Luce, a hypothetical.'

Lucy stood from her slumped lean against a wall. 'Shoot.'

'You're early twenties, you want to drop off the radar. Completely. Totally. No communication with the family or anyone you know. Just drop out entirely. How do you do it and where and how do you live?'

Lucy smiled to herself and sat. Dana glanced at Bill, who raised a querying eyebrow that Dana didn't quite follow.

'So, it would depend on circumstance.' Lucy bit her lip in a way Dana couldn't stop noticing. 'I mean, do I have access to a new identity? Do I know the kind of people who could do that? Getting a false driver's licence, Medicare card, passport, and so on?'

Dana leaned forward and tried to focus on the paperwork in front of her. 'I don't think so, no. We've still to find any employment record, but he doesn't really strike me that way, no. And I don't think it was necessarily planned either. He might have simply upped and left.' She looked to Bill for a confirmatory nod. 'So let's say you don't.'

'Then it's not as if I can start again, as such. I have to stay me, with my identity. Which means either I have to move right away – so people don't know me and I can start afresh. Or I stay where I am, but no one can see me.'

'Moving away's more plausible to me,' offered Bill. 'We simply haven't widened the net enough. We're near the meeting point of three states here.'

'Confluence,' said Dana. '"Confluence" would be the word.' Lucy smiled to herself.

'Pee-dant,' grinned Bill.

'It's pronounced "ped-ant",' chorused Dana and Lucy, laughing.

'Anyway,' Bill continued with an exasperated hand-wave, 'he'll have slipped across a border or two, into another jurisdiction. Like I said: cash-in-hand employment, drifting. But maybe, in the last few weeks, staying somewhere he can get clean and neat. That would partly explain his appearance.'

Lucy raised a finger. 'But if he's clean and neat, and staying somewhere decent, why burgle the store? I mean,' she went on, 'he's only in that store for one of two reasons.' She counted them off on her fingers. 'One, to burgle it. Or two, to kill the victim. If we're assuming that he might not be a murderer' – she looked pointedly at Dana – 'and I think that's how some of us are leaning, then he was going there to steal. Why do that if you're already some place that's comfy and you're well looked after?'

'There you go again, Luce,' said Dana, 'coming at us with your "facts" and your "logic".' Her smile faded quickly. 'You've got a point. There's another thing: the way he is with people. He doesn't seem like he knows how to relate at all, or even fake it. It's not all shock, or being arrested. I'm sure that's part of it, but I think he's this way anyway. I'm struggling to see how he could get a job, or hold one down, with those kinds of people skills. Something that involves zero interface, maybe? Hmm. In fact, the more I think about that, the less likely it seems.'

Lucy and Bill had no reply. It struck Dana that no one but her had spoken *with* Nathan since he had arrived at the station. Everyone else, including Bill, had spoken *to* Nathan. The doctor's checks amounted to little more than a concussion test – Nathan had given single-word answers to direct questions. The custody officer, Simpson, had asked Nathan a couple of questions, but the replies had been nods or head-shakes. Bill had run through the prisoner's rights and got the legal waiver signed. But Dana had been the only one to get a word out of Nathan about anything other than his most basic details.

'Okay,' said Bill, 'we need to move forward. I want Dana back in the room quickly, Luce. The court's clock is already going, and there's no telling when Whittler will change his mind and lawyer up, so we have to exploit the gap while it's there. Wherever he's been living, we have to find it. There might be crucial evidence there, but at the very least it'll be a measure of the man – something we're severely lacking at the moment. Check databases interstate to see if he shows up there. Run his prints across the state, and across the border – I want to know if he's even been suspected of anything else. And I think Dana needs as much information as possible on the family, especially Jeb. Something under the waterline set Whittler off – would help to know what it is.'

Lucy gave a mock-salute. 'All over it, boss.' Dana watched her walk away.

After she left Bill turned to Dana. 'When your head's back, Dana?'

She looked absent-mindedly at him. 'Uh? Oh. Yes, we need to get Whittler to open up on where he's been living. That might give us a whole new ball game.'

Bill nodded slowly. 'It would be good to know. But go gently. He has to have faith in you, Dana. That's key.'

Dana smiled. 'No pressure, then?'

Chapter 7

Before facing Nathan a second time Dana crossed the corridor to check with Mike. Her office had been Mike's: he might have been the first public servant to voluntarily give one up. In truth, he'd found it isolating being on his own: he much preferred sharing with Lucy, and any hapless uniform seconded for a particular case.

She could smell the polish he'd applied to his desk that morning. Even the papers in the recycle bin were folded, not scrunched. Bill had assured her that Mike was fine with Dana catching this one, because Mike had worked four nightshifts in a row. His bad luck this had turned into something bigger.

'Got over your hissy fit about the water cup yet, Mikey?'

He gave one final click on the mouse and stretched back in his chair. 'Convincing enough?'

'I think so, yes.' She perched on the edge of another desk. 'Whittler certainly bought it. You should have your own star on that street in Hollywood.'

'Undoubtedly. But cops are always actors, aren't we?' He shrugged, as though he couldn't hold back the world. 'Always pretending we aren't surprised, appalled, scared, turned on, sickened – whatever.' He shook his head, answering a question she hadn't asked. 'Keep the mask up so we come off as reassuring, not just as frightened as they are.'

Sometimes Mike needed yanking out of his own head. 'Yer preachin' to the choir, sister.' She smiled.

'Touché. Oh, I have a photo of the victim's wife . . .'

'Megan.'

'Megan, yeah. From the insurance company's website. She's a quiet looker, and the victim's . . . not.'

She shook her head. 'A quiet looker? As opposed to . . . ?'

'Sorry, my dad's expression.' His placatory hand gesture didn't stop Dana's frown. 'Two types of beautiful women, he always said. Loud lookers knock you out: drive-into-a-tree gorgeous. Quiet lookers can be just as good-looking, but you need a second glance; they don't flaunt it. Might be in the eyes, or the smile, but they won't be dressed to the nines or anything.'

She raised her eyebrows a touch and whispered, 'That Human Resources tape's running, Mikey. Better cover yourself.'

He coughed and took a deep breath. His voice turned loud, flat and robotic. 'It is a reprehensible and sexist attitude which I don't support myself and which does not reflect my thoughts or actions within this unit. I throw it in as an interesting historical aside. Esteemed colleague.'

She grinned and gave a thumbs-up. 'So she's an eight and he's a five. Or . . . she really likes tall, wide, non-handsome bald guys. Which means what?'

'Possibly nothing. Maybe she was tired of him, wanted him out of the way. Or maybe he thought she'd leave sooner or later, so he starts playing around – like a pre-emptive strike. People sometimes do that: create the situation they fear.' He didn't seem to be directing that at Dana, but she took it to heart just the same.

Mike was scrolling down the screen, looking at three months' data from the store's alarm system. 'I see an unlikely amount of "sleeping at the store to catch a burglar" going on.'

Dana nodded. 'Yes, I wondered if all that was above board. Help Nick with the CCTV, if you get a chance. There might be something to suggest whether this vigil was an ingrained habit or cover for a quickie.'

Mike looked doleful and disapproving. 'Not very romantic, joining your paramour on the floor of a stockroom in a deserted store.'

'Mikey, you're a prince among men.' She mimed a fluttering heart.

He raised a finger. 'However, the floor of a stockroom in a deserted store, with a candle and a rose – now *that* would be seduction.'

'Strange idea of "going the extra mile" you have. Check with the Cassavettes' lawyer if they've been talking separation or moving back to the city. I sensed she didn't really want to come out here in the first place.'

Mike made another note. 'Shall do. There's nothing on CCTV close to the timescale for the stabbing, by the way. We've gone through the thirty minutes prior to the alarm and thirty minutes after. One camera on the cash register – that has a slight shadow in one corner for a couple of seconds, around the time of the stabbing. Probably Cassavette moving into position. Then nothing, until the uniforms come through the door. The other one, by the stockroom, shows Cassavette stretching his legs occasionally, harrumphing and eating chocolate, until' – Mike checked his notes – '0527 precisely. At which point he moves out of his sleeping bag and heads for the main part of the store. No sign of Whittler, or anyone else, for that matter.'

'Crap.'

'As you so eloquently say, crap. Sorry 'bout that.'

Dana pursed her lips. 'Any evidence Whittler knew Cassavette? Some kind of prior relationship?'

'None whatsoever that I can see. No record yet that he worked there or had an account with the place.' Mike tilted forward and waved a pen in her general direction. 'We're starting to round up the staff and former staff, so that might yield something. But no, nothing yet.'

Dana thought for a moment. She was already invested in Nathan Whittler, already trying to coax some form of relationship. He was the man arrested at the scene, bloodied and blinking. Yet they currently had no scope on his psychology, or pathology. It would be a long, arduous battle to open him up – plenty of thankless efforts, blind alleys and failures. But it was important that he wasn't the only game in town.

'Talk me out of Nathan Whittler,' she said.

Mike tapped his pen against the desk. This was what they did – the primary detective pursued what seemed like the best live option and the other detective mopped up the rest, chewing on alternatives and constantly chipping at assumptions and lazy groupthink. Dana had introduced the concept when they first met, and Mike liked it. Not only was it effective, but it spoke to Dana's commitment to finding truth, rather than guilt.

'Okay. At the moment the evidence is strong but circumstantial. Forensics probably won't completely prove anything but will tilt you in a particular direction. Barring a major shift, that direction will be Whittler. Yes?'

She nodded, settling back down on to the corner of the desk, tweaking her kneecap as it threatened to lock. 'Yes. Bloodied hands always makes an impact. So what's wrong with that picture?'

Mike wasn't veering towards the most common kinds of stabbings – drug arguments gone bad, gang wars, 'disrespected' teenagers. Partly because they usually happened in the street, or at a location known to police already. Partly because those kinds of crimes rarely if ever happened just before dawn. They were daytime or evening crimes – done by 2 a.m. Plus, there was nothing right now to suggest Lou Cassavette knew that kind of person – at best, it would have to have been an accidental meeting.

'So, first, if Whittler's the burglar with the rucksack, he's forensically aware. Very much so.' Mike nodded to himself, as if working through the idea on the run. 'He was leaving no trace at that burglary. So why be found with a dead body and blood on the gloves? That's a major flip. It's possible he was caught out, but even so. Anything that cuts across his previous behaviour should make us wary. And his behaviour up to that point was to yield no forensics whatsoever.'

Dana agreed but had an alternative. 'What if he had an accomplice for the burglary, who scrammed? The accomplice could be the forensically aware one, and Whittler is the dim one left behind with a dead body. He might be too scared to give up his partner.'

'True.' He liked the comeback – she wasn't simply soaking up what he was suggesting. His previous partner had been a little lazy and very passive: he'd accepted instantly anything Mike said, even if it contradicted a conversation from five minutes before. Dana did not do that. 'But Whittler strikes me as brighter than that, and nothing about his demeanour suggests he's a team player.'

Yes, thought Dana. Nathan Whittler's demeanour loomed large; she had a nagging feeling it was crucial. The type of person Nathan Whittler was, could be decisive.

'All right,' continued Mike, 'so there's the deviation from known behaviour: both forensically, and to commit a murder. Because we've nothing on him, and certainly nothing violent.' He tilted his head to indicate either/or. 'But he does have means and opportunity, which is why we count him in. That leaves . . . motive. He has no apparent motive.'

That was, at this juncture, true. But they might find a connection later.

'So who has?'

Mike pointed at the screen, where Megan Cassavette's picture held his gaze.

'Well, *she* probably has. Or drives the person who has. *Cherchez la femme*, and all that. When you first came from Fraud, you looked for rational and logical connections that led to motive. You wanted, especially, a financial reason for crimes. You still do, to some extent. If you want me to pick up on potential missed opportunities, I'll always go back to that. You want motives from spreadsheets. Whereas I want motives from bedsheets.'

She had no problem yielding that point. It was in her nature to go digging in data, as though every answer lay there. She was still learning – usually from Mike – about all manner of alternatives. Learning, in her view, too slowly.

'You think she has a lover and *he* killed Lou Cassavette?'

Mike grinned. 'Or she. Twenty-first century, right? Or maybe Lou has a lover and it's her angry husband. Or Lou finished it and the lover objected. Stabbing is close up, personal; often driven by passion, even if it's in the moment. Nathan Whittler doesn't seem like a passionate person, does he? I don't see him as someone driven by high-enough emotion to stab someone in the heart, and high emotion is what it takes.'

Dana chewed her lip. It was a strong point. Nathan Whittler was too frightened even to look at her and had broken down in the first interview. Did he have the ferocity, the heightened anger or jealousy? He didn't seem to, and she couldn't yet picture something monstrous enough to cause it. Whereas a jilted or determined lover? Maybe they would.

'Good job, Mikey. If we're going to pursue that angle, then the rubbish bin on Megan's lawn looked out of place. No other house had it. That could be a signal, if Megan is the one with the lover. Or maybe

Lou left it out last night, to signal no-go to his paramour: hence, they meet at the store. See what Tech can find from the laptops: lovers usually give themselves away. So I'm told.'

Mike made a note.

'Where are we with the rest of it?' she asked.

'I have a call in to a buddy in Intelligence, so waiting on him. Financials and phone records will be through shortly. I put in a call to the store's bank to check the business finances, too. Waiting on a reply. Dennis is starting on the computers from the Cassavette house. Search of the house turned up nothing significant, but Megan's going to stay at her mother's for a few days, so we have a clear run if we need to go back there. Inventory of that rucksack from the store is on your desk – eclectic mix of ridiculously cheap items, for some reason.'

'You're so all-encompassingly thorough, Mikey.'

'The phrase you're looking for is "obsessive neat freak with a control fetish".' To prove it, Mike tapped a pile of papers into a flawless bundle.

'Ha. I bet they all swipe right when they see that under your photo.'

'My zany single life ended many years ago.'

'And a nation breathed a sigh of relief that day.' Dana stood up, a zing of pain from her knee as she did so. 'Okay, thanks, Mikey. I'll go push Whittler for a firmer fix on where he's been hiding out. Keep Bill in the loop as you work through those details – he can feed me anything vital.'

Chapter 8

Nathan seemed more relaxed when she looked in through the mirror. Slumped casually, holding the paperback in one hand and gently swirling the water in his cup with the other, he looked placid, almost contented. Already she considered herself so connected to him that she felt responsible for his wellbeing. She had to consciously note that her primary duty was to Lou Cassavette's memory and to finding the truth.

But when the door handle squeaked he snapped to attention. Jumped, almost. He spilled a few drops of water as he put the cup back on the table. His posture became stilted and wary. She'd broken into his own peculiar brand of reverie.

Dana took a deep breath and entered. She resumed her seat and flicked on the tape machine.

'How's the book, Mr Whittler?'

Nathan glanced at the cover – a weathered man in a black hat squinting as he fired at a dusty foe, Monument Valley icons behind him. 'Terrible, I'm afraid.'

Dana nodded as she set out her paperwork and files. 'Yes, I'm sorry we couldn't find anything better at short notice. The best thing about Zane Grey is the name of the author. After that, it's downhill all the way.' She looked up at him. 'I sense you're a big reader, Mr Whittler?'

Nathan reached for his cup again but merely held it in two palms, like hot chocolate on a cold night. 'Yes, whenever I can.'

She waited for him to expand, as most people would, then chastised herself. That was not how he operated. The rhythm she was trying to engender would have to be driven by her.

'Soothing, isn't it? Someone else's world?' She tilted her head to one side and was silently thrilled when, seeing her shadow move, he unconsciously mirrored it. 'When you get a good book, it's like someone gifted you a piece of their imagination.'

Nathan blinked hard at his cup. 'Yes, quite so. You were a child who escaped to the library, then?'

'Oh, yes,' she replied. 'There were a bunch of us who did that.'

Although, she recalled, never together: just an archipelago of individual, quiet souls among the shelves, breathing slowly, grateful for the solitude and acceptance. They didn't have to justify or explain themselves – they were appreciated for their mere presence. She would see the others like wraiths, a horizontal splinter of another child between book and shelf. Like her, she imagined, praying the sun would magically stop setting and the clocks become still.

'What sort of thing do you normally read, Mr Whittler?'

This seemed to stump him. He looked again to his hands for telltale blood lines. 'Uh, well, anything I can get, really. I don't always have a full choice, so I pretty much read anything. Especially in the evening.'

'Too busy in the daytime?' She left the question hanging.

Nathan took a sip. She understood that he wanted the water as much as a prop to hide his unconventional body language as for the refreshment. Dana pondered whether he'd be more forthcoming without the cup to hide behind, or if it was helping him to feel more respected and trusted – because he had asked for something and got it.

'Well, actually, I find my eyes get strained if I read too much.' He nodded to himself, as if he'd escaped a tight corner.

Dana pretended to write – her own prop. 'Mr Whittler, I mentioned the last time we spoke that I'd return to the subject of your address. May I do that now?'

'Yes, Detective Russo. If you wish.'

She tapped finger and thumb together under the table. 'We established previously that you've not had a formal address that could be found. Is that a fair summary?'

'Of what?'

She'd stumbled. 'Of your living arrangements, and our current understanding of them.'

'Yes, it is.'

She inwardly cursed herself – inaccurate language was going to be picked up: it was a given. He had to respect her intellect in these 'conversations'. If he didn't, she felt sure he'd close down and cut her out entirely.

'We also established that the most recent address was not a boat, or a caravan. But we can't find a fixed residential address. I wonder, therefore, if you were out of state during the period from 2004 to 2019.'

His slight smile told her that he wasn't, even before he confirmed it.

'I haven't been out of state since I was a child, Detective Russo. Never felt the need.'

'I see. In that case, I would tend towards the idea that you've been living in the countryside.'

He tried to remain flintily neutral, but a muscle near his collar bone twitched. He stayed silent and touched the water-bottle cap again.

'I'm assuming, Mr Whittler, that you haven't been living in any of the cabins near the tri-lakes?'

He looked up sharply at the mirror. 'No. I have not. Those cabins belong to other people.'

His voice was steelier than she'd heard it before. She decided not to react, not to confront him with his own answer. She needed him talking, so on this issue discretion had to be the better part of valour – for now. She should park it; discuss it with Bill later. It was a potential line of attack: his bristling defence of his own ethics about where he slept, when he was the primary suspect for killing a man.

'Quite so. In that case, Mr Whittler, I'm left with the only reasonable alternative – that you've been living in the woods' – he flickered – 'recently?' He stopped flickering. 'No . . . for a very long time?'

He pretended to cough and opened the water bottle again. She sat motionless while the glugging filled the crackling air between them. In the distance, a freight train's shuffling seeped through the wall insulation. When he finished pouring he carefully replaced the cap, twisting the bottle so that the label faced him, and touched the cap. He left the cup alone.

Again, she waited him out. While he was clearly comfortable with his own space and silence, she now sensed that this operated only when he was alone. When there was someone else engaging with him, he was acutely aware of their need for him to respond. Nathan Whittler seemingly comprehended enough of social graces to know people's expectations. His first response would be flight, she was sure; when that wasn't an option, he floundered. He found it easy to wipe out for a minute, maybe two. Most people would have given up by then, she reasoned, so he could get away with it. The uniform officers, the doctor, the cell duty, Bill: they'd all quit a few seconds after asking him something. If you could bear to stretch it for three or four minutes, there was the chance he'd break first.

He whispered. 'Since 2004.'

Suddenly the air felt saturated. She could imagine Bill behind the mirror, punching the air at the breakthrough. All they needed now was . . .

'And where is that camp of yours, Mr Whittler?'

He squirmed under the question. She felt she'd pinned him, like a butterfly in a collection. His hands performed a writhing, dry-washing motion and he looked rigidly at the label on the water bottle. His lips moved slowly and silently – possibly some kind of mantra – and he scratched his face hard. It was painful to watch; Dana toyed with the idea of reaching across and gently squeezing his hand in consolation. It would have been a monstrous and hugely counter-productive gesture to make, but his anguish was plain to see and physically difficult to observe. Being Nathan Whittler was clearly not easy and the sudden insight into what it involved jarred her.

'I'm sorry to ask something so personal, Mr Whittler,' she began. 'I can see this is distressing for you, but it's something we must know in this situation.'

'You can't . . . don't you see? I can't tell you. Won't tell you.' He folded his arms and hunched forward. But it was the movement of a small child who knew he'd lose in the end and was making himself feel better with apparent defiance.

Dana considered for a moment. There were any number of reasons why he wouldn't divulge where he lived. She didn't discount the possibility that the camp held key evidence that would implicate him. He might simply be covering his own back and hoping that, at some point, he could return to camp and destroy what might bring him down. He was, after all, the main suspect in a homicide.

But she felt that wasn't at the root of it; or if that was the case, it was incidental to his main problem. It felt to her that he simply found it a grotesque intrusion, a physical assault on his privacy. Perhaps she could attack it another way.

'Mr Whittler, you said that you'd lived in this camp since 2004. Have you lived anywhere else in that time, or has this camp been your only home during that period?'

Nathan took a sip. 'It's my only home, Detective Russo. My only home. I'm sure you understand someone's need for their home to be their refuge. I'm sure you're very careful who you let into your space.'

He said it to the floor, almost to himself, but she still shook when she heard it. Despite his disconnect, he seemed able to strike at the root of her. Yet there was no malice in it, she felt; his words appeared to be benign and open to a simpler interpretation.

'I understand your reticence, Mr Whittler, but—'

'Would you?' he asked.

'Excuse me, would I what?'

'Answer questions about your home. From a complete stranger?'

It was not an idle enquiry; Dana could sense that Nathan did not ask such things. If he posed the query, he meant for it to be answered. She needed his co-operation and this might be a way to secure it. But she felt he needed her honesty just as much. She gambled.

'To be honest, Mr Whittler, it would depend on the circumstance. I'd have to weigh up some factors.'

'Such as?'

'In no particular order, then. In this context, am I guilty or innocent? Who is asking? Exactly what are they asking? What does it cost me to tell them? What will they do with the information? What I might gain by telling. What will be inferred if I don't. Whether it's acceptable to withhold in the face of a reasonable question, from a reasonable person, who can be trusted with the reply.'

He didn't answer, but chewed on her response.

'I live in an old house near here. I let very few people into it. I wouldn't want to live anywhere else. It's filled with things I love, and many that only I could love. I can't imagine my life anywhere but that house.'

Nathan bit his lip and stared solidly at the floor. Then he nodded slightly and took a sip of water. It seemed to be a prelude, an acquiescence of some kind.

Dana reminded herself that she wasn't only asking questions here for her own knowledge; there were people behind the glass who wanted, and needed, information to act upon.

'Am I correct to assume that you lived there by yourself?'

Nathan nodded slowly.

'Has anyone, at any time, visited the camp?'

'I hope not. No one to my knowledge, Detective. That is, I didn't want or need anyone to visit. So no. I don't believe so.'

Again, thought Dana, that running over of the sentence – continuing long after the point had been made. There was something about that which signified desperation on his part, she was certain of it. This desperation would, she already understood, make him clam up. He was buckling but also closing down; she needed to change tack.

'May I ask some questions about the practicalities of your living arrangements, Mr Whittler?'

She was offering him firmer, more neutral ground. He took it.

'Yes, you may, Detective.'

'Thank you. We're unaware of any movements in your bank account. What did you use for money?'

Nathan's face reddened. For a moment she thought it was anger. But then she recognised the emotion and felt the irony that she, of all people, hadn't picked up on it straight away. It was shame.

'I . . . I had no need of money, Detective. I wasn't paying rent, or things like that, you see.'

Dana considered backing away, coming at it later. But no, this was a legitimate line to take. 'I can see that it would be possible to live frugally, if you so wished, Mr Whittler. But you would still need to buy food. Wouldn't you?'

Nathan stared icily at the edge of the table. There was a quick glance at the mirror, as though his conscience were glaring at him from beyond it. The shame brought forth a flash of anger.

'Why are you asking me that, Detective? Why? What business can it be of the police what I eat? In what way is that relevant?' He raised his voice but studiously avoided eye contact. 'You're the police, not doctors, isn't that so?'

She shuddered, grateful that in his fuming belligerence he didn't see her reaction. She'd anticipated frustration, but this was raw anger, and she hadn't expected that. She and Mike had discussed whether Nathan had the high emotion in him to commit a crime as potentially passion-led as stabbing. She considered the possibility as she listened to Nathan's breathing. But this was, surely, an opportunity.

Dana dug into her training. He'd lost his temper – albeit for a few seconds. She knew – simply knew – that he would now be contrite and embarrassed. She held the moral high ground for the first time and he would feel obliged to repay her. She could make use of his need to atone, if she held her nerve.

He scratched his head and rubbed his face sharply with his palms. His breathing slowed. 'I'm sorry, Detective. I apologise.'

'That's quite all right, Mr Whittler. Police interviews are always stressful.' She moved some papers around needlessly and turned to a fresh page in her notebook, simply to show him there was a break with what had gone before.

'I wonder how you managed in this cold weather, Mr Whittler. In your camp.'

He inclined his head once, to acknowledge her good grace, before replying. 'Many layers, Detective, many layers. You have to understand the importance of insulation. And you have to develop a system – of when you'll be awake and when you sleep.'

'How so, Mr Whittler?'

He steepled his fingers, like an aged teacher imparting wisdom. 'Most people sleep at night, but that's when it's coldest. The coldest time is just before dawn, and that's when most people have been asleep for many hours. Their metabolism is slowest; they're at their most vulnerable. The trick is to do it the other way around: wake up hours before it's coldest and move about. Then you can sleep in the afternoon, when it's safer to do so. You see.'

Never in her life would Dana sleep outdoors, so in that sense the information was utterly irrelevant. But it was the first freely given insight he'd offered.

'Ingenious. I can see how that would work. Did you have this kind of survival knowledge before you went into camp, Mr Whittler?'

'No, no. Trial and error, really. You need to think it through, is all.'

'And this week – with the very low temperatures – was that especially hard for you?'

He nodded. 'Yes, I haven't felt that cold in quite a while. But you get through it. You get through it. Everything can be survived, if you go about it right.'

This new silence felt different. Nathan had pulled inside himself again – his speech tailed off to a whisper near the end, and Dana sensed he was tired. She wanted to push but knew she shouldn't.

'Perhaps we should give you some rest, Mr Whittler? And some food?'

'Thank you, Detective. And an aspirin, please, if you can find one.'

As she closed the door Dana saw Bill approaching. She made a T-sign with her hands, indicating she needed to recalibrate. He nodded and turned his attention to Lucy as she passed in the corridor.

Chapter 9

The foot bridge over the train lines passed about twenty metres above the track. These days, the freight was largely imported foreign goods headed to the city, which in reply exported only garbage, washed-up politicians and patronising day-trippers. The rails went through a natural gorge at this point: the bridge had wire fencing up and over, making it feel like an elongated aviary. It was to stop suicides, she reminded herself with a shudder.

Like most mining areas, the region's progress – and the location of the two main towns – was dictated largely by geology and wind direction. The geology meant that development in Earlville cascaded down three snug river valleys, clutching the coat tails of coal and tin, spilling and tumbling along whatever was near-horizontal. The valleys trapped the foul air, the people and their ambitions. Tight communities with narrow horizons and fierce loyalty; they still clung to a notion of duty to each other. Some early philanthropic money-throwing produced the requisite library, school and church, but little else after that. Now, with the coal gone and religion's bindings loosened, the town festered and grumbled – disappointed to be left behind but secretly wallowing in it.

The wind direction chose the location of Carlton. Ten kilometres from Earlville on a shallow slope, upwind from the industrial belching in the valleys, Carlton was a place of clean air, strong limbs and the spoils of others' labour. It was initially built in a grid pattern around a central square, before a trend for crescents began to hold sway. All the municipal buildings for the region were located there, along with a proprietorial air that said Carlton knew what was best for Earlville. The result was broad, tree-lined streets, with most houses stemming from a golden pre-war era: verandas, widows' walks, hanging baskets and a studied but aloof and time-frozen affluence. The poorer districts were merely scrunched and hunched versions of the same. Too far from the city to be commutable, Carlton grasped its heritage tight and left economic development to others. Dana liked it.

Some schoolchildren were being ferried from their classes to the nearby swimming pool. They crocodiled in bashfully linked pairs, then stopped to point excitedly down an alleyway between a carpet store and an office block. The buildings sandwiched a large water butt: the water's silky dark surface held three bright yellow rubber ducks, grinning in the shadows.

When Dana was taken for compulsory school swimming lessons there had been a craze for 'mushroom floating'. It involved cramping into a tight, foetus-like ball and surrendering to buoyancy. After a while, the coiled form would softly roll on to its back, allowing it to unravel in the light like an emerging bloom. Except Dana didn't. Her ferocious knee-hugging would not be weakened. She would not rotate gently, nor even float serenely; instead, she remained face down, slowly subsiding to the floor of the pool until she ran out of breath. Then she had to fight her way to the surface, thrashing through the bubbles. No one could explain why she didn't float; no one comprehended her body's wish to fall to the depths and remain there.

She walked down a recently resurfaced lane: New Walk was four hundred metres of dry-stone walls, punctuated by large metal gates bracketed by columns. Carlton always looked after those who had shaped its past, rather than those who might lead the future. Old school, old money: the homes were impressive yet strangely unemotional. People had hired other people with exquisite taste.

The owners would be gone by now – into the city for business or shopping. They set the tone for local elections; they were the ones who needed to be impressed. Without their fickle patronage, the foundations of every public service buckled. Entitled, one-eyed, privileged and ignoring anything that disquieted them, they treated the police as bespoke security guards.

St Vincent's Church was tucked into a corner at the end of the lane, hunched below a beautiful copper beech. In the day's sunlight the beech presented filigreed shadows, flickering gently across the clapboard exterior. In summer, the congregation stood below its branches in welcome shade, sipping the lemonade sold to pay for the ever-atrophying roof. The roots slithered away below tufted grass to the small car park and burrowed under the church to prop it up.

She'd been brought here when she was eight years old: a port in a storm, a place of responsible adults. Somewhere that could wash the cut and ice the bruise; a location the cops knew; people who'd fuss and make tea for an hour, who'd bring biscuits and sweeties to her. They'd meant well, those Samaritans rescuing her from her own garden. But really: the idea that this place was any better than home. It was less visceral, but ultimately proved just as dangerous. The ripples still slid outwards, even now. Twenty-five years wasn't enough to still the waters.

She stopped at the threshold. It was an achievement to be here at all – a marker of progress, but at the same time a necessary evil. For

Dana, this was still something to be pushed through, to be accomplished and rewarded later. She could have met Timms elsewhere, but she knew she had to keep crossing this Rubicon every few weeks. If she didn't, it would build even more in her mind and become another crippling obsession.

'Bless me, Father, even though I haven't sinned.' Dana's voice struck the stone floor, her steps echoing in the icy space. Churches made her shiver regardless of temperature, drove her backwards in her mind. She always felt she was scrabbling for grip, fighting to stay in the present despite a brutal dragging force. She looked up at Christ, bleeding and suffering.

'Red! Wasn't expecting you today. Of course. Well. Anyway. What have you to confess?' Father Timms looked up from a stack of paperwork and pushed his spectacles up so he could focus. His voice shimmied off the stone walls and fluttered past her, out into the crisp air.

'Uh, nothing. At least, I think I've been blameless.' She dropped her bag by the door and stepped forward tentatively. 'Does it count as a sin if you didn't know it was a sin?'

'"Sin"'s an over-used, emotive word. Try "cock-up", "screw-up". Something like that.'

They grinned and hugged. Timms stepped back to look at her properly. It had been only days since they'd had coffee, but he sensed a change in her. It wasn't only setting foot in here – though that was part of it. There was a gnawing uncertainty around her eyes and a bashful reluctance to meet his gaze. Notwithstanding the date, he thought he recognised Case Face; he'd seen it in her a number of times. She'd be sublimating everything to focus on a crime, but some things couldn't be held down.

'What was this sin that isn't really a sin, then?' He motioned to a nearby pew and they sat, legs facing front but bodies corkscrewed towards each other.

Dana coughed into her scarf, more to buy time than anything else. 'Was hubris a sin?'

Father Timms waved a hand dismissively. 'Ah, we had lots of odd ones back in the day. Coveting: coveting was big for a while. We've had to invent a few to keep up – taking selfies, that kind of thing.' He nodded. 'I think hubris was fashionable at some point, yeah.' He paused, and his smile faded. 'Not one I'd associate with you, Russo.'

'Yes, well. Me neither. Although, if I was actually hubrissing, I'd be the last to know, wouldn't I?'

'That's very true. If only the word existed, it would be true. Tell.'

Dana looked at the organ, which skulked by a velvet curtain in the corner. She could almost see her mother playing it still: the hunched back of a weaver, the dancing fingers, leaning her flimsy weight forward because her legs alone wouldn't move the pedals. A spindly, gimlet-eyed spectre of a woman. Interminable hours after school: Dana scrawling in notebooks and reading novels while her mother worked herself into rapture. Then the scrubbing; the endless scrubbing.

That was after, of course.

And before, of course.

'Well, all this feels . . . pre-emptive. I mean, I might be jumping the gun, but I need to get ahead of it now, before it causes real problems. I feel like I've taken on a task I don't know how to complete. And there are very real implications if I don't manage it.'

'Imposter syndrome again? We've talked about that before. You have very keen self-preservation skills, Dana, but they come at the price of underestimating yourself. You know where all that comes from, don't you?'

Yes, she knew. It was where everything came from: good or bad, useful or self-destructive. All from the same locus.

'We have someone in custody for the Jensen Store homicide. You've heard about that?' This place was not quite a confessional, but almost. She knew he would respect the sanctity of this discussion just as much: their friendship had reached that plane a while ago.

Father Timms nodded. Soon the local newspaper would clatter against his porch, sodden by morning dew at the first bounce. There would be lurid details and ill-informed speculation, but he already knew the bare bones. Carlton was still a small town with a hive mentality. 'Yeah, I heard. Poor guy. So, you've got a suspect?'

'Yes . . . technically speaking.'

'But?' he prompted.

Dana looked away, struggling to frame it right. Father Timms was smart – sometimes too quick for her own good – but her problem was mainly professional, not pastoral.

'But . . . it doesn't feel right. This, uh, suspect. He's off-beam. Not in a mental-health way – at least, not that we can ascertain. But something . . .' She paused. Saying it out loud made it seem even more nebulous. She couldn't really explain what felt wrong. 'There's a big "something" I'm missing.'

In the mist beyond a car alarm sounded for two seconds then switched off. Father Timms flipped a hymn book over and over, like a card sharp idly toying with the pack. 'You rely on your intuition, Dana. Why doubt it in this case?'

'Not sure. Bill gave me a run at this guy and I think – no, I *know* – that I'm getting more from him than someone else would. But still I feel I'm falling short. We have twenty-four hours – crap, less than that now. But maybe four hours of actual talking to him. We might not get enough for a murder conviction without this guy opening up – confessing – and I'm the only person who's getting anything from him; it's all on me to break through and find the truth.'

'Lot of pressure.'

'Yes and no. There's always pressure to close a case, especially one like this. But no, I wasn't moaning about that bit.' She scratched her nose. 'I thought I could do it. I thought – since he seemed to trust me a little – I could get through his defences. Hence – the hubrissing thing.'

She faced the organ again, stuttered at the memory, and recovered. 'Because I'm not sure I can. I feel like I can't really get through to him. All I'm doing is getting little slivers off the corners, you know? Bill would say it's early days, but it seems to me like a window that's closing. This guy will lawyer up and clam up at some point, I'm sure of it. I need to be right in the guts of it by now, but I'm out in the margins. I'm going to run out of ideas and out of time.'

She squeezed the bridge of her nose and rubbed her eyes. 'He keeps saying he doesn't want a lawyer and we can maybe get extensions, but our luck can't hold for ever. Sooner or later a judge is going to call "enough", whether this guy agrees or not. Then we'll be properly screwed. Father.'

Timms turned slightly and leaned back against the hard wood. 'So where's the logjam, Red? There's always a logjam of some kind when you show up here.'

She shook her head. 'Ah, sorry. Feels too much like cupboard love?'

'No, no.' He dropped an octave and looked up at her. 'Although you're welcome to participate, spectate, or just plain donate . . .' He smiled. 'No, it's more that if we meet away from church, it's not the same thing driving you. I know what it costs you to meet here, instead of anywhere else.'

In the silence that followed Dana's eyes were drawn back again to the organ in the corner, to the pipes reaching for heaven, to the black pedals with their scuffmarks and ingrained polish. Their walks home had been silent – scuffing steps and the hissing backdrop of her mother's fuming breath. The walk gathered her mother's desperation, built the momentum, raised steam. While little Dana – she knew what was coming but could do nothing but clack her patent shoes obediently on the pavement.

'I'm hardly likely to view this place as sanctuary, am I, Father?'

He gave her a sidelong glance and hastened to cover his tracks. 'No, you never will. And I respect your courage, still setting foot in here. Especially today. That's all true, but you do come here to clear away something that's blocking you. We do serve some purpose for you, Dana.'

She thrust her hands into her coat pockets, to keep finger from thumb. 'Okay, we're currently grappling with where this guy might live. Have lived. Since 2004.' She looked back at Timms, noticing a wrinkle on his forehead that she'd have sworn he didn't have last week. 'He's adamant it's been his location since then. But he's not on any database; he's not showing up anywhere at all. We're stuck: he's been living in some kind of camp, but we don't know where to start.'

'Hold on, hold on.' Timms frowned. 'For fifteen years, he's been *camping*? What, winter as well as summer?'

Dana could see that, once again, they were on the same wavelength. It was simultaneously reassuring and spooky that he did this so often. 'I know. Surely he'd find shelter in winter? He doesn't look like he's been camped out that long. He's got short hair, decent skin, soft hands; he's clean.'

He leaned forward and rubbed his ring finger absent-mindedly. 'You've considered, Detective, that he may be – oh, I dunno – lying to you?'

She smiled at the altar. 'Ha-de-ha. Yes, I thought about it. But my instinct tells me he isn't.' She put up placatory palms. 'Might be way off – he's so unusual he could be throwing my radar. But no, I think he's holding back something fierce, but he's not actually lying. I'm not asking the right questions.'

Timms shook his head slightly. 'So who's he spoken to; where's he worked, where's he shopped? Friends? Relatives?'

Dana stood; her knee was starting to grind. The cold made it worse. She rubbed it as she spoke. 'Big fat zero. No employment records at all, no friends we can find, hasn't spoken to his family since 2004, allegedly. Nothing. Totally off the grid.'

He glanced to his left, to a triptych along one candlelit wall: Moses. 'Like a hermit?'

She followed his gaze and noticed the images. 'Like a hermit. Yes, exactly like that. But without the whole tablets-of-stone-God's-word thing.'

'Hmmm. And he's given no clue about the nature of the camp or the location?'

'No, he's very reluctant to give any details.' She thought for a second. 'Strike that. He actively doesn't want us to find it, although I haven't worked out why not. And before you ask, yes, he might have incriminating evidence there, and that might be the reason.'

'No, no, I wasn't going to say that. It strikes me there would be other reasons. An acute sense of privacy, maybe – that's been his home, and maybe his protection, for so long he can't bear the thought of anyone seeing it. As if it's a part of him, somehow, and you'd be looking inside him by looking at it.'

'That was my idea, too. It chimes with his pathology – or what we know of it.'

Father Timms shrugged. 'Well, it's just a stray thought. But in the olden days hermits used what they could find as shelter. The easiest – no preparation, no building anything – was a cave.'

Now she stared, open-mouthed. 'Yes, yes. Good, good thinking, yes.' She swallowed hard. 'I've got to go.'

She wrapped her scarf around her neck, not quite sure how to end the conversation without simply rushing out. She stood still, caught in the moment. He did it for her.

'Go. Go, Dana. It's okay.'

She smiled weakly, half in apology.

'But remember!' he shouted at her departing frame. 'I do know what Day it is. And I am here all Day. In church, on the phone, anywhere you want to meet. I am here for you. Deal?'

Chapter 10

When she got back to the office Dana riffled through some papers in a lower drawer before coming up trumps. The telephone rang so long she was about to give up, and then someone croaked a greeting.

'Billy Munro? It's Dana – Dana Russo, from the book club?'

'Oh, hey there. How's things? Are you ringing to tell me to finish that Ishiguro? Coz I have to tell you, I was losing the will to live.'

She smiled. 'No, I'm with you on that one. No, it's not about the book club, actually. I wanted to pick your brains on something else.'

'Oh.' He sounded surprised, disappointed and cautious in one word. Quite a feat, she thought. It flitted through her mind that she seemed to evoke that combination in a number of people and had no idea how.

'Billy, I have in my feeble brain some notion that you're a potholer. Is that right?'

She could almost hear him nodding that broad, bald head of his. Billy had a near-permanent blush to his skin, making him look either angry, squeezed or hurt most of the time. 'Well, I used to be, till the arthritis hit me. Can't get in and out of gaps like I used to. These young guys are like greased otters.'

'But you probably know most of the caves around here, yes?'

'Oh, sure, it's not like they change from one year to the next, is it? What's on your mind, Dana?'

She thought about how to frame it. As far as she was aware, Billy wasn't a gossip, but you never knew these days. She read with horror about people photographing their junk right, left and centre and posting it for the world to see. Not difficult to imagine a middle-aged guy talking out of turn in a bar.

'Okay, so this is strictly off the record: police business.'

'No problem. Twenty years a rural firefighter, and SES. I know how the cops work.'

'Cool. So let's say someone's been hiding out in a cave. For quite a long time. Has to be big enough for them to live in, but far enough out of sight that they aren't bumping into hikers and rubes. And not interesting enough, or unexplored enough, for potholers to show up. Where would I start looking for that kind of cave?'

'Well now,' Billy replied. There was a short grunt as – she presumed – he sat down and gave it serious consideration. 'Let's see. There's plenty north of the tri-lakes, but there's people in and out of there all the time. Tourist central, there, in summer. Those caves are on the ridge above Miller's Point campground, and there's that outdoor sports place next to it. You know, with the zip-line and all? So they're big enough, but you'd probably be noticed. Some people are just plain curious, you know? See caves up on the hill: take a look. Plus, it's also popular for, uh, how to frame it for a lady . . . courting couples? So I doubt your man picked those. Hmm.'

Dana liked the old-world courtesy. Made her feel she had been born in the wrong era – something that infused her thoughts whenever she saw a black-and-white film. She waited patiently. Billy needed to go through his thought process, whittling down the options. He was an engineer by trade, she remembered. So maybe he had to be methodical no matter what he was doing.

'So, then there are some west of that pine plantation, over by Wilmslow Creek. That would be pretty off the grid. But as far as I know, those are really small. I mean, you have to shuffle in through some little gaps and you can't stand up in 'em. At least, not unless you shimmy some more and get into the next chambers. I'm guessing your guy didn't do shimmying?'

Did he? Was Nathan Whittler the kind of man to do that? She didn't think he was. It would be difficult to keep doing so without getting covered in dirt, and he seemed to her too nervous to start exploring caves which needed skill to navigate. She had the impression that his would be a cave he could stand up in. Assuming she wasn't off down a rabbit hole of her own, she reminded herself.

'I don't think so, Billy. We haven't got a sense that he's the adventurous type, not like that. I'm thinking somewhere hidden but big enough to walk around when you're in it. And way off any trail, I would imagine.'

'Ah, well. In that case, you probably need areas that are mainly limestone. They have caves that form naturally – the ones near the tri-lakes are small natural holes that the old indigenous tribes hollowed out into something bigger. They're big enough to fit tourists, so they're the right size but the wrong type, if you get my drift. Nah, you need limestone areas. There might be plenty of caves that we don't have on any map, of course.'

'Really? Oh, I was hoping there would only be a handful. Or one, would be even better.'

He chuckled. 'I know what you mean. Yeah, the more I think about it, the more it sounds like some natural limestone formation. Let me have a discreet little chat with some people, see if I come up with anything.'

'That would be great, Billy. Caves aren't really my thing.'

'You and my Tina both. She can't have a closet door shut without panicking. It's not for everyone. Teaches you about yourself, though.'

Yes, thought Dana. *I don't want to know any more about myself. Kinda know way too much already.*

'Okay, let me know if anyone has any winning ideas. Appreciate it, Billy. See you next week.'

'Adios, amigo.'

'Adios.' Before she realised it she'd mimicked his farewell. *People pleaser*, she cursed herself.

'Adios?' Lucy had arrived while she was speaking; a packet of soggy-looking sandwiches had also appeared on her desk. 'You calling Mexico or something?'

'Yes indeedy, one of those tiny little wrestlers they have. With the masks that apparently mean something culturally important.'

'Oh, simultaneously cute and a little weird? Yeah, understandable. They'll probably bust the case wide open, I would think.'

They both grinned then descended into silence. It felt uncomfortable for Dana, even though Lucy didn't seem to mind.

Dana pointed doubtfully at the sandwiches and deadpanned, 'These look so nice.'

'Don't they?' Lucy gave it the full mock-enthusiasm. 'I like the way the description's in bold on the label – you wouldn't have a clue if you had to work it out.' She shrugged. 'That's what you get buying food from somewhere that mainly sells petrol.'

'Next time I'll send you to a cute pop-up gastro experience.' Dana sat and prodded the sandwiches with the end of a pen – the closest she wished to get. 'Maybe an old Streamline trailer – buy something organic, single origin, fair trade, gluten free and paleo from a guy with a perfectly trimmed beard and a flat cap.'

'We don't have those kinds of places in this town, thank God. Too relentlessly old-fashioned here.' Lucy nodded at a new clutch of papers as she placed them on the desk. 'More forensics.'

Dana picked them up and shook her head ruefully. 'What did

detectives do before forensics? And why don't forensics solve everything?'

Lucy reflexively touched the glasses that hung from a chain on her neck. 'Before forensics, we just guessed. Or executed a poor person. Or both. And forensics don't solve everything because science doesn't. Medicine, clean energy, engineering – all flawed and limited.'

'You're wasted in admin, Luce. You should be a philosopher.'

'I'm both. I'm multitasking.'

Dana had suggested Lucy consider joining the police. She'd be great at it. But it always quickly foundered on 'unruly working hours', an objection that Dana never bottomed out because Lucy studiously avoided letting her.

'So what am I looking at here, Luce?'

'They're still searching for the weapon. They've done a metal-detector search of the surrounding woods; they're on to a finger-search of the store perimeter. Working outside–in, Stu said. It'll take a while. The missing knife from that packet is still favourite.'

Dana frowned. 'Perhaps the killer didn't use the weapon they already had. Maybe they had a gun but didn't get to use it?' She corrected herself as Lucy looked doubtful. 'Okay, unlikely – if they had time to open a packet and take a knife, they had enough time to draw a gun. Maybe they had a cosh or a Taser or something: then they decided they needed something lethal and not temporary.'

'Or maybe,' countered Lucy, 'whoever it was had to improvise a weapon. You're looking for reasons Whittler didn't do it, when he's the obvious suspect. That guy with the razor – the obvious answer is usually right.'

Dana dropped the papers on to the desk and leaned back, tapping finger and thumb. 'Occam. William of Ockham, in fact: he had the razor. Yes, fair comment, but it's nagging me that Whittler isn't the type.' She rocked forward and pointed to the third paragraph. 'I mean, look here: no hesitation marks and just one stab. And the trajectory, straight between the ribs and into the heart.' She looked up. 'That sounds a little slick for an apparent hermit who didn't take a weapon along, don't you think?'

It made Dana think, too. About the point Bill had raised earlier – that since they had no radar on Nathan Whittler for over a decade, he could have done anything. Been anything. Someone that capable of survival was smart, resourceful and might become desperate. The forensics suggested that, in a dark store, Nathan could have wielded a knife with fatal accuracy, at the first time of asking. As if . . . he'd done it before.

Lucy shrugged. 'Yeah, you might have me on that one. I'll have a cogitation, get back to you. I think Bill wants you to go at Whittler again.' She made to leave, but at the doorframe she turned again. 'Oh, who was that you were talking to, if not a *luchador*?'

Dana couldn't help smiling. 'Ooh, label me impressed. I was talking to someone who might know about caves.'

Lucy wagged a finger. 'No, Dana, you weren't talking to someone. Remember your management module. You were "reaching out" to part of a "wider network".'

'Oh, that's right.' Dana air-quoted: '"I was facilitating some stakeholder engagement to in-source some alternative skill sets." Mmm, guy from my book club knows a bit about caving. By which I mean potholing – not about giving up. Speaking of which, can you find me something about limestone areas in this region? He thinks a suitable cave might be within a limestone area, so some kind of geological rundown would be good.'

Lucy nodded. 'You think Whittler's been hiding out in a cave?'

'I'm going to ask him, but yes, I think so.' Dana stood and glanced down the corridor to find Bill. 'We need to find where he's been: if he clams up, we get no motive. There's a chance – if it was him – that he'll walk on a lesser charge, simply because we can't compete with his version of why he killed Cassavette. We only get a wrapped-up murder charge if he talks; and we only get him talking if we know enough about him to open him up.'

Chapter 11

Nathan was smart. Dana had accepted that from the beginning. Now she had to rise to the challenge he was creating.

As she'd said to Father Timms, it felt as if she was pushing against something she couldn't break through; a fence that wouldn't yield. Nathan was used to withdrawal and Dana could hear Bill's concern in her head: what might Nathan have done in those fifteen years? What might he get away with, if she doesn't get the truth from him?

It was partly also because she was afraid of pushing, fearful of Nathan's disintegration. She didn't handle outpourings of deep, gut-sourced emotion well. They pushed her off balance, spun her backwards. She went blank, stared and gawped and lacked the words; wanted to run. Sometimes, it was easier with the criminals who accepted the outcome as the cost of doing business. Harder with the newbies who were forced to experience the full magnitude of their failure and its consequences. Dana had been grateful that Megan had been stoic enough, for long enough, that she could escape unscathed.

The Day still slid a blade through her defences. The problem never got easier: sometimes her mood lifted a little and sometimes it darkened further, but the burden remained permanent and inviolate. The Day was an attempt to rupture the rhythm, throw a spike into the wheel of her struggle and try to force a change. That was why it needed time and space away from everyone. That was why this particular Day was hurting even more: she was trying to cheat.

Many suspects – especially first-timers such as Nathan – thought detectives simply walked into the room and started asking questions. They didn't. She didn't. The best detectives might seem like they are firing scattergun bullets, hoping one will hit home. But their questions were nearly always carefully planned. It was a key advantage the detective held over the suspect: only a fool would discard it because of ego, complacency or contempt for the person sitting across from them.

Dana's strategy was carefully calibrated. For each of her early questions she would have a number of possible pathways to pursue, or escape routes. Ask A, and if the suspect says X, ask B. If the suspect says Y, ask C. If the suspect says Z, leave that aside and go elsewhere: return to it when the suspect's feeling more off-guard. Maybe ask A twice; probe for weakness. Or A is a one-shot deal; take whatever comes and move on. Perhaps hold back the forensics until the alibi is weakened. Or dive in with the existence of a witness. Or hang back. Dana always pondered the options before striking.

She was sure Nathan didn't have a clue she was doing it. But he would, with each passing dialogue. He'd sit in the room, or in his cell, and think back over their 'conversations'. Gradually he'd come to understand the way she was playing it: at which point she'd have to bring different tactics and a fresh approach.

So far, she'd concentrated on winning his trust. She had to be someone he could speak to, given that he'd refused any discussion with anyone else. It was a major bargaining chip. His communication in the last fifteen years seemed to have been severely limited. No matter how much he was at peace with that, she was certain there was a lingering need to talk and, more importantly, to be heard. To be listened to, and reacted to, was an element of feeling human. Surely Nathan wasn't immune to that?

She'd focused on showing herself to be a polite, well-spoken, grammatically aware, book-loving, civilised person. The kind of individual Nathan might like to know, and the type of human being he thought he was. That had worked up to a point, but he would start noticing it. The more he considered it, the more he would see that she was, in an arms'-length and subtle way, befriending him. He was close to that point now.

Before long, he would kick against her approach. He would do so, she believed, not only because he would see it as a subterfuge and therefore lacking authenticity, but because he defined himself as an outlier, an individual with few or no friends. Accepting her would undo the core belief that must have sustained him these past fifteen years. So he'd rebel against it, even as he welcomed it, to affirm what he'd been most of his adult life. She should expect that.

She closed the office door and drew down the blind. Everyone in the station knew this meant she was not to be disturbed for anything short of an earthquake. She sat quietly in the dark, slowing her breathing and consciously feeling the air fill and leave her lungs. After physically counting each finger in turn, in her mind she moved around her body, labelling each part. It was a way of ensuring she had her mind focused on what was now, what was her and what she could control. She'd been taught it at the age of eighteen and had never stopped using it. All her life there were wolves circling the campfire of her mind; this was a way to keep the flames high.

After a few minutes she snapped on the desk lamp, winced at the sudden light and began writing her next interview plan.

Nathan had stacked the used water bottle, tissues, the sandwich wrapper and the Zane Grey into a neat mini-tower. There were no crumbs or smears on the table; not even a watermark where the bottle had stood. This time, he didn't jump when Dana entered the room.

Dana winced as she went to sit. She tried to straighten her leg while seated, noticing Nathan stare at her knee.

'Sorry. Cold weather and my kneecap don't mix. It's about sixty per cent plastic.'

'Was that from illness?'

She was startled by his interest in someone who wasn't him. 'Uh, no.'

'Really? Was it injured in an accident?'

'No, it wasn't.'

Even Nathan seemed troubled by the silent pause that followed.

'Then what was it?'

The question was eminently reasonable. Most people knew, if they ever asked, not to ask again. Her acute discomfort, the formidable effort she made to wave it away; every vestige of her reaction combined to say it was *verboten*. But Nathan Whittler simply asked the obvious question and waited for the answer.

But she couldn't answer it. She was unable to say because it might open up a fissure that would bubble with something she struggled to contain. Especially today, on this Day. She couldn't say because it might expose her to things she couldn't fight, couldn't beat. And, underlying all that, there were legal issues.

'I'm afraid I can't tell you, Mr Whittler. Everything we say in this room is recorded and, as such, is admissible in court. Not only what you say, but what I say as well. The story behind my knee problems is *sub judice*: it can't be discussed. Suffice to say it happened five years ago, it was not accidental and it was not a medical problem.'

He was perplexed. 'Everything you say here can be played in court?'

'It can. I expect a law suit from the estate of Zane Grey, at the very least.'

Nathan gave a watery smile and shook his head.

'Fresh water, Mr Whittler.' She waggled another bottle and turned it deliberately so the label faced him.

'Very good, Detective Russo.'

Dana smiled at her notes. He was beginning to consider her a kindred spirit in some way. She needed that but wasn't altogether comfortable with it.

She swept the remains of the earlier session into a plastic bag and let him watch while she tied a precise trucker's hitch with string. He almost certainly knew some woodcraft; maybe he knew knots as well. It would be these little points of connection that she felt would, paradoxically, unravel him.

Lucy and Bill were behind the mirror. She'd asked them each to focus on different things while watching – Bill on what was said, and any semblance of a way in, or leverage; Lucy on the body language, and what that might imply. Dana planned to be braver this time around. She'd established politeness, grammatical rigour and awareness. This needed to go further, and faster, without letting him come apart.

Again there was a loud glugging as Nathan poured a cup of water. He took such forensic care: like he was in a lab and pouring acid into a beaker. One stray drop would be some kind of failure. She switched on the tape.

'So, Mr Whittler, if we might return to your address and accommodation?'

He nodded. She noted that he was no longer focused on his shoe, as he'd been initially. Now his basic responses were directed to the corner of the table.

'I've been doing some thinking.' She set the files to one side and framed a new page in her notes with both hands. 'As we established, you've had the same home for the past fifteen years, but not a permanent address that would appear on any database. I'm thinking, therefore' – she glanced pointedly at him – 'that you have been living in some kind of cave.'

He blanched. She could see emotion swarm across his face, like a storm sweeping over a prairie. He scratched at his nose, then his chin. His hand brushed the back of his neck and he shivered as he tugged at a sleeve. Her mind drifted to what Lucy might have found out about limestone areas, and she had to force her concentration back while she waited for Nathan to laugh nervously then recover his poise.

'What makes you think that?' His voice was thick and crackly, as if he hadn't spoken in days.

She knew he was stalling, that his mind was racing and reaching, flooded with implications. But she also understood that process mattered to Nathan Whittler. It was not all about the result, but also the manner of getting there: one influenced the other. He had an old-fashioned belief in the virtue of doing things in the right way.

'Well, I don't believe you lived in some tarpaulin-and-ferns contraption. It would be too temporary and too uncomfortable. I can see from your skin, your hands, and so on, that you've taken care of yourself, that you've been relatively comfortable. And I think you were in it for the long haul right from the start. I don't believe that you would go for something interim: you'd want a shelter that would last a lifetime, first time.'

Nathan nodded slowly. 'Possibly.'

'Well, as you've implied, where you've been living must be some sort of weatherproof, or weather-resistant, shelter. It wouldn't be considered by most as a permanent dwelling, but I can't see anyone surviving fifteen winters entirely in the open air. To say nothing of the storm season.'

She resisted the urge to say *someone like you*. He still looked to her the indoors type, unlikely to relish the rugged and harsh life he was claiming. Instead, she clasped her hands and put some weight on her elbows. Her knee spasmed again.

'So I believe that you've been living somewhere that's sturdy enough to allow you to stay away from other people, but within reach of them. I say that because you must have periodically needed supplies and food. You previously indicated it wasn't a caravan, or a boat, or part of someone's dwelling. And we also confirmed that you have the integrity not to use someone's cabin. It's really a process of elimination.'

He continued to stare at the corner of the table. She could see his eyes move slightly, as though tracing the grains in the wood.

'Did you consider a tent?'

She paused deliberately, slowly writing nothing of consequence on her pad just to see if he leaned slightly towards it. He did.

'Yes, Mr Whittler, it did cross my mind. More specifically, a large and heavy tent, like the army use. I thought that might be hefty enough to see out fifteen seasons and survive the weather. I came down against that because I felt you'd established the camp entirely alone; that kind of tent would be too heavy for you to carry to a fairly isolated location, away from any tracks or roads. Oh.'

He looked up at the final word but quickly glanced away again by way of the mirror. She tapped her pen against the desk twice then flicked back a page in her notes.

'I apologise, Mr Whittler. I forgot to ask you about your car. In 2004 there was a Toyota Corolla registered in your name. Have you driven that car since 2004?'

Nathan sat back. She figured he was considering what answer would be in his best interest. If he said he still had the car, and he hadn't, it might send them off on a wild-goose chase looking for it: that could buy him time. On the other hand, if he wanted time, he could simply lawyer up and not answer anything at all. The clincher, in her mind, was that she believed he was withholding but would not outright lie: not if she gradually brought him to the truth. He might stop talking altogether, but he wouldn't lie.

'I have not, Detective. I'm pretty sure no one else has either.'

They'd need to chase it up, all the same. Her finger and thumb were tapping below the table.

'Korea.' He said it softly.

'Excuse me?'

'The US army in South Korea, in the 1950s. They ran a campaign for many years in similar weather. They lived in tents. It is possible.'

'Hmm, that's true, although they had many other facilities you lacked – medical support, warmish vehicles to travel in, periodic leave which they spent inside buildings or on the beach at Okinawa. I understand your point, but I think the balance of all circumstances leads me to believe a tent is improbable. I may be wrong, of course.'

'I'm glad you've thought it through, Detective Russo.'

Dana wasn't sure what to do with the compliment. Or if it was a compliment. In every interview his tone was neutral and his body language so strange she struggled to nail it down.

'Thank you, Mr Whittler. So as I said, in the absence of a car, or any assistance, I felt it doubtful you could have lugged a large tent to your camp. And a smaller, flimsier tent wouldn't have worked.' She paused and underlined a line of her writing slowly, carefully. She was certain he couldn't read what it was.

'In addition, I thought it possible that any tent would have been seen from the air. Around here we have helicopter joyriders, some forest rangers, leisure flights, crop-spraying and other aircraft. And, latterly, those remote-control drones. However well it was camouflaged, a tent might be spotted. I believe you wouldn't take such a risk, given the importance of retaining privacy.' She leaned back, primarily to release the grinding contact in her kneecap. 'So, as I said, it's a process of elimination.'

Nathan pursed his lips as he thought, re-consulted the lines on his palm. She was just as fascinated with his hands. If he'd lived in the wilds for fifteen years, how could they be lily-white and pristine? Judging from his soft skin alone, he looked about ten years younger than his chronological age. It was one of the markers that jarred with his claims: he insisted he'd lived wild, but he didn't look that way. Mikey, for one, was unconvinced, and she sensed Lucy wasn't wholly on board yet either.

'That's very good, Detective Russo. I suppose that's what you do, you detectives. Deductive reasoning, and all that.'

Dana breathed an inward sigh of relief. It had started to feel as if they were getting nowhere, but this was genuine progress. It seemed to grate on Nathan, however.

'May I ask you some hypotheticals, Mr Whittler?'

He twitched his mouth, as though swallowing a smart answer that he had suddenly decided might be counter-productive. 'As you wish.'

'So, let's say that my forensics report here' – she tapped a file with her index finger – 'shows that you have sand in the soles of your boots, in addition to the soil from near Jensen's Store.' She paused, to ensure she framed it correctly. Nathan was making her think about her phrasing. 'Where would that sand have come from, Mr Whittler?'

He picked at a hangnail and spoke to the corner of the table. 'Lots of places have sand, Detective Russo. Is this one of those things where you find an exact chemical balance in the sand which occurs only in one place in the entire country?'

She pondered for a second whether he'd recently seen television crime dramas, where that kind of story was more likely than in books. She wondered again about his claim to have been out of sight – possibly in a cave and away from people – for fifteen years.

'No, it's not. Unfortunately. But there aren't, as far as I'm aware, areas of sandy soil in this region generally. We're boggy marshes and mosquitos, for the most part. It would be quite a specific location. In fact, it would probably be next to a river or a lake.'

This one was a reach. Five minutes before they started she'd been planning her strategy. This was a byway she could shut down quickly if it was leading nowhere, but pursue if something opened up. Her level of geological knowledge made it a total guess.

It hit home. Nathan blanched once more, took an unsteady sip from the cup. His delayed touch on the bottle cap seemed almost an afterthought. She felt she'd shaken him out of a deep-rooted compulsion, and that counted as a win.

His tone was sharper. 'Well, it's possible I've walked near a river or a lake lately. Isn't this called "the land of a hundred lakes", Detective?'

'It is, Mr Whittler. Well, a few lakes and a hundred swamps would be more accurate. But the fact that the sand is underneath the soil on the boot suggests that you were walking on sand just before you approached the store. And there's no sandy ground near the store. The closest lake is a few clicks from there.'

Even with his mouth closed she could now hear his breathing. It seemed impatient, almost belligerent. He raised his voice.

'I thought you were asking hypotheticals? This seems very . . . *precise*, Detective Russo.'

Dana took the shot across the bows with a slight incline of the head, which he would have observed as a vaguely moving shadow across the table top. She gave a slight pause, to indicate the separation from the next question: he seemed to appreciate that kind of etiquette.

'My apologies, Mr Whittler. You'll no doubt understand that not every question I ask is of my own choosing. I operate within a structure, a command structure.'

There was a pause while Nathan considered and Dana held her breath.

'Of course, Detective Russo.' His voice had lowered again. 'But if you wish to discuss hypotheticals, they should be hypothetical and not rooted in current situations.'

Apparently, failing to stick rigidly to the definition of a word was the problem. 'I understand. Perhaps I could, instead, ask some more general questions about your survival in such unusual circumstances?'

Silence. She took nothing as being consent. She sought a question that would pique his indignation.

'Many of my colleagues would find it difficult to imagine being so isolated, so lacking in human contact. They would ask how you managed to bear that.'

'Hmmm. Yes. I'm a little familiar with people's habit of always taking their telephone with them. I ask myself how they bear *that*, Detective Russo. To be at everyone's beck and call at all times, even at home, or at night. To be constantly a second away from someone intruding into your time, your thoughts, your privacy, your intentions. It's difficult to imagine why people would put themselves into that situation – often willingly.'

Her finger and thumb reflexed beneath the table. 'I'm with you on that, Mr Whittler. Personally, mine is switched off to a degree my colleagues find baffling. I suppose they would answer that, firstly, they don't find it intrusive. For many, it's a positive decision and they like, uh, "being in touch", as it were. Secondly, they accept the trade-off: limited privacy in return for the convenience. Being able to book or cancel appointments, let a friend know that they're running late, find a recipe or contact details, manage without diaries and pieces of paper and all that paraphernalia. They regard it as progress.'

Nathan pulled a face – the first time he'd shown outright displeasure. She was surprised how easy it was to spot. Many of his previous expressions had been impassive, or contrary; she'd regarded them as opaque, or detached from their cause. It was almost as if, when strong disgust came through, he was transparent. He became more like . . . any other person. She found herself a little disappointed by that.

'Hmmph. Progress? I see it a little differently, Detective Russo. What do their messages to each other say? What important subjects are they discussing? All I've heard of it is shallow and empty. How are they informing each other, adding to debate, enlightening? Your colleagues find it hard to imagine how I would do without a bunch of wittering nothing in my life. I think it's self-evident how "hard" I find it.'

'As I say, I'm with you on the mobile phones and the banality it often brings. But I think their amazement runs deeper than that. In those fifteen years, how many people did you speak to, Mr Whittler?'

The question struck him as fully as if she had leaned over and slapped his face. He physically shook, and recoiled. Part of her regretted asking because of the wash of emotion across his features; part of her relished the impact she'd made.

'No one, Detective Russo.'

His reply took her down. The euphoria flushed away instantly. She'd expected a small number, but not that. It couldn't be so.

'No one, Mr Whittler? Surely some people, intermittent contact? Accidentally bumping into people, coming across them? Someone?'

'As I said, Detective Russo. No one.' His voice wavered between a whisper and defiance.

She reconsidered. Could she pursue this? And why? She could tell herself she was establishing the absence of alibis, building another necessary brick in the wall. But perhaps it was simply the prurience of incredulity. Even she couldn't imagine such a thing.

'That must have taken enormous . . . discipline. Willpower.'

'How so?' He shook his head a little. 'Oh, no, it doesn't. There's nothing *heroic* about it, Detective Russo. Don't imagine me as something unique, someone who discovered some special truth about humanity. No, don't think that.'

He was fuming now; his fists balled up, his breathing strong and furious. His voice rose and he directed it at the wall below the mirror, as though he couldn't bear to throw this at Dana herself.

'It's no more virtuous than any other preference. You wouldn't think it took strength of character to continually surround yourself with people, to be constantly in their orbit, never alone. It wouldn't be remarkable discipline to be afraid of being by yourself, even for an hour. You'd simply view that as the person's preference, their personality in action. So why think the reverse has any hint of heroism to it?'

He was getting close to her heart now: she could practically feel him brush past it. Soon he would want – or need – a *quid pro quo*, and it was too personal to give. She was supposed to empathise to some degree, but this felt too close. He was drifting on to land she'd struggled to understand her whole life, which had made her do things she couldn't undo. And he'd clumsily run aground while a tape was running – a recording with an audience.

She wanted out of this conversation. Wanted out right now. It was starting to slice her to the bone. But it wasn't possible to simply cut and run, not without a departure that would reduce her status in his eyes. She had to stay with it.

'I can see, Mr Whittler, for a deeply introverted person – in the true sense of the word – a relative lack of direct contact might be preferable, or desirable. But truly, your experience seems to go way beyond that. In that sense, it's so beyond mainstream that it could only be reached by an unusually strong personal choice and an unusually strong willingness to see that choice through, regardless of consequence.'

'What consequence?'

She'd slipped. He'd challenged an assumption she'd made, but she couldn't quite grasp what that assumption had been. It was obviously counter-productive to suggest that he'd gone mad after fifteen years of complete silence.

'Well, most people in, for example, solitary confinement, find their lives extremely difficult. The lack of communication, and validation, plays on their mind.'

'Do I seem crazy to you, Detective Russo?'

He was looking straight at her. Not at the mirror; not at his foot or the corner of the table. He was staring at *her*. She could feel herself flush – all her thoughts of being a kindred spirit seemed to fold at once.

Her assumed 'connection' was so flimsy that two seconds of eye contact could unravel it. He'd neutered it in a heartbeat. For this moment he was not supplicant and she wasn't in charge. Unprepared for his sudden change of body language, his near-instant display of belief, she'd yielded control and made herself the recipient. She didn't like it.

'Well? Do I?'

'No, Mr Whittler, you don't. You seem remarkably – totally – lucid and sane. I didn't mean to imply that you weren't.' He had sea-green eyes and long eyelashes that seemed to make his blink slow and drowsy. Dana felt skewered by his gaze. She could see herself in it: desperate, keeping the worst fears at bay with stoic suffering. It hurt when Nathan demonstrated how similar they were.

'So what was this "consequence" you said I risked?'

Dana thought for a moment – she felt Nathan would grant her that. He was running this conversation. Had he reeled her in? Or had she been complacent? She swallowed and tried to refocus.

'I think many introverts struggle with the dichotomy presented by their preferences, Mr Whittler. So they wish for some communication, but according to their choices and on their terms. Too much human involvement leaves them exhausted and unhappy. If the balance goes too far the other way and they get little or no communication, it can affect their general sense of perspective; their view of themselves and their lives. It can cause depression, heartache; a sense that they can't break free from those problems.'

Dana could feel the internal heat of confession and shame and the rancid memories that combination created. She tried to keep her voice from shuddering, became conscious of where the breaths should go. Nathan was watching her intently, focused on her words. Now she was the one talking to the corner of the table.

'So,' she struggled on, 'in your situation you already had a circumstance that leads to considerable solitude. You chose to compound that by avoiding all contact. As opposed to, say, living where you lived but working locally and mixing with colleagues. In those terms, you expose yourself to all the potential consequences faced by introverts, but to a far greater degree. There is no counterbalance in your life, Mr Whittler, nothing to break the sequence. People will wonder why you didn't crack under those conditions, as they would. That's what I meant by "consequence".'

Nathan looked down at his hands, turning his fingers and rubbing once again along his fate line. 'I see. Yes. Hmm. Put like that, I understand where you're coming from. But I think you have to see the bigger picture, as they say. My life – my choice – wasn't something I feared. I preferred it: sought it. Silence is not nothing. It's not an absence. It's a full experience in itself. People who are scared of silence are scared of the nothingness of it – they think it's a void, a vacuum, a danger. But it isn't.

'My solitude is total. If I keep the modern-day mind-set, then yes: the seclusion will probably kill me. At the very least, it will grind me down and leave me exposed to the kinds of problems you so eloquently laid out, Detective Russo. But consider another view: instead of fighting the solitude, you relax into it. You slow all the rhythms of your day, of your life. You throw away the telephone and the computer and the clock. You allow the isolation to be yours, not you to be a prisoner of it.

'Lo and behold, Detective, a different life comes into view. You don't rush, you don't care how long something takes. So it takes two hours, or four – what do you care? It takes what it takes, and you have no other appointment you must make, anyway. Once you go with it, then it becomes like sea legs – you don't feel the motion because you're moving with it, part of it. Then you come to relish the peace, love the silence. The opposite emerges: instead of fearing solitude, you embrace it, and fear losing it.'

That one phrase – *fearing solitude* – made Dana end the discussion. Her energy had disappeared with his words. Breathing was hard and her flight instinct took over.

'I see. That's an interesting proposal, Mr Whittler. I'll have to think about that. I must also meet with my colleagues, if you'll excuse me.'

She snapped off the tape hastily and was halfway to the door before she turned. 'Thank you, Mr Whittler. We'll talk again, soon.'

He looked straight at her again. As though he could see through her to the doorway. As though he knew what he'd just done.

'I'm sorry someone did that to your kneecap, Detective.'

Chapter 12

In the women's bathroom harsh light slapped around on shiny surfaces; a mirror occupying one wall, blank white tiles on the floor. Grotesque reflections curled across the metal hand dryer. The legacy of bleach and perfumed sanitiser saturated the air. Two stalls were empty and one was occupied. Lucy tapped on the closed door.

'You okay, Dana?'

There was a pause and a muffled voice. 'Could be anyone in here.'

Lucy smiled and leaned back against the countertop. 'Nine women in this station. I'm one. Three are in admin and I've just walked past there. Sue and Nikki are on an interstate warrant all day. Miriam's on reception – her voice would go through sheet metal – and Ali is off with flu. Process of elimination. The application of logic, Dr Watson.'

Dana emerged, looking sheepish and tired. It felt ridiculously hot in the bathroom. 'Yes, hmm, maybe that wasn't too difficult.'

Lucy turned to face her. 'He got to you, didn't he?'

Dana nodded to her reflection, unable to face Lucy directly. She didn't want to have this conversation – not here, not on this Day, and certainly not with Lucy. All three dimensions made it raw; amplified her vulnerability. She could feel her skin sing.

'Yes. Not crying, though. Didn't sniffle. It's a little close to home, some of it. Which is ironic' – she patted at her face with a tissue – 'considering I'm the best person to be going at him.'

'Double bind, huh?'

'Exactly, Luce. I have to understand him enough to get inside his head. If he doesn't give up more than he has so far, a murder conviction's going to be a reach. He can claim all manner of accidental in that store: we have almost nothing to contradict him. But to understand him, I have to empathise, and that's a little . . . exposed.'

She washed her hands while Lucy waited. Despite being the older and senior woman, Dana felt the more fragile: gauche, awkward, in need of consolation. In need of babbling on, too.

She batted at the soap dispenser which was, not for the first time, too gunged up to live up to its job description.

'So, talking to Whittler, it's problematic,' she continued. 'Not least, everything I say in that room is courtroom-admissible. So, effectively, it's public. He wants me to open out, but I still don't think he fully gets the legal implications.'

She rinsed under the tap. 'At some point, he'll lawyer up: he has to get wise to that eventually. Even if he doesn't, the court will make him take a lawyer at 0600 tomorrow. So I have that in my locker.'

'What do you mean? Won't he be harder to talk to, with a lawyer there?'

Dana dried with paper towels. Part of her wanted to rush back into the cubicle and slam it shut. A piece of her always wanted to run, to hide, to cover her face and hope 'it' mysteriously went away. The kind of magical thinking she should have left behind long ago. What had she been told by more educated minds than hers? *A life script you no longer need, Dana.*

'It's . . . it's not that simple.'

Lucy hefted up on to the counter, swinging her feet like a child on a playground swing. 'Got as much time as you need.'

Still Dana couldn't meet her eye; she tousled some items in her handbag and talked to that.

'Sometimes, no matter where I am, who's there, what I'm doing, I feel like a total outsider. I don't understand the people in front of me, what they think, how they think. I don't get it, and it drains me trying to work it out.'

She paused, subconsciously giving Lucy the chance to judge. Lucy didn't move.

'So when I'm interviewing suspects I like it when the lawyer's there.' Dana chucked the paper towel at the bin, lipped it and missed. 'It's a structure, a framework. I'm supposed to be the outsider.

'They're the suspect and the suspect's lawyer: I'm the only cop in the room. Often the only woman in the room, the only one with access to certain information, the only one with the state lined up behind me.' She paused, grabbed a breath in an airless room. 'So when it seems like they're aliens to me, there's a certain logic to that. I feel less of a freak for thinking it. If that . . . you know, makes the slightest sense.'

Lucy narrowed her eyes, stared at the far wall. 'So . . . you and Whittler – you don't have as much to lean on?' She turned back to Dana. 'It's purely you and him and you have to understand him?'

Dana nodded silently. A conversation from the corridor outside rose and subsided. The room still felt blindingly hot. Her blouse was sticking to her: it made her feel ugly and wretched.

Lucy continued. 'But you *do* get him. I can see it. Hell, he can see it, and he's supposed to be . . . socially maladjusted, or whatever. So it must be shining through: your empathy, your comprehension. It must be so clear even he can see it.'

'Forgot I asked you to watch body language.'

'Well, I can tell you he's shifting. Pretty slow, but he's changing. Stopped staring at the floor for a good twenty seconds, there.'

'Ah yes, but I panicked when he did it. It felt unnerving. Came out of the blue. I should have been ready for it.'

Lucy shook her head. 'Ready for it? We all thought he'd thaw out by degrees. That was a major shift, looking straight at you.'

Dana didn't know what to say. In truth, she'd been embarrassed by the way Nathan had sideswiped her, without seeming to try. It added to her sense that these interviews could veer off course in a second: she was never truly in control. If only Nathan had a plan, he'd be dangerous.

Lucy gave her a way out. 'Oh, and he's now fascinated by your knee. We all are.' Lucy grinned and forced Dana into a watery smile.

'Hmm, not much to tell. I've had it, uh, nearly five years now. Sort of used to it. It's mainly plastic: a slightly soft plastic that bends a little. It doesn't like cold, damp weather or sitting in one spot for too long.'

'I know you have this day off each year.' Lucy seemed to be circling, not wishing to land in case the runway was a quagmire. 'I, uh, I think this is a tough day for you. I just want to help.'

Dana blew her nose, mainly to hide her face. She felt the heat of shame, of desperation, of hopeless gratitude and fear. They all mixed to flush through her like fire.

'Thank you. It's not the ideal day, and I usually make sure I'm not here. Don't think I've told you why, before.'

Lucy shrugged, her voice softer now. 'Well . . . you said a while back that it's some kind of anniversary. And whatever it is, you're not over it.'

There was an impact to someone else saying it. Harsher but more honest than when Dana said the same thing in her head; as if her own opinion didn't count and needed verifying. Talking about it now would undo her, she sensed. She would be remarkable, and then remarked upon. She clenched her fists as though she could retain the truth within.

'Yes . . . the double problem. Two different events. But connected. One begat the other.'

She paused. The old-fashioned word felt like a sliver of her mother, creeping through her body and out of her mouth. Words like *begat*, *Jezebel*, *smite*: Dana remained soaked in her mother's Biblical rage. A malign influence still nestled somewhere deep: capable, planning.

'Urgh, how to explain it? Jeez, I've explained it so many times I've forgotten the explanation. Okay, okay, think of it this way. If you're an alcoholic, you're always an alcoholic. Always. Every day. Each morning when you wake up, you have to make a conscious decision to fight it that day. There's no escape, no let up. The disease is always with you, waiting for an opportunity, forever seeking your weakest moment, your laziest thinking. And then it's in, and hooking its talons so it can stay. You have to damage yourself, to work it loose. So you fear it – you rightly fear it.'

Dana leaned on the sink, terrified to look up at her reflection.

'That's what it's like with this . . . whatever this is. Depression, post-traumatic things, anxiety. Whatever. It all melts into one. But the dynamic is that every day it hurts, and claws, and wants. So every day I push back, and hang on. But on this date each year I try to change the fight, try to get ahead of it somehow. Except today I can't, because I'm here instead, and the thing is punishing me for that.

'This Day, it's . . . it's complicated. I suppose it's an anniversary. I normally don't . . . usually I'm not here for this day. So I'm probably on edge a little more than I would be; not quite myself, in some respects. Anyway. Need to be better. Can't let a murderer get away because I can't have some downtime. Uh, so, yes, it's a long-term thing. I'm trying. Really, I'm trying. Working isn't really helping, even though I thought it might.'

Lucy was looking at her but not *at* her. She was clearly paying attention but somehow managing not to stare. Dana couldn't work out how Lucy was doing that. Or how she knew to do that.

Dana took a deep breath.

'But, whatever, tell me about caves, Luce.'

Lucy waited a beat then pushed herself off the counter and grabbed at a blue folder. She moved her hands like a fortune teller with a crystal ball. 'Maps. I have maps from the interweb. Maaany maps, most excellent price. Very reliable, very good, you have fun times. I guarantee big happiness.'

'So tell me, oh mystical one, where's the only cave I need to search to find Casa Whittler?'

'If only it were that simple. So, your caveman – see what I did there? – was right. Limestone in various locations: they're all shaded blue here. But once you add in the possibility of sand near water – you spooked Whittler with that, so I'm guessing it's correct – then you come down to A, B, and . . . C.' She tapped at three locations on the acetate covering the map.

'Okay.' Dana pored over it, primarily looking for roads and contours.

She didn't think Nathan had some benign benefactor leaving goodies at prearranged drops every month. Dana wasn't picturing him trapping rabbits and gutting fish – she believed he stole absolutely everything he ate or used. This, as much as the killing, was why Nathan Whittler was sorry: in his moral code, she was convinced, they were somehow practically on a par. It made her move away a little from the idea that Nathan was a consummate, experienced killer who'd remained hidden for that reason. The 'terrible things' he'd confessed to Dana early on, she believed, referred to multiple acts of low-scale burglary and theft. The location of his cave would be related to this. While Nathan would have wanted to be in the wilderness, he'd have needed to be someplace that didn't require going up and over three mountains to get anywhere.

'Now this one' – she tapped at an area in the high mountains, a col between two peaks – 'is the least likely. Coronet Heights is too far away, too steep, too wild. To get to anywhere he might burgle is a monumental hike. He'd be limited in what he could steal and carry. Too isolated, I reckon.'

'No, you're right, I think,' said Lucy. 'So which of the other two should we start with?'

'This one's a little too close: Miller's Point is . . . a kilometre from this beach, and I know that gets plugged with tourists. Discussed this earlier with Billy, and I'm not inclined towards it. There's a boat-hire place there in the summer – someone would have seen Whittler, and anyway, it would all have driven him crazy. Reggae music, jet skis, drunks in canoes – he'd freak.'

'Which leaves this Goldilocks area here – the Dakota Line.' Lucy's finger swept a chain of four large ponds and stopped at a kilometre of shoreline along a finger of water. Piermont Lake was at the northern end of Baker National Park – perhaps not majestic enough for casual tourists needing selfies, nor hardcore enough for serious hikers and adventurers.

'Is that all Baker to the north as well?' asked Dana.

'Uh, nope. After the river there, it's Silver Ridge State Forest.'

'Not that I have a clue what the difference is,' said Dana. 'I mean, it's all wilderness, basically.'

Lucy leaned in. 'Lookie here – no cliff faces, judging by the contours, so no climbers. The opposite shore is swampy – maybe birdwatchers, but not much to see. No road access to Piermont Lake at all. The nearest road is maybe . . . five clicks from the shore.'

'Yes,' replied Dana. 'From that western side, eight kilometres' tramp to Jensen's, but that might be the closest store. And there's surely bound to be some kind of trail from the shore to the road, even though nothing's marked.'

'How does he usually get to civilisation? Walk?'

'Maybe hiking. Perhaps he boats it to the southern end, then hikes. Get Mikey to pull together the search team, please, and we'll think how to tackle it. Sunny today – might use the drone.'

Lucy carefully folded the map. As they reached the door, Dana turned. 'Luce? Thanks for listening, and keeping all this to yourself.'

'You're welcome. Discreet is my middle name. I keep it totally separate from my other names.' She laughed as they came out into the corridor. 'Now, you must have seen what I did there.'

Dana smiled and threw the comment back over her shoulder. 'I surely did, I surely did.'

Chapter 13

Bill was not one for case conferences. He preferred to control the investigation with a series of one-to-ones. It left him at the centre of the web: he could always be sure what was said to whom and what they were required to do. But occasionally he relented. Whenever Dana asked him to relent.

Already the incident room was amassing heavy air, partly organised detritus and a sense of expectation. In a semi-rural area like this, homicides were few and far between and often easy to detect. Usually domestic, or occasionally neighbours feuding, it was seldom they needed to go deeply into the background of complete strangers. The sense of a tragic waste of a life sat uncomfortably with the tingle of professional anticipation.

Dana pretended to be studying her notes ahead of time; in reality, she was fending off her own mind. This was still her Day: still the morning of it, in fact. Her brain snapped like a dog at the end of a chain. She underlined some notes for no other reason than to physically move – she felt calcified, unsteady. Her vision floated for a second then she swallowed hard. Best to get on with it and pray she could cope.

Along one wall was a series of whiteboards. One was headed

'Cassavette': a potted history and scanned photos of Lou and Megan from their kayaking triumph. In black: known facts. In blue: likely data that hadn't been verified. In red: supposition and questions. The same system for the next whiteboard, headed 'Nathan Whittler'. The third board held underpinning investigation data: who was responsible for what, contact details, information on duty rosters and support such as Forensics and Tech.

Dana loved preparing for these but hated doing them. She always felt she was treading a poor line between giving everyone their say and providing firm direction and leadership. She believed Bill and – especially – Mike did them better. But the lead detective couldn't avoid leading the detecting.

'What we know so far,' she declared, quelling the low-level murmurs. 'Lou Cassavette – thirty-five, owner of Jensen's Store, on the Old Derby Road. Bought the place around a year ago. Thought staff were stealing stock then decided instead it was a burglar. Camped out last night in the stockroom. Someone entered the store, possibly via a window; Lou was stabbed at 0530 this morning. One entry wound, no hesitation.' She pointed at a forensics photo. 'The knife is still unfound – we're doing a close search. I believe it's still in the vicinity. Arrested one Nathan Whittler, who was kneeling by the body. He has the victim's blood on his hands, and there is significant evidence that he was the burglar. No known connection between the two men.'

She paused, wondering if the silence was rapt attention or merely politeness. Dana took the bull by the horns.

'You might be asking yourselves why we're bothering to investigate at all. Why this isn't a slam-dunk.'

The mutters and shuffled movement told her she was dead-on.

'Lou Cassavette died this morning, at someone's hand. He is the one we owe a duty of care: he deserves the truth to be known. It's easy here to get drawn into just one story, just one narrative. That isn't serving Lou Cassavette's interests. A comprehensive and careful investigation, however, will do so. Let's all keep that in mind.

'The store was illegally entered via the window, but there's no physical proof of who did so. Whittler is favourite. He could claim that he's the burglar but not the killer. While Whittler was found in the store, there is no evidence that proves he stabbed Cassavette. If his fingerprints eventually turn out to be on the knife, he could conceivably have been trying to remove it. He has Cassavette's blood on his hands – through gloves, mind – and nowhere else. That can be argued as an attempt at first aid – we have no splatter or spray. There are no other forensics – so far – relating him to the body prior to the stabbing. There are no fingerprints of his – yet – anywhere else in the store; nor are there fibres. Forensically speaking, he floated into the store, hovered above the dead body, maybe attempted first aid. And that's it.

'Equally, we have no motive whatsoever for the killing. Not for anyone, including Whittler. We can't connect Whittler yet to the Cassavettes, or to the store. As far as we can prove, he hasn't even shopped there. Instead, we have a total vacuum about his life for well over a decade. So, ladies and gentlemen, this is far from a done deal. And while it remains that way, we look at every angle and every conceivable alternative. Mikey, anything coming up on background?'

'Getting there, yeah.' Mike stood and picked up a sheaf of papers, which he used like a laser pointer towards the whiteboards. 'Lou had a substantial debt. Most of it to buy the place outright, but he'd borrowed again to turn part of it into a café. Last month he loaded up a business overdraft to cover day-to-day losses. He was going backwards, basically.'

'So any kind of stock loss would be getting on his nerves, yeah?' Bill chirped from a half-shadow in the corner, his arms folded.

'Absolutely,' replied Dana. 'According to his wife, Megan, he also thought it was a point of principle. So maybe that made him more belligerent when the burglar turned up.'

Lucy raised a hand. 'Hi, devil's advocate here. So that supports a view that the fight in the store was accidental. So that Whittler – sorry, the assailant we haven't confirmed yet – didn't go with any violent intent. Hence the packet-of-knives routine. Cassavette comes over all outraged, there's a scuffle that won't stop, the assailant grabs something handy, and *boom*.'

'That's a plausible scenario,' agreed Dana. 'I think that might be Whittler's story.'

'We haven't asked him yet. We've spoken to him twice, yeah?' Stuart Risdale, a twenty-year veteran and leader of the search teams as required. A man with a padded and ageing Labrador, and becoming more like his pet every day. His tone was polite enough. She noted the collegiate 'we' when he meant 'you, Dana' – Bill encouraged team vocabulary – but the question was valid.

'Three times, actually. I get it, Stu. Other than the victim, he's the only person we can currently place anywhere near the scene at that hour. When we initially broached it in Custody, he physically recoiled. It's a fine line, and we'll probably only get one realistic shot at it. So this one needs a slow build-up. Plus, at the moment, we're getting Whittler with no external edit. We're on the twenty-four-hour limit with that – the court will step in tomorrow morning. Once he lawyers up, we lose all the information in Whittler's head. His lawyer will make it very clear he's to say nothing until a trial. And believe me, this guy knows how to stop talking.'

She turned from Risdale to the room in general. 'We need to approach it gradually, and we need to acquire information that helps us challenge or confirm anything he says. That's our advantage right now: he's speaking without a legal filter. That's a limited-time offer: we can't afford to waste it.'

Bill nodded sagely from the touchline and Dana felt boosted by the support.

She turned back to Mike. 'What else on the Cassavettes?'

Mike nodded at the use of the plural. 'So, neither show up on any local intelligence. Nathan Whittler's brother does: twice. For assault, and for threatening behaviour.'

Dana leaned in. 'Hmm. Circumstances?'

Mike flipped through some more notes. 'Ah, here we go. Jeb – for that is his name – was twice cited for incidents outside locked construction areas. Looks like both times were arguments with union reps who were trying to stop non-union labour such as Jeb walking through. Scuffles, big talk, lots of that bristling thing, and presumably some shoving. No blood, no fractures, no charges, no convictions.'

'But a propensity for violence. We need to speak to the brother anyway, as he's the last living relative for Nathan. But dig some more on that, please, Mikey: it might be ammo.'

'Shall do. So, as I say, neither Lou nor Megan show up locally. But Lou is on the state system, according to my source at Central.'

Lucy nudged Mike's leg. 'All your sources at Central, Mikey. Are they one person who's very busy, or lots of different people?'

'I can neither confirm nor deny either of those options, or any other. So Lou shows up as having links to some regional players in money laundering. Old buddies, neighbours from way back – nothing official. Central thought he might be using his previous store to wash cash; but the investigation never got far. I've asked my source to dig deeper. I'll get back to you on it.'

Dana nodded. 'Okay. Background on the couple so far?'

'They married three years ago. I found one of those newspaper articles they only publish after the happy couple get back from honeymoon – so they don't get burgled while they're away.'

'Or in case they die doing the parascending thing,' chirped Lucy.

'Optimist. Anyway, their heart-warming backstory is that they were teenage sweethearts. Lost touch after school, met years later in a supermarket car park. Be still my bleeding heart . . .'

'Wait,' interjected Dana. 'She's the same age as him? Truly?'

Mike checked his notes. 'He's thirty-five, she's . . . yeah, thirty-four. Both thirty-one on their wedding day. Yeah. She's aged better than him, huh?'

'Definitely. I'd have put her mid-twenties. Anything else?'

'The phone records and computers from Lou turn up nothing unusual. Except porn-site visits.'

'That's unusual?' Stuart glanced around the room. 'Asking for a friend . . .'

Mike chuckled. 'What's unusual is an uptick from a fairly steady routine. I wondered if it might suggest tension within the marriage. Sure enough: Megan's laptop says she's had three meetings with a lawyer in the last month: Spencer Lynch. This guy specialises in divorce. Last meeting was yesterday – a one-hour conference at his office.'

There was a slight frisson in the room. This station was used to domestic-led homicides in all their forms: this new option fitted their comfort zone.

Bill's voice drifted in from an angle. 'Lynch? Met him. Bottom-feeder. Only does divorces and challenging pre-nups. No slicing up your ex – no fee. He's exactly like you'd think he'd be.'

Dana nodded and turned back to Mike. 'Does anything confirm Megan's alibi for the time of death?'

'Nope. Waiting on Megan's mobile records. Uniform will be canvassing neighbours after this meeting, in case they saw anything for that time. According to Lou's phone, she sent a text to Lou at 2330 – he replied 2331. There's nothing on her home phone after 7 p.m. until 0628, which was a call to her mother.'

Dana nodded. 'Yes, she rang her mother while I was there doing

The Knock: I can verify that. Are we sure we have all their phones covered?'

'I've checked all the networks for Lou, for home and work addresses. Still waiting on Megan, so not closed yet. It's possible someone has a pay-as-you-go hidden away, but otherwise, we're good.'

'So Megan has no alibi. Any signs of a lover, or is she only disgruntled?'

Mike swapped one sheaf for another, this one stapled. 'Okay, so her laptop was more useful than Lou's. She's booked a trip to Paris for next month. One ticket, return. She's been chatting on social media with a number of people, most of whom look to be old friends from the city. Nothing there to suggest anything other than being fed up of living here, wishing she hadn't come. *I never see my husband, the spark's gone*, etcetera. If I was guessing – and I am – I'd say pissed off, but maybe hadn't decided to leave yet.'

'That fits my impression when I spoke to her. So no one's cheating?'

'Not yet, no . . . as far as we know. Lou has nothing suspicious or flirtatious going on. She has a few possibly overly friendly colleagues, judging by the emails. But without knowing her or the kind of work atmosphere, that might be a reach. She's very attractive, judging by the photos, so the flirting might be one-way.'

'Okay.' Dana looked around the room in case there were any further questions or clarifications. 'So, actions around Cassavette. One, I want to know for sure if he had a weapon on him, or any trace of one. If we're calling murder as the charge, it matters. Stuart, please take that: the forensics on Cassavette's body should be nearly finished by now.

'Two, I want to know about the lawyer – that bothers me for some reason, and I want it cleared up: why the visits, how far down the line was Megan, and so on. Mikey – either you or I need to speak to that lawyer today, please.

'Three, uniform will be doing house-to-house. As we know to our cost from last year, failing to do it right causes a lot of heartache. It's a new estate in Earlville they live on; someone will be stuck there all day with nothing to do but twitch the curtains – you can count on that. Whoever finds that person gets themselves a goldmine.

'Four, we need to get through all the current and recent employees at Jensen's Store. Mikey will kick that off, supplemented by uniforms as they come off the house-to-house. Lou thought his team were ripping him off – the only two cameras were on the cash register and the stockroom. If someone working there had a grudge, we need to be able to pin down their alibi. I don't want Whittler's lawyer – when he gets one – having an alternate explanation based on bitter ex-employees. Luce, can you co-ordinate those, please?'

Dana paused; her mind began to stumble. Like grabbing something underwater, her perception was a little off, the target drifted away from her grasp. She pretended to cough so she could draw breath and refocus.

'Forensics have already done a sweep of the area around the store. No witnesses; no apparent signs to follow up. We're – sorry, *Lucy's* – chasing down any CCTV from around there, but it's a mainly rural area with a few choice properties. All the wealthy homes might have their cameras pointed at themselves, not the end of the driveway. We'll keep on that, but it's yielding nothing yet.'

Dana turned to the second whiteboard as Lucy wrote up the policy book – the official record of how the investigation was conducted.

'Sooo . . . Nathan Whittler. I suppose I should introduce you all to Mr Whittler. He's uh, quite something.'

She glanced at Bill, who grinned.

'Whittler was born in Earlville in 1980. Son of Martin and Pamela, who are no longer with us; one brother, Jeb, as Mikey outlined. We're hoping to speak to the brother soon; he's arriving from overseas.

Everything in Whittler's life appears to stack up until 2004. He was living with his family up to that point. Luce, what was he doing for work until then?'

Lucy flicked back a page in a file, although Dana knew she had the entire thing memorised. It was a Lucy gesture to sometimes play down her capability to a group; Dana still couldn't quite fathom why she did it.

'Living with his parents, as you say. He was . . . an apprentice cabinet maker, at Pringles Furniture. It's an antiques place in Earlville. Apprentice since he was eighteen, so six years. Either cabinets are more complicated than I thought, or he's a slow learner.'

Letting the chuckling ride, Dana added, 'Based on talking to him, I'd say he's a perfectionist. Probably learned quickly enough – he is bright – but couldn't bear to finish anything until it was perfect.'

'Okay. But that was pretty much all he did, that we have records on. Other than learning to drive, and in 2004 buying a second-hand Corolla and breaking an arm. So, you know; dream life.'

Dana took a deep breath. 'In 2004 he pretty much falls off every radar we have. Just goes. Nothing. Everything we have on him after that time is based purely on what he's told us, which may be a pack of lies. He has no credit card, no phone, no Medicare use, no employment or social security details from Centrelink, and no movements in his bank account; he's totally off-grid for all records that we have. Luce, interstate?'

Lucy shook her head. 'The ones we border: zero. Same as us – never heard of him before, have no records.'

'Thought so. And nothing abroad . . . ?' – she glanced at Bill for a confirmatory nod – 'that we've caught up to, either. We don't know what kicked off him walking out on the family. He won't say, and the parents are both now dead: a tragic but routine car wreck in 2007, apparently. So Whittler went off in 2004 and didn't look back; we have no idea where, why or how.'

She moved closer to the second whiteboard and pointed to the red writing – the supposition, the assumptions.

'What little he's told us so far is that he went into the woods in or near the national park, constructed some sort of camp and stayed there for fifteen years. He existed by stealing, I believe, though he's reluctant to discuss it. I don't think he built a farm or turned into a master fisherman, and we have no evidence of him generating an income. So it looks like he lived wild, stealing food and other things he needed.'

A hand went up. Rainer Holt, a very keen uniform.

'Yes, Rainer?'

'To steal all you need for fifteen years – wouldn't we have come across that? We don't get so many burglaries. Unless he was driving into the city to do them.'

Dana jolted. She hadn't really considered Whittler lying about the car, keeping it somewhere and riding at night into the city to burgle there. She'd made a crass assumption about his honesty and that this was all local. She could feel her face tingle.

Rainer continued. 'To steal all that you need – not only food, but everything – you'd have to be pretty prolific. We've caught all our regulars at some point in the past fifteen years, no?' He glanced around the room at some of the older uniforms.

Risdale nodded, and so did Mike. Dana could see that the room was fifty–fifty on whether Nathan was spinning an outrageous lie, or had done what he claimed. Maybe the suggestion of living wild locally was all talk – throwing her off the scent of a burglar with wheels. An image flashed through Dana's mind of Nathan's hands – white, well kept, neat . . . *indoorsy*.

'It's a good point,' she admitted. 'I haven't bottomed out the MO yet. As I say, he's reluctant to discuss it. Primarily because I think he's ashamed to have done it. But my gut says that's how he survived.

Maybe he took a little from a lot of places – that way, they don't notice or think it's not worth reporting. Cassavette suspected it was his own staff at his place: that suggests low-grade, frequent, petty pilfering. Difficult to confirm, difficult to prove, too small to invest resources in stopping it.'

Rainer thought for a moment. 'Yes, I can see that. But should we discount the possibility that he was doing city homes and not locals'? Or perhaps he had a friend or relative giving him supplies? His brother, maybe?'

Dana nodded. 'Absolutely right. Until we can confirm it, then all options stay on the table. But one reason I'm inclined to think we're on the right path is the other information he's given. The key part being this: he says he hasn't spoken to another human being in fifteen years.'

The room stopped. Dana waited for the immediate howls of protest – that this was impossible, that Nathan was clearly unhinged and unreliable. And guilty. But they didn't come straight away. After a few seconds, Mike chimed in.

'I'm going to call it, from a personal point of view. This, more than anything else, is what I find difficult.' He stood and spoke to the room in general, turning towards Dana every few seconds so she wouldn't feel he was undermining her. Mike got office politics.

'To back up a little, I'm not convinced he's spent fifteen years in the wilderness. Oh, I think he's spent spells there – maybe the summers, maybe even the past few months. But he doesn't have the look or feel of someone who's been beyond civilisation for such a long time. He's too aware of current events, his skin isn't right, his clothes aren't used enough. And I don't think he's got the skills. I know a couple of people I think could maybe do that if they had to – *maybe*. They've been specially trained, have some killer equipment, and the *cojones*. Whittler looks like a mousy indoor worker – neat hands, newish clothes.'

Lucy tapped his leg. 'As a rodent-like employee in an office, I will be suing you, Mikey.'

Mike laughed. 'Have your people call my people. But really, even if I possibly buy that Whittler camped out all this time, it's a stretch. Some of these winter nights have been brutal. I reckon he's used cabins and got away with cleaning up before the owners came back in spring.'

He paused to take in the room. He and Dana were usually rock-solid in their agreements: this was holding the squad's attention.

'But the no-talking thing? Nah. No one can do that. No one *has* done that, ever. People in solitary confinement – still get to speak sometime. People who go off and become hermits – only do it for a short time. Some of them have to talk daily: it's part of their job. The conversation might be low level, or short. But I don't think total silence can be done for that length of time.'

Dana's thumb and forefinger worked again. 'So what you're saying is, you find that no-speaking aspect impossible for anyone to pull off. And therefore, everything else he claims is suspect?'

'Yeah, I think so. I don't believe any human can do that. So yeah, credibility shot for me.'

'Hmm. Thoughts, people?'

No one blinked until Rainer offered, 'I think it's possible. It's only one month, multiplied, isn't it? Some people could do one month. Maybe it gets easier the longer you go? But I reckon you could tell that from how he behaves. Was his voice croaky? Did he want to talk all the time to make up? That kind of thing.'

Lucy came in. 'Oh, I know this one. The croaky thing doesn't apply. I checked with a website on mutism, and with a doctor. Turns out your vocal cords can work fine, no matter how long you've been silent. Especially if Whittler's in the middle of nowhere and can sing, or yodel, or whatever. And I think the other thing's a judgement call:

he might feel the need to jabber non-stop, or he might be addicted to clamming up.' She glanced to Dana. 'Right?'

'Yes, he hasn't been exactly a motormouth since he arrived. In fact, I'm the only one he'll speak to at all. But your point's well made, Rainer. We'd need something to corroborate a claim that unusual.'

Bill stood, and the room turned to hear him.

'All right, I've said this before to Dana, so it's not a surprise to her. But I'll reiterate it here. First off, we need to cover all the bases on this, because if there's even a chance that Whittler isn't the murderer, we're currently losing evidence, forensics and time. The killer might be strolling away while we're focused on one guy stealing beans. So let's keep our options open as long as possible.

'That said, Whittler has been off the radar for every agency we can find for over a decade. There's a chance that he hasn't done anything wrong – or maybe nothing significant – for that time. But he chose carefully how to become hidden and stay that way. It's setting off alarm bells for me. If I wanted to commit multiple crimes and get away with it, I'd start by trying to be invisible. If the police don't know I exist, how can they pin me for the crime? We didn't know Whittler existed – had no reason to. He might have done anything – and I mean *anything* – in those fifteen years. Let's bear that in mind. He may not be a hermit: he may be something else entirely. Dana has that in her thinking already.'

The room bubbled with uncertainty. She'd had them with her at first, until she suggested Nathan hadn't spoken in over a decade. Like Mike, many imagined this was physically impossible – at least without going nuts – and therefore it threw all Whittler's other statements into doubt. Then Bill's warning about seeing Nathan too benignly: it was timely, accurate and necessary. Dana covered her disappointment with an attempted display of command.

'Bill's right. We don't assume anything about Whittler unless or until we can prove it. All options on the table until then. Okay, actions. Mikey, thinking about it, I'd like you to take the lawyer, Lynch, please. I want to know the state of the Cassavettes' marriage and what was being planned. Megan obviously held back – bottom that out with Lynch.

'Lucy, I'd like you to please focus on Whittler's family. All the background we can get. As I understand it, the brother is some kind of international businessman. I want some more detail for my chats with Whittler. Thanks.

'The uniform officers, on the list for door-to-door around the Cassavettes' street, please. Lucy will co-ordinate who's doing which homes; Mikey has prepared the strategy and questions for you to follow. Anything out of the ordinary, anything about their lives and habits, anyone asking questions about them in the neighbourhood.'

Conscious they were starting to gather themselves to leave, Dana raised her voice.

'Two points before we move. Thank you. First, let's not forget that someone died today – they were murdered. For us, there are processes and work to be done, and that's our day-to-day. For others, it's the worst day of their entire lives and they'll never recover. We owe it to them to remember that a human being is gone. Secondly, the door-to-door is important, everyone, it's not a motion to go through. Last killer we caught came from those apparently routine conversations with neighbours, so don't treat it as a chore, please. It matters. Thank you.'

She was flushed with the sense that she'd lost the room before they'd taken it all in: that she'd failed. She beckoned Rainer over before he left with the gaggle of uniforms. He approached cautiously and it struck her that perhaps he thought he was in trouble for speaking up.

'Hey, Rainer,' said Lucy as she passed him.

'Oh God,' muttered Dana. She glanced up at him: he was basketball-tall, with a thin face and long fingers. 'Is it pronounced *Ryner*? Jesus, I've been calling you *Rayner* for weeks, and now in front of everyone. Sorry, sorry.'

He grinned. 'Ah, I think it's either way, to be honest. My mother was German, my father wasn't, so I guess it's a fifty–fifty.'

'Even so, I've, uh, disrespected your culture and all. I should have checked at some point. Bad Dana.'

'Not sure I have a culture, as such. No problem, boss. Was there something, or should I go with the door-to-door team?'

'Uh, no. I've a job for you, actually. Good comments, by the way. They caught me in a stupid assumption – that Whittler had burgled and done it locally. I'd dismissed the car. So: two things, please. When you get back, I want you to chase up anything to do with the Corolla – Lucy ran the basic checks, but anything else you can track down: to either confirm it still exists or it's been totalled somewhere. That'll get us on firmer ground about where Whittler might have been stealing.

'But first, I want you to go over to Earlville.' She was momentarily distracted by Lucy's return, and then skipped a beat as she wondered if Rainer had noticed. He seemed to be focused on making notes, she believed. 'Speak to Pringle, the furniture guy.'

Lucy looked up. 'But don't hammer him. Or nail him.'

Rainer caught it straight away. 'He's a chip off the old block.'

'Oh yeah,' said Lucy. 'He could open doors. Hope he's not unhinged.'

Dana tried not to laugh, failed. 'Okay, enough. The English language has officially lawyered up; we're no longer allowed to abuse it.' She gathered herself. 'I want to know what Whittler was like before he went away – type of person, habits – especially sociability. Plus, I want anything we can get on why he went: it was almost certainly some kind of family mess, but I want some leverage on Whittler if we can. You have good instincts, you'll be fine.'

Rainer blushed momentarily, which Dana found sweet. He turned to Lucy. 'Do you know if the old man's still there, Luce? It was a long time ago.'

'Yeah, he still runs the place. I spoke to his new assistant this morning. He might be . . . nah, I'm out of puns now. He's working today, I know that.'

Rainer turned back to Dana. 'On it, boss.'

As he walked away Lucy leaned into Dana, their arms touching, and asked, 'Was I ever that keen?'

'I don't think either of us were, to be honest.'

Chapter 14

Billy Munro had left a message.

'Yeah, couple of the older guys I know reckon your best bet for those caves is around Piermont Lake, about nine or ten clicks north of the Old Mill Road. Seems there's some caves on the western shore, though they're mighty hard to get to. You may have to canoe into them. Could be they're full of bats, so to actually live there you'd have to be batshit crazy. Hahaha . . . uh . . . Yeah, well . . . the dinosaur club here thinks there might also be a couple upstream from the lake a ways. 'Course, they've got memories like a sieve. But it might be worth a thought. Adios.'

Dana reached for the map Lucy had marked up.

Piermont Lake was 'C'; the third and most likely alternative she and Lucy had discussed. Billy had said that there might be some options upstream. Her finger followed a thin blue line snaking its way north from the top of the lake, until it wiggled its last and ended where the contours jammed together.

Stuart Risdale coughed at the doorway.

'Hey, Stu, pull up a chair.'

Risdale sat carefully, as though landing on sprigs of holly. A back injury from falling off a motorbike: his wife had regaled Dana with the details at some compulsory office picnic a few months ago. Mrs Risdale had put it down to a mid-life crisis with a tutting weariness: a women-together, what-can-you-do shrug that Dana identified only retrospectively.

'No sign of the murder weapon yet. I just checked. But I asked them to work outside–in, so they could pick up other traces as they went: if the knife's near the blood, it might be another hour or two before we find it.'

'Okay.' Dana was more interested in the map at this point.

'You wanted me to push Forensics about Cassavette having a weapon? Well—'

Dana nodded. 'Ah crap, yes, I did. Good catch. Any news?'

'There's no sign of a weapon of any kind – no ad-libbed grab item, and no gun or anything like that.'

Dana was surprised. Given Cassavette had been running a vigil for a few months, she'd figured he'd be carrying some kind of weapon. Maybe something like a heavy bottle: then he could claim he'd simply grabbed it from a shelf without planning it, if the burglar sued later.

'So he went at someone armed with righteous indignation? Didn't get something from the stock?'

'Apparently not.' Risdale shrugged and turned over a page in the bundle he was holding. 'Well, in truth he might have been spooked. There was no weapon, but where he was sleeping we did find red hairs and a hairgrip.'

Dana smiled. Mike's hunch about Cassavette using the 'burglaries' as a cover honed into view. 'Oh, did we now? Cassavette's as big and bald as they come. Mind you, that's a stockroom and all the staff use it. So it's possible it belongs to one of them. Could be an innocent reason.'

Risdale ran his tongue around his cheek to demonstrate his scepticism. 'Sure, sure. Could be. Not quite so innocent if you find it *inside* the sleeping bag, though.'

'Ah, and there was me thinking that if anyone was messing around, it was his wife.'

'Hmm. She might still be: wouldn't be the first couple where they're both playing away games. There could also be a reason that doesn't involve screwing around.'

'That's true. I mean, it might not be his sleeping bag, or he might have loaned it to someone who lost a hair grip. But . . . really . . . I'm not seeing that. Could you sleep in that without the grip poking you at some point?' She considered. 'Unless it only arrived there, you know, *last minute*.'

Risdale grinned. 'My thinking, too. I've mentioned it to Mikey to pass on to the uniforms. Luce is searching the records on employees to narrow down the redheads; we can try them first.'

Dana stood, buckling for a split second when her knee didn't lock into position. 'Good, we'll leave them to that. Take a look at this map, please, Stu. I've narrowed down the search area.'

Risdale had those kind of stiff army-style boots that strapped halfway up the calf; they squeaked when he stood up. Dana's finger traced Piermont Lake.

'I think Whittler's been hiding in a cave somewhere on the shoreline here, or maybe upstream slightly . . . here. There's sand in the soles of his boots.'

'Yeah, Dakota Line. My brother goes fishing near there sometimes; not all of those lakes are sandy, but yeah. If I could?'

She stood back when Risdale bent over the map, as though his eyesight were as bad as his back. He straightened up with a grunt.

'I suggest we start upstream and work down. Reasons being: your man would need water, and unless he has millions of purification tablets, he has to take a chance there isn't a dead animal polluting the water. Hence, upstream is less risky. It's safer to take the water where it's running, not static: the faster it runs, the safer it is. Also, it's partly psychological – white water looks cleaner than water that isn't moving. Plus, it makes sense to camp as near to the water as you can without risking flooding.'

'See, I'd never have thought of any of that. Yes, makes sense. The kind of cave I'm thinking of is going to be quite big; tall enough to stand up and move around in. Whittler isn't wriggling through some tiny gap each time, I don't think. But the entrance would be pretty well hidden, including from above. He might have camouflaged it.'

'Okay. We'll do some extra research online: we can access some military maps and photos. But we'll be in the air in fifteen minutes, and there soon after. I'll take three guys, an inflatable canoe and a drone. We'll do an initial sweep and email some images.'

'Excellent. Make it to Mikey, actually. I might be back in the ring with Whittler.'

Risdale moved to the door, turned. 'I didn't mean to sound bitchy in there, Dana. I saw the footage of the guy when he came in – I can't believe you could even get a word out of him.'

'Appreciate it. You were right, though – I haven't asked him yet. It could well be the last question – *What happened in the store?* Either he'll spill his guts, or he'll look daggers and never speak to me again.'

'True, true.' He paused. 'He probably did it. You know that, right?'

Dana smiled. 'Quite possibly. But I'm guessing his home is going to be a hell of a window into his soul. Thanks, Stu.'

There was a small gap – maybe half a metre wide – between the rear wall of the vehicle servicing shed and a two-metre metal fence at the back of the station. The space was carpeted with tenacious tufts of grass and hosted a few brambles climbing a concrete post towards the light. Where the gap emerged on to the parking area there was a collection of windswept cigarette stubs. Dana could recall figures hunched from the chill, cupping their smokes and simultaneously cursing the weather and their own weakness. A metre past that, the gap turned and was hidden from view. In the narrow channel backed by weather-lashed breeze blocks the noise from hydraulics and drills punctuated a steady wind.

Dana stooped there, and vomited.

At first it was a dry retch. She'd been too wound up this morning – awake since midnight, in fact – to have eaten anything. Eventually, her stomach muscles produced some yellowish bile, bitter as it left her. She gasped and spat for a couple of minutes, feeling her facial muscles quiver back to normality. Then she wiped her mouth with a tissue and popped a couple of mints.

Her temples hammered with a pressure headache. Right on the psychopath zone, she thought: the area on the lobes where human empathy lay – or didn't. She sometimes worried that her emotional freezing – the sense of standing helplessly outside normal human behaviour – was her mind telling her she was psychopathic. Maybe she was simply covering her pathology with a brittle coating of humanity, a veneer that would shatter like spring ice if she didn't fight to protect it.

She tried to tell herself that the shakes were from the vomiting or from a lack of food. But the Day was clawing at her, reaching, taking. She thought again of the revolver, how it had felt in her mouth. That metallic coin-taste, the heaviness of the barrel on her tongue, the collision with her lip as it left. As though it were angry at her, disappointed that she lacked the courage. She felt nauseous again and leaned against the wall until the feeling subsided.

It was difficult to tell whether working this Day was making it worse. It *felt* worse. It had never happened before – she'd previously gone to extravagant lengths to make sure she was away from the station and uncontactable. Leaving the waterfall this morning, she'd believed the current distraction might be a good thing; maybe being around people would intrinsically make her less suicidal. But all it seemed to do was compress her anguish into little bullets of time, which sank through her guts every couple of hours. It was less drawn out, less debilitating, but sharper and more persuasive. When it bit, it bit hard.

Partly, it was a sense of failure. Or, more accurately, a sense of shame about failure. All this had first been triggered twenty-five years ago. She'd had psychiatrists, psychologists, therapists and counsellors down the years who'd dug at the surface; moving soil around but never getting to the core of her. She hadn't let them. Dana had always believed, ultimately, that only she could find the solution. Yet here she was, twenty-five years later, puking behind a wall and hiding everything from her colleagues. Still denying that anyone had a right to know what was in her heart. The bile at her feet, the shaking, the finger-and-thumb, the clutching of a nebuliser, the shimmering vision – all said she couldn't provide the solution. She was still failing.

Trying to trammel it into one Day was not possible: she knew that, even though she clung to the strategy. Using the Day was supposed to adjust the dynamic: to delay, postpone, almost *trick* the heaviest shadow into waiting until it was supposed to be exposed to the light. As if there were an etiquette, understood by both her and her suicidal tendencies; social graces to be followed. Her attempts to control it and structure it were flimsy, but they were all she had. Trammelling was the only thing she could do that demonstrated she could do anything at all – the only overt sign of agency.

She thought of ringing Father Timms but decided against it. Perhaps if she was back in the office, concentrating on Nathan Whittler, it would all magically subside.

Dana stopped off at Custody, to check on the requirements for Nathan's ongoing detention. The station had eight cells, including the suicide-watch cell, which was visible from the main desk. The other cells stretched away down a corridor of rough render walls, the concrete floor worn smooth by dragged and scuffed feet. Occasional cries, seemingly random and directed at no one in particular, split the air. They disrupted what was otherwise calm acceptance and stoicism: regulars who knew the routines as well as the officers. Martin Simpson was today's custody officer, pottering around his small kingdom: blond wood, filing, CCTV and a radio tuned low.

Closest to the custody desk was the Lecter Theatre. Near floor-to-ceiling glass at the front, it was a cell where the edges had all been smoothed off and where the underfloor heating was turned up so that no blankets would be needed. Ligature points were minimised by flush-fitting doors and locks, and a sink recessed into the wall. Everything that could be done had been done; everyone knew it wasn't always enough. Each custody officer held the nagging, insistent fear that this shift might be *the* shift.

Like most stations, Carlton had an ever-increasing problem with the mental health of prisoners: it had become the agency of first and last resort, because they couldn't get places in hospitals. It was categorised as the police region's biggest organisational risk: no one knew what a prisoner had taken, was suffering from or would do. Almost everything was guesswork and hope – humanity and awareness would take the custody officer only so far.

The doctor had assessed Nathan Whittler as high risk. The main problem was that no one knew – or could verify – where he'd been or what he'd done, nor could they find any evidence of medication. That, plus his clear discomfort at any human interaction, made him a concern. Dana didn't want Nathan to be pitched into the humiliating visibility of the Lecter Theatre, but for now they really had no choice.

'Hey, Dana.' Simpson would be finishing his shift soon and clearly couldn't wait.

'Hi, Martin. How's our new guest doing?'

She made sure she was around the corner from Nathan's cell and couldn't be heard. Somehow, she felt it would add to Nathan's shame to be aware that she could observe him, see his degradation and lack of privacy.

Simpson puffed his cheeks as the printer hummed out more warm paper. CCTV screens flickered behind his shoulder.

'So-so, at best. He's, uh, really uncomfortable with the whole thing. I can't, in all conscience, give him any more privacy than he has – not in that cell. Unless the doc says otherwise, he's stuck with it. You can see him flinch, though: light, people, noise – anything. He's a flinch machine.'

Dana nodded. 'He's like that in interview, too. Okay, I'll be calling him back soon. If you can please find him anything sugary – chocolate, something like that – I'd appreciate it.'

Simpson grinned. 'Keeping him sweet?'

'Literally, yes.' She smiled. 'Lovin' your work there, Martin.'

On her way to Bill's office Dana poked her head round the door and spoke to Mike. 'Anything more on that intelligence on Lou Cassavette?'

'Yeah, actually.' Mike lifted one file to extract another, then patted the pile twice until it was perfect again. 'So, the hassle was because he went to school with two of the Alvarez brothers.'

Dana looked blank.

'Ricardo Alvarez? Biggest drug dealer in the state? Jeez, you need that bit of general knowledge. Not everything is a specialism. Okay, so the Alvarez family have been up to their buckets in various aspects of organised crime. Currently drug kingpins, though the word is they're trying to diversify.'

The whole world of sources bewildered Dana. It wasn't how she operated, as a detective or a human being. She couldn't imagine cultivating someone who would want to tell her something dangerous to them. She never knew what 'the word' currently was, or what the street thought.

'How is Cassavette attached?'

'Maybe not at all. He went to school with two of the brothers. One of the brothers is the financial chief of the family empire, another is in prison for murder. Cassavette's previous business was a corner store in the city – they're a natural for laundering money. I mean, high turnover – and much of it in cash – with plenty written off for shoplifting or damage. So it was a potential link that Central never followed up, but it stayed on the radar. The Alvarez family like doing business with people they know.'

'Relevant to this investigation, though?'

'Still chasing. Cassavette might have moved to get away from that sort of thing. Maybe it followed him down here. Perhaps they leaned on him, and he leaned back. It's an option.'

'Okay. That lawyer of Megan's – Lynch. Is he here yet?'

'I imagine he'll be here shortly. Because I set Lucy on him.'

'Ah.'

Lucy's view of lawyers was a conversation piece: she basically saw them as vermin. Her 'tolerance' was narrower than a human hair, but more fragile.

Dana turned and headed down the corridor. She could hear Lucy before she reached the office door.

'Mr Lynch, I'm not inviting you to an elegant soiree with canapés and we don't have a lawyer quota to fill each month. This is a serious crime that requires your immediate presence.' Lucy looked up, saw Dana and tapped the button for conference call.

Lynch's delivery sounded odd in the echo-ridden, tinny speaker: a well-educated fox purring in a drainpipe. 'Seriously? I haven't committed any crime, and I mainly deal in divorce law. I think you're getting a little, uh, dramatic. Matters are rarely as urgent as people think they are. I can fit you in . . . around four?'

'Mr Lynch, I am not asking you. I'm telling you to come to the station straight away. Now. This minute.' Lucy did a cross-eye and puffed her cheeks. Dana raised an eyebrow.

'Really, I'd love to help, but I'm tied up in client meetings for at least two hours. Can't it at least wait until lunchtime?'

Lucy sucked her gums for a second and took a deep, long breath before launching.

'Mr Lynch, are you currently talking down a novice pilot whose trainer has had a heart attack? No? Are you currently guiding someone in the Congo jungle to perform surgery on themselves before they bleed out? No? Client blubbing on a ledge somewhere? No? Then what *you* are doing isn't as important, or urgent, as what *we're* doing. I know where your offices are. It takes six minutes to walk here. I expect you here in under ten, or we'll march over there and we can all do that "perp walk" thing. Personally, I love that, but those on the receiving end seem to find it embarrassing. Not to say a career-screw. Under ten minutes, and counting, Mr Lynch.'

She stabbed the end-call button with the tail of her pencil. Her face shifted from glowering to perky. 'Hey, Dana. I'm practising my people skills.'

'Jeez, Luce, you're terrifying. Let me apologise in advance for anything I ever do to upset you.'

'Nah, you're gold. Lawyers, on the other hand: their sanctimonious, patronising crap. They aren't even the bottom of the barrel. They're the thing you use to scrape it.'

Dana grinned. 'When he gets here, stick him in Interview Three. No drinkies, no one with him. On his own to stew for fifteen minutes, then Mikey can have at him.'

'Ooh, gently simmering lawyer. My favourite. Will do.'

Dana gave her a thumbs-up and walked on to Bill's office. There was a small window in his office door, and she peered through it as if it were a speakeasy entrance until he waved her in.

'Hey, Dana. Grab a chair. I just need to sign off on these.'

She sat and gazed out of the window, watching the breeze pick up on a pair of trees that had finished with the scenic gold and were now turning bare and frigid. Up here, it was difficult to hear much of anything. Dana could understand why some bosses stayed in their office the whole time; dealing with politics but relishing the serenity.

Bill's sideboard had a picture of his wife: clearly professionally taken and, Dana reckoned, about a decade ago. Melinda's face had a calm assurance and self-possession, like an early Bacall, with a glint that said she knew more than she'd ever need. Dana briefly wondered if anyone – no matter the equipment, diffusers and post-production software – could get her anywhere near looking like that.

Bill perused a report, running his pen rapidly down the centre of each page. Speed reader. Dana had always wondered about taking that course. Central offered it, but it was a three-day residential and she didn't like being away from home for that long. It spooked her. She'd had to do a week's residential on investigative techniques, and she wound up driving in and back each day, even though it was a six-hour round trip. She had to admit, though, Bill's ability to absorb and retain vast chunks of information was impressive.

'Test me.' He slung over the report.

'Hmm. Page seventeen, there are two photos. The upper one – who took that?'

He closed his eyes, and the pupils danced like REM sleep. 'Top right, italics, Brian, Brian . . . Mulcahey.'

She put the report back on the desk. 'That's creepy – and a really flimsy super-power.'

'Yeah, I was offered invisibility or flying. I went with "memory for trivia". A mistake in retrospect.'

'On the other hand, PrettyGoodMemoryMan doesn't have to wear tight spandex.'

He smiled. 'For which we're all grateful. Especially me. Something on your mind?'

'I wanted to collect your thoughts before the next go at Whittler. Lucy thinks his body language says he's softening.'

'She's right,' agreed Bill, 'although some of that is him simply adjusting to being around people generally, not necessarily warming to you. That particular road is limited, though. Be ready for him to pick a fight about nothing.'

Dana tilted her head. 'Because?'

'Because he's spent the last fifteen years being a particular person with a particular view of the world. You being pleasant to him puts a dent in that.'

'Ah, yes, that occurred to me, too.' Dana settled back and rubbed her recalcitrant knee. 'He's defined himself by that "lone wolf against everyone" personality. Getting on with someone, and not getting screwed over, undermines his sense of self.'

'Exactly. Don't get me wrong; he welcomes what looks like friendship. You're doing an outstanding job: being precisely the kind of person he'd warm to, in exactly the right way. But be prepared for his long-term persona to give one more kick, one more moment representing him.'

Bill took off his glasses to rub his eyes. It struck Dana that he had been there when she arrived at Jensen's Store; he must have been at work before 5 a.m.

'You believe he went fifteen years without speaking?' Bill asked.

'Yes, I think he did. There's a . . . spirit, a determination. I think he found his niche out there. Around people, that single-minded independence would have grated; they wouldn't have appreciated it. The modern world rewards confidence and self-absorption: he'd have been derided.' She could feel herself blush with emotion. 'But out there? Oh, he's king of his own little world, and that world doesn't need any chitchat, does it?'

'Mikey doesn't believe it. Personally, I'm agnostic. What matters is that Whittler feels believed by you – which he does.'

'I get where Mikey's coming from. Stu's the same.' Dana nodded and paused. 'I wanted to ask you something specific. When I asked Whittler early on if he'd slept in any of the cabins, he got very indignant. I actually thought I'd blown it at that point.'

'Yeah, in retrospect that was a tight squeeze. At first, I thought maybe he *had* slept in them and he was getting agitated because you read him so quickly. But now, I'm not so sure. I think maybe he hasn't. Partly, I think he has his own very black-and-white ethics. People who live alone don't have them modified by messy compromises: they harden them.'

Dana raised an eyebrow ironically.

'Oh, crap. No offence.'

She smiled and waved it off.

Bill coughed a recovery and continued. 'Also, he's secretly really proud of the home he got together and how he survived. I think he has an ego about it, and you need to play up to that. He hasn't had an audience in fifteen years. You played it exactly right, saying how it spoke to his integrity not to use the cabins.'

'Hmm. Lucky door back in, that was.'

'No luck in it. Told you, Dana – you're exactly the person for this. My advice? Keep going how you're going. Hopefully we'll find his magic secret lair and that'll give you a whole world of ammo. But until we do, maybe keep on the philosophy track a little more. When you talk about that, his sentences get longer, he opens out more. It makes you a kindred spirit. For all his independence, I think he wants one.'

'Cool. We're on the same page.'

'Singin' from the same spreadsheet, sister. I want you to focus on Whittler – the how, and the why. He remains prime suspect for very good reasons, Dana. If we're going to get full value out of him, we'll need to nail the details and the motive. That's your aim in there. We'll keep Mikey and Luce focused on other options – other people, other scenarios.'

As she got to the door Bill's voice rang out. 'Hey, you know Holt's name is pronounced *Ryner*, right?'

She laughed. 'Don't start with me, Bill, I swear to God . . .'

Chapter 15

Nathan was sitting upright. He was about one third through *Animal Farm*, seemingly engrossed. When no one was around he demonstrated the extreme ease with his own company that Dana found almost inspirational, and Mike had labelled 'weird' when he passed the room. Nathan exuded a serene stillness that seemed practised yet unforced.

As she glanced through the glass she looked for signs of fatigue. If he really hadn't spoken to anyone in fifteen years, she guessed that this intermittent conversation they were having would be draining him. He would, at some point, find it debilitating. She was trying to gauge when that moment would arrive and how she could spot it, because knowing when he was waning would influence her strategy. So far, Dana was struggling to detect it. His fatigue seemed apparent only when he was at his limit, or in tears: then, she knew to give him a rest. Perhaps she wasn't giving him enough credit for resilience or reserves.

After dispensing with the preliminaries and the tape machines once more, Dana prepared to poke again at Nathan's philosophy. She paused momentarily, wondering who was now standing behind the mirror or when the tape of this conversation might be replayed. Since it was entirely possible her words would be broadcast in a courtroom – and shortly after, in the media – she wasn't sure how much to personalise them. Authentic feelings from her unravelled Nathan's defences more quickly; getting answers to his questions pleased and emboldened him. But Dana loathed sharing emotions with anyone else, let alone *everyone* else.

'I assume we've been taking care of you correctly when you're outside this room, Mr Whittler?'

'Adequately, thank you. Although . . .'

Dana looked up. 'Yes, Mr Whittler?'

He winced before replying, as though his request were an imposition and likely to induce scorn. Or punishment.

'I wonder if you could remove the Bible that's been placed there?'

'Of course. Does it offend your religious preferences?'

'Not at all. Inasmuch as I still have them.' He shrugged and paused. 'No, it's more . . . grew up in a household where Bibles and crosses were everywhere. I mean, everywhere. Iconography of every kind on every flat surface. Bad associations. I, uh, don't need to be reminded of my parents' bedroom when I'm in a cell.'

'I understand.'

'Do you?' He lifted his gaze quickly from foot to table-edge: his mannered facsimile of sharpness. 'That's the sort of thing people usually say as a platitude, I think. I believe you always mean what you say, Detective, so I'm intrigued that you say that.'

She had to frame this right. Nathan wanted a *quid pro quo* from her; she wished to convince him she'd kept her end of that bargain without actually having to keep it. She had no wish to travel back in her own time. But she needed Nathan to regress at some point and explain what led to him leaving the family home. The pay-off wouldn't come now, but later.

'Well, religious iconography always carries hefty meaning, Mr

Whittler. That's what it's for. There are certain households where every angle contains a vision of piety, or suffering, or pious suffering. Where every action is infused by a sense of being watched, judged and found wanting. Where ordinary events are smeared by moral finger-wagging, or worse.

'However, I believe there are also households where such objects hold a different interpretation, or perhaps a further one. Places where it's possible to see the objects as emblematic of how some people behave: more specifically, they are used to justify or explain such behaviour. If that conduct is a bad memory, then I'm aware that seeing those objects again, even in a totally different context, can drag you back to a place you wouldn't like to revisit. Drag you back every single day of your life, without you being able to stop it, in fact. That's what I understand, Mr Whittler.'

He nodded slowly, reflecting on what she'd said.

'Then you do get it, Detective. You understand very well. I knew you would.'

His statement of knowledge, of certainty, jarred her. She disliked even the notion of being an open book to anyone, let alone to a suspect in an interview. It implied that insight was mutual, rather than her advantage over him. Even, it suddenly floated past her, as though he had a plan of his own for these conversations. But she had to give him some wins when he asked questions: the give-and-take built his confidence in her.

Once again, Dana used the turning of a notepad page to indicate a change in the conversation's trajectory. They had something of an easy rhythm now: Nathan comprehended the signal.

'I've been thinking on some of the things you've been talking about, Mr Whittler. I'm very interested in what you feel you learned, out there.'

Nathan smiled, staring at his foot. 'Ah, yes. The wise man in the woods. Perhaps people will think I have some kind of dazzling awareness to offer – I'm going to be some sort of crystal-clear thinker. Ha.'

Dana noted the sarcasm but continued. 'Yes, Mr Whittler, many people will. Once your story emerges in the media – which, unfortunately, it eventually will – there will be people who feel your, uh, circumstances gave you some unique insight into the human condition.'

'Those that haven't met me.' Nathan brushed at his jumpsuit: perhaps fastidiousness, perhaps just keeping his hands occupied.

'But I've met you, Mr Whittler. And I believe you have an insight to offer.' She noticed Nathan's raised eyebrow and pushed on. 'I believe that for two reasons. Firstly, you did step outside most human experience – you see much of our lives from the viewpoint of a genuine outsider, and I don't think you should discount the importance of that. We can't have that perspective: you may have it.'

She waited for a response that was never coming.

'Secondly, you're an intelligent person who has had the time to think on these things. I know, if I'm alone, I can clear my mind of everyday concerns. I think better, I'm sharper; I'm more creative with my solutions. I believe you had those advantages when you reflected on the world. Don't you agree?'

'Not sure I do, Detective Russo. Maybe I'm only a man in the trees, eating baked beans from a can. Maybe I wasn't bright enough to begin with, and all this is a wasted opportunity for mankind. Perhaps I survived on bad food, good luck and stubbornness. Hardly a philosopher king, is it?'

She tapped her pen against her pad. 'One thing doesn't preclude another, Mr Whittler. I imagine that not only did you think about life, but you also thought about the process of thinking. If you see what I mean.'

They both let the silence ride. Nathan seemed to be weighing something up. Dana tensed for the shutdown she felt was coming: even though she agreed with Bill that Nathan was more forthcoming on the philosophical side. Maybe Nathan indulged her because he felt such discussions kept them away from specifics like his hideout location, his potential burglaries and whether he had knifed a man to death a few hours ago.

Nathan considered, then adjusted his posture. He leaned forward, matching palm on palm and rubbing them together slowly, fixated on his shoes.

'So let me tell you how my thinking went, Detective Russo. Because it's not so mysterious after all. When I first went into the wide blue yonder, my only focus was on survival. It was a few weeks before the winter started in earnest: I had a small and closing window to get myself straight. I'd been living rough for a few days when I started to truly appreciate the importance of not getting wet.'

He shook his head ruefully. 'No great philosophy there, Detective, no remarkable insight: just *don't get wet, Nathan*. I can't emphasise enough – the cold when you're wet is so much worse than dry cold. So my early time was centred wholly on shelter, on warmth where I could create it and on food. Who was it, Maslow? Food and shelter first on the list.'

Dana nodded. Was there a cop in the Western world who hadn't stared at that famous pyramid at some point in their training?

'Once I had some kind of handle on where and how I was going to live, I found my brain creeping around, looking for work. I had that modern mentality that my mind must be busy. In your world – my former world – it gets engaged, stimulated, and deliberately so. You can't even handle a day without it. You create a life where you have that relentless occupation – telephone, work, television, music, people – because you think your mind requires it. You believe your brain will turn to soggy mush without some kind of constant external intervention.

'So my unprepared mind looked for work and found it. It had a rich vein of loathing on tap: looking back and criticising, damning myself over what I'd done or not done, said or not said. My mind liked the negative – it was sustenance. It fed itself by eating into me. I found I had to pay more attention to the practicalities of my new life, purely to shut my mind off from doing that. I recognised it was doing me harm to retrace the past, but it was like an addiction – my brain wouldn't stop. That retribution had to be crowded out by current activity. I organised and reorganised, overdid the attention to detail, let myself become obsessive about things that didn't matter. I did that deliberately, Detective Russo, to stop my mind from killing me.'

Nathan stopped, as if seeking absolution, or forgiveness. It wasn't Dana's to give, even if she wanted to: he'd seemingly selected the most unreliable and atheistic of priests. She recognised the theory, though – trying to crowd out the negative by filling the dangerous mental space with activity. It was, she thought, exactly what she was doing with this Day.

Despite her empathy, all Dana could do was nudge and listen.

'At some point, Mr Whittler, you pushed through that phase?'

'It lasted maybe two years. A horrible time – gruesome. I couldn't see how it could end. I had no endgame in sight beyond continuing to live – this was it; and it seemed to be devouring me from the brain outwards. I was still trying to live at a modern speed, you see. Still thinking there was urgency, or requirement, or others who should be considered. I was scared of the idea of being bored. I mean, Detective, truly bored. Not simply at a loose end but with literally nothing to do that day, and comprehending that fact even as the sun rose. Days felt absurdly long; unnavigable.

'But gradually, things began to shift. I started to experience periods of nothingness – whole hours, or afternoons, when I took no action whatsoever I could recall, had no thoughts I could remember. At first

I was puzzled, and worried. Maybe I was losing my marbles, out there in the wilderness. Perhaps it was sending me crazy, and those "lost hours" were proof of that.'

He took another sip of water then touched the bottle cap before continuing.

'Anyone living in the rough has that as a prefix, don't they, Detective? Crazy hermit, crazy man in the woods. I'd drifted into the notion that living without human interaction, without that all-consuming stimulus all the time, would drive me nuts. But no, I had that wrong. It took a while, but I came to recognise the good in it. That was the key.'

He shuffled forward, warming to the subject. 'We spoke about silence before, Detective; the silence was part of that blankness. I could never have done it with noise. Not even the noise of my own thoughts was tolerable: I had to have perfect peace. I began to organise myself to have periods of nothingness; timetabled spells when I could do nothing, think nothing. I started to understand the importance of that – how it healed my mind to let go of the chains and drift. It came to me how nourishing that was, how vital to my wellbeing.'

Dana was thinking that this sounded like heaven. She wasn't sure she had that relationship with seclusion; she both wanted it and feared it. Or perhaps, she feared others' reaction to her wish for that much solitude: maybe their conditioning shaped hers. That would explain her envy – that Nathan had gone ahead and lived the kind of solitude that she yearned for but didn't trust herself to grasp. Nathan's world seemed to her almost idyllic; to be floating through isolation. Most importantly: to be absolutely certain that the absence of people – or the lack of any goals – were virtuous aims in themselves, and not signs of an abjectly failing human being. She caught herself: back to investigative mode. Nathan had induced a reverie.

'So, Mr Whittler, those brief periods when you had to then engage, on some level, with the world you left behind: they must have been particularly painful.'

Nathan looked again for his fate line. His voice dropped towards a whisper. 'I don't really want to talk about those . . . times. I know you're a detective, and this is a police station, but all the same . . .'

'Don't misunderstand me, Mr Whittler. I'm not asking now about the what, where and how of those moments. I'm asking about the contrast between understanding how solitude can work for you, and having to spend any time in a world inhabited by others.'

'Ah, I see. To be honest, Detective Russo, I'd struggled with that most of my life anyway, albeit in a different setting. As I assume you . . .' He collected himself. 'Well, anyhow, it wasn't a different trade-off as such, just a different *balancing point* on the same set of scales.'

For a moment she feared he'd clam up, just when she sensed he was revealing something deep inside himself. She felt her breath resume when he did.

'I'd always wanted more solitude than my life could practically offer. Now I was much further along that spectrum: but the same spectrum, and essential issue, were there. I still had to engage with people in some way, at some point. This time the engagement was more about observation, planning. It was, what's the word? More . . . anthropological, I think.' He nodded to himself, as if the exact word had only now occurred to him. 'I studied humans for a particular reason, for a particular end: how to avoid them for the few minutes I was in their world. I could choose, after a fashion, when and how.'

'I understand, Mr Whittler.' Dana paused then almost whispered, 'And yes, you're correct in the assumption you made.'

Nathan nodded solicitously, and both were silent for a moment, almost as an act of commemoration for Dana's admission. She swallowed hard as she realised this was a disclosable, legally usable declaration. People would know: it felt like cutting open a scar.

'It's impossible, you know,' he said suddenly.

'Excuse me?'

'To get that kind of total internal silence. In the modern world, I mean. There's too much in the world to allow it, too much stimulus. There's noise, distraction, obligations, people, the need to earn money, the pressure to engage, the reactions of others. Too much. I mean, that's what you're reaching for isn't it, Detective? I could tell, when I was speaking about it.'

She had to judge swiftly. 'I, uh, I can see the virtue of it. But I think most people wouldn't be able to cope as well as you, Mr Whittler, with that degree of solitude. Both practically and emotionally. Some of us believe we need a ladder out of the pool, no matter how much we enjoy swimming.'

Nathan inclined his head in a touché gesture.

She was about to ask the next question when there was a double rap on the mirror, swiftly followed by another. Each officer had a distinct knock, so the detective knew who was interrupting. Two doubles was Bill's call sign. She couldn't ignore it.

'Would you excuse me a minute, please, Mr Whittler? I need to speak to my boss.'

Nathan nodded and sat back to examine his fingernails. Dana noticed again how fastidiously clean and neat they were. She confirmed to the tape that she was leaving the room.

Bill was there when she closed the door behind her.

'We found his home. Got video and everything. You need to see this.'

Chapter 16

Rainer Holt left the patrol car two hundred metres down the street from Pringle's, on a herring-bone park with a needlessly steep pitch to the drain. Earlville's inhabitants had plenty of observational skills, and the time to deploy them. Better to seem to be on a lunch hour and a little aimless than striding deliberately into any particular establishment. So he paused to window-shop in a place selling handmade leather boots, rain slickers and other paraphernalia it claimed was 'vital for the wilderness'. He wondered if Whittler had much of that kind of gear; or whether he'd disproved the shop's hectoring by surviving fifteen entire years with pretty much none of their stock.

The main street in Earlville had been pedestrianised last year. He'd seen an old photo of this street with a line of momentous fig trees down the middle, planted to commemorate WW1 diggers. They'd been ripped out 'for safety reasons' and replaced with some shade-free human-sized saplings and silver waste bins with ads for flavoured milk. It didn't seem to Rainer like a reasonable trade-off. An ugly multi-storey car park loomed over the back of the main shopping centre. Designed in the seventies with a deliberately brutalist air, the centre's concrete now barked harshly at on-comers, the childish font over the entrance failing to impart joy. Off this main strip, older stores remained: the wilderness store, and larger units of pharmacy, grocer, baby clothing and shoes. Pringle's had been there since the thirties, as the art deco lettering overhead implied. Hipsters from the city weren't put off by the location. They found it 'authentic' and 'old-school': they treated the trip like a journey to a living museum.

He strolled into Pringle's Furniture, immediately spotting the old man himself. The store itself was unpretentious. The walls were the bare metal of a warehouse, the floor unpolished concrete. Furniture wasn't laid out in 'inspirational designs' of fake rooms: this wasn't a series of lifestyle scenarios and concepts. The items were placed individually and haphazardly, with enough room to walk around each piece, feel the wood and the fabric, and appreciate both the time and effort of creation. It was less a shop, more a space for admiring craftsmanship.

Chatting to a spotty apprentice-type in a space between two expensively distressed armoires, Rufus Pringle flicked a double-glance at Rainer and dismissed the young employee. Rufus wore an old-fashioned brown overall with frameless spectacles peeking from a front pocket. Underneath the overall was a red tie and a collared, checked shirt. He had stubby fingers that toyed with a well-used pencil. Rainer tagged him as a 'measure twice, cut once' kind of man.

'Mr Pringle? Rainer Holt. Police.' He held out his ID and was unsurprised when Rufus retrieved his glasses, put them on, read every syllable of the card front and back and returned it with a quiet nod.

'What can I do for you, sir?' Rufus's voice was slightly raspy – either the remnants of a cold or he was a reformed smoker.

'To be honest, Mr Pringle, I'm not sure. I'm testing your dim and distant memory. Nathan Whittler?'

Rufus reached within his mind for a second as he pocketed the spectacles, then shook his head and whistled.

'Ah, Nate. They found him, eh? What happened?' There was a disappointed resignation to his tone.

'You don't seem surprised he's resurfaced.'

Rufus shucked off the comment with a wave of the hand and leaned against one of the armoires. 'Ah, well, he took off like that; always possible it wouldn't work out. Where did they find the body?'

Rainer paused. His first instinct was to disabuse the old man of the notion. But then he wondered if delaying might eke out something that would otherwise remain hidden.

'Took off, you say? It was before my time, obviously. Could you talk me through his last few months with you?' Rainer was just boyish enough for the wide-eyed ingénu shtick to work.

'Sure.' Rufus pointed to a bubble office up some rough-hewn stairs. Rainer followed him up, reluctant to touch the handrail for fear of splinters. The office was a repository of invoices with handwritten comments, some sawdust on the floor, a calendar still showing last month, a lousily made mug holding pens, and a crayon drawing of a stick man with *Gradad* written lopsidedly on the top. Rainer sat on the only other chair, feeling it tilt and groan – he hoped the furniture Pringle sold was more solid than the furniture he used.

'So, little Nate. Yeah, 'course I remember him.' There was a slight smile around Rufus's mouth. 'Quiet little thing. So damn conscientious. Never really got to grips with any idea of time management. He'd fuss over some little thing for ages, when he should have been on to gluing the joints, or whatever. Steady as, mind; nice kid. Young.'

'Young?' Rainer was fond of the one-word prompt.

'Young for his age, always.' Rufus stopped, found a throat lozenge from a pack hidden behind some paperwork. When he spoke again, it was quieter and half an octave lower. 'Probably due to his brother. Piece of dirt, that one. You arrested him yet?'

Rainer hedged. 'Early days, Mr Pringle. I'm only collecting the background on Nate.'

Rufus harrumphed and picked up another pencil to occupy his fingers. Rainer imagined Rufus couldn't go long without touching something; feeling it against his skin, working it in some way. Rufus's life was defined by what his hands could shape.

'Yeah, okay. So Nate came to work for me straight from school. Nice to find someone who wanted to, if I'm honest. He sought me out – said he wanted to learn a trade, a craft.' Rufus tugged at his ear, leaving a smudge of sawdust that drew Rainer's eye. 'Everyone else at that school either took off for some university as fast as possible or joined the smelting company. Better pay, see? Either way, they blew town the moment they could. Nate was on minimum wage with me, but he seemed okay with it.

'Yeah, so Nate used to walk here each day, even though it was six kilometres. I offered him an old bicycle, but he was as stubborn as all that. I think it stretched his time out of the house, if I'm honest.' Rufus shook his head and paused, as though the recollection was becoming painful. 'Nah, walking was fine, he said. Kid was like that – got something fixed in his head and nothing would shift it. Nothing. Anyways, he was working fine for me – a little slow, like I said, but thorough. Definitely thorough. Always left the workshop nice and tidy, too. So his big brother, what was his name, now?'

'Jeb?' Rainer was surprised he could recall the name.

'Yeah, that was it. Jeb. Older than Nate, way bigger. Head like a buffalo; nasty attitude. Acting like the king of the world all the time. I know he used to sneer at Nate for his job, you know? Jeb was more the quick, easy-money type. Wheeler-dealer, corner-cutter. Bully.'

'Bully?'

Rufus tapped the pencil against a blotter. 'Uh-huh. You could see it if they were ever in the same space. Not that Jeb came here much:

this was all too slow and steady for him. But if you ever saw them together, it was like watching a croc and one of them little birds that cleans off the insects for 'em. I mean, Jeb rolled around like he owned everything in town; Nate was flicking around in the shadows, here and there, quiet, trying not to draw attention. Every now and then Jeb would lift his hand – scratch his head, or whatever – and Nate would flinch: like it was coming, you know?'

Rufus stopped, leaned in. Rainer felt compelled to come closer, and their heads were barely half a metre apart when Rufus resumed in a conspiratorial tone, 'And I tell you, that carried through to here. If you ever had to walk behind Nate for some reason – get a tool or whatever – it was like you'd already doused him in petrol and he was waiting for the match. Yeah, spooked real easy. Real easy. That kind of thing, well, it's *in the grain*, if you get my drift.'

Rainer nodded. 'The period before he left, was there any indication he was going?'

The old man chuckled as they drew back. 'Oh hell, yeah. He came to see me. Ah, when, now? Spring. Would be late spring. He flew in the autumn, but this was late spring. I'd emptied out a section of that little place over there.' He pointed to a boxed-in corner, maybe three metres square, which Rainer had guessed might be the toilet.

'Hmm, he noticed me clearing it out and asked how long it would be empty. Well, I was going to use it to store some wood burners, but they were being hand-cast in Hobart, wouldn't be arriving for months. So I said he could use it if he needed. The next week, little camping things started appearing. A tent, groundsheet, sleeping bag, and so on. It crossed my mind he was going to camp out right here, hide from his family. So I asked him straight out, said he couldn't actually live here. He laughed.'

Rufus pointed with a stubby, spatulate finger. 'I distinctly remember that, because I don't think I ever heard him laugh other than then.

Anyways, he said he was planning a long trip, but he had nowhere to store the stuff at home. Well, that was crap and I knew it – his folks had about fifteen hectares, and a couple of barns. Right there, I knew he was planning to fly, and I thought, "Good for you, son." Coz that family, they were . . . hmmm . . . awkward.'

'How so?'

Rufus folded his arms and splayed his legs out: Rainer's girlfriend called it 'manspreading'. 'Well, Jeb I've told you about. He was about a metre ninety when he was twelve. Little bugger was hard to control once he got big enough. Sly thing, too. Good at sniffing out weakness, I reckon. But then, bullies are, right?'

Rainer blanched at a schoolyard memory.

Rufus continued. 'The parents – I wanna say Pamela, but that might be wrong; can't recall his name – they were real God-fearers. Don't get me wrong, I'm not saying anything against the Church. Just that they, I dunno; it felt like they took it to extremes. They always looked like, what's those people? Amish, yeah, Amish or Quakers, or whatever. That real old-fashioned thing, like another century. Didn't see them too often, but they always seemed spooked by the real world. I got the feeling their farm lived about eighty years behind the rest of us, you know? Poor Nate, what a waste.'

Rainer couldn't bring himself to leave Rufus in ignorance any longer. The old man was talkative enough: there was no need for any more leverage.

'Sorry, Mr Pringle. Maybe you got the wrong impression there. Mr Whittler isn't dead. He's alive: at the station, in fact.'

'Oh.' Rufus looked up, eyes shining. He swallowed and put down the pencil shakily, as though he no longer trusted himself to hold anything. He took a moment. 'That's . . . that's good. A relief. Well. Hmmm. Is he okay? Is he in trouble or something?'

Rainer nodded, touched. 'He's being looked after, yes. But we're trying to piece together some of his past, Mr Pringle. You mentioned Mr Whittler was bringing camping gear into the store?'

'Mmm, he'd go to the old outdoor store used to be over on Bramston. Behind the cinema that closed? Yeah, once a week – bought something for his trip. Compass, penknife; usually something small. Maybe his family would have spotted him spending anything more. I used to ask him where he was headed. I thought he had a destination in mind – some place he'd always wanted to see, photo he'd cut out of a magazine, or whatever. But he didn't seem to know. Knew he was going, but not where.'

'Did he have any friends? Someone he might turn to, or travel with?'

Rufus puffed his cheeks. He flickered when a phone rang downstairs but brought himself back to the conversation. 'Oh Lord, no; he didn't do friends. Never saw him with anyone but family. Not sure he was allowed friends, as such. I don't think anyone would have been welcomed on the farm, that's for sure. No, he was, uh, what's the word, "self-contained"? Yeah, I think that's it. Self-contained. He was his own friend, that kind of thing.'

Rainer had run out of questions, for now. He felt the need to check with Dana; she might have follow-up. He put his hands on his knees. 'Well, that's a great start for us, Mr Pringle. Thank you.'

At the foot of the steps Rainer turned and, as he always did with everyone he interviewed, shook hands. Rufus held on a beat longer than needed.

'Nate: if he needs anything, I'll stand for him. Will you tell him that? Supplies, whatever; will you tell him?'

Chapter 17

Dana joined Bill in looming over Mike's shoulder. She was trying not to shake, nervous about what Nathan Whittler's home would be like. She didn't want it to look bad for him: squalid, somehow, or amateurish. She found herself hoping the others would look at Nathan's efforts with admiration. It was proprietorial on her part, and maybe inappropriate, but she felt it nonetheless. It had only been a few hours since she took the call at sunrise, but she was so drawn in that the Whittler case now drowned out almost anything else.

Almost anything.

'Where's this feed from?' asked Mike.

'Dakota Line,' replied Dana.

'Why's it called that?'

'Oh, I know that one,' interjected Bill. 'Didn't you do it at school?'

Mike held his hands open in ignorance.

'Right, so the Dakota brothers owned all this stretch of land: the chain of lakes, and about a click either side, down towards the Old Mill Road. This is, oh, well over a hundred years ago. Eighteen nineties, I think. One day, one of them discovers a few crumbs of gold in the river. People are finding gold all over Australia around this time, so they think it's a new rush. One wants it for himself, but the other

Dakota says, "Share." Well, they can't agree like two adults so they split the land in two, with the boundary running down the middle of the river. That way, they each have an equal shot at further gold – which, ironically, neither ever finds. They hammered spikes into the middle of the riverbed all the way down, to mark the border – hence, the Dakota Line.'

Mike shrugged. 'Cool story, bro.'

The video had been emailed: an initial edit that was simply streaming the footage from Stuart's helmet cam. It was barely thirty minutes old. The audio was scratchy and sometimes the images broke up or jammed for a second. The flaws gave the evidence a retro feel in an age of high-definition digital, as though it had regressed to match the era when Nathan had begun his new life.

Stuart was at the front of the inflatable canoe, the helicopter nowhere to be seen. Ahead of them Piermont Lake narrowed sharply to the north; bubbling white water glided towards them from green folds of thick foliage. The current didn't look that strong, but they could hear Stuart's grunts with each paddle stroke. Overhead they got occasional subliminal flashes of silver from a blue sky as the small drone flew back and forth in a rudimentary search grid.

Now the canoe was simply holding station; small half-paddles kept them around twenty metres from the bank. Stuart took a slow sweep in either direction to show the context. The lake appeared maybe two kilometres long. On one side, forest-cloaked low hills slid to the shoreline. Pines curled outwards and upwards over the water, their reflections flickering. On the other side the shore was mainly reeds seething in the breeze, with a couple of small areas of grass further south. Some black swans and a couple of herons prodded and nodded in the shallows. Not a soul and, when Stuart looked up to locate the drone, no sign of any jet trail, either. To Dana, it seemed bucolic and beguiling. She thought back to Nathan's quest for 'nothingness'.

There was an indistinct shout, and then a mixture of static and chatter on the radio attached to Stuart's shoulder. He gave a little commentary.

'So, Al's picked up something on the drone. Thinks he can see a canoe, might be tethered. He's going to guide me in. This might be it, boys and girls: a hit first time of asking.'

The canoe zigzagged, the current faster the nearer he came to two large rock formations, each about nine metres high, rounded at the top like an elephant's profile. They appeared to be jammed together, with a faster flow of water around the right edge. The drone shivered directly above them.

Stuart found some deeper, darker water under the first rock's overhang. He abandoned the paddle and started to hand-walk along the rock's surface, effectively dragging the canoe with his fingers. On the audio they could hear the steady rush of fast water – it wrenched Dana back to sunrise and she had to swallow hard. She glanced across to Bill, who, thankfully, hadn't noticed her anxiety.

The footage juddered as Stuart fought the current. 'Gotta be a way in . . . somewhere. I don't think our man's doing kayak rolls to get in; must be a way that leaves him dry.' The three of them twitched and leaned in unison with the camera.

'Ah, gotcha! Oh man, that's clever, that's really clever.'

The folds of the two rocks parted slightly in an 'L' shape. The tail of the 'L' allowed the canoe to float through with about twenty centimetres to spare above it. The vertical part of the space, while it curved a little, allowed Stuart to ride through by turning sideways; they saw the camera bounce slightly as it nudged the rock and heard the rustle of Stuart's back against the wall as he passed through the gap.

The entrance had enough arc that Stuart could no longer see back to the lake. He emerged into a pool of quiet water lit by a vertical breach – almost a natural chimney – about four metres in diameter.

Sunlight bounced down and on to the surface of the pool, reflecting back in a series of shimmering gold lines on the overhangs. Stuart grabbed at the camera – they could see his fingers swamp the lens. He held it in front of him and swept a 360. The little landing area to the right held a Canadian canoe: originally red, it had been carelessly painted with some kind of dark paint, possibly a waterproof primer. The paint might have been simply to break up the shape for camouflage rather than change the colour itself.

The canoe was tethered against a flat rock, a natural stepping stone. Beyond this was the entrance to the cave itself, which was around two metres high and just as wide. The floor looked like stone giving way to sand. The rest of the 360 was sheer rock face, sweeping upwards. Except for another gap to one side, starting at head height. Perhaps fifty centimetres wide, it was plugged by several heavy branches: Dana guessed that might be a land entrance.

'Yeah, I'm going to get out of the canoe and step around for you. The picture might not be ideal coz I'll need the torchlight to see anything, but I'll give you a guided tour. Back in a moment. Don't touch that dial.'

Mike turned and gave a grinning thumbs-up to Dana. 'Your guess was right. Score one for the Russo.'

She nodded. 'Looks that way.'

It was a strange mix of elation and trepidation. Dana was thrilled to have found Nathan's cave and she knew this provided the rich mix of information that would change her strategy completely: it was the break she needed to open him up some more. But she knew him well enough to understand his intense humiliation when he found out everyone had seen inside his little world. She knew what *she'd* feel if anyone was broadcasting from inside her home: Nathan would suffer even more acutely.

After some shuffling, the video restarted with a view of Stuart's boots. He tugged the camera upwards until it showed a view of the pool.

'Ah, welcome, one and all. So, this water entrance. It's genius. You wouldn't find it unless you were right by it *and* searching for this kind of thing. If Al hadn't seen the canoe from the drone, I probably wouldn't have found the way in. May be tricky in flood, or in winter with any ice – the water's fairly calm here, so it would ice up before the lake itself. But unless you actually witness anyone coming or going, you'd never find it.'

The camera swung vertically in a drunken loop. 'Up there he has daylight, and about . . . two, three hours of sunlight; more in summer. Again, any kind of height and all you'd see looking down is rock and water. It's only because the drone was so low it had the angle to see the canoe.'

Bill nodded at no one in particular. 'Your guy's smart. That's impossible to find, even from a helicopter. No wonder he stayed hidden for so long.'

Dana felt a bizarre swelling of pride. It actually felt, in a strange way, like *her guy*. She reminded herself he was almost certainly a killer. Ingenuity in his hiding place was hardly exonerating evidence.

'So, in the entrance here we have a flysheet. These cords under it – I'm guessing this is where he dried his clothes after he washed them in the creek. Or got water on them. Speaking of which' – he moved sharply over to his right and pointed at the end of the flat rock by the canoe – 'yeah, in the corner. That gush of water coming through the gap is probably his fresh-water supply – moving nice and quick, and he doesn't really have to leave the cave to get to it. It's also an entrance by foot, I reckon.'

Stuart moved to give them a slow sweep of the land entrance. There were a series of steps crudely carved out of the rock's incline; effectively a ladder up and over the artfully placed branches. From outside, it would simply look like shrubs growing in a shady crevice. Like the water entrance, it would be impossible to detect unless you witnessed anyone using it.

'Ah,' said Dana, suddenly comprehending. 'I'd been wondering why the canoe was there, if he'd been to Jensen's Store. But I get it now.'

Bill looked across quizzically.

'I mean, he used that land entrance and walked cross-country to Jensen's Store. He didn't need to canoe to the southern end of the lake and go on foot. The store is west, on that side of the lake. He could walk it. That's why the canoe is still in situ.'

As Stuart made his way back to the entrance, Mike pointed at the screen. 'Did you see the poles on that flysheet? Same paint as the canoe. Why paint the poles?'

It came to Dana. 'Sunlight. Glinting off the metal poles. He'd be paranoid about being seen from above. When I talked about his home not being visible from the air, and that's why he wouldn't use a tent, he smiled. That's what he meant. He is using a tent, but it can't be seen from the air, not even if the sun caught it.'

Stuart was now back at the entrance. There were two metal spikes, also painted, driven into the threshold wall, with water bags suspended from them. A canvas camping chair was parked in the sand, next to a milk crate that served as a table.

Stuart moved in close. 'Just for you, Dana. His reading habits.'

Several books were piled perfectly on the crate – Clavell, Hammett, Dostoyevsky.

Dana grunted. 'That's ironic. I was going to give him *Crime and Punishment* to read here, but I thought it was too cruel.'

Stuart stepped gingerly past the chair and into the chamber. His torchlight was strong but the beam was narrow; it swept across items in a way that was almost too quick to take in. 'Yeah, this probably isn't coming across well, so I'll give you what video I can and talk you through it. We'll get the tech boys out from the city with the heavy gear, now we know what we're about.

'On this side are towers of plastic boxes. All airtight. Hard to see what's in them, but uh . . . yeah, first aid in that one. I can see bandages and stuff. This one has crockery, I think. Plates, spoons, dishes. Can't tell what's in the bottom one. Maybe tools – he'd need hammers, pliers, that kind of thing.' Stuart shuffled across to the next tower. 'Clothes. Hmmm. Maybe in order of season. Probably changes the sequence of the tower every few months. On top here are sweaters, heavy-looking trousers, maybe a coat. The lower ones have T-shirts, I think. Yeah, he has a little annual wardrobe thing going on.'

The next tower was slightly apart from the other two; jammed up against a wall of the chamber. These containers were transparent while the others were opaque. Above them, a series of rough-hewn alcoves had been cut into the rock. Maybe fifteen centimetres deep and twenty centimetres of space on them, they were occupied by perfect pyramids of tins.

'Oh, food. This is the pantry. Nice and dry, and away from the water even if it floods a bit. These beauties float, anyway, so he'd be fine in an emergency. I can't see' – another drunken loop upwards and back, making the three of them slightly queasy – 'nope, no hole in the roof anywhere, no damp runs. This place is watertight. And look how crazy neat he is. Not a qualified medical opinion, of course, boss.'

He pushed the torch closer to the shelves and containers. 'Canned stuff, mainly. Tinned fruit, cans of vegetables, that beans-and-sausage seems like a favourite. Sweet tooth – chocolate, grain bars. Guy ate like a king. This store would last eight, ten weeks easy.'

Bill grunted. 'How did he get all that stuff out there?'

'The clothes?' asked Dana. 'Or the food?'

'Clothes and camping gear, I get. Standard hiking procedure. I mean several months of canned goods. They're heavy.'

Dana thought how methodical Nathan would be, how he'd think slowly and deliberately.

'One piece at a time, like the Johnny Cash song. Each time, he acquires more than he needs for a week or two and stores the extra. Over time, he builds up a cache. Then he manages it using sell-by date; probably has a system where the near-overdue stuff is at the top of each container.'

Bill gave her a raised eyebrow that said, *That's exactly how you'd do it*. Dana gave a half-grin, and they both looked back at the screen.

Stuart turned and scanned the chamber. It was only three metres across yet the light seemed to die in it.

'Stu, what's that to the left?' It was out of Mike's mouth before he realised.

Dana caught it. 'Yes, Stu, travel forward in time to get Mikey's message, then go back to your own time and turn left.' She shucked him in the shoulder. 'Seriously, why isn't he doing that, Mikey?'

'Boyish enthusiasm. My bad, people,' he said with a raised palm.

All three laughed when Stuart did indeed turn left.

'That's freaky,' said Dana.

Stuart tracked to the corner, where a sheet had been pinned up against a wall using a small hook. He dragged it back by one corner and looked beyond. 'Ah, bedroom.'

Dana wondered briefly why Nathan would want to shut off the bedroom, in an isolated cave in the middle of nowhere, known only to him. She assumed it was simply Nathan being Nathan – privacy to the power of privacy; solitude squared.

The room contained an inner tent – the little brother of the flysheet outside. Pegged out and tied off, it was fully zipped up. Stuart peered through one of the mesh windows. There was a bed inside. He moved across, opened the zip door and crouched at the entrance.

The bed was a single blow-up mattress, partly covered by a thick sleeping bag. Milk crates kept it off the ground. Stuart bent so they could see underneath it – an insulating mat and what looked like raw wool bundles to stop the worst of the damp seeping up. To prevent it sliding around on top of the crates, it was largely hemmed in by more containers, which seemed to store books and food cans.

Stuart's torch beam landed on some maritime flares. 'Not sure why he'd need these. Maybe if he got too ill to carry on, he could let these babies go and hope to be saved? Dunno. That's one for you to work out, Dana.'

No, thought Dana, it would never be for that. She couldn't imagine Nathan doing such a thing. He would literally rather die.

One container had the lid slightly ajar – batteries, spare torches, pens, what looked like a journal. Dana's heart yelped with empathy – she would kill anyone looking at her journal. She physically squirmed when Stuart knelt down and picked it up – as if he were holding a toddler over a fire. He held the book out of view; in the corner of the screen they could see pages flicking and they all strained to see what was written.

'Some kind of diary? I'll bag and tag it for you.'

The camera looked back to the bed. A radio, with a set of earphones trailing from it to the pillow. Even out there, she thought, in the midst of the wilderness, Nathan was so paranoid about discovery he would listen only with ear buds. Dana shivered.

Stuart stood again and looked around. In one corner of the chamber there appeared to be a fold in the walls. It turned out to be another semi-chamber, the furthest part of the cave from the entrance. A hole had been dug, and Stuart peered into it.

'Now, I'd been wondering since we got here how he did this. Toilet and waste disposal. Without attracting wildlife. I'll need to explore this a bit more to work out how he's doing it, but I'll spare you the footage. Let's say he has a system, and it looks like he was running out of room.'

Stuart turned and went back towards the light. As he replaced the sheet curtain he leaned into it. 'Hmmm. Bug spray. He saturated the edges of the sheet to keep the bedroom as free from bugs as possible. It uses less repellent than spraying himself all the time. Smart.'

Stuart grabbed the camera and, switching it around, loomed into it.

'That's all for now, folks. I'll get this emailed to you as fast as I can. Hope it helps. We'll seal the place off, grid it and get some heavier duty effort into it. Let me know if you want anything specific explored. I'll drone the diary to the base team, and someone can drive it over to you. Might even get there before this footage. Back to you in the studio.'

Bill stood up and massaged his lower back. 'Thoughts?'

Dana leaned against a bookshelf. 'No fire.'

'What?'

'There was no fire, or barbecue, or any way of cooking anything. Or sit by, in the cold. Given how paranoid he was about discovery, he probably didn't want any fire or smoke either. He's seriously lived for fifteen years on cold or raw food. Even in winter.'

Mike nodded at the darkened screen. 'My kids would live on cereal and chocolate if I gave them half a chance. To be fair, Whittler had a fair sprinkle of fruit and veg there, but it was all canned. I guess you get used to not cooking stuff.' He shrugged. 'Maybe there's more nutrients that way.'

Bill interjected. 'Mikey, you were sceptical about the fifteen years; about whether he'd actually done that. This change your mind?'

'Yes and no.' Mike swivelled so that he faced both Bill and Dana. 'On the logistics side, I'm more convinced. Seeing how he set things up, seeing how well that was all hidden; yeah. He could hide that long, not be seen for that long; eat and sleep and crap for that long. But I still doubt he could *live* for that long. By which I mean the lack of speaking, the human contact, and so on. I still think that's impossible.'

Bill scratched the back of his hand. 'Hmmm. Dana?'

Dana puffed her cheeks. 'I'm kind of the opposite. Talking with him, I'm totally convinced he could manage without people. He has that within him. There's a resilience which could do it. Plus, I think he worked out *how* to do it: how to make the silence an advantage. It already suited his personality, but he worked out how to be that way without going crazy. So he could do that, I reckon.

'On the other hand, I'd always been sceptical about the logistics. Just the practicalities – what if he got toothache; why he didn't get bothered by snakes, dingoes, spiders; how he survived the cold and the heat and the bugs. I'm not practical, so I couldn't see how the day-to-day could be handled. Nothing in the world would persuade me to live in anything like that. But seeing it, yes, it's fairly clean and bug-free. He's worked out the water, the shelter. He seems to have plenty of food. Seeing it tells me he sorted out the practicalities as well as the psychology. So I'm sticking with yes. See it as a serial killer's lair, Bill?'

'Hmm, not especially. Though the detailed search might produce evidence of other crimes, so I'll still hedge my bets. But, point taken. Okay.' Bill clapped his hands once. 'Gather your thoughts, then my office in ten minutes. I want to know what this means for our approach and any research we might need to do.'

As he left the office Bill held the door for a uniform, who passed Dana a clear plastic bag. It contained Nathan Whittler's journal.

Chapter 18

Dana saw Rainer Holt from the other end of the corridor. He waved, and mimed going into her office. She nodded and muttered, '*Ryner, Ryner*,' as she walked. When she got there Rainer was waiting like a soldier reporting for duty. She locked the journal into the top drawer of her desk. She'd have to at least skim it before she spoke to Nathan again.

'Hey, how'd it go?'

Rainer stood a little too rigidly as he spoke. Dana kept waiting for an opportunity to tell him to sit down and relax a little. But he seemed to have the ability to continually speak, whether he was breathing in or out. He rattled off his discussion with Pringle without a semblance of a break for oxygen. Dana made a mental note to suggest he consider a career in politics.

'So, in your view, much of what Whittler became was essentially set by the time he left Pringle's?'

'Looks that way. I haven't met him, of course. But the loner thing, fear, stubbornness; that was there when he was a teenager.'

It had struck Dana earlier that Nathan's time in the cave would be a distillation: a pure and concentrated form of the person he'd always been. Being alone for so long, as Bill had said, left no need for adaptation imposed by compromise. Nathan had been free to be Nathan in unalloyed form. It followed, therefore, that Nathan was more likely to talk when Dana agreed with his general train of thought, but be spiky or belligerent the moment she contested things.

'Pringle doesn't know what finally made up Whittler's mind to run? Why then, and why there?'

'No, he doesn't. In his view, "there" seems to have been anywhere. Whittler had no real destination in mind, except for "not here".' Rainer hesitated, before following through with an observation. 'That suggests running *from*, not running *to*, doesn't it? Anyway, it was some months in the making – collecting all the stuff and storing it at Pringle's. Maybe "then" was a general plan, and it got hurried up by some event. Or maybe he'd always intended to go then.'

Dana liked the amount of thought Rainer had put into this while driving back from Earlville. She held up a finger.

'I'm inclined towards a precipitating event. If it was a general plan he could activate at any time, or he had a planned date in mind, he'd have gone late spring or summer. That would have given him months without cold weather to get everything set up. I don't believe he knew about this cave before he started running – I think he lucked into it. So he actually went at a dreadful time: winter was about to begin and he had to set things up fast. He isn't a "fast set-up" person. He's methodical, everything in its place.'

'Like Pringle?'

'Hmm. Good point. Pringle as a father figure, a role model? Yes, that fits. Sounds like his own family was the polar opposite of that. So anyway, the decision to go then, in the late autumn: that's because a key event made him do it.'

She had to flex her leg against the desk to free her kneecap. 'Have a dig around of incident logs in early to mid 2004, please, especially related to the farm Whittler lived on. Including paramedic and firefighter attendance – it needn't have been criminal to have been the last straw for Whittler. And ask Lucy what she can get about the parents' car accident. That's bothering me now.'

'And hunt some more for the Toyota?'

'Ooh, yes. Do that. I think it's buried under fifteen years' worth of foliage somewhere, so you'd be trying to prove a negative, really. But yes; any sightings, any traffic offences, etcetera. Good stuff, Rainer. I like your thinking about this. Thanks.'

With Rainer gone, Dana was about on schedule for the strategy meet with Bill and Mike. As she turned to gather a file, she was seized by a sudden panic. Her vision began to swim, like a bookshelf in an earthquake. She clutched the desk to stay upright. Oxygen left her, a slight whistling sound as it passed beyond her control and away.

Hoping she wasn't groaning or screaming, she turned her back on the corridor and felt blindly for a pocket. From the moment she grabbed the nebuliser, the fear stabilised. She grasped it tight, squeezing desperately. Facing the wall, she took a big hit from the inhaler, and waited. For twenty seconds she allowed the gasping to subside, holding her file in front of her so anyone passing would think she was reading. Eventually she felt the heat dissipate, the vision calm and the wheezing recede.

She'd faced it down again, thanks to the enduring, resilient power of placebo.

Her own self-doubt whined that she should be able to cope by now: that since she had faced some version of this at least once every day for years, she should have a better means of coping. But while she was darkly familiar with panic attacks and feelings of utter hopelessness, on this Day they were fiercer; more sure of themselves and the vulnerability they induced.

How many times could she get away with it? Each incident was a lesson. They seemed to be random – certainly beyond her control – and once started, they had to take their course. She couldn't imagine an incident in front of Nathan or in a meeting with Bill. She didn't want to think what they'd see in her during those moments. For now, she was trusting that an incident would punch through at a time when she could hide and ride it out. Luck. She was hoping for luck. The thing that was forever in short supply.

She passed Lucy's office on the way to Bill's and caught the latest catch-and-throw with Rainer.

'How'd it go with Pringle? Did you *chaise* him down, *drawer* him in? What did it hinge on? Could he handle it?'

'I kept chiselling away. Sofa so good, but now I've had to shelve it.'

They both chuckled then fist-bumped.

'Here we go. Toyotas and their secret lives . . .'

Mike had propped himself up against a filing cabinet, checking his messages. Bill was sitting in his comfy chair, a desk chair shaped like the driver's seat in a sports car. It was the only overt display of masculinity in the whole room. Bill's wife, Melinda, was an interior designer and she'd made over her husband's office. She'd done ridiculously well: Dana wanted to live here.

'Stu called me,' began Bill. 'He tried you first, but you must've left the office by then. And, for the hundredth time, turn on your damned mobile.'

Dana's hand reflexed to her pocket and she blushed when she realised she didn't even have the phone with her, let alone on.

'Sorry. What did Stu want?'

'They found the knife, eventually. Wedged under a freezer at the end of the murder aisle. Not, in his view, hidden there deliberately. The angle it was – accidental, he thinks. Maybe kicked there in the scuffle. Anyway, it has blood on it. He had it bagged and driven to Forensics: they're working on it now.'

'Hmm, unlikely there'll be fingerprints. Whoever did it might well have been wearing gloves. So it's handy but might not be conclusive.'

That was true, thought Bill. He remained convinced it was Whittler, simply because nothing was as compelling as finding the man there, hands on a dead body and blinking in torchlight. They kept finding maybes and could-haves on the motivations of others – Megan, Lynch, the Alvarez clan – but it still turned in Bill's eyes to Whittler.

'What's your plan of attack, Dana?'

She checked her notes. 'Well, I think two main areas. First, the cave.' She focused primarily on Bill, knowing Mike's role in this discussion was devil's advocate. She and Mike had an unwritten understanding that they would push each other in this kind of meeting – the reasoning and justification it required made them think better.

'Whittler needs to know we've found it. It's crucial to him, and we'll be asking things that show we now understand where he's been. It would be silly to deny it, and I think we need to face his pain up front. He's going to be very upset, I think. It's so personal to him.'

'Yeah, totally,' interjected Mike. 'We're opening him up, and he's not used to having anything in his world disrupted.'

She turned back to Bill. 'So, my plan there is to focus on wonderment and marvelling on what he created. In time, I'll need to segue into getting from the cave to all the places I'm sure he robbed, but I think that might need to happen gradually. I can be an utterly convincing know-nothing rube, for some reason. And I genuinely couldn't live in such a place myself. So I think I'll seem authentic to him.'

'Yeah, I think if you can settle the fact that we know where it is, and that we're being respectful in how we search it, you're going to have to ride out the rest. As we said, he'll pick a fight over something as part of his adjustment process. The more I consider it, the more I think it'll be this. The other area?'

'Rainer did some interesting work on Pringle, of Pringle's Furniture. I want to ask Whittler about his time there: looks like it was quite formative generally. I think I can work in some questions about why he ran, and why then. There's some kind of family iceberg there we're not seeing yet. Talking it over with Rainer, I think Whittler was spooked by something particular which made him run then, rather than later.'

Mike shifted slightly. 'I think that's more solid ground than the first one, isn't it? I mean, beyond knowing that we have his cave, there's no need for questions about how Whittler ate or crapped. It's not, uh, germane to the investigation. Unless we find DNA or something incriminating about the stuff he owns, and we're just starting on that. Maybe focus on the history with Pringle?'

For a second time Dana found herself questioning whether it could be, once again, the prurience of incredulity.

'I get you, Mikey. But a lot of this is about Whittler's fragile state and ego. We're still treading a fine line to stop him lawyering up. I've puffed up his ego and built up a rapport. If I ask anything that shows we know his cave, without telling him first that we've found it, I lose some of that trust. Praising him for the home he built increases the trust. Plus, as Bill says, there's going to be conflict sooner or later. He'll lash out for his own reasons. I'd rather have that happen in relation to something that isn't, as you say, necessarily germane. That way, I can reward him by backing down once his tantrum blows out, without actually losing anything relevant to the investigation. As we've said this morning, we may well have no witnesses at all, and only circumstantial forensics. We have to get Whittler's full story from him – if that's a confession, so be it.'

Mike cogitated for a few seconds then gave a thumbs-up. 'Yeah, yeah, I can see that. Put that way, I'm in.'

Bill beamed. 'I love it when a plan comes together.'

Dana raised a finger. 'Can I ask a wider strategy question? Are we still thinking Whittler might have committed other crimes? I mean, besides this one and maybe burglaries? I ask because if we think he's an experienced killer, I need to cast a wider net with my questions.'

Bill palmed the question off. 'Mikey? Thoughts?'

'Yeah, initially, I was with you, Bill. Whittler threw me with his strangeness and his lack of any history. I still think that isn't an accident – he's hiding something deep. All that talk earlier about "doing terrible things"? If he had killed previously, then all that jazz of being a hermit loner is great camouflage. But I haven't seen any evidence, aside from potential burglaries, that might be criminal. And I still like other angles – the Alvarezes, Megan, maybe Lynch. They still make sense to me as viable people and motives; Whittler still doesn't. Yeah, no . . . if it was him who killed Cassavette, he was very accurate. When he's that proficient at wielding a knife, it's hard to believe it's his first time.'

Bill nodded slowly, and Dana waited. Bill steepled his fingers.

'Yeah, I still have that same reservation, too. I'm not putting him down as a serial killer or anything, but it's hard to see one stab, literally in the dark, that just happens to be perfect. That reeks of practice, and there's no nice way to practise that. However, as you say, other than the burglaries, we have nothing: fingerprints and DNA don't connect him to anything.'

'So,' asked Dana, 'I stay focused on the Cassavette killing in interviews; don't try to broaden it?'

'Yeah, stay fixed on that.'

Mike went off to face the Cassavettes' lawyer, Spencer Lynch, who was holed up in Interview Three. No doubt, thought Mike, stewing at being hauled in after Lucy's intervention.

'Following on from that, Dana,' continued Bill, 'are you finding Whittler convincing? I mean, if he's survived in the wild like he says, it makes him resourceful and capable. Are you certain he's channelled that into something legal?'

'You still think he has a credibility gap? I've been asking myself that. It's easy to get thrown by his body language, his reluctance. Put it this way, boss. Everything he's admitted stacks up to what we know; everything he's claimed, that we can verify, has come back a yes. But whatever is still inside his head remains a maybe. There's a big something we haven't unearthed yet. My gut says his ingenuity and ability are all directed inward – he's been totally focused on himself and on avoiding others. But while we don't know that big something, we need to hedge our bets. That's why Mikey and Luce are tracking down alternative options: just in case Nathan Whittler isn't the guy.'

'Speaking of which,' said Bill, 'I appreciate how much you're letting others work on this.'

'Of course. Team game.' Dana stood.

Bill's hand gestures invited her to close the door and sit.

'I know that's what I preach, and I do mean preach. I know you're a solid player. But we both know you'd run this whole investigation completely solo if I let you.'

Dana gnawed on a hangnail to avoid eye contact. The silence was warm and humid.

'I mean,' Bill continued, 'it's an essential part of your nature. The working-alone thing. The lack of chit-chat. I get it. And I can't say you wouldn't wrap the whole thing up in a bow – signed, sealed and delivered – without anyone's help. That's why you're lead on this case. Whittler is, in some respects, you *in extremis*.'

She considered disagreeing, but it would be hard to fight the weight of evidence. Bill was smart enough to nail the argument if he had to.

'We're not totally alike.'

'No, you're not. Otherwise, you wouldn't be working with your colleagues, and doing it well. You'd have overcome your squeamishness about creepy-crawlies and kicked Whittler out of his cave.'

She smiled at the floor. 'No TV there – disaster. Couldn't live on cold food. Not enough bacon.'

'Amen to that. I'm not criticising you. It's very lucky for us that someone with your skills and your view of the world is right here when this case drops in. We'd be floundering without you: totally reliant on limited forensics and with no co-operation from Whittler.' He leaned forward, elbows resting on the desk and hands clasped like a prayer. 'The flipside of that is you need to think harder than most – more consciously than most – about involving others. And I appreciate that you are. Is all I'm saying.'

She couldn't bring herself to look at him, flush with embarrassment. 'Thanks, boss.'

He smiled at her. 'Go get some more on Whittler.'

At the doorway, Dana turned. 'You know that *A-Team* quote dates you really badly, right?'

'Don't start with me, Dana, I swear to God . . .'

Chapter 19

Mike tapped the file against his hip as he approached Interview Three. Early forensics had dribbled through: enough for a first run at Lynch. Even though the store had a thousand and one fingerprints, they'd identified some already.

It felt good to be first assist on this one, and not lead. A few years ago he'd have railed against the idea. Top-dog status was hard won, and the climb had required patience. Yet here he was, effectively splitting the seniority with Dana. That sharing thing had coincided with Bill's arrival last year. Mike had termed his new boss *Mr Collegiate*. Others sneeringly coined *Billy Win-Win*. Mike could have dug his heels in at that point, given that many in the station thought of him as the senior detective. But he'd seen both the way the wind was blowing and what was in it for him.

Partly, he was getting older and didn't need the same stress. Perhaps he quite enjoyed supporting Dana a little – he knew she was happy to learn and they had complementary skills. Between them, they made one mighty detective. Individually, they were deeply flawed, but in different areas and bright enough to acknowledge it. He, for example, would have been patient with Whittler but would have got nowhere: Whittler would have shut down like a petulant child. While Mike had empathy skills and verbal agility, he found reluctant interviewees more difficult. He worked them better when they were responsive and could be moved around the chess board. Dana was a queen of outwaiting the opponent, and her bookish manner had caught and held Whittler's attention.

He'd even donated his office – something that apparently had never occurred before in public service history. Several people thought he'd been made to do it and called it *emasculating*. But for him, it was simply practical. Dana was an introvert who craved and fed off time alone: she needed that space to be a better detective. He didn't – he liked bouncing ideas off Lucy and he enjoyed the energy of there being several people in the office.

Mike still wasn't wedded to the idea that Nathan Whittler had lived for fifteen years without speaking to another human being. Nor was he convinced Whittler was the murderer. While it seemed a reach in some ways, Mike was still wavering between a domestic issue involving the Cassavettes, or some left-field intervention around the Alvarez family. He was waiting on some more intelligence on the latter so had to make do with pursuing Lynch for now.

Interview Three was off to the side of the main interview suite, an add-on created a few years ago when they realised that they were giving suspects too much opportunity to collude or intimidate. It was cheaply built, with inadequate insulation: it felt cold in winter and gave off a permanent musty air of disdain. Important suspects, sympathetic witnesses and victims went in One or Two. Unreliable witnesses, or those whose professional aims cut across police work, came here. Anyone placed in Three could be in no doubt what the police thought of them.

Lucy was pretty much standing guard at the door.

'Ms Delaney.' He mock-saluted. 'We could get you a bearskin hat for sentry duty, if you think it would help.'

Lucy gave it genuine consideration. 'I'd prefer a red hat, to match my eyes. I thought he might be a potential runner. I can't run, but I love tripping up those who can.' She jerked her head at the closed door. 'He was less than impressed by me. Imagine that.'

'I physically cannot imagine that.'

Lucy smiled. 'You read that forensics update really thoroughly, didn't you, Mikey? Lists and all?'

'I hear ya. I was super-diligent, Luce, have no fear.' Mike glanced in through the window. 'Do I need a password? I'll go with "let's kill all the lawyers".'

She pushed off the wall she'd been leaning against. 'The Bard knew what's what. All yours, Mikey.' She threw a final comment over her shoulder. 'Don't forget to wash your hands before you come back to the office.'

He grinned at her departing back but knew she wasn't entirely joking. Her loathing for lawyers was entrenched for some reason. He'd never found that reason.

Spencer Lynch was flicking the edge of a silver business card with a manicured nail. His watch, Mike noticed, was so expensive it was surely one of those that was 'looked after for the next generation', rather than owned.

'You drive a 5-series, am I right?' Mike strode straight into it, extending a hand for a pumped greeting that suggested a mutual admiration team was about to form.

'I would be impressed, Detective, but you no doubt have access to the vehicle register.'

Lynch's voice was like warm chocolate. Mike predicted it would slide down easily with about half the judges in the region; the other half would gag on it. He therefore estimated that Lynch won around half the time. Divorce lawyers were like baseball players – anything above thirty per cent was a good hit rate.

'Ah, haven't checked that source, to be honest. I'm Detective Mike Francis. Thank you for coming in at such short notice.'

Lynch took a seat, smoothing down his tie and pinching his trousers to retain the perfect seam. 'I was told to. In no uncertain terms. By a woman who let me believe she was a detective but turns out to be some kind of, uh, secretary.'

The final word seemed to imply that Lucy's occupation was somehow catching and wouldn't respond to antibiotics.

Mike breezed through it. 'Ah, she's a force of nature, that girl. When she's full on, few can resist. Look, I know you're anxious to get back to something billable, so if you can give me a couple of answers, we'll get done as fast as possible. Deal, counsellor?'

Lynch gave a smug inclination of the head.

'So, Megan Cassavette. I've only seen photos. Do they do her justice?'

Lynch smirked. Mike reminded himself to keep his composure; easy to flail about and drown in this much oil.

'She's a very attractive woman, Detective. Occupational hazard of being a divorce lawyer. You meet the good and bad.'

'A little like my job, Spencer. Can I call you Spencer? I mean, we both meet people of all sorts, often at the worst moments of their lives, and at their most vulnerable.'

Lynch crossed his legs, inching the chair back as he did so to ensure no part of his bespoke tailoring touched a police table. 'I'm their lawyer, but often they want a . . . human touch.'

Mike crossed his arms and gave a level gaze. 'Must be a tricky balance, Spence, what with your iron-clad code of ethics.'

Lynch tried to control a flicker but he had a slight blink that would lose him a fortune at poker. A little unlucky for a negotiator of divorce spoils, Mike thought.

'Oh?' Lynch asked. 'Is there a point to this line of questioning?'

Mike jabbed at the file with an index finger. 'Witness: saw your BMW Fiver driving away from Megan Cassavette's early this morning. It's been seen near there many times before. The rubbish can on the corner of the lawn – that's the signal, yeah?'

Lynch's embarrassment rose from collar to scalp in two seconds.

'House-to-house, Spence. Apparently mundane and random. Actually, carefully planned and nearly always useful. We're very diligent about that sort of thing.'

Mike paused. Lynch coughed and glowed red, like a ripe apple.

'We searched the Cassavette house: used bed sheets in the washing machine. We called on Megan before she could switch it on. Sheets still . . . moist.' Mike raised an eyebrow. 'Care to bet your lucrative career against the DNA lab? My money's on the lab.'

'I . . . we . . . is that a crime? I suppose no detective ever slept with someone other than his wife?'

If he was hoping to guilt Mike into backing down, he'd misjudged. Mike was squeaky clean in that department; he radiated the confidence of a loyal person with a strong marriage. Not something Lynch was necessarily used to seeing.

'Isn't Megan your client, Spence? Aren't you in a professional business relationship? Duty of care, code of ethics, position of trust, appropriate behaviour – all that stuff?'

Mike saw Lynch hesitate. Presumably he was about to launch into some diatribe about how they were both men of the world, how these things happen, how Megan would be hard for anyone to turn down, how he would ensure it wouldn't happen again. Then he saw Mike's face and gave up that option as a very bad idea.

'Look, Detective . . .'

'When did you arrive at Megan's house?'

'What? Is this an alibi check? What?'

'I'll know if you're lying, Spence. You have a tell, by the way. Once we're done here, I'll explain it to you. For now, it makes lying very foolish. Timescale, counsellor.'

'Uh, around midnight. Meg made sure Lou was definitely out all night. Then she . . . well.'

'Hardly the Bat Signal, is it? For future reference: if a woman puts out the rubbish can on random nights when there's no collection, and then someone who isn't her husband turns up late at night? Gets noticed. House-to-house lives for stuff like that: cheery anecdotes, cheesy anecdotes.' Mike cupped a hand to his ear. 'If we're both really quiet, you can probably hear the laughter from the canteen.'

'Look, I admit it. Me and Meg, we've been seeing each other for a few months. We try to, well, be discreet.'

'Oh, sure. We wouldn't want her husband to be upset, right?'

'That's over in all but name. I should know, Detective. See?'

'Yeah, I see. I'm trying to work out who's using who the most, to be honest. I mean, she's literally getting your services, uh, *pro bono*.'

Lynch frowned. 'That's crude.'

Mike nodded in agreement. 'It's crude but in Latin, so it doesn't count. Spence, have you ever met Lou Cassavette?'

'No.'

'Hmm.' Mike flicked through a couple of pages in the file, ran a finger down a list. 'That's strange, because we found your fingerprints in Lou's store. On a shelf, near the sweeties. One of twenty-odd we've already sussed. Care to explain?'

Lynch's eyes widened.

'I can't . . . there's no way. I mean, I . . .'

'You what? Wore gloves, like a forensically aware legal expert? Took special precautions? What?'

'How would you even have my prints?'

Mike shrugged. 'As a lawyer in this state, they'd be on file until you officially retire. In case you accidentally handle evidence, for example. Don't you recall giving them when you first qualified? That rule came in twenty years ago, Spence.'

'I, uh.' Lynch held up his hands. 'I wasn't lying, Detective. I've never actually met Lou.'

He paused. Lynch had been a defamation lawyer before he started swimming in the infinity pool of divorce. Mike felt Spence would like to be on his feet about now, pacing, before leaning in a folksy way towards one of the jurors – the one his assistant had picked out as the most malleable. Rooted to a chair like this, he was robbed of his sleek body language.

'Last week – Thursday, actually – I was driving back from a meeting and I went past the place. I was . . . curious. A piece of me wanted to observe Lou: all I've ever had is Meg's take on him. He doesn't know me from a hole in the ground. So I thought I could, you know, take a peek.'

Spence shook his head and looked at the ceiling.

'And then I had a stupid idea that maybe I could talk to him, or whatever. Crazy. I was brave until I got in the store. Then I thought how utterly brainless it was, and what Meg would think of it. I pictured her expression if I told her I'd chatted to Lou and . . . so I left. Never saw him. Bought some chocolate so they wouldn't think I was a shoplifter.'

Mike pondered. It was ad lib enough to be genuine. At the very least, it would give him leverage if he talked to Megan, which he was now convinced he needed to do. Dana wanted a second opinion on her anyway; this would be useful as a bombshell if he felt she was holding out.

However, he still had the besotted puppy-dog lover of Lou's wife, definitely in the store where Lou was stabbed. And recently, too.

Mike leaned forward. 'You've seen the photos of Lou, right? In the living room? By the marital bed? Big, meaty guy; tall, shaven head; put you through a wall if you're screwing his wife?'

Lynch re-smoothed his tie. 'Whatever.'

'And you know that, well, Lou's dead.'

'Dead?'

Mike thought Lynch's tell would seep through if he'd been the killer – Lynch wasn't that good a liar. Or he'd reckoned Megan would have told Lynch straight away – the next call after ringing her mother this morning, in fact. They were still waiting on the final phone records to prove it either way.

'You didn't know?'

Lynch's skin slid to ashen. Mike had known a couple of people – professional actors – who could make themselves do that to order. But Lynch probably wasn't one of them.

'What happened?' Lynch's wide eyes narrowed suddenly. 'You haven't got me here . . . you can't . . . wait . . . no.'

'No? Your fingerprints are a corpse's fall from the dead body, genius. You know exactly who the victim is. You've admitted you know where the store is, and having been inside it. A small child could see you have motive. I'm betting you alibi Megan, and Megan's your alibi; and neither of you has corroboration for the time in question.'

Mike stopped. He noticed that Lynch's breathing seemed a little laboured and a little noisy. A small rattle in it, as though someone was shaking a packet of peanuts in another room. Lynch lurched forward and fell to his knees.

'Are you okay, Spence?' Mike stood up.

'Water, now, please. Heart.'

Mike rushed out and grabbed a water bottle off a colleague's desk. 'Emergency!' he called as he went.

Lynch was grappling with the blister pack, his fingers now inept and useless. Mike helped him out, hearing a whispered 'two' from Lynch as beads of sweat formed on the lawyer's nose.

After swallowing the tablets and glugging half the bottle, Lynch puffed his cheeks several times and gulped in the air. He rubbed his hand across his face, seemingly disgusted by how wet it was. Mike nodded to two colleagues watching anxiously at the threshold. When they closed the door behind them Mike settled back in his chair.

Mike passed him some tissues. 'Need a doctor?'

Lynch smiled weakly as he re-sat. 'No. Good, thanks. Touch of angina. Pills control it. Doesn't usually come that fast. Sorry to worry you.'

'Let me know if you need the doc.'

Lynch nodded and put down the water bottle. 'What happened to Lou?'

Mike considered how much to tell. Lynch wasn't the prime suspect right now, but he was a chance. So was Megan. Mike had to hedge his bets. Lynch's ignorance had taken Mike by surprise. Even in the most benign scenario, he was still sure Megan would have called Lynch straight away; was bemused that she apparently hadn't done so.

'He was stabbed to death in his store. Early morning, dawn. Megan didn't mention you when she told us her own whereabouts.'

Lynch fiddled with the blister pack – his fingers still trembled. 'No, no, she wouldn't have. But I was there . . . at her place, I mean. All night. Left about six-ish, as you say. Is that after time of death? Or do you need to know where I went after that?'

Mike wouldn't be committing to anything at this point. 'Where'd you go?'

'To my golf club. There's a gym and showers at the clubhouse. Cameras everywhere in there.' Lynch paused, took another swig. 'Neither of us had any idea something had happened to Lou. God, how awful.'

'You a gym-bunny, Spence?' Mike sat back to overtly appraise

Lynch's waistline. 'Doesn't show. Or is there a Mrs Lynch you were trying to avoid?'

Lynch sat back, grabbed yet more water. 'The only Mrs Lynch in my family is a ninety-year-old who sits around playing bridge with her cronies, bemoaning that her only nephew never married, Detective.'

'So I was right to say you and Megan alibi each other?'

Mike had to remind himself that Lynch was a clever guy, not to be taken breezily. Maybe he was planting enough innocent-ingénu and improvised responses to throw Mike off the scent. Personally, Mike couldn't stand infidelity. He thought it was lazy callousness – someone could always end one thing before starting another, if they really wanted to.

'Smart meter. Meg has a smart meter. For the electrics? One of those boxes tells you how much power your washing machine used, that sort of thing. We both got ready around dawn. So that'll show us moving about: lights, and so on. Electric hot water, as well. I couldn't be making the tea and Meg showering, and we're simultaneously killing Lou in his shop. Have you tried that?'

Mike had to admit that was a new one: being cleared by an electricity bill. He really should stay on top of this new technology: it increasingly placed people geographically and demonstrated their actions and he ought to understand what options that gave him for tracking witnesses, suspects, and others. At the very least, he should make sure Lucy was on top of it.

'We'll look into it. You have to admit, Spence, both you and Megan have a strong motive for wanting to lose Lou.'

Lynch shook his head. 'Wasn't like that. Meg isn't like that. She's a good person, good instincts. A better person than me, you'll be amazed to learn. But no, it's not like that.'

Lynch scooted his chair and risked putting his elbows on the interview room table. The tailor of his handmade suit would have wept.

'I'm leaving the firm, Detective. Moving to the city, with Meg. Teaching divorce law at the university next year. I, uh, haven't told the firm yet, you understand.' He glanced up and appeared mollified by Mike's raised palm. 'Anyway, Meg was going to divorce Lou, that's true. He's a nice man, but they've drifted, and he's married to the store, really. They lead separate lives. I'm helping Meg with the details.'

Seemingly more than mere lovers, the couple were actively looking to move on together, leaving Lou twisting in the wind. Maybe Lynch, or Megan, was too impatient to wait for due process and paperwork. Quicker if the impediment died.

'How kind of you.'

Lynch slapped the table. Mike actually jumped.

'Look, Detective, be as suspicious as you want to be, but don't judge me, or Meg. We were trying to be nice about it all, trying to do it right. They're business partners as well as married. It isn't easy extricating yourself: not without wrecking things for the person you're leaving. We didn't want to do that. We just wanted to start our own lives. Is that so wrong? So terrible? Or are people only allowed to be happy if they meet ideally; under perfect circumstances, both free and easy and no one else in play? Life's messy, as I'm sure you know. And I don't have to account for myself morally to you. Neither does Meg. Check the smart meter: I'm sure you can. And then either piss or get off the pot, Detective.'

Mike recovered from the surprise. Perhaps Megan knew Lynch had killed her husband but was distancing herself from it in case Lynch was caught. His voice was low and even.

'Why didn't she call you first thing today, tell you Lou was dead?'

Lynch waved a hand. 'Don't know. Probably to protect me from this, uh, friendly chat. If she'd called me, she'd surely know that you'd find that out. Then our relationship becomes, as you know so well, the property of mature professionals who laugh at others' private lives in the canteen. You know what? People tell me the most intimate things in my line of work and I never repeat them to anyone. Why aren't your colleagues able to say the same?'

His insinuation hit home. Mike knew he was right: it was a shabby part of the culture Bill hadn't been able to eradicate.

Lynch continued. 'Maybe she wanted to spare me all that, and spare herself that.' He leaned forward. 'Don't know, Detective. Don't really care. Meg's a smart woman and I trust her implicitly. There's no gap between us for you to dig into, sorry.'

Mike nodded. That was probably all true, but he'd need to talk with Megan, and without Lynch being able to forewarn her. Lynch had been made to leave his phone at the front desk when he arrived: standard security process in an era where every phone was a camera and a recorder.

Mike stood up. 'I'll need to verify some things before we can let you go, Spence. Should be routine, but might take an hour. I can get Lucy to bring you a coffee.'

'A coffee would be nice, thank you. But not delivered by that young woman.'

Mike smirked. 'As you wish.'

He made it to the door before Lynch spoke again. 'What's my tell, Detective? You said you'd let me know.'

'Oh, that?' It was subliminal, and only in certain lights. But Mike wanted Spencer's shiny veneer scratched a little. 'You blink three times when you've been caught out. It's quick; like a reflex. But it's there.'

Lynch pursed his lips sceptically. 'Funny how no one's ever mentioned that. All the negotiating I do.'

Mike shrugged his shoulders. 'Not a mystery, really. Your friends are too polite; your opponents like it.' He held the door handle for a second. 'Ask Megan about it. She'll tell you straight. She's a smart woman, and you trust her implicitly. Don't you, Spence?'

Chapter 20

Dana had prepared most of her strategy for the next phase with Nathan. The endgame – the prize – was Nathan telling what took place in the store. He had no innocent reason to be there that she could see; he had blood on his hands. If there was a confession to be had, she meant to have it. If there was a viable alternative explanation, she intended to get it. But her strategy for now was to move Nathan closer to that prize without rushing him into closing down. Each conversation still held a tripwire in the dark.

Previously, she'd had various channels and escape routes. But now, armed with the knowledge of the cave and her previous discussions with Nathan, the strategy was becoming more linear and less nuanced. This part wasn't vastly complicated. Once she started telling Nathan that his inner sanctum was now on video, viewed by strangers and being catalogued and sifted, he would freak. No, wait, she thought: he wouldn't actually freak. More likely he'd simmer, or withdraw, or try to avoid her entirely. Because that was how he dealt with things.

She was prepared to let him; viewed it as both inevitable and necessary. As long as Nathan was free to simply be in his cave and avoid people, he'd achieved a type of serenity. She truly admired it, envied it. But that calmness was brittle by definition; it couldn't survive sustained human contact. He hadn't learned to bend and would therefore surely snap. She suspected that even he didn't know how it would go, once she cracked the surface of his fragile wounds.

She put on some latex gloves and opened the evidence bag containing his journal. It was unlikely anyone else had touched it, but you never knew. Since Stuart had been wearing gloves and so was Dana, it meant the forensics were simple – any fingerprints other than Nathan's were immediately of major interest.

The journal started six weeks after he disappeared. She'd thought that it would be reflective, philosophical. She was disappointed. It was not so much a journal, more a ledger. It held details of what food and first-aid equipment he held at any one time. It gave the impression he conducted a comprehensive stocktake at least once a day.

But on each left-hand page was a log of what he'd stolen. And where he'd stolen it. She held her breath – it was a complete inventory of his crimes.

She turned it over and saw the manufacturer spec: it was a 256-page book. By flipping quickly through the pages, she could see none had been ripped out or left blank. She counted from the back – twelve pages unused; so 244 pages filled. Each left-hand page held two separate dates and two separate burglaries. That meant 244 crimes in fifteen years – one every three weeks or so.

Stuart had reckoned on the video footage that Nathan's current food stash would last at least eight weeks. Dana thought he was underestimating Nathan's capacity for delayed gratification and fortitude: she was convinced Nathan could stretch that to three months if needed. Taking one or two extra items each time would build up the reserve stocks Stu had witnessed earlier.

Presumably, this morning's foray into Jensen's Store had been an attempt to build excess resources for the winter. Dana reasoned he'd probably eat more in winter, when the temperature required more energy. It would make sense, she thought, to stock enough for weeks when he might be hemmed in by poor weather, or it was simply too cold or uncomfortable to want to go out. She recalled what he'd said about wet cold being so much worse: he'd want enough resources that he could stay dry for as long as necessary.

All the same, the inventory was proof – in Nathan's own hand – of exactly how many burglaries he'd carried out. Dana couldn't recall any period in her time at the station when anyone had suggested such a spree. She wondered how he'd managed to get away with that. It seemed impossible to believe no one had truly cottoned on, or seemingly reported it.

Dana phoned for the exhibits officer and watched him sign for the journal. She asked for a photocopy of every page to be put on her desk while she was with Nathan: tomorrow, someone would have to check each claimed burglary against reports of that time. Something told her they wouldn't find any matching reports at all. Somehow, Nathan was getting in and out of places unhindered and unnoticed and his haul wasn't being missed.

At the very least, she mused, it cleared up the possibility Rainer had raised about Nathan keeping the Toyota and carrying out burglaries in the city. And the journal most likely precluded Nathan having some kind of sponsor or patronage; no dropped sacks of provisions at pre-arranged points.

Nathan had sneaked around the district for over a decade. They'd never even known there were crimes to investigate.

Mike's fourth call to Central Intelligence finally yielded Peter Kasparov, the detective he really needed to speak to. Kasparov had spent most of his life dealing in snippets and slivers of information, splicing them together to gain a vague sense of what was going on out there.

But, like Dana, his best work was done by his brain, in the darkest and quietest place that could be found.

'Kaspar, just the man I wanted. You know more about the Alvarez family than the Alvarez family, isn't that right?'

'Very kind, Mikey. Possibly true. The Alvarez clan run the gamut from incredibly clever to dumb as a rock. I certainly know more than some of the rocks, since I haven't been addling my brain from age ten. But the smartest ones? I'm not in the ballpark.'

Mike doubted that was the case, with one possible exception.

'Well, you know more than us down here.'

'Ah, that's undoubtedly true. How's the saintly Barb?'

'She's still more than I deserve but with that bizarre blind spot that stops her divorcing me. Strangers still think I'm her dad, of course. So, we have a little murder here, and I wanted to check out any possible link with the Alvarez family. Have you ever heard of Lou Cassavette?' He repeated the last name with NATO phonetics.

Kasparov's mind worked more like an old-fashioned card index than a modern computer file. When reaching for data he would physically move his hands as if he were opening and closing drawers, flicking through cards. It would look weird to the unwary. Mike could picture Kasparov in his office, one desk lamp and no other illumination. He'd be dressed in some form of sleeveless cardigan, likely one with a diamond pattern. He'd have nail polish, probably a dark shade for work. There would be a silver flask by his left hand, containing only chilled water. By now, orange peel would be in the waste bin by his right foot.

'Lou Cassavette. Hmm. Yes. Got the report now. Went to school with Alfonse and Miguel Alvarez. Ricardo, the eldest, was already beyond education and into career by then. Alfonse, as you know, Mikey, is doing thirty to life for being a complete psycho. Despite his shenanigans in maximum security, he's basically out of the game.

Whereas Miguel . . . yeah, Miguel is the one that might be relevant. I take it Mr Cassavette had a sad demise?'

'He did. Killed in the store he owned, out here near Earlville. Knife through the heart at 5.30 a.m. We have a primary suspect, Kaspar; I'm covering angles.'

Kasparov harrumphed, but Mike could hear the clatter of fingertips across the keyboard. Kasparov had a feather touch.

'Now, Mikey, as you know, Miguel is something of a master at hiding and moving the money. Much as I'd like to catch him, I have to admire the skill. As they start closing in on the various tax shelters around the world, Miguel is focusing more on nearby channels, where the Alvarez tentacles can easily reach. They want their money hidden, but where they can see it. If you see what I mean.'

'I getcha. Go with what they know, stick to the knitting, that kind of thing?'

'Exactly. You're a quick learner.' More clicks, and typing. 'There's a lot of people that hate you, Mikey, and wish you dead. But I think you're okay.'

Mike sniggered. 'Your majesty both embarrasses and entertains me.'

'Ha. Yes, here he is. Your dead man. Cassavette. Ugly bug, isn't he? Used to be the manager of the Lightning Quick store on O'Brien Street. Which would have been perfect as a laundromat for the likes of Miguel. Let me delve . . . tax authorities liked him for it, to be honest. But he had an accountant called Duran, kept them at arm's length. Ah yes, Hector Duran. One of Miguel's protégés and, I believe, on his way up the food chain as a result.'

'Dana always says to follow the money.'

'Ah, the fragrant Ms Russo. Send her my regards – Fraud never recovered from her leaving. She's absolutely right, too. The Alvarez empire is changing from illicit goods into just dirty money. They never handle the merchandise any more, only the financial fall-out. It's their big USP over the other drug gangs – they know how to finesse the cash. Others lose most of their profit margin turning hot money into cold, but not the Alvarezes. In fact, they might be acting as bankers for some of their rivals, weird as that sounds.'

It was a tighter connection than Mike had bargained for; he'd thought it would be old school pals at best. A mid-range financial adviser beholden to the main Alvarez brother was tying up the books for Lou Cassavette.

'So Cassavette was connected?'

'Ah, not so fast, Mikey. In the dreamy world of intelligence, things are seldom as they seem. Put it to you this way: if you set up as an accountant and your only clients are called Alvarez, you attract attention. So to establish bona fide credentials, Duran also has plenty of genuine clients – Cassavette may have been one of those. But if I check . . . yes, Duran is still his accountant, as of now. He kept him when he moved and bought . . . Jensen's Store, in lovely old Earlville. I was punched in the face there once: I bet most visitors say the same. So there is a tenuous connection, but don't leap at it, Mikey.'

That was true, thought Mike. As Dana constantly reminded him, connections had to actually do something, not just be nearby. *Correlation is not causation, Mikey.*

'Any evidence Miguel ever leaned on Cassavette, to help with the magic tricks?'

'Not that I can see. Though messages routed through Duran wouldn't show up, necessarily. But it's fair to say Miguel's main weakness is a nostalgia for the good old days of his youth. Which of course were absolutely terrible – poverty, racism, crime, violence. And that was after he came over on a boat, where two thirds of them never completed the journey. I wouldn't rule out some financial connection to Miguel – he might have had Cassavette washing cash, or he might have loaned him some for old times' sake. Give me a couple of hours, Mikey. I have minions. They'll check it out.'

'Much obliged, Kaspar. Barb would send her love.'

'Ha. If only. Bye, Mikey.'

Spencer Lynch hadn't occupied Mike's mind much in the previous ten minutes. He wondered why he wanted the killer *not* to be Nathan Whittler. He suspected it was because he was picking up on Dana's wish for it not to be Nathan. Assuming the Alvarez angle didn't pan out, that meant it would most likely be Spencer and/or Megan. And so, he needed to get his own view of Megan Cassavette.

Chapter 21

Megan's mother, Rita, lived on the outskirts of Gazette. Mike had acquired Megan's mobile phone records and made a few notes: Lucy would go through them with a raptor's eye.

Gazette was a weird little place almost midway between Earlville and Carlton. Originally merely a stopping point on the road for fuel and supplies, it was gradually morphing into a mid-price village that majored on the older clientele. A large billboard on the edge of town for a 'managed lifestyle facility' happened to asterisk that it was seven minutes to Earlville Mercy Hospital. Probably five, Mike thought, with the lights flashing. Eucalypts went with the breeze as the clouds rolled in from the west. Off the main road through town, the traffic noise ceased entirely.

The townhouse sat at the end of a walkway; vehicles were parked in bays near the entrance to the complex, and the footpath wound its way through easy-maintenance shrubbery, past six front doors. The attempts at Spanish colonial were half-hearted: white stucco streaked with stains from draining window boxes, anti-burglar grilles given a curlicue at the end. The week's blustery weather had thrown bark cuttings from the flower beds on to the path. Rita's house was at the far end, meaning several pairs of eyes on every visitor to the place.

He could see a porch of terracotta tiles extended out into a scrubby lawn. A couple of metal chairs and a small table topped with colourful mosaic almost gave a Mediterranean feel, except that the sun had shuffled away and the westerly was gathering strength.

Megan answered the door. Barefoot, tight-ish jeans and a biscuit-coloured sweater that was too large and fell slightly off one shoulder. She held the door like it was a protective lover, one thigh pressed against it. Suddenly, whole chunks of Lynch's behaviour appeared perfectly reasonable. Mike gave a neutral smile and showed the badge.

'You're the detective?'

'Mike Francis, yes.'

'C'mon in. My mum's gone to the supermarket but, being her, she's left freshly baked croissants.' It flashed through Mike's mind that Megan was the kind of woman that men, by and large, would love; women, by and large, wouldn't like at all.

They sat at a small round table in a nook designated for breakfasts and light meals: Mike could see through a doorway to a larger dining room to the left. Megan had a pastry in front of her but sat on her hands and blinked a lot. In the living room, desiccated heat belched from a fireplace glowing with a faux flame on faux pebbles. On the kitchen radio, middle-of-the-road rock from the eighties.

'I'm sorry for your loss, Mrs Cassavette.'

She shook her head. 'Megan, please, Megan. That other detective – the quiet woman? She was ridiculously polite. And Mum's treating me like a rare artefact. I am not, in fact, made of spun glass. I could fall on the floor without shattering.'

Mike knew to wait it out then ride the apology when it came. She fumbled with a sleeve.

'Sorry, Detective.' Despite the trauma, her gaze was clear and direct, confident. 'Can I ask you something?'

'Sure.' He took out a notebook and pen and watched her watch him do so.

She swallowed. 'Why do you say that? That thing: *sorry for your loss*. That thing?'

'Honestly?' Sometimes people asked but didn't really want to know. Especially when the statement had been directed at them.

'Naturally.'

He counted off the reasons on his fingers. 'Well, firstly, we are. Sorry, I mean. We see lots of bereaved people – often we're delivering the news. So, in many ways, it's heartfelt. We know precisely what loss is, and what it means, and what it does. So we are sorry.'

He paused to let that sink in. Megan clearly thought it was only a platitude and he could see her eyes mist slightly when he corrected that assumption.

'However, we've also been told to say it and police officers are good at following instructions. We have a command structure for a reason. Thirdly, it's been picked by smarter minds than mine as politically, psychologically and religiously neutral. It's sympathetic, without being drawn into your emotional state ourselves. Also, it's neutral, in case you're a potential witness. Or a suspect.'

He gave her a significant glance, but she stared back evenly, as if that last sentence were peripheral to her question. 'Fourthly, there isn't much anyone can say that makes a blind bit of difference. We're not really allowed to give hugs or wipe tears, or anything that actually might help. The only way we *can* help is to find the truth of what happened.'

She went back to picking at the sleeve; an unwound stitch he guessed she'd been worrying at since she put on the sweater. 'Hmmm. Thank you. Your colleague didn't say it, by the way. I liked her for that.'

She pushed the plate back.

'See, I'm struggling with other people's reactions to my grief. It's the first time I can remember losing someone close – Dad left when I was three – so I'm finding their behaviour a little weird. Even though I'd be doing the same things if I was them. If you see what I mean.'

'We see people in all different stages. Believe me, whatever you're doing is spot on, and no one can say it isn't. No one knows what to do for you. Even if they somehow went through the same thing themselves, it would've been different. They kind of understand. Everyone wants to help you, but most of them in a vague way that doesn't put them out too much.'

Megan managed a smile then looked up to the ceiling in frustration. 'Well, frankly, I'd rather be at work. I'd rather be doing something. Probably sounds callous. But work would fill my mind up, I think.'

'Not the introspective type, huh?'

Her eyes dropped to his suddenly, the sharpness deadened by disappointment. 'Nope.'

'In that case,' he said, opening the notebook, 'shall we do something by dealing with some questions?'

'Shoot.' She bit her lip and raised a hand. 'Wait, that's a bad thing to say to a cop, right?'

'Ah, they teach us early about figurative requests to shoot.'

They shared a grin and Mike saw how easy it was to be beguiled by Megan Cassavette. She was sharp, self-deprecating and had confidence without aggression. Lynch was not, as Mike had previously thought, a middle-aged fool. Lynch had seen a star and reached for it. Possibly overambitious in the final analysis, Mike thought, but it was a justifiable leap into potential oblivion. In Lynch's eyes, Megan was worth the jump; worth the fall. Mike had the same question in his mind as Dana: how had *Lou* impressed Megan enough? Assuming he had.

'So I wanted to ask you about last night and this morning, if that's all right.'

She crossed her arms as she leaned forward, resting her chin on her forearms and staring at the fireplace. It made her look child-like, lost. Unkempt dark curls drifted across her temple.

'So, Spencer Lynch arrived at what time?'

She closed her eyes for a second. 'Ah. Okay.' She looked up at him. 'Spoken to Spence?'

'Twenty minutes ago. So all those cards are on the table.'

'Damn. No point trying to keep him out of it, then?'

'He's front and centre right now. Timescale, please?'

She lifted from her arms, as if to concentrate better. 'After I'd texted Lou and he'd texted back, I went out and . . . uh.'

'Gave the Bat Signal?'

She sat back sharply and rolled her eyes. 'Jesus, we really became an open book, didn't we?'

'Some neighbours read a few pages weeks ago.' He let her take in the fact that their subterfuge hadn't survived a couple of nosy citizens. 'Okay, you did that at what time?'

'Lemme think. Uh, after eleven but before twelve. Spence arrived just before midnight. The clock in the hall strikes on the hour and we were standing next to it at midnight: made us jump. Um, he left about six, I think. Yeah, maybe a few minutes after.'

So far, so good. Mike recalled the records showed she'd texted Lou at 2330. If she was telling the truth, Lynch wasn't there at that point. If she was lying, however, she might have bloodlessly texted Lou good-night from underneath Spencer Lynch. Her reply wasn't precise enough that it would look like a concocted story; it was merely close enough.

If he believed her, there was no way either could have been at the store to stab Lou. Right now, Lucy was contacting the electric company: analysing the smart meter's data may alibi both Megan and Lynch. If he didn't believe her, she or Lynch had time to go to the store and kill Lou and then return. Meanwhile, the other person might try to convince the meter there were two people there.

He couldn't shake something about Megan. He was suspicious of her motives in choosing Lou as a partner. Maybe Lou had been as together as she seemed to be, but he doubted it. He concurred with Dana that Lou had married up and Megan had settled. Maybe Megan liked being with someone and knowing she was smarter than them. Some people did: it topped up their self-belief every night. His suspicion of her earlier motives for marrying Lou seeped in; something felt off-kilter.

'You see, from my perspective, Megan, you alibi Spencer, and he's your alibi.'

She didn't swallow, look away or bat an eyelid. 'Yes. Yeah, I can see that. Well, we sure didn't invite anyone else around. And we both switch off phones . . . you know, kind of a golden rule. So no, I can't think of how you'd prove we didn't go out. No. Can't help, I'm afraid.'

If she'd mentioned the smart meter, he'd have wondered. Lynch had raised it, and it was a left-field idea: if Megan had also done so, it would have felt forced and conspiratorial. Omitting it gave her credibility. Unless . . . maybe not mentioning it was a double bluff: a pre-arrangement she'd cooked up with Lynch. Dana had mentioned that her radar had pinged when she spoke to Megan, but she hadn't known why. Mike had the same sensation now.

Nothing more to gain from the alibi angle, so he switched. 'You were beginning divorce proceedings?'

Megan rubbed her wedding band, seemingly without irony: something to occupy her hands. 'Well, depends what you call beginning. Hadn't filed the papers.' She paused momentarily. 'It was tricky to do it right. That's how Spence and I met.' She shook her head. 'You'd worked that bit out already, sorry.'

'Why so tricky?'

She sat back and stared at the pastry on the plate. 'Look, I didn't want to hurt Lou or harm anything he was doing. And what he was doing was trying to run that store, build it up. The revenue the store generated wasn't enough to secure the loans it needed.' She looked up. 'You know: the exact same loans that enabled the shop to generate the revenue? Banks live inside circles like that. Anyway, for us to get the loans in the first place I had to co-guarantee, based on my income with City Mutual.'

Mike sat back himself and put down the pen. 'Ah.'

'Exactly. The moment I file for divorce, the bank figures my income's disappearing and the business loans aren't viable any more.' She stopped, and when she resumed her voice was further away. 'Lou loses a wife and the shop; probably declared bankrupt. Spence and I were trying to work out the, uh, transition.'

'I see now. Finance was never my strong point.'

He hadn't quite twigged when Lynch had mentioned all this. He'd presumed it was tricky to sell property or they'd had a joint investment fund or something. Now that he thought about it, unwinding the intricacies of such a relationship – without anyone getting pulled to pieces – wouldn't be simple.

'Oh, I'm pretty good at it, actually,' she replied. 'No good at sport, can't sing, but okay at finance. We were looking at me moving out and not telling anyone; carry on helping with the loan until Lou could get on his feet. But it's a small town and the bank would hear about it. Spence said that'd be worse, because we couldn't control the when or the how. Besides, it might prove never-ending; you don't get much closure on either side if you're still that entwined. Spence's happy to pay the loan himself or guarantee it himself. But, of course, Lou would rather d— I mean, Lou wouldn't accept that: his wife's new partner keeping him afloat. So, as I said, tricky.'

'No way he could reschedule the debt? Get an investor?'

Megan smirked. 'So you do know something about it? Ah, the banks would never play ball. They slice and dice people like us every day; barely ruffles a feather. Lou had some guy who seemed interested in taking a share, but it was wrong from both sides. The guy wanted the site, not the store; thought he could get it re-zoned for executive homes. He drifted off a couple of weeks ago when that was a non-starter. Besides, Lou'd fought to get a store he could build up himself: kinda takes the point away if you're doing someone else's bidding.'

'I getcha.' Megan had an interesting choice of words there, he thought, recalling what he now knew about Alvarez. That angle wasn't going away; it kept peering out from the shadows. 'And all the loans were through the banks? No other partners, no family or friend money involved?'

Megan frowned. 'Not that I know of, only the banks. That was the problem, Detective – there were no other sources to tap.'

Maybe there were, thought Mike. He wondered if Megan – who'd helped to run the Lightning Quick store before moving here – knew Miguel Alvarez. He decided to hold back that particular ammunition.

'Your husband, Megan. Was he someone who suffered fools gladly? I'm wondering if he pissed anyone off, or they pissed him off.'

'Your colleague beat you to it,' she replied flatly.

No, she didn't; we're each asking, to see if the answers tally, thought Mike. He waited patiently until Megan huffed, and continued.

'He wasn't violent, no. He originally came from a pretty bad neighbourhood, Detective. Out on the Flats. He showed me the block, once. Needles everywhere, burning tyres and scraggy horses in the middle of nowhere. You could put your finger through the render. All the walls dripped. Every day of Lou's childhood his snot was black, and he coughed like hell. He also saw what resorting to violence did to people. So no; not aggressive. That said, he could mix it if he had to. But here, he didn't have to. Does that cover it?'

The Flats was an area of sixties architectural disasters on the east side of the city, built on land that was cheap because it flooded. Mould flowered in every house and stairwell; kids died of asthma; property got ruined every few years. It quickly degenerated into a semi-slum and never recovered. If Cassavette had survived there, thought Mike, then as an adult he was either a broken toy or tough as they get. Or maybe both.

'Why haven't you contacted Spencer since you got the news this morning?'

'Hmmm. Precisely to avoid this kind of conversation. And for him to avoid this kind of conversation.' Her response came quickly – it felt rehearsed. She'd been preparing for police questions about her actions and motives. Not grieving. 'You embarrass Spence at his office?'

'He came to my house for a playdate.'

She smiled. 'Oh, that's a little better.' She glanced at the window, maybe hoping her mother would return and distract them both. Her smile faded fast.

'They're a bunch of snobs at that firm. Fire him at any hint of police action. Ease him out if he helped break up a marriage.' She jerked a thumb at herself. 'Ostracise him if his new partner lacked the right . . . pedigree.' She looked back at him again and he felt slightly skewered, in a pleasant way. 'I didn't want any of that to fall on him, if I could avoid it. I figured you'd be pulling phone records right away: if all it showed was a woman talking to a divorce lawyer, things might have stayed below the radar.'

'It's a homicide inquiry, Megan,' he reminded her. 'There's no space for anything below our radar. And nor should there be, for Lou's sake.'

'Yeah, yeah, 'course, you're right. Sorry. I wasn't . . . well, wasn't thinking straight. Sorry.'

Mike thought she might rush to fill a silence, but he underestimated her. She was very controlled. Almost too much.

Time for the bomb.

'Has Spencer ever met Lou?'

She shook her head. 'No. They lead very different lives, Detective: I'm the only link between them. I can't imagine how they'd ever bump into each other, even in a town this size. Not that Lou would know who Spence is, anyway. Spence knew who Lou was and where he worked, so he could easily steer clear of him.'

Mike took a couple of breaths as a run-up and made sure to take in all of Megan's body language in her response.

'So can you explain how Spencer's fingerprints are in Lou's store, about three metres from this morning's incident?'

Megan's eyes widened, then she frowned.

'No, I . . . no, you must be wrong. Why would Spence go to the store?'

'You tell me, Megan.'

'I, uh, no. No, I can't. In fact, I don't believe it. Spence and I talked about this, talked a lot. He was tol— we *agreed* he wouldn't go near Lou and we'd sort it all out like adults. Why would he go there?'

Answering an obvious question with a question felt like a distraction tactic more than incredulity.

'Off the top of my head? Check out the opposition. Threaten, cajole . . . murder.'

She was adamant. 'No, no. Spence isn't like that. No. We were going to get divorced one way or another, that's all. Spence and I were prepared for a long haul. We wouldn't need to . . . I can't believe Spence has been there. Did you ask him? What did he say?'

'I can't answer that. Ongoing investigation.'

Although he had no doubt she'd soon be ringing and leaving increasingly belligerent messages on Spence's voicemail. Mike would need to have a listen when he got back to the station.

'But this, uh, divorce trickiness thing, Megan. It offers motive, as I'm sure you can see. A cynical detective might conclude that the easiest way to solve the dilemma would be if Lou wasn't around.'

He expected some outrage, some anger. But she'd regained her balance after finding out Spence had gone freelance. Back in control. What Mike got was an appealing tilt of the head and an intelligence he was now regarding as feline.

'I think your quiet little colleague thought the same thing. That I killed Lou. That I didn't love Lou. Fair enough: she's a smart cookie. I guess if you all see life through dark glass, it always looks black. Let me guess: Lou looked older than me, I'm the one having the affair, I'm the one wants out. So either I went to the store and killed him or I sent Spence to do it. How'm I doing?'

'Not bad, Megan. We try to look at everything.'

Megan's frown and clenched hands displayed a hint of annoyance. Maybe impatience. Maybe insulted dignity. Possibly, Mike continued to think, she was annoyed that he wasn't swallowing everything she said.

'Well, for the record, I loved Lou, even though we weren't getting along. I married him because I loved him; because he was sweet and strong and because he had a moral compass I could only dream about. And no; I'd have kept paying his loans. He bailed me out plenty since we met, in every way. So don't think I didn't care just because I'm not all tears and snot now. Don't think I hated him because I met Spence. Sometimes life isn't fair, or reasonable, and the good ones get the crappy end of the stick. Doesn't make it anyone's fault.'

Whenever he heard an outburst like this, Mike thought of two things. First, was it authentic? Did they run words together because they couldn't tumble them out fast enough? Did they look hot inside, flustered and emotional? Did they repeat themselves? Heartfelt emotion could be inarticulate, repetitive. And second, in all those words, what were they refusing to answer? What was it that their invective might be hiding? What were they dissembling?

The answers he wrote – for now – were yes; and maybe nothing.

Chapter 22

Dana had discussed the physical conditions of Interview One with Bill. She wanted to turn up the heat: figuratively and literally. They had perhaps three hours of interview left before a lawyer became compulsory: they kept having to provide breaks and refreshments to avoid later accusations of bullying or pressurising. This time, she aimed for quicker answers and less thinking time. She needed Nathan off balance slightly: it would help if another bottle of water seemed benevolent, felt like a reward. When Nathan was taken for a toilet break Bill authorised the new temperature and the lighting dialled up a notch. Nathan would assume, on his return, that nothing had changed and he'd simply forgotten how warm it was compared to the corridor. Bill had the prisoner log updated to show Dana requesting a warmer environment because of her kneecap.

Nathan was sitting upright this time, a measure more alert, more involved. Dana was about to demolish part of his faith in her: she might have to begin anew with him. She hoped it was one step back to take two paces forward, but she had no real way of knowing.

He hunched down again as she entered the room. It was an attempt to hide his engagement with proceedings, an affected air of relative disinterest. She could see when she put her notes on the table that he attempted to read them upside down.

Dana wondered what kind of impression she was giving: whether her new-found knowledge was palpable. She did the preliminaries, gave her kneecap a tweak and started the tapes.

'Mr Whittler, I know you're not one for small talk. So I'll cut to the chase. About an hour ago, one of our search team found your home.'

She watched him very closely. There was a quiver, a shuttering around the eyes, as he looked at the floor. His breathing became louder, but not faster. She thought she detected a slight blush around his neck, though it could have been a trick of the light. As she'd anticipated, there was no immediate ranting, only a nascent fury simmering near the surface.

'I wish to reassure you, Mr Whittler,' she continued. 'Only one person has set foot in your home and, apart from maybe me, only one person will. The scene has been sealed off. That person will conduct any searching inside the cave that needs to be done.'

'Too. Late.'

It was a whisper, the cautious murmuring he'd first used this morning. A solid indicator that Dana had lost much of the ground she'd gained.

'Excuse me?'

It flitted through her mind that perhaps some incriminating morsel had long since been removed; that they'd find nothing of evidential value. She knew that wasn't the case with the burglaries – maybe it was true of the killing.

'Too. Late. Detective Russo.' His voice grew sturdier, steelier. 'Your attempts to mollify me, to suggest no harm has been done. Too late. The place is ruined: *poisoned*, the moment your colleague entered it.' He gave a dismissive flap of an arm and turned away.

Dana understood this. The emotional importance of his home was something she had comprehended long before they found the place. Nathan's sanctuary – his perceived safety – was now compromised. It also meant, she'd realised, that he could never go back to it. Since it was sullied and tainted, the discovery meant a burning of the bridges: a blunt end to the life he'd been living for fifteen years. She'd taken away his peace when she took away his concealment. She'd done that: her mind, her insight. He was right to blame her personally.

'I have some awareness of what this place means to you, Mr Whittler. We've videotaped footage that shows us the layout, and only one person is allowed in there, or to touch anything. We don't wish to cause—'

'What? Unnecessary suffering? Trauma?' He was shouting now, wagging a finger at his own foot. '*If you really cared*, Detective Russo, you wouldn't have touched it in the first place. You wouldn't even have gone looking. The moment you decided to do that, we were always in a messy compromise.'

Dana decided to sit for a moment. Her sense was that Nathan was so unpractised, so unused to argument, that he really couldn't do it. Little flares of temper might come and go quickly but he didn't understand how to fan the flames. He seemingly had no template, no memory, to draw upon. It struck her that perhaps he hadn't argued as a child either. Perhaps this was another extension of his suppressed boyhood self, a stretching of adolescent emotion.

It also came to her that, for the first time, he had used the word 'we'. Somewhere in his psyche, Nathan now accepted that he and Dana were joined together in an endeavour: maybe not quite as adversaries or buddies, but as two people doomed to be on the same trajectory. Which must signal that, on some level, he understood why Dana had to have the cave.

'You're an intelligent man, Mr Whittler. You appreciate why you're here; what we found at Jensen's. We must understand the past few years of your life if we're to unravel what might have happened in the store.'

He suffered silently. Twice he opened his mouth then realised he had nothing to say, or maybe no way to say it. He grabbed handfuls of his jumpsuit and sat quietly, sinking in the chair. Dana could see the cords of his clenched jaw. Eventually, words squeezed through and into the room.

'What would you do, Detective, if strangers walked through your home, touched your things, had a good snoop around? What would you think?'

Another *quid pro quo*; another test from Nathan about whether she was being honest with him. But again, her answer would be courtroom admissible – a potential lever for the defence if she judged it wrongly. She couldn't afford to appear to be manipulating him, not when he had no lawyer to safeguard his interests. Dana had to be looking for the killer but simultaneously protecting Nathan's rights.

'If they had no reason? I would feel angry, violated. I would feel my privacy had been compromised: I would hate it. That's how a burglary feels. If, however, they were executing a lawful warrant because I was clearly a significant person in a crime investigation; if they had observed due process; if they were led by a detective who understood exactly what was involved and made sure the space and property were respected? Then I would be upset, but I'd accept it, Mr Whittler. I'd recognise their legitimate right to do it, provided they did it with care and respect.'

'That was my home, Detective. It's like someone's been in there and spat on everything I have.'

There was a screech as he slid the chair, turning away from her and towards the blank wall. Childish: it was exactly like a small child's tantrum. She found it reassuring that she could still read him.

'No, Mr Whittler, it is not. It's not like that at all.' She tried to keep her voice coolly intellectual and not hectoring. 'In fact, it's quite the opposite. I rarely see my colleagues impressed by other people. But they can't imagine how you managed to achieve all that. The level of thinking, the level of will – it's beyond them.'

'Flattery?' He choked a little on his contempt. 'You must understand I'm immune to that.'

His voice was muted, and turned away from her. Dana briefly wondered if the microphone was picking it up, but she felt the momentum and control were too important to risk interruption. The little red light was still flickering.

'Not flattery, Mr Whittler. I don't do flattery. Ever. But if I'm impressed by something, I say so.'

He ran a sleeve across his mouth, wiping spittle from his upper lip. 'Milk crates, cold vegetables from a can, second-hand books and a toilet full of plastic bags. And you're impressed, you say?' He snorted.

Dana pushed on, certain that she could impart a sense of wonderment that would thaw him. 'Mr Whittler, I'm a clever person. Often, I'm creative. But there's no way I could create a home of that . . . order. That organisation. That sustainability.'

She paused, wondering if any of her words were even registering. He was still belligerent, shutting her out as he'd done early this morning.

'It took skills that you clearly didn't have when you began. You had to think through every detail on your own: no help, no teacher. Just you, and your mind, working through it. And you achieved something that people will still find astonishing a decade from now. Yes, I'm impressed by that.'

Still nothing.

Dana didn't want to overplay her hand here. If she pursued this line too much, it might drive Nathan deeper within himself: his avoidance reflex. He couldn't physically run away and hide, so he'd indulge that reflex by putting up the shutters. Or she might aggravate him enough that he called for a lawyer. All the same, she still felt she was turning the right key in the correct lock.

'What was it you said to me before, Mr Whittler? "*Everything can be survived, if you go about it right.*" Hmmm. I didn't appreciate the full intent behind those words. My apologies. Now that I've seen what it's taken, what it cost, what you had to build and protect, I can see a little more clearly.'

She'd believed repeating his own words would break through. Perhaps the fact that she remembered them might draw him out. Yet, more silence. Nathan began to tap one palm with the fingers of the other hand, a gesture almost of boredom, like an ape in an empty cage.

Dana reached for something more specific.

'The maritime flares in the bedroom. It would never be a signal that everything had failed and you needed rescuing, would it, Mr Whittler? My colleagues think so, but I don't. You didn't keep those flares in case you gave in. Because you'd never give in.'

She leaned forward, peering intently at his profile as he stubbornly stared at the wall.

'I mean, you'd never use those, *vertically*. Would you?'

Just a flicker, the tightening of a grip on a sleeve. A sense that he was available to be in the same room as her next words.

'Dingoes. Snakes. A weapon of last resort; am I right?'

His voice sounded sticky, coated with reluctance. 'Never needed them, thank God. I had no gun, no actual weapon, you see. If a dingo or a python got in there, especially if I was asleep . . . I was hoping to panic it, disorient it, maybe. Had nothing else.'

Dana could suddenly sense it again: that feeling she'd had this morning, late morning. The rest of the room was fading from her mind. The only things in her consciousness were her words, his words, and her tenuous hold on what he meant by flicks, gestures, silences and absences. It was triggered by the sense of a way in, a concealed doorway opening. Her finger and thumb tapped together under the table.

'I'm surprised you weren't bothered by snakes, or spiders, or whatever.'

He nodded at the wall but turned towards her. 'So was I. When I first found the cave I was paranoid: funnel webs, brown snakes, maybe. Even a possum's risky if it felt cornered – I would have been vulnerable. Not just immediately; an infected wound would have been a major problem. I assumed some animal or snake would have colonised the place. I have no idea why they didn't. The only creature I had a problem with was a rakali.'

Dana flicked another grab of the kneecap. The pain was getting worse – little stabs.

'Ah, super-smart, aren't they?'

'One of them seemed to work out the clasp on the plastic boxes. I left a box open and put a mousetrap in there. He didn't bother me after that. I hope he was okay.'

He stared at the wall again. He was mentally back in his cave on the Dakota Line, on some bucolic day when he was neither hot nor cold, when he had boxes full of food, when he had books he'd yet to read, when the radio was playing Bach. She still envied huge segments of his life.

She had to move the conversation on. He'd no doubt peak and dip as they went on, but for now his anger seemed replaced by resignation. She almost wished he'd fought harder – really gone at her. She felt as though he'd subsided in the face of opposition too quickly, that he hadn't done justice to fifteen years of determined stubbornness. It occurred to her that, when the problem was in the room with him and he couldn't avoid it, he was quite . . . *compliant.*

'You only went into stores. Never homes.'

He leaned back and looked at the ceiling, his pupils dancing as he sought reassuring patterns in the plaster. She'd broken through his defences: they both knew it.

'No, I'd never visit homes. I didn't want to run into anyone, of course, but it was more than that. I guarded my privacy; I didn't wish to invade theirs. I was worried someone might feel their home was no longer their castle. Got to admit I thought about it, with some of the holiday homes, in winter. Many were left unlocked for months – some sort of country code about travellers in dire need, I think. A lot of them kept supplies, and they probably wouldn't have been missed. You come back in late spring, open the place up – were there three packs of batteries or two, when you left? But in the end, I couldn't bring myself to do it.'

He twisted and looked at the tape machine. 'You found my journal. Of course you would. Something else that was private and now isn't.'

Dana took a deep breath. 'I was worried it was a diary. Hoped it wasn't. I wouldn't want to read your diary, Mr Whittler. I wouldn't want to intrude in that way.'

'How do you keep people out? If they're constantly around you, I mean? I might have to learn how, I suspect.'

It was his first intimation of life beyond today; the merest glimpse into a mind that was starting to see ahead, to a future that might be behind bars. At the very least, he could surely not return to his previous ways.

'Well, turn everything back on them, Mr Whittler. Ask open questions about their lives. Feign interest. Most people want to talk about themselves more than they want to talk about you. So there's that. Also, you can draw clear lines on certain matters and always stick to them. Keep to those lines about yourself, and others. That's the only way some people comprehend there are boundaries. Consistency, determination.'

He scratched at his fate line, as though committing her suggestions to memory.

'You need to know about the stores? For confirmation?'

Dana nodded and opened a fresh sheet in her pad. 'I have to, yes. If you could confirm what's in the journal for the tape. To wrap up some things. Then we don't have to speak about that again.'

She stopped and glanced at the mirror, her heart yelping. She shouldn't say this – had no obligation to do so, and every reason not to . . .

'I should tell you at this point that you don't currently have a lawyer, but you have a right to one. Mr Whittler, I . . . I, uh . . . strongly suggest you get one before we go further.'

She could feel the heat from her face. She waited for the rap of knuckle on glass from a colleague: perhaps the double-double-tap that was Bill's. She'd be prepared to ride the inevitable argument. When the sound didn't come, she looked back at Nathan.

'Mr Whittler, you need someone in here who has your best interests at heart.'

Nathan turned slowly. 'But I'm certain that you . . . thank you. I know what I've done in those stores. And really, you have the journal. There's little point arguing about it.'

There was a short screech as he turned the chair back again. The room was exactly how it had been before.

'Will we find evidence of you gaining entry?'

'I doubt it. I was pretty careful. I'd seen enough television before I left to know how to avoid fingerprints, footprints.'

He sat back a little, hands cradled in his lap and eyes fixed on the table's edge.

'When I worked at Pringle's I used to build cabinets and armoires. They were a big seller. Everyone was building modern homes and they wanted something in it that looked old, established.

'Anyway, Mr Pringle taught me about the locks we used on the armoire doors. I'd worked with wood, mostly, so I had to play with the locks to understand the device. Most locks are basically the same, Detective. You can tamper with them in a way that means when you turn the key you hear a noise and feel a click, but the mechanism hasn't locked. It's tumbled around itself and gone nowhere. The thing isn't locked.'

Dana made a quick note to ensure the window lock at Jensen's was forensically examined. She wrote it in Pitman so all Nathan could see were squiggles.

'The shorthand,' he observed. 'For security?'

'For speed, Mr Whittler. So I don't interrupt your flow. The locks?'

'I doctored particular window locks and door locks the first time I entered an establishment. Always more than one, in case one of them was discovered. Unless the person actually tried to open what they thought they'd just locked, they'd never catch on. If they did, they'd assume the lock was faulty, not rigged. It was pretty rare to return to a place and find they'd caught up. People are lazy, Detective Russo: especially when they only work there.'

'So when they locked up they'd hear the lock click and think it was secure, but you could open it up from the outside?'

He took a swig of water from the mug. There were beads of sweat on his upper lip.

'Exactly. They weren't really high-security places, were they? Most had no cameras, except perhaps by the cash machine or the checkout, and I never went near money. And they'd never notice anything was missing.'

He put the mug back on the table and touched the cap on the water bottle. The outside of the bottle was covered in condensation. Dana continued in Pitman and passed a tissue to him without looking. He wiped the bottle fastidiously, then folded the tissue four times and palmed it.

'Yes, Mr Whittler, I was particularly intrigued by that. I doubt anyone will turn out to have reported the stock loss.'

'Oh, there's an art to it, Detective. Firstly, people neither notice nor care if certain things go missing. They aren't expecting someone to take cans of peaches but leave the cash. So you're taking things that wouldn't be spotted immediately, if at all. Just like, if someone entered your home but only took a pencil, and some kitchen roll from under the sink, would you even recognise they'd been there? I doubt it.

'Secondly, you take from the back of the display or the shelf; only with things where there's plenty there already. Say there's fifty cans of beans, with a row of five at the front. You carefully take five from the back, leave the rest of the display untouched. You need to be careful of stains, markings in the dust, and so on. No one will ever spot it. By the time they've sold forty of them the cans have been replenished, moved around so the older cans are at the front, and so on. There's nothing for anyone to notice. Often, the items are displayed in a way that makes it easier – they're thrown into a wire basket or heaped up in a corner. You make a mental note of how the display looked and, as long as it looks like that when you're done, the shop won't realise.'

'Computerised stock control, bar codes?'

'Bar codes are usually only to get the correct price when you sell. Computerised stock control? Never saw any such systems out the back: I don't think many places had anything like that. If they did, they'd count them when they first unpacked them, I suppose. And they'd count each one when they sold it, I guess. But in between, there's a whole lot of nothing. At least, that's how it seemed to me.'

Dana tried to think the process through from Nathan's viewpoint; sneaking around a store in the darkness with a mental shopping list. 'But sometimes you'd need something that was right by the checkout, or there were only two on display. Surely?'

'Yes, occasionally. I tried to keep well stocked so I was only ever topping up. That meant I could afford to go without on one trip or another. Batteries, for example.'

He bit his lip before carrying on, as though betraying a confidence. 'But if there were, say, only two of something: I took one and placed the other on a different aisle. That way, the store would think that one of their dumber staff had put both in the wrong places, but they could only find one. It wouldn't occur to them that the other one had been stolen.'

She reminded herself that Nathan had had hundreds of hours to think this through in fine detail. 'Ingenious. No wonder we had no idea this was going on in a regular way. Or at all, for that matter.'

'It wasn't simply to avoid detection. Please don't get me wrong. I only took what I needed, when I needed it. I didn't want to damage the store. I hoped one man's needs, every few months, wouldn't kill their business.'

They both paused. The room became heavy; the heat was beginning to bite. Nathan took bigger swigs of the water. Sweat was beginning to form on the back of his hands. He seemed aware of the glow of his skin but apparently connected it with his emotions, not the temperature.

'You were ashamed of doing this, Mr Whittler.'

He pushed the palms of his hands into his eyes, and sniffed. 'Yes, I . . . yes. I was. Very much so. Horribly so.'

More gulps of water, and a deep breath. The increased temperature was working; making him rush and blurt, and feel obligated. 'The first few times, not so much, strangely. You might think I was mortified to begin with and gradually got used to it. In fact, it was the other way around. The first few times I was so focused on how to get in and out undiscovered I thought less about the morality. It was later on, when I was practised and somewhat skilled – when it was almost banal, usual – that I really felt the shame.'

He placed both palms on the table. 'I'm . . . I'm so sorry. For those people, the people I stole from. I'd never done anything like that before in my life, Detective. Never. It was not nice, to be dragged down to that level. To drag myself to that level.'

And that was the deepest cut, thought Dana. The guilt wasn't merely that he was robbing stores on a regular basis. It was the knowledge that he was deliberately leading a life that made that theft inevitable. It was the knowledge that he chose *and continued to choose* that life and never tried to change it: that would eat Nathan Whittler from the inside.

Had done so.

She couldn't allow this self-flagellation to continue. He would fall into a morass. Dana had seen that kind of spiral thinking, the circular drain of self-loathing. She'd seen it in a mirror. Felt it today, in fact. If he continued down this path, she'd lose his co-operation. Perhaps for the final time.

'You never tried to fish, Mr Whittler? Or grow things?'

She wondered if she'd framed the question diplomatically enough; whether he'd see it as an implied criticism.

Three tears stopped at his jowl, fading. Nathan tapped his fingertips together. 'Considered it. The main problems with fishing were being exposed, and actually eating it. I never saw edible fish in the pool by the cave. It doesn't have any weeds in the water – I suppose that's why. I would've needed to be out on the lake itself and I didn't want to risk being seen.'

He shook his head, as though replaying that very debate in his mind.

'Occasionally there were hikers; not just near the cave, but up on Dakota Ridge. Even if I wasn't recognised or bothered, the fact someone was fishing on that lake might lead others to try their luck there. I saw a few people try to fish on the far shore, but they didn't seem to catch anything and rarely came again.'

'And eating fish? Don't you like it?' she asked.

'Assuming I ever caught something. Well, for one, I'd have to gut a fish and prepare it properly. I might have acquired a book about that, I suppose. I would have been concerned about the risk of getting it wrong and poisoning myself. Disposing of the offal without attracting animals would have been one more chore. But mainly, I would have needed to cook it. I wouldn't risk a fire. So no; no fish for me unless it was already canned.'

Dana could understand his reasoning in refusing a fire. Cooking, not so much. Without being an expert, she thought a small gas camping stove wouldn't have made him more visible. At least it would have been warm food in winter. Clearly, once Nathan had a concept in his head, he followed through in a blinkered, linear fashion. All or nothing. According to Pringle, he'd always had that streak.

'And you mentioned the fire. That struck me in particular. You daren't risk any means of cooking?'

'No. I periodically considered gas: maybe a barbecue, or maybe constructing some kind of hearth from stones. But by then I was sort of used to it – the cold food. Any smoke, out there, Detective: it can be seen. I worried the rangers would always investigate smoke, in case it was the start of a major bush fire. In winter, it would be a dead giveaway that it was man-made and not some lightning strike. And you could spot the smoke from a plane, no problem. No, it was too risky. I only had to get it wrong once for the whole thing to fall apart. I couldn't experiment.'

'But that also meant you had no heat. Ever.'

He nodded. 'Pretty much. I'd made sure the sleeping bag was outstanding, though. And I did a decent job of stopping the damp rising to the mattress: raw wool is fantastic stuff, Detective, amazing. I did cheat a little: I had some pocket warmers for the very cold nights.

I could use them if I really felt my hands or feet were in serious danger of frostbite. But generally, no; heat and cooking were non-starters.'

'And no agriculture?'

'I tried a little. I mean, I was worried that someone from the air might spot a garden, as such. You know, I thought it would stand out from random nature to have man-made furrows and vegetation. I didn't want to give anyone a reason to hike out that way. But I attempted little efforts under trees or bushes. They either didn't take or animals ate them long before I could. Again, I didn't want to encourage wildlife, especially animals that might attract predators.'

'Thank you, Mr Whittler. I'm pretty certain we have everything we need on that score. I don't think we'll need to revisit it.'

'Detective.' Nathan gave no hint as to whether he'd found the latter admissions humiliating or cathartic. She realised she was too tired to read him well. She worried that, in the back of her mind, another panic might be forming. Sometimes, it was a self-fulfilling prophecy.

'Some more water for you, Mr Whittler.'

She waggled a bottle at him and he passed the empty one to her.

'Can I bring you anything else, when I return?'

He thought for a moment. 'No, thank you, Detective Russo. I'm okay for now.'

She sensed that he was mulling something over, something vital. But he wasn't ready to give it up yet. He needed to think through the ramifications, and she had to give him the space to do so.

Chapter 23

Mike stopped off at Custody when he returned to the station. He authorised Spencer Lynch's release, but schlepped on some gloves and played Spence's voicemail before releasing the lawyer's phone and personal effects. Four messages: three were banal crap from the office about upcoming cases and a charity dinner. The last – left six minutes after Mike left her mother's townhouse in Gazette – was from Megan Cassavette.

Hey Spence. Me. Just had that detective, Mike Something, here. I know he spoke to you before he turned up here. Uh, look, hang in there. Call me when you can. We need to talk. Miss you special. Bye.

Mike played it twice, listening the second time for the rhythm, intonation; what was said in the gaps. Megan had been deliberately neutral. There was no drama, no edge and no emotion in her voice. The last part sounded like the kind of saying two people shared. But she might have been ringing to arrange for a parcel delivery, the amount of emotion she put into it all. Very poised and very controlled for someone who became a widow nine hours ago, he decided.

Lucy was at the spare desk in Mike's office, sitting up very straight and looking triumphant.

'That's one happy Delaney,' said Mike as he came in.

She smiled. 'I love adding new strings to my bow. In fact, my bow is getting heavy and cumbersome, it has so many strings.'

Mike carefully placed his jacket on the back of his office chair, smoothing out any perceived wrinkles, and rubbed his eyes. 'You need a bow assistant to help carry your many and varied talents.'

'Ooh, a talent monkey. Yes, please.'

'Anything show on the employee interviews yet?'

'We're about two thirds through; notes are on the shared drive. Frankly, they're a sorry bunch of misfits, never-saw-nothings and people who remain startlingly unaware of everything around them.'

Mike took out his notebook and re-read the last two things he'd written: 'yes' and 'maybe nothing'.

'Megan's a catch, am I right?' Lucy looked at him from below her fringe.

'I'd say so. Did you see Lynch's interview?'

'I was behind the mirror the whole time. At least, until he mentioned the smart-meter thing. Then I had to get researching. He wasn't quite as much of an idiot as I first assumed. Not that he gets a free pass, or anything.' She mock-pouted.

'I know what you mean. I think we can take it that he's genuinely besotted with Megan. No mid-life crisis or quick liaison going on there.'

'Yeah, disappointingly lacking in sleaziness. You said you'd let him know what his tell was. You follow through with that?'

'Sure. Promise is a promise.'

'Wouldn't that compromise any future confrontation?'

'When you say "confrontation", you mean constructive dialogue? Unless we come up with something radical, there might not be another chat with the lovely Spence. Nah, it plants a double bluff. He doesn't really have much of a tell as such. Now he *believes* that blinking is his giveaway, he'll go absurdly over the top trying to hide it. Much as we try, it's a natural instinct to overcompensate. He'll think he's hidden it but the remedy will be obvious: like a drunk person trying to act sober. All the advantage would still be with me.'

Lucy smiled. 'What about his fingerprints in the store? What sayeth he on that score?'

'Ah, well. He claimed he went there eight days ago – had a mad moment where he wanted to see his rival. Then had an even madder moment where he contemplated talking to him. Some kind of man-to-man bull, or size him up, or whatever. Ended up realising how nuts that was, bought some chocolate and left.'

'You believe him?'

'I sort of do, actually. It's the kind of dumb thing you do when you're smitten. And I think when he stopped to think it through, and imagined Megan's face when he told her, it brought him up short. That rings true. Most of my dumb ideas can be stopped by me picturing Barb's face when I have to explain it. So yeah, in lieu of anything substantive against it – yeah.'

'Not all your dumb ideas, Mikey. Even Saint Barb's powers don't run that strong.'

'So show me the future, Luce. What can the brave new world of computerised billing tell us?'

Lucy eased her chair to one side, so that Mike could scuttle his across next to her. He checked the doorway before propelling himself across. 'I nearly hit someone doing this last week.'

'Mirror, signal, manoeuvre.'

They did their little fake battle for pole position, and bumped chairs.

'Okay,' she began, 'so this is a little freaky. That estate the Cassavettes live on? It's got a smart meter fitted in every home. Apparently the plan was to fit solar panels on each house, then the market tightened and they cut corners. Unheard of – a property developer not following through.'

Mike placed his hand on his heart. 'Once again, I physically cannot imagine that.'

Lucy grinned. 'So, the meters were partly to show the lucky householders how much income their panels were generating. Obviously, no longer needed for that, but these meters do so much more.' She opened a spreadsheet. 'You can set them up to read each socket – how much electricity is running through it, for how long, and when. If you programme it to know that socket A is the fridge, socket B is the television, etcetera, then you can see which appliance is on, and when. It's supposed to help you economise, and save the planet. But it's a nosy person's charter, if I'm honest.'

Mike stared at the spreadsheet but all he saw were boxes with tiny numbers in them. 'And that's bona fide evidence?'

'You mean can someone tamper with it? Well, I guess they could reconfigure what each socket meant: they could re-programme it to say socket B is a clock, not a television. But there'd be an audit trail if they do.' She tapped the keyboard to refresh. 'And the electric company – the very well-spoken Jason – assures me they haven't changed from the original settings.' Lucy turned to face Mike, her face sombre. 'I believe Jason. As you would.'

Mike nodded. 'I've never been lied to by Jason. He's good people. In fact, I've never been lied to by *any* Jason. It's an intrinsically trustworthy name. So what does the data say?'

'My new bestest friend Jason and I agree that the pattern the previous evening looks kosher. TV goes off just before midnight; so do the lights. Bedroom light the last to go off. Bathroom light is on for fifty-two seconds at 0314.'

Mike grimaced, then chuckled. 'You get to Lynch's age, that kind of goes with the territory. Let me see . . .' He ducked back a few pages in his notes, finding the timelines from his discussions with Megan and Lynch. 'Yeah, that fits with both of them claiming he arrived just before midnight and they went to bed.'

'See here? Or is that too small for you, old-timer?' Mike squinted. 'Two sockets running low level and briefly until 0030 – my buddy Jason says that's usually phone-charging. Here's where it gets really interesting.'

Lucy highlighted four columns in the spreadsheet, zoomed in and pointed at various cells. 'Lights on at 0522 – main bedroom, then main bathroom. Hot water in the bathroom 0523 to 0536. En suite lights 0527. Hot water in the en suite 0528 to 0537. Second socket in the en suite 0539 to 0543 – that'll be a hairdryer. Then, lights off upstairs, lights on downstairs. There's a kettle . . . and then a toaster. Only thing still on when Dana arrived was the kitchen light. And the data for after Dana arrives fits with her description of what happened: lights, coffee-making, and so on.' Lucy tapped a file in her in-tray. 'I have her notes here.'

Mike puffed his cheeks and sat back. He hadn't expected it to be so comprehensive, so definitive. Like the technology on phones and fitness devices, the level of data allowed rapid and detailed inferences about private lives. As a detective, it was extremely useful, but part of him was a little queasy about it.

'Jesus, Luce. That's uh, *fulsome*. Not to say Stasi-like.'

'I know, right? All they need now is a jam jar with your scent in it and they have the trifecta. If you don't deliberately sign against it, the electric company can see all this data. You know, so they can, uh, '*make sure you're on the best possible tariff*' and all.' Lucy tutted. 'I mean, it's spooky: worrying, in the wrong hands.' She laid a reassuring hand on his. 'It's fine with upstanding citizens like me and Jace, of course.'

'Of course. So we agree they couldn't have tampered with the actual meter itself – the recording mechanism?'

'Only by leaving a trail that would be pretty obvious. Jason says the settings haven't been touched since they were originally created, a week after the Cassavettes moved in. Apparently, that's fairly common – set and forget.'

'Yeah,' replied Mike. 'I sometimes don't bother to change the clock in the car when it's daylight-saving time. Just do the calculation in my head for six months. So I can relate.'

He looked to Lucy, and was embarrassed at her mouthing *you old man*.

'But,' he continued, 'if they can't tamper with the recordings, then . . .'

'Way ahead of you. Here's how they could do it.' She leaned forward and pulled up the reports from other teams that morning. 'Search team says there's no burglar alarm in the Cassavette house, and the clocks by the bed, judging from the search photos, are battery-powered. Door-to-door says Lynch parks round the back of the property, next to some waste ground. So it's possible to leave the house and drive to the store without leaving a trail of smart meter, lights or any CCTV between one place and the other.'

'No cameras at all?' Mike had hoped that a second sweep might have found at least one that faced the road. Even something that identified the car type, if not a number plate, might have been effective leverage face to face.

'There is . . . *there are* some in homes along the route, but none that has any view of the road. They all face the houses, or face inwards from the electric gate to show the visitor's face. So, effectively, no. It's ten kilometres – seven minutes if you're busting it through the backroads – from that edge of Earlville to Jensen's Store. Dana did the exact route on the way back from Megan's and timed it, clever girl.'

'All right – Lynch or Megan could have got to the crime scene and back unhindered. But how would they fool the Stasi-meter?'

Lucy sat back a little to explain. 'So they get up – in the dark – at 0500. They know not to switch on the lights. No burglar alarm to switch off, no electric clock with a spurt of power when it wakes them up. So far, so good. One of them – let's say Lynch, but it could be either of them – slips out in darkness, into the car and over to the store. Megan stays in the dark until 0522, then she starts switching on lights and showers in both bathrooms, as if they're both there.'

'That's feasible.' Mike joined fingertips in a prayer motion. 'Pray continue your bold narrative, madam.'

'Lynch does the business, gets back by 0545, has breakfast with his lover and toddles off to the gym, where he has the shower they pretended he took earlier. Maybe ditches any bloodied clothes along the way. Megan is about to wash the tell-tale sheets when Dana shows up.'

'Ah. If one of them is the killer, and they're hiding their activities, why not put the sheets in the wash earlier? Why leave evidence that Lynch has, uh, stayed over?'

Lucy thought for a moment. It was a reasonable question. If the couple were being so forensically aware, and wanted to keep Lynch's presence a secret if they could, why not wash the sheets straight away?

'Because . . . Dana's there earlier than they expected.' Lucy was thinking it through. 'They thought Lou would only be found when the shop staff arrived, not before. Which would be around 0730. Lou was discovered about two hours earlier than the killer would have anticipated. We found the body thanks to the silent alarm at Jensen's Store. Maybe Megan doesn't know the ins and outs of the store's alarm system. Perhaps she thought it would be switched off since Lou was inside the store: she didn't realise Lynch would be setting it off.'

'Assuming he did set it off.' Mike tapped his pen against the corner of the desk, until he sensed it was driving Lucy up the wall. 'That bit – the entry into the store – is still the trickiest bit for me. We're assuming Megan knew little about the security in that store, but that might not be entirely true. I mean, she co-signed the loans that paid for it, she co-owns the store, she's still talking to Lou. Maybe he updated her each time he ramped up the security.'

They sat for a second.

'Dana,' they both stated at once.

'We need to talk to Dana,' said Mike.

'She's in with Whittler again,' said Lucy. 'Explaining how his lovely little cavern is being sullied. He might be sulking and refusing to speak by now. Let's check.'

Chapter 24

Dana closed the door on Nathan. What she really wanted now was what she couldn't get: an hour by herself in a darkened room with no noise and no people. She could feel she was near the edge. Her thinking was becoming ragged and distracted, buffeting from idea to idea; not fully taking in what was said, or how it was said. It was a warning sign: this time she'd had to finish talking with Nathan because *she* was exhausted, not because he was too drained to continue. She needed to be better than this, she told herself; had to be sharper. If she couldn't grab that hour, she'd have to make do with a ten-minute island: drinking in some deep breaths, she texted Father Timms, requested a meet outside the station.

The investigation had accelerated: she had to run at the same pace.

Back in her office, she re-checked the canisters in her drawer and tapped her pocket. This time, she remembered to fish out her mobile and switch it on. Three messages from Stu.

First, he'd requested heavy-duty back-up machinery for tomorrow to help him sweep the cave and surrounding area. As per Dana's instructions, he'd be the only one inside the cave: she was keeping her promise to Nathan.

Second, he'd pushed Forensics on the knife.

Third, she should check her email: knife details.

The email from Forensics was perfunctory. The store carried more fingerprints than brands of lollies. Twenty-five sets of fingerprints identified, including staff members and customers on police file. Seventy-seven sets with no identification in the system. A full list of current idents had been sent through to Mike and Lucy earlier, before Mike tackled Spencer Lynch.

Dana considered the implications. Mike and Lucy would have already cross-referenced the twenty-five against anyone knowing Lou or Megan or potentially involved in the case. That would narrow down the numbers considerably; it would be their responsibility to chase any emerging leads. The seventy-seven were a worry: the killer could be among them, and already had half a day's start. He or she might be across the country, or overseas, by now. If the killer wasn't anyone they already knew existed, the possibilities blew out exponentially. The investigation would be weeks and months, maybe years. She shuddered.

Blood on the knife in question matched Lou Cassavette's type: but nearly forty per cent of humanity was also A+. DNA to come in a day or two, but not even conjecture at this point. There were no fingerprints of any kind on the blade or handle. Any drops of blood from the blade when it came out of the wound had been smeared by the body falling to the floor, therefore there was no blood trail to indicate how the knife came to be under the freezer. Skittled there inadvertently was most likely but, pending further reports, impossible to prove at this point.

Dana had spent half the day waiting to find the knife, assuming it would be a major turning point. Some cases squirmed out of reach that way – killer facts turned out not to be so killer, while minor points eventually became crucial. This case was one of those. Almost certainly, the knife they had was the murder weapon: that alone indicated the killing was improvised, in the sense that someone pulled a knife from a packet in the store. It demonstrated a lack of overt planning to kill. But beyond that, it still didn't prove who. And *why* remained the biggest question in her mind.

She was missing something she shouldn't miss. And she knew it.

There was a knock on her door and two heads poked around, one above the other, in *Scooby-Doo* style. Mike and Lucy had emerged from their office. It was possible they'd caught the latest interview with Nathan from the CCTV feed.

'Thelma and Freddy! Come in, guys. How'd it go with Lynch?'

'I don't like being Freddy,' pouted Mike as they entered. 'He was impossibly camp, always wore a *cravat*, for crying out loud, and he never solved anything.'

'Yes, all true.' Dana shrugged. 'He was outperformed by a brainless dog. Your only other option is Shaggy, though; I can't see you eating a sandwich taller than your upper body. Or saying "zoinks".' She tapped her pen against the desk. 'On the other hand, Freddy got to drive the van; and I'm pretty sure he ended up in bed with Daphne, in the raunchy adults-only sequel they never made. So, you know, all good in the end.'

Mike remained unconvinced. 'Still . . . I never sit with my back to a bookcase. And I don't trust janitors, managers of old mines, or fairground owners.'

Lucy sniggered behind a fist.

'Okay,' said Mike. 'Lynch? He opened up pretty well; he has motive, and he knows the place. But I kinda believe his answers, oddly enough. I went to see Megan after; checked up on some of the things Lynch had claimed. They pretty much corroborate each other, but their alibi is still flimsy.'

'Crap.'

On the one hand, Dana wanted Megan and Lynch to be cleared

unequivocally, so she could put all her thought into unravelling Nathan. However, Nathan's motivation was mystifying.

Lucy added her news. 'When I cross-reffed the list of fingerprint idents from the store, guess who came up? Spencer Lynch.'

'Spence blustered about having a brain snap,' added Mike. 'Visited the store intending to check Lou out, then bottled it. Megan apparently had no idea he'd ever been there.'

Every time Dana was preparing to concede that Megan had no part to play, something cropped up that put her somewhere near the frame.

'What's your take, Mikey?'

'I think, reluctantly, he might be telling the truth. His fingerprint was there, but partially smudged with another from a store employee, which supports his claim that his visit was last week, and not this morning. Megan's surprise seemed genuine: I think she'd made it clear Spence wasn't to do that, and, uh, his job was to agree and obey.' Mike shook his head. 'That's how I see their dynamic, too, by the way. He's more educated, but she's smarter. He's older, but she holds the reins.'

'Yes, that tallies with everything I've seen and heard so far. She has – *had* – two equally grateful men in her life: now she has the one she apparently wants. Yet, so far, I can't see the whole jealousy motive quite sticking.'

Dana was suddenly hungry. Adrenaline made her feel over-caffeinated and shaky. She indicated the stairs towards the canteen. As they ascended, Lucy updated Dana about the smart meter and what it might mean. Dana cursed herself for not mentioning it at the briefing – it had taken Spencer's alibi claim for it to resurface. Another slip that others had thankfully caught. Another indication that the Day was stealing her professional expertise. She'd spent longer, she calculated, vomiting behind a building than she had thinking about the smart meter as an alibi.

'Jeez, I'm hopeless today, Luce. Megan mentioned that this morning. Ages ago. I should have told you, even if I didn't share at the briefing. We could be hours into that if I'd concentrated.'

Lucy waved a hand. 'Ah, I'm a woman ahead of her time. So I've caught us up. No harm, no foul. Besides, I'm not happy with it,' Lucy continued. 'It looks like it's providing an alibi but it's possible to fool it.'

They paused at the top floor, Dana out of breath and tweaking her kneecap. 'I hear you. So, as an alibi, it's weak. In which case, the other evidence becomes more weighty. We need full value on the will and the other paperwork. At least that might help us decide if they had enough motive.'

Dana's phone went: Rainer. Mike mimed swilling coffee and went ahead. Lucy skulked on the landing while Dana took the call.

'Uh huh, okay. Good, that's one less thing to worry about. And definitely not last night? Right, right. Yes, start on that. Hospital records, too. There's something there, I'm sure of it. *Danke*.'

'So international right now,' Lucy grinned. 'Spanish and German on the same day?'

'I'm a global village. Rainer found the red-hair source for Lou's sleeping bag. One of the girls who works shifts at Jensen's. Uses the store as a rendezvous because her parents consider her boyfriend a bad influence. Apparently, the alarm code is so widely known it's useless. But the redhead wasn't there last night – at a concert interstate and definitely got back this morning.'

Lucy folded her arms and tapped one foot against the other. 'So no evidence Lou was cheating?'

'Absolutely zero. Which makes me feel pretty crappy now. I jumped into suspecting him because he's not as good-looking as his wife. Clearly, being the cuter of the two should have made her more likely to be the cheater.'

There was something underpinning Dana's comment. Lucy thought of pursuing it but bit her tongue and instead said, 'Rainer was smart about it. There were three redheads on the employee list I gave him. He rang Forensics and double-checked if the red hair was natural or dyed, then tried the youngest first, because she had the pale skin and freckles to go with it. He's a bright spark.'

'He is,' replied Dana as they came through the canteen doors. 'Might be able to find him a secondment, or something.'

Dana's mind was still on the potential to fake alibis. It meant she couldn't drop Megan or Spencer Lynch as suspects. Like Mike, she hadn't fully appreciated what technology could do to place people at particular times and locations. The public sometimes seemed to imagine the police had an infinite array of databases that placed everyone to the minute and to the millimetre: the curse of television, she presumed. They forgot that the police had no such thing; and that even if they did the data might be unreliable, insufficient, out of date, manipulated or contradictory. In short, it would need checking out.

All the same, the smart meter appeared to Dana to be a viable resource. But Lucy was adamant that the smart meter was as much a red herring as proof: it could provide false assurance without the data itself being doctored.

The cloud was now low and glowering, threatening heavy rain later in the day. Dana's knee felt better for the walk, despite the stairs. She checked she still had the nebuliser in her pocket.

They grabbed a table by the window. The canteen had once been split into a highly civilised senior officers' lounge, and a scrappy set of tables and chairs for the grunts. Bill had the divide ripped out in his first week, cementing his reputation as Billy Win-Win. Now they all shared the scratchy plastic chairs, smeared cutlery and wobbly tables. One wall was lined with the photos of fallen comrades, another with posters for an upcoming three-legged race for charity. From the sublime, to ridiculous.

The canteen was on the third floor, high enough to see beyond the outbuildings and most treetops to the horizon. In the west the stacks of the smelter punched the skyline. At night, they took on a science-fiction hue; all hulking metal, warning lights and billowing vapour. By day, even from this distance, they looked like rusty, clattering steam-punk: a relic from another era.

'How're you holding up?'

Lucy managed to look at Dana without staring or demonstrating pity.

'Uh, hangin' on grimly. Like most days.' Dana puffed her cheeks. 'Well, not great, as you can imagine, but I haven't got long to get through now. Break it down into bite-size pieces, I guess. Thanks for asking. I'm all right. Really.'

In truth, all the decay was taking place under the surface, like a rivet below a ship's waterline. Everything in daylight looked okay; normal and survivable, somehow. In the deep, it was dark and everything was unravelling.

Lucy took off her shoe and massaged a heel. 'The interview with Whittler. We only caught the second half of it, of course, but I don't think that went entirely as you planned.'

'No, I was braced for more conflict than I got. Not sure if I'm happy with that or not. There's something big behind the dam, waiting to burst it. I'd rather Whittler was letting the water out a bit at a time.'

'Did he give in after you told him we'd found the cave? I was expecting a battle royal.'

Dana nodded, angry at herself for misjudging the strategy so badly. 'So was I. So was Bill, for that matter. We mis-calibrated. In fact, we were way off.'

She paused, sifting through the recollection in her mind.

'When he acquiesced so quickly it threw me off balance. I had to give too much of myself to get the information I did get: that's a bad long-term tactic for me. We're still on the edge here, Luce: he could shut up – or lawyer up – and I don't think we have a lot of options if he does. So I have to be right, all the time. But Whittler did shout at me, which he hasn't done before. Or, sort of at me. Shouted at his feet. But all his anger seemed to last about three minutes.'

'Why?'

Dana glanced at Lucy and smiled wearily. 'Why did I get it wrong? Ha, I get things wrong all day.'

Lucy laid a placating hand on Dana's then withdrew it. Dana fizzed at the contact. 'No, I mean why did he run out of anger so quickly? I had him down as a monumental grudge-bearer.'

And you'd know, thought Dana, recalling Lucy's lacerating phone call to Spencer Lynch.

'True. Well, in part, Whittler's no good at arguing. Can't do it. Probably never has. I bet he's either caved in – see what I did there – or withdrawn, over every argument he's ever had. The bigger the battle, the more he's pushed to extremes.' She felt a moment from earlier was calling to her: relevant and important but out of reach. 'Something major tipped him into running and hiding for fifteen years.'

Lucy raised an eyebrow. 'But he can't run here. He's got to face it.'

'Exactly. He has to react in some way, in front of me.' Dana sat forward and concentrated. 'I think you only have major arguments with two sets of people. One, someone you really care about: like couples who fight but know the underlying relationship is rock-solid. Then you can tee-off and really vent, knowing the basic mutual respect makes it a freebie. Or two, if you really don't give a crap about the other person. Then you can say what you like because you don't care how that makes the other person feel.'

'But . . . Whittler is kind of in between with you?'

'Precisely so. He has enough respect for me that he reins in his rage. He can't cut loose at me – he'd find it unforgivable. Assuming he knows how, of course. But equally, he doesn't know me well enough to become angry and still be certain he's not losing a relationship. Such as it is. Being caught in the middle like that, plus his lack of match practice, made it a pretty weedy effort at getting enraged.'

Lucy shielded her eyes from the low sun, which now flashed from below a sharp edge of graphite cloud. 'So when he's put on the spot, he's weak?'

Dana considered if that was quite the right word. Nathan was open to persuasion in some ways and utterly immovable in others. It wasn't accurate to sum it up with 'weak'; it was more nuanced than that.

'He can be . . . compliant. That's what I'd call it. If he can't run away – or run away inside his head by shutting up – he turns biddable; stubborn in some respects, but submissive. I suspect, to some extent, he's always been that way.'

'So what was the incident that made him leave home and find the cave?'

Dana shook her head. 'Don't know. We're inching towards it, but not there yet. It's a question for my next session with him.'

'I need caffeine. Want some?' Lucy slid on her shoe, grabbing the strap as she squeezed her foot back in.

'Just water, thanks. Actually, can you get two bottles, please? I'll give one to Whittler. Thank you.'

Lucy stood up as Mike arrived. They'd agreed a few minutes ago that they'd need to tag-team Dana. She was showing her obvious signs of people-exhaustion, and one-on-ones were now generally preferable. They surreptitiously low-fived as they passed.

Mike slid a bar of chocolate across to her. 'There you go. Dark chocolate's good for you, apparently.'

'Thank you.' Dana smiled, peeled the wrapping and broke off a corner. It felt luxurious and smooth on the tongue. Her mind snapped to the sunrise, and she had to wrench it back to the present before Mike noticed. 'Hmm. Anti-oxidants. The science is on my side. *Gracias*, Mikey.'

'*De nada, gringo.*' Mike took a bite of sandwich: half of the contents squeezed out of the side. 'Saw bits of that discussion with Whittler. If nothing else, we've cleared up lots of burglaries we didn't know existed.'

'Over two hundred. So the crime rate'll go up, but so will the solves. Makes Bill happy, I suppose. One for his "proactive media stance", I'd think. But here's something I don't get, Mikey. Three people: Lou, Megan and Spencer Lynch. I'm guessing Lynch thinks Megan's a better person than he is?'

Mike nodded. 'And Megan said Lou was a better person than her. Said he had a moral compass she didn't have.'

'Okay. All of which puts Lou top of the ethical pile, right? The most righteous and upstanding of the three. Yet he's the one who's dead.'

'No one said life was fair.'

'True. But I find it ironic.'

'It's more than ironic, though. It's likely. Murder's inherently immoral – or amoral. It's logical, then: it would usually be committed by the less moral against the more moral. Wouldn't it?'

Mike had a point, she thought. 'You think Lynch did it? Sneaked out early morning and stabbed Lou?' It didn't make sense to her, but it was a point she had to follow: they couldn't blindly focus on Nathan. 'Then Whittler shows up, entirely separately, to burgle the place. Instead, he's clutching at Lou's blood when the torches find him?'

Mike shook his head between mouthfuls. 'Would imply that Megan was some kind of femme fatale. Can't see Lynch getting out of *her* warm bed on a cold morning, driving to the store and stabbing her husband, all off his own bat. It would need her connivance, her encouragement. Or, at the very least, her tacit approval.'

She thought back to her own discussion with Megan – the sense that Megan was not aware of quite how much she could control others with her looks, her smile, or the withdrawal of a smile. 'Think she's capable of that? Think it's likely?'

'I think she's capable of it, if she had a mind to. By which I mean she's attractive enough that getting what she wants is usually possible. I imagine there's men Megan could persuade, no problem. She isn't vampish, or anything like that. Just someone men would like to please. She has a low-level fatal appeal.'

Oh, thought Dana, *you named my indefinable impression of her*. 'Low-level fatal appeal. Yes. Interesting description.'

Dana counted off her reasoning on her fingers. 'So, Megan's smart enough to think of the plan. Clever enough to run a trick with the bathrooms to provide an apparently bullet-proof alibi. Hot enough to make a man's ethics run cold.' She didn't notice Mike's grin at the turn of phrase. 'And there's motive: she wants out, but the divorce is tricky to prosecute.'

Mike sat back. 'All truc. But firstly, I don't think she's minded to do that. You thought she underestimated her own charm, didn't you? I agree. Megan understands she's very attractive but doesn't quite know she has that power, or what she might do with it. She thinks all the usual rules apply to her, even though they probably wouldn't. Plus, I think she genuinely liked Lou. I can't see her poised over a cauldron, wishing curses on to him.'

He considered how Megan had opened his eyes to the complexities of leaving a marriage that was also a business partnership. 'Third, if she was that ruthless about getting rid of Lou, she'd have walked out and left him to lose the business. This possible investor seems to have been a bust: Lou would go belly-up.'

Dana snapped another two squares of chocolate. 'Yes, true, there's that. Plus, the burglar alarm data for the store shows it wasn't off at any point before 0530, when it was switched off by the officers. The alarm covers the perimeter, not internal movement. So how would Lynch have gained entry? The data suggests the only time anyone came into the store in any way was when Whittler climbed through the window.'

Mike offered a hypothetical, solely so she could shoot it down. 'Unless it was Lynch who opened the window – which we now know was unlocked – and committed the crime. Then Whittler, a couple of minutes later, comes through the same window. The alarm's already notified the station – Whittler doesn't affect it. If Lynch closed the window behind him when he came in, it would've appeared to Whittler as unopened. Whittler would be none the wiser.'

She countered. 'I don't see how *Lynch* would know which window, or that the window was unlocked. Whittler said it looked locked and would seem locked when you last turned the key.'

Dana didn't like the messiness of who knew about the locks. It was too difficult to pin down and she liked her cases when the logic flowed consistently. 'Unless Megan knew,' she went on, 'and told Lynch which window to use. In which case, surely Lou would have known as well and it all breaks down.' She shrugged. It was too convoluted to seem credible, relied on too much secret knowledge and coincidence. 'Leaving that stuff about the locks aside, there's a "but" coming, right?'

'But – I still don't see it. Megan and Lynch want to be together. They can do that easily, but they'd screw up Lou's business. Sure it's tricky, it's awkward; probably slower and messier than they'd want. But they're two intelligent people, and one is a lawyer with twenty years' experience of exactly this thing. I think they'd have waited it out and worked it out.'

'So you don't see enough of a motive?'

'No. No, I don't.' He paused. 'I do see Whittler, with a knife, in the dark.'

He was right, thought Dana. They could run around in circles trying to prove or disprove the potential to fix an electric meter; they could play at the margins of divorce settlements; they could check wills and bank accounts; they could trade hypotheticals about window locks; they could look for a money-launder gone awry; they could do what they liked. In the end, someone had to have wanted to stab Lou Cassavette. Lynch and Megan didn't really have a reason. But then, neither did Nathan. There was no evidence he even knew who Lou was, let alone had met him.

No one had a motive for this murder.

Lucy returned with an apple and two bottles of water. She pointed and gave a cartoonish disapproving look at the half-consumed bar of chocolate.

Dana looked contrite. 'You're probably wondering why I'm eating this, Luce.'

Chocolate guilt was the worst. Lucy put on a pout. 'After I brought you those lovely sandwiches from the garage; a byword locally for cordon-bleu cuisine.'

Dana took another bite of 70 per cent cocoa, fair trade. 'Appreciate the effort, Luce. But it was hard to tell where the packaging ended and the sandwich began.'

Mike spoke up. 'I have a problem, ladies.'

Lucy beat Dana to the reply. 'Admitting it is the first step, Mikey. Let me see . . . it won't matter if she really loves you. That reassure you? Barb sees all; Barb forgives all.'

Mike gave a theatrical thumbs-up and shook her hand. 'Thank you, wise laydee. By the way, Barb does not forgive all. The Christmas Present Debacle of 2005 proves that.' He raised a finger. 'I have a second problem. Why didn't Whittler, or whoever, grab the biggest knife? Doesn't make sense.'

Dana cursed herself. She'd noted that back at the crime scene, but hadn't given it a second thought since. Stuart had needed to remind her about chasing forensics; Lucy and Rainer were catching balls she'd dropped all day. Dana felt she was skating by, getting away with it because she was making progress each time she faced Nathan. Not organised enough, she told herself. Not on top of it.

'I haven't fathomed that either,' she said. 'Let's assume it's Whittler for the moment. Maybe he only wanted the threat. I mean, we're guessing Cassavette's blocking his path to the window. Whittler's a burglar, not an assassin. He doesn't want to hurt the guy but he needs to escape.'

'So?' asked Mike.

'So he grabs a knife that's big enough to be a credible warning. It says he's a threat to Cassavette. He can hurt him; he's *prepared* to hurt him.' Dana shrugged. 'A little knife – maybe Cassavette thinks Whittler isn't serious, or thinks he can take him down.'

'Yeah,' agreed Lucy. 'Cassavette's a tall, chunky guy – way bigger than Whittler. The knife would need to be large enough to be intimidating, something that can do damage.'

Mike pursued it. 'Still, why not the biggest one? That's even more intimidating.'

'Yes, true.' Dana tried to picture it in her head. She couldn't frame the image: Nathan with a knife. He'd baulked at a mousetrap to scare off a rakali, for Christ's sake. Surely Nathan would only want a knife for the shock value, the threat? 'Maybe the biggest blade ups the ante too far. It says, "We're on. This is it. Fight Club." '

She could see Mike wasn't convinced, and she wasn't entirely sold herself. But this was what they did: bounce ideas.

'The knife Whittler chose is the Goldilocks weapon,' she continued.

'It's too big to be some kind of idle boast – it's not a kiddie knife. But it's not so big it's too much peril and makes Cassavette feel he has no choice but to fight. Instead, it makes Cassavette wary, but maybe not desperate enough to start the battle. Because all Whittler wants the knife to do is intimidate; get Cassavette out of the road so Whittler can run.'

Mike sat back. 'That's a lot of clear-headed, logical thinking going on if he's a panicking burglar who wants out. Panic and darkness make everything instinctive, primeval. All that thinking seems too rational for that situation.'

Dana nodded. 'That's because it is. Good shout.'

The three were silent for a minute, Dana finishing her chocolate. Now Mike had raised the question of why that knife had been chosen, it was bugging her. If he hadn't mentioned it, she'd probably have forgotten until tomorrow.

'Wait, I've got an idea,' said Lucy. 'All this is speculation. I've got an idea based on what we actually know.'

'Which is?' Dana and Mike in chorus.

'The food on the shelves.' Lucy presented this as if it spoke for itself, sitting back with a satisfied expression.

'What?' asked Dana. Her eyes narrowed. 'Assume, in a wild and unlikely scenario, we don't know what you're talking about.'

'No, think back to Whittler's cave.' Lucy bounced forward again, animated. 'I saw Stu's footage on the shared drive. That cave is Whittler's personality in three dimensions, right? He used OCD, deliberately, to keep his mind from wrecking him. Checked stocks over and over, every day; those lists in his journal are positively weird. All to give his mind work to do. He said that himself, in fact. It's ingrained now; hard-wired. He can't stop. Those cans in the cave – perfect pyramids; threes and fives, no fours. Even the junk in the interview room today – he stacks it in a tower, he cleans up; it's neat, balanced. That's what he does. Because that's what he *is*.'

Lucy leaned in close to Dana, almost whispering. 'So he took the middle knife . . . because it's the middle knife.'

It felt like a dull thud in Dana's chest, as though Lucy had struck her with the heel of her hand. 'Oh God, you're right.' She nodded. 'Taking that one leaves two either side of the space – the balance is still there.'

It was Nathan, she thought: it was definitely Nathan. It had always been Nathan. Now she felt certain.

'Wait, wait,' said Mike. 'He'd do that in the dark? In an emergency?'

'Especially then,' replied Dana. 'Like you said, Mikey, he panicked – he thought the place would be empty. He needs to get out, needs his escape route. He's not thinking, as such, it's all instinct. So he grabs a pack of knives and opens it. The patterns he's ingrained over fifteen years; they make him do things automatically. Preserving symmetry is automatic.'

She scrunched the chocolate wrapper. 'It's not the third-smallest knife, or the third-biggest. It's the *middle one of five*. And that's all.'

Chapter 25

After collecting her thoughts in her office and texting Father Timms again, Dana joined the other three in Mike's office and doled out some more chases for the team. Paperwork was starting to pile up on the spare desk, which now doubled as the physical repository for shared documents for the team. Dana liked the growing evidence that they might be getting somewhere. In a digital world, she still took comfort in rising towers of filing. She began with Rainer.

'Rainer, please carry on with the checks for the period leading up to Whittler leaving. There must be something in some official record somewhere.'

He nodded, but she paused. *Losing it, again.*

'Sorry, Rainer, that's vague and unhelpful. Okay. First, I need to know if or when the parents' finances changed – sudden loan, change of will, power of attorney, selling off property, transfer of deeds, setting up a business, that kind of thing. Anything that looks like a trigger for Whittler running, or the outcome from a trigger. Second: any reports of disturbance at their home or work: illness, any intelligence connecting them with emergency or social services. The parents appear to have had some, uh, old-fashioned values. Thank you. Good work on the redhead, by the way.'

Rainer scribbled notes but then raised his pen. 'Thanks. I was wondering – does it have to be a one-off event we're looking for? I know Whittler went off at a bad time of the year and that's why we're thinking there's a precipitating event. But I'm wondering if it was simply the straw that broke the camel's back. Whittler's boss thought there was a problem building up for some time. I mean, it could have been long-term and one more tiny incident made him think it would never stop.'

Dana considered. Given Nathan's pliability under duress, she still felt there had been one overriding event: something Nathan couldn't stomach, something he knew would lead to disaster. Otherwise, he'd surely have continued to silently acquiesce or suffer. But Rainer had a point – perhaps it could have been cumulative.

'Yes, you may well be right. I was thinking bullying from the parents, perhaps. They had that stern, ultra-religious lifestyle. Maybe the Bible-bashing was choking Whittler. Or his brother. Speaking of whom?'

She turned to Lucy.

'Jeb texted he was coming straight here. Depends on the traffic.'

Lucy clicked on a company webpage. It was Dana's first look at Jeb. She was surprised he looked nothing like Nathan. 'I looked him up,' continued Lucy. 'Import/export. Mainly steel assembly kits: instant warehouses, hangars, that sort of thing. Apparently, he's rolling in it. Spooky guy in the photos, though: not someone to bump into on a dark night.'

Dana stared at the screen. Again, her inner radar pinged without signalling why. Further evidence that she was off her game and sliding downhill.

'Okay, Mikey and Luce. I want to wrap up Megan and Lynch if I can. After our little chat about the knife, I'm more certain it isn't them. Plus, we haven't broken that alibi and their motive looks insubstantial. But let's ensure due diligence on the paperwork.' Dana looked at the ceiling while she worked out what was needed. 'Please complete the audit trails on the telephones and banking. Check the exact ownership of Jensen's Store and its contents. Anything else you can think of that might suggest a motive. If we tie all that with a bow, we can at least park it until I've exhausted the chatter with Whittler. I want to be able to focus on him and not have any other options in my mind today. Mikey: if Jeb arrives while I'm prepping, or in interview with Whittler, can you take first crack at him? Thank you.'

Mike nodded, and Dana took that not only as an acceptance of her instructions but also affirmation that she'd asked for the correct action. She had no doubt he'd have suggested something else if he felt it was required. She relied on it.

'One current line of inquiry,' said Mike. 'You'll recall Cassavette is an old school friend of Miguel Alvarez, the king of money laundering for the Alvarez drug empire. Turns out Lou has an accountant who's prominent in Miguel's A-team of people who can make money disappear. I've got someone checking if there's any actual connection.'

Dana frowned. Now she was thinking it was an unnecessary distraction from focusing on Nathan. She had to rein herself in: this was a viable alternative theory and she should welcome the chance to bottom it out. It would almost certainly be raised by a competent defence counsel. More evidence her thinking was crumbling under the pressure of the Day.

'You're thinking his store might be a front? Or this Miguel might have wanted it to be, and Lou turned him down?' She couldn't picture it, but that didn't mean it couldn't happen. She'd spent half her life learning – the hard way – that she knew almost nothing about anyone, really.

'Maybe.' Mike paused, noting the stress on Dana's features. 'Actually, I'm thinking Whittler did it. But I'm covering the money-laundering base. More to follow.'

Dana nodded. Anxiety and exhaustion were starting to bubble.

'Okay. Next interview, I'm going to tackle Whittler about that precipitating event: what made him leave home? I think we have all we need from him about his cave and the burglaries. We can tie up the rest with forensics from the cave. Stuart's emailed me. He's closing it down at the cave for the day; running out of daylight, and he was part of the search team at dawn in Jensen's. I want Stu fresh for tomorrow, to start with the heavy search grid and the indexing. Mikey – can you liaise with Stu from now on? Just keep me up to date with anything unusual emerging from that. Thanks.'

Lucy coughed. 'Don't forget, Whittler doesn't know his parents are gone. If it was me, I'd end up blurting it out without intending to . . .' Dana knew Lucy was too smart to do such a thing; it was a diplomatic reminder. She tilted her head to acknowledge it.

'He doesn't, does he? Good catch, Luce. Okay, I'll have a quick chat with Bill, then back in the ring.'

Bill Meeks' office had a camera and audio feed from each interview room direct to his desktop, so he'd witnessed the previous interview with Whittler. He still thought it hilarious to call the access his 'window of opportunity'. Dana smiled each time he said it: not because it was funny, but because his puppyish amusement about it was funny.

'Two hundred-plus burglaries?' Bill mimed touching something hot. 'We needed those detections – this month has been a bust. Plus, charging him with those gets us another twenty-four hours without having to charge or release on the homicide. Speaking of which . . .' Bill leaned forward. 'You pushed Whittler about getting a lawyer *before* he spilled his guts on the burglaries.'

'Yes, yes . . . about that.' Dana shifted uncomfortably in her chair, unsure whether Bill wanted to reprimand her, or thank her. It was a sign, she felt, of her increasing weariness that she couldn't tell.

'So, several reasons. First: whatever we think he's done, and however strange he may seem, he's a vulnerable person. I think we always need to bear that in mind. The court certainly will; we need to regularly show good faith, in my opinion. Second, I knew he was about to confess to two hundred crimes: we had the journal and he was only confirming what we knew. I didn't want a subsequent defence to claim he was manipulated because he didn't have support. I told him to get a lawyer and he expressly refused: I wanted us to have that transparent indemnity. Third, I need him to trust me. Especially after telling him about finding his cave, I had some bridges to build. I think that helped to build them. That's why I only pushed for enough details to confirm the journal. He was pleased not to have to dwell too much on something that was humiliating. So I won back some trust. Was my thinking. Boss.'

He broke into a smile. 'And mine.' He sat back again and she breathed out. 'You're right. He thinks you have his welfare at heart. He thinks you're his only buddy in a world that's let him down.'

It seemed to Dana that everyone was patting her on the back for pretending to like Nathan and care about him just to open him up. Which would make her what? A liar? An actor? A hypocrite? Whichever; she wouldn't want to look in the mirror. And it made her wonder about how Machiavellian her colleagues thought she was; how inauthentic and calculating she appeared to them.

'Well,' she replied, 'I'm about to burst what bubble he has. We're going to talk about why he left home, and why then. Which means it'll probably come out about his parents. Maybe we should prep for that.'

She wasn't surprised that Bill was way ahead of her. 'I've asked the doc to be ready. We should re-check anyway on Whittler's fitness for interview: it's coming up on ten hours in custody. And Whittler's going straight back to the Lecter Theatre after this interview. I still want uniform watching him, with a ten-minute signature log. Agreed?'

'Totally.'

'What about this possible Alvarez connection?' asked Bill. 'Think that has legs?'

No, she thought, *I don't. I'm all in on Nathan Whittler now, even though I probably shouldn't be.*

'Possible. Lou certainly knew Miguel Alvarez, by all accounts, and corner stores and restaurants are the preferred washing machines for bad cash. Mikey has someone at Central digging deeper.'

Bill tilted his head. 'How're you doing with all this, Dana?'

She could feel herself blush: pastoral questions made her self-conscious. 'Uh, fine. Bit tired, but we're gradually clearing impediments. Mikey's emailing you updates about Megan Cassavette and the lawyer, Spencer Lynch.'

'Piece of work, Lynch, isn't he?'

Surprisingly, no, she thought. Mike had a fairly benign view of him, and even Lucy had softened slightly. It was one of the reasons they'd downgraded Lynch's chances of being the killer.

'Kind of, but not really. Mikey will explain. I also think we have a handle on why that particular knife was used, and why it means Whittler used it.'

'Oh?'

Again, Bill's face was hard to read. Or rather, hard for her to read. Holding back the Day was taking an increasing toll: the exhaustion was seeping through. She had maybe ninety minutes of her professional self left today, before she'd have to stop and go home.

'So, the knife from the packet was an ad-hoc, panic measure: in the dark, in an emergency. So we infer it was done quickly, desperately;

totally on instinct.' She looked to Bill for a confirmatory nod but got nothing. 'In which case, instinct has to guide the choice of the third-largest knife, rather than the biggest. There's no rationale in that situation to select a smaller knife, is there?'

'No, there isn't. In for a penny . . .'

'Exactly. So, selecting the middle knife was entirely because of the chooser's underlying, unstoppable instincts. It was the middle knife because that preserved the symmetry. It kept two knives either side of the empty space. Only Whittler would do that. Only Whittler's OCD tendencies would make him do that.'

Now she said it out loud to Bill, it seemed flimsy, plucked from the air. The reasoning felt tinny and insubstantial. Yet she was sure they were right.

'Okay.' Bill thought for a second. Then nodded. 'A little weird for my tastes, but I can see where you're coming from. At the very least, it makes Whittler more likely. When will you tackle him on that?'

'I'm still thinking it's the last call I'll ever make with him. If we go okay with this session, I want to bottom out everything else I can before I take him on about Jensen's. I can't afford to try it twice: either he tells, or he clams up for ever. I still think that second option's how it could pan out.'

Bill closed the paperwork. 'Yeah, that might be a confession too far, for today. We'll review after this session, see if we need to put off that final scenario until tomorrow. Judges hate the idea of us leaning on someone because he doesn't have a lawyer.'

Dana had thought the same thing. In truth, she calculated that the five interviews so far added up to only ninety minutes in the past nine hours. The number had surprised her; the level of concentration Nathan required, plus her own gradual debilitation, made it seem like days of effort. But she didn't want the appeal court to have a reason to even read the file. Everything had to be done right.

Chapter 26

Mike looked through the glass door at the figure sitting in reception. A huge splayed insect of a man: limbs stretching out towards the main desk, pate gleaming under the fluorescent light, slight gut visible below his waistcoat. A clean-shaven head ended in a near-monobrow that made him appear permanently frustrated. His face looked angled forward even when he leaned back against the poster behind him; like an Easter Island statue with the body added.

Jeb Whittler was hard to read from a distance; something about him said aggressive and intimidating, but perhaps that was simply his size. He was dressed in the kind of suit Mike would need a mortgage for – probably by putting up one of his children as extra collateral. Although Mike had stated outright to Dana that if, or when, he was in the business of sacrificing offspring, it would be for a new car. At the very least, a demonstrator.

'Jeb Whittler? Hello, I'm Detective Mike Francis. We can talk in here.'

The handshake was grabby and fierce, the eye contact a little too assertive. But again, Mike reprimanded himself for equating physical size with aggression. He indicated a little anteroom off the reception area and slid the tag to 'occupied'.

'Thanks. Got here as fast as I could. The call said you've found Nate. That true? I mean, is it definitely him?' Jeb's voice was the kind of bass rumble that Mike expected, but with a strangely whiny tinge to it, like a sports car with a fading gearbox.

They sat facing each other across a Formica table which had three blistered burn marks of the kind that seem to find only Formica tables. The room echoed with each of Jeb's booming sentences – he was the kind of person who didn't adjust his volume for the location.

'Oh, it's definitely him. We found ID; everything matches. DNA confirmed against hospital samples. There's no doubt.'

Jeb shook his head. There was a slight sheen of sweat around his temples, but Mike suspected that was caused by rushing down the freeway; thinking the whole journey that his long-lost brother was alive and well after all.

'Okay. Is he all right? Can I see him? I really need to see him.'

Mike held up a placating hand, intrigued by the choice of words. Not Nathan Whittler's needs – Jeb's needs.

'He's been checked out by our doctor several times. He's basically fit and well but . . . look, he's fragile.'

Jeb puffed his cheeks and reached reflexively for a pack of cigarettes. He'd almost retrieved them from his inside pocket before he realised and dropped his hands.

'I don't believe it, really. I mean, fifteen years. We'd all given up. And your guys said something about . . . charging? Nate?'

Mike was sure Lucy wouldn't have given that detail; yet Jeb clearly thought it. He must, therefore, have at least one contact inside the station; a contact who presumed Nathan had been charged. It made Jeb a connected kind of person; Mike disliked them.

'He was at a crime scene when we got there. We haven't charged anyone yet. Your brother is helping us with the investigation. It all takes time, Jeb, lots of time. We're still piecing things together at the moment, so I'd appreciate talking to you about your family life; the time before your brother went away.'

Jeb shook his head, as if the news couldn't settle.

'Are you sure I can't see him?'

Mike placed a notepad on the table and clicked his pen. 'Not at the moment. He's being well taken care of but he's easily overwhelmed; we have to be cautious. Plus, we specifically asked him, and he said he didn't want anyone notified on his behalf at that point.'

Jeb looked . . . what was it? Disappointed? Calculating? Mike was finding it hard to read a face so massive – he was drawn back again to the sheer volume of Jeb's skull. He rushed to continue, feeling Jeb's need to control the pace and direction.

'Jeb, we've contacted you ourselves, off our own bat. We're talking to you because it aids the investigation but we have to follow Nathan's wishes. He's, uh, not able to deal with too much at once. I'm sure you understand.'

'Okay.'

Mike concluded that was the best he'd get. He was trying to distinguish between Jeb's shock at the news and how sudden it was, and anything else he might be thinking.

'So you're . . . how many years older than Nathan?'

'Uh, eight years, give or take. He was, um, not totally planned.'

'Tell me a bit about your parents, and the farm.'

Jeb sat back a little. It would be reasonable, Mike thought, to assume he was collecting his thoughts, trying to frame a coherent timeline for a stranger. Eminently reasonable: yet Mike found himself seeking another motive, for reasons he couldn't yet fathom.

'Well, I think we lived a couple of places just after I was born, but the farm was all I could ever remember. I say farm: twelve hectares, more of a backyard by Aussie standards. Previous owners had sheep back then – Merinos, actually – but a few dry years ended that. Bank foreclosed, we got it cheap. There was still a couple of barns away from the house, and some old machinery in them. But we never ran it as a farm. I think our parents liked the extra land.'

'Because?'

'Because . . . they didn't like people very much.' Jeb shrugged. 'Not sociable. They liked the isolation.'

That word again. Mike had rarely come across so many people who'd viewed it so positively.

'Was there something in particular they didn't like about people?'

Jeb gave a slight grin, as though Mike had asked a naïve question.

'No, no. Everything. They thought the world was a sinful place, Detective. They were very religious, very Christian. Took the Bible at its word.'

'Regular churchgoers, then?'

Jeb's smile broadened. It lacked mirth, warmth.

'Ah, not as much as you'd think, no. How can I explain it? They went to church each Sunday because they were Christians and they thought all Christians should do that. But they didn't think much of the church in this town; weren't very impressed.' Jeb paused. 'Preacher was too happy-clappy and tolerant for them. It was over-modern: too free and easy. They liked their Christianity to be . . . in no uncertain terms.'

'Quite fundamentalist about it?'

'In many ways, yeah. Don't get me wrong – decent people. But strict parents, and pious. No flashy modern clothes, no jewellery, no TV. We had a radio, but only the spoken word, no pop music. Just Radio National, or Christian stations. A lot of modern life left them cold.'

For Mike, Nathan's world view – and his reactions to life – were starting to add up. Raised in a preachy atmosphere that was suspicious of modern life: his running to a cave and hiding no longer seemed quite as much of a stretch. It would explain why he ran – to get away from the strictures, the unyielding doctrine and its enforcement. But Mike's misgivings continued, as though he were missing something obvious and important.

'So you grew up in a home at odds with the world around you?'

'Yes, I did.' Jeb stopped, then seemed to realise he didn't want to finish the statement. '*We* did. Had to adapt and live two different lives, really.'

Jeb mopped his glowing temples in a way Mike found curiously effeminate. He patted at them with an immaculate handkerchief – there was something precious about the gesture that didn't fit his overbearing presence.

'There was no church school in town and they couldn't afford private education for either of us, Nate and I. So we had to go to the local school. I think our parents thought it was bad for our discipline but they never had the money to do anything about it.'

'Discipline?'

Jeb looked up at the light then down again. 'I don't know how you were raised, Detective, but in my house there were rules, and a price for disobeying them. There was a strict hierarchy, a known code of conduct. Retribution was swift, the consequences of action were clear. Our house had a lockable cellar; dark, cold – full of spiders, snakes in summer. The threat was often enough. Let's say the upper hand was what worked in that house. Nathan never got to grips with it. I was a quicker study.'

Mike concentrated hard to make sure he would recall the exact wording of Jeb's answers. He felt they needed unpicking, somehow. For such a solid physical object, Jeb was a lot of smoke.

'I see. How did your parents react when Nathan came along?'

'Oh, mortified. Something'd gone wrong, hadn't it?' Jeb put his hands flat on the table, appearing to warm to the conversation when it turned to his parents' potential hypocrisy or humiliation. Mike made a note as Jeb talked on.

'Either they'd had sex when they should've had the faith to resist temptation, or something failed in the contraception department. Only two options, right?'

'So Nathan was seen as . . . ?'

'A mistake. A horrible and obvious, walking and talking mistake. Anyone who'd thought they were a strict, holy, righteous couple were sniggering and pointing. They were a laughing stock. The devout couple and their nineteenth-century ways – and here was proof they had *fornicated* when they weren't planning for a child. Everyone could see it: like catching an Amish with a laptop, you know? Nathan was their own weakness reflected back at them.'

The last struck Mike as the result of plenty of brooding; possibly, of therapy. Jeb's dislike of his parents – and the discrepancy between their preachiness and behaviour – was apparent. Parents like those produced offspring like these, Mike concluded.

'That's a very deep-thinking view. Did they treat him any differently?'

'From how they'd treated me?' Jeb puffed his cheeks and rolled his eyes: the theatre of years of exasperation. 'Oh, yeah. They indulged him. For all that he was a mistake, they knew it wasn't his fault he'd been born. So they cut him some slack. I'd been on a tighter leash: classic first child. I was way older, of course, but I was the upcoming man of the house and Nate could just moon around, reading and stuff.'

This was all useful background – but Mike knew Dana would need some concrete examples to throw at Nathan: an inside hook that would open him up further.

'So discipline continued to be a significant factor in your own upbringing?'

'Oh, absolutely. As I got older, it became clearer to me about who instilled discipline and who controlled things. The rules got a little sharper, the punishments a little more imaginative. Next level, so to speak. The longer it all went on, the more it became a "my way or the highway" kind of thing. I guess Nate took the highway.'

Something about Jeb's tone, or maybe his language, had shifted. It wasn't quite in Mike's grasp yet, though.

'Was it a surprise, when your brother left?'

'Oh, totally. I mean, who'd have thought? I never picked Nate as the leaving type. I assumed he'd be staying at the farm for the rest of his life. He had this little job in a furniture shop—'

'Pringles? Yeah, we've been there.'

'Really? Oh. Okay. So you know about that.' The news obviously rattled Jeb. 'Well, I suppose I thought Nate would carry on there indefinitely. He didn't seem the type to break away, you know?'

'Surprised he was allowed to work. Tight rein, and all that.'

'Well, money was always tricky. My mother didn't work. My dad was an accounts clerk – that's not a big earner. My brother had to contribute what he could, when he could. Nate was expected to pitch in, play his part.'

Nothing about Jeb's own contribution, Mike noted. 'So, the day of his leaving?'

'Just like the day before it. Walked to work, apparently left at lunchtime. No one from Pringle's contacted me or anything. I had no reason to think he wasn't at work. When he didn't show up for dinner I rode around trying to find him, but no luck. Next morning, I spoke to Pringle. Said Nate had taken his pay, picked up all his stuff and left.'

That was it, thought Mike: the pronouns had moved. By the time Nathan was leaving it was all *I*, *I*, *I*. The parents had melted into the background; Jeb was front and centre in his own play. The power must have shifted.

'And there was no trail? No further contact at all?'

'Not a thing. I even tried a private detective, but Nate had disappeared into thin air. No letters, no phone calls. Nothing to say he was okay. I would really like to know where he got to, Detective.'

Jeb leaned forward and glowered as he said it. Mike sat impassive and Jeb seemed to realise who was who and where he was. He sat back and linked hands in his lap. Supplication didn't suit him.

'We can't discuss that aspect right now, Jeb. There's an ongoing investigation, so we have to be discreet. I'm sure it'll all come out in the fullness of time.'

'He can't just have disappeared into nowhere. Someone must have known where he was, what he was doing.'

You'd think so, wouldn't you, reflected Mike. *I'd have thought so, too, until today.*

'And you, Jeb, what did you do when you left school?'

'I started in construction. Steel frames – I helped put them up. After a couple of years I thought I could do better than the guy running the company, so I started my own.'

'And did you? Do better, I mean?'

'God, yeah. It's not so hard. Gradually expanded out of state; now we're international. That's where I was – up north. Deal for five warehouses.'

'Congratulations.'

'Thanks. I have good people in the major positions now. They're the real asset.'

It didn't sound right: too trite, too business-book. Jeb came across to Mike as someone who ran everything exactly as he personally wanted it – no opposition, only implementation.

'To be honest,' Jeb continued, 'it's losing its challenge. I've been looking to diversify. I have a couple of irons in the fire.'

'To keep your hand in?'

'Exactly.'

Mike couldn't see this line of inquiry going anywhere. He wanted follow-up on what he'd heard. Someone would have to go to the farm and see if they could find anyone who knew the Whittler parents.

'Well, that's great, Jeb. It's really been useful, thank you. If you could give me your mobile number?'

Jeb reeled it off quickly, almost too fast for Mike to note.

'As I say, we're looking after Nathan just fine. He has all the medical and other services he needs right now. But we're taking it nice and slowly – short interviews with rest periods in between. So you don't need to worry about his welfare.'

'But I do, Detective. I'm his brother. Last relative, and all. I'd really like to see him, talk to him.'

Mike waved the notepad.

'I have your number. You might as well grab some food or something. Get unpacked from your trip. As soon as Nathan indicates he's ready to see his brother, I'll call you straight away.'

Jeb sloped out of the main door and Mike made sure to watch him from behind a pillar. As anticipated, Jeb turned when he thought no one was watching and scowled at the station.

Chapter 27

People were beginning to seep out of offices towards their cars: Carlton was going home. A bus growled on a side street, swamped by ads beseeching viewers to watch Channel 7's latest reality show: some people would be cooking some things, and apparently 'all Australia' wanted to see. A gaggle of female students – all in tight jeans and overlong knitted scarves – crossed Dana's path. She had to stop to avoid a collision and they passed on, oblivious and assured. If it's a murder of crows, she thought, what's the collective noun for a group of pretty, entitled college girls? A meanness? A stiletto?

Father Timms was tucked up in a dogtooth coat that made him look like a noir extra – the guy who delivered proof the girl was still alive. Their bench was well away from the flow of footsteps across the plaza.

Timms passed her a coffee: single-shot, one sugar, whipped slightly by a chill breeze that had imposed itself on the plaza. She liked that he knew her regular order.

Dana suddenly recalled it was Friday today: that fact had escaped her totally since midnight. The sunlight was hazy and milky; maybe forty minutes of daylight left. It made her realise how long the day had been, and how long the Day was.

Timms had a dishwater-colour tea in a Styrofoam cup. She thought tea should be in a proper cup, or at least a mug. It looked . . . unseemly.

'Today's the anniversary, isn't it?' asked Timms.

He'd said that this morning, Dana realised as she sat. She'd been on her way out of the church, desperate to escape the iconography and everything associated with it and had pretty much blanked out Timms' offering.

'How come you remember that?'

Sometimes, key chunks of the moments in question were a little confused in Dana's head. Incidents, faces, words: all too real and all too visceral. They could reduce her to near-catatonic panic. But dates, and the sequences where people arrived and left the scenes: not so much. Details had dissolved into maelstroms of promises never kept, assurances that wilted, denial made truth. It was almost as if she deliberately dissembled that aspect for self-preservation – purposely scrambling the jigsaw pieces in her mind. Remembering everything would be too vivid, too much impact. She knew this was the Day, but other specifics often eluded her.

'A week or two after last year's . . . well, *after*, I made a note in my phone. Just of the date, you understand, not of the details. Such as I know them.' Timms paused and they watched a woman pull frantically on a lead as a large dog quite literally followed its nose towards the fountain. 'So, you know, my phone remembered.'

She couldn't turn to look at him: she spoke to her cup.

'That's, uh, impressive. Weird.'

'None taken.'

She smiled and shook her head. 'Sorry. I tend to carry stuff in my head, not on spreadsheets, or technology, or whatever. If someone gives me a telephone number, I memorise it; I don't punch it into a phone.'

'Memorise? Jeez, Grandma, no one outside a spelling bee memorises.

They know which website it's stored on in case they need to get it. The modern world is about access, not ownership. Take music, for example. We used to own records, cassettes, CDs; now we have access to a website.' He took another slurp. 'But you're trying to distract from the point here.'

'Yes. And it was going quite well.'

'So it is the anniversary today, Dana?'

Sometimes she forgot how much Timms knew. Or exactly where his knowledge came from. Dana had confessed some to him in conversations such as this; a bit had been reported in the media ages ago; parts of it were dusty public record – if you knew where to look, had the right names and understood what you were searching for. Much of what Timms knew – or thought he knew – would have been half-gleaned from his colleagues down the years. It would be a sketchy mosaic of rumour, innuendo, bearing witness and reading confidential documents. The Church recorded everything, then protected some of it. Some of them.

'Yes, it is today. I keep getting flashes.' Dana shook her head. 'Which is odd: they feel like they might be out of sequence.' She was aware her chronology was hazy at times.

'Hmm,' he replied. 'Memory doesn't work in a straight line. Each memory has a different type of emotional pull, a different sort of . . . gravity.'

'True enough. People's blame always sticks in my mind.'

'You were a child. Only one person ever truly blamed you, Dana, and they were wrong in every way.'

She thought about that, before turning to face him.

'That isn't true, though, is it? I can't pretend that it is. You weren't there: let me promise you, there were plenty ready to buy into it. The idea that only one person thinks a particular thing? Doesn't stack up. Even Hitler wasn't the only person who believed in what Hitler was doing. There isn't a thing in this world that only one person believes. Nothing so vile, or ludicrous, that there aren't a phalanx of people out there ready to credit it.'

She waited for a comeback; none came. Only her own words flowed on.

'There *were* others. Complicit, acquiescing supporters. Every bully needs an audience. There were followers, believers. I know it wasn't only one person. I've never been able to wish away that knowledge, no matter how much I wanted to.'

He had no answer to that.

Dana glanced across the sweep of people. A street-cleaning truck winked its orange warning lights near the junction, easing around a ute replete with fishing gear. The columns fronting the town hall took on a more honeyed patina as dusk approached. Civic reassurance was always a solid Carlton virtue: it was a town that knew how to carry on gracefully, even though it was merely managed decline. The immaculate streets, preserved heritage, hanging baskets and air of civility couldn't beat the numbers: employers and talent were seeping away to the city, unnoticed but inexorable. Earlville wore its winnowed heart on its sleeve; Carlton suffered internal bleeding.

Timms broke the silence. 'You called me. So you must have something specific on your mind?' A priest's ability to ask an open yet prodding question; not so different from Dana's job after all.

'I don't know that I do, necessarily. Just. I'm finding this Day, uh, hard to handle.' The temperature change from indoors to outdoors had made her scalp itch; she scratched at her head and rubbed a cheek. 'I always do, of course. Every year. But I'm, well, I'm working a homicide today. Usually I have a day away and try to do some thinking.'

'Maybe it's better to do less thinking. At least about that. For today.'

She swirled the cup, her breath beginning to mist as the temperature slid. 'Hmmm, I'd thought that. Hoped that. But it isn't.' She looked across to him briefly, then away. 'It comes like little bursts of heat. I don't know when, or why. Gushes through when I don't expect it. And it's all I can do to stop it overwhelming me, bring everything to a halt.'

She stopped, embarrassed by her inability to cope with simply being at work. What would people think if she couldn't handle it? What would they think, but never say?

'If I'm not working, I *can* halt. I can stop the car, or turn off the TV, or whatever; I can stop and let it happen, let myself roll with it. But today, I can't. When a wave hits me like that, I get paralysed. I stand there and pray it won't swallow me.'

'You pray?'

'Turn of phrase. Don't get your hopes up.'

'Well, I can't give you lots of platitudes about this, can I? We both know you've heard them a thousand times.'

Yes, thought Dana. A thousand times from fifty different people, for years. It all poured through, downhill and out of sight. There was no phrasing, no combination of words, that washed it all away.

'So all I'll say is this,' continued Timms. 'Everything else can keep. Your killer – you'll catch them tomorrow, or the next day. Sounds from the news like you might have them locked up already. There's no need to do everything this moment. Your number-one priority must be you. Always. But especially today.'

It was exactly the advice she'd give to someone in her position. She could step outside herself long enough to share that wisdom, but not long enough to take it.

Timms seemed to sense this. 'Look, make a deal with me.'

'A trade-off? That doesn't sound like it's in the Bible. They literally had words carved in stone.'

'My particular god is extremely pragmatic. As you know.' He looked away and she diplomatically avoided giving a sidelong glance.

'So here it is,' he continued. 'It's four o'clock now. Promise me, no matter what, you'll be home by five thirty. I know it's a short walk from the station to your home. Five thirty: and text me when you reach the sofa.'

She turned and offered a handshake. 'Deal. And thanks, you know. Just. Well, thanks.'

Timms was the only person in this town who knew anything much about the Day, and he didn't treat her like a victim. He didn't offer pat advice, or homilies, or some stupid little psychobabble game where the aim was to fool herself. For years, experts had offered her a series of programmes, therapies, action plans, exercises to do and report back on; each devised to allow her to 'take control' somehow. They all required that she either try to outsmart herself or wilfully become more stupid.

Father Timms knew not to dabble in that kind of suggestion. Instead he offered non-denominational, non-judgemental support and the kind of advice that took a slight edge off the worst of it. Which was pretty much all Dana felt she could do for herself. She and Father Timms were of the same mind on this one: it was all about damage limitation and staggering through. That was the basis of trying to shutter everything off into the Day: trammelling the worst thoughts and attempting to corral them into twenty-four hours.

Which meant every minute she spent on this case made the Day more desperate.

Chapter 28

Rainer was filling in. One of the other uniforms was supposed to ride out to the old Whittler farm for Mike to see if they could turn up anything useful. But then a call to a four-car pile-up on the freeway took almost everyone's attention. Lucy had basically instructed Rainer to come here, and he'd surprised himself by immediately doing so, as if she were his boss. Though, reflecting on it during the drive over, it wasn't such a surprise. Lucy said stuff, and he did it. They all did.

The farm was five kilometres from Carlton, up on a hillside of open pasture with several pockets of Tupelo trees which fizzled burnt orange as autumn died. Rainer presumed the farm had once been livestock – sheep, probably – but it was now an equestrian centre. Lucy had pulled the website and suggested it fostered some regional champions and Olympic hopefuls, so it was no hick operation. Freshly painted white fencing ringed the property and sectioned off the driveway and buildings. A line of rich volcanic soil spooled over the ridge and away – presumably the training track for stamina work.

The approach road was turning grey in a gauzy late afternoon, early tendrils of mist rising from a nearby copse that held a small brook. The tarmac ended by a farmhouse which looked carefully restored: right down to the wagon-wheel propped up against the front and the requisite wheelbarrow-as-flowerbed by the entrance. To the right, a gravel path led to the stables, behind which was a large metal shed that Rainer presumed was for indoor work, or dressage, or whatever. To the left, a wooden cabin served as an office.

Rainer didn't like horses. They were too big. His girlfriend had a niece who rode and he'd occasionally driven the kid to events. Horses were too large, made random noises, almost constantly changed their foot position in a way that caught him off guard, and stared with those large, liquid eyes.

He wiped his shoes on a doormat that squelched with disinfectant. The cabin had four desks, all swamped with badly filed paperwork. He or Dana would make short work of tidying this to a proper standard; Lucy or Mike would simply never allow it to happen. He could feel his fingers twitch. A brunette with glasses noticed him and nudged a colleague. The middle-aged man sauntered across with the air of someone who'd been there for years.

'Can I help you?'

'Rainer Holt, police. Is the owner of the centre around, please?'

'You're looking at him, son. Dan Mathers. Co-owner, I should say. My better half owns the other half.' Mathers offered a hearty country-welcome handshake. 'Police, you say? Is something wrong?'

'Oh, no, nothing like that. Is there someplace we could talk?'

Mathers strolled around the desk. 'Well, I'm going back to our cottage to get some papers. We could talk on the journey.' He looked down and grinned. 'Don't worry – gravel path all the way. That shoeshine isn't in danger.'

They re-crossed the courtyard. The clop of distant hooves punctuated birdsong; Rainer noticed some fading saplings near the shed.

'You bought this place from the Whittlers?'

'Ah, well, Jeb Whittler. Yeah, his parents died before. I think the place was too much for him on his own, and anyway, he had some construction business that needed investment. Yeah, a while ago now.'

Rainer did a 360, certain that Mathers was the type who responded to flattery. 'It wasn't in this condition, though? It all looks immaculate.'

'Thank you. Number of staff here, and how much we pay 'em, bloody well should look perfect. Nah, it was a mess,' Mathers continued. 'The main house there? Just about habitable. We lived there while we knocked down the old barns, built the stable complex and the dressage arena.'

He pointed to the large metal shed and Rainer wondered if Jeb had been involved in its construction.

'That doubles as riding space when it's too wet or hot outside. At that point, it was day-trippers only, but the big money is in residential. So we built this little cottage over here for ourselves and converted the main house into a bed-and-breakfast arrangement. Customers like being in and around the horses the whole time. And it keeps the insurance down if the owners live on site.'

'I see. And you've produced champions, I read?'

'Ooh, more Marlene's department than mine. She's the horse whisperer; I'm the accounts whisperer.' They crossed a cute little bridge over a brook, the smell of freshly mown grass stronger here. 'That's where she is today – looking at some potential new horses up past Earlville. Yeah, we've had a couple of regional champions. Nearly had an Olympian – Suzanne Doyle. Got *that* close. Would have made it next Olympics, but she had to give it up. So yeah, pretty good.'

They stopped near a picnic bench beside the cottage. The owners' home was built of the same stone as the main house: Rainer guessed they'd re-used the stone from demolishing the old barns. The cottage already had creepers winding to the first floor. He could see the fence to one side and the road beyond, flashes of colour through the branches as cars whipped past. Dan Mathers seemed reluctant to show him inside, so they managed an awkward shuffle to the bench.

'So, Dan, I'm here to learn as much as I can about the Whittlers, and about the farm as you inherited it.' Rainer put his forearms on the table: the wood felt rough and unfinished. 'Did you meet Jeb's parents at any point?'

'Nah, they were dead before we even moved to the area. Car crash, as I understand. No, we had to get out of the city and stretch, you know? It was only Jeb by then. We asked around the neighbours before we bought, though. As you do. They thought the Whittlers were creepy. All of them, mind, the kids included. Quiet, closed in; wore old-fashioned clothes.' Mathers glanced back towards the main house. 'The parents preached Bible a lot; I know that much. When we moved in Jeb had pretty much taken his own personal stuff and scarpered. If you'd told me he ran off the morning we arrived, I wouldn't have been surprised. I mean, everything else was left as it was – like a ghost ship, or something. Bibles everywhere, oodles of crosses, lots of religious tracts on the bookshelves. It was weird. We offered it all to the local church – come and take it away. They said no. I think there was plenty of friction between the Whittlers and that church. We didn't want to get into all that so we threw it all out.'

It interested Rainer that Jeb appeared to have moved suddenly, as though there was some final-second imperative to being gone. Presumably the legals of the move would have taken weeks. Jeb could have sorted out both his stuff, and his parents', while the contracts were going through. He had been clinging on, seemingly reluctant to actually let go. Or he'd been doing something specific, which mattered and couldn't be interrupted, up to the last minute.

'You didn't keep any of it?'

'Sorry, son. Never thought the police would come looking for it years later. Why, do you need it?'

'Oh, it's an ongoing case: it would have been background, mainly. So you moved in after Jeb moved out. Ever see him again?'

'He still lives in Carlton. We used to wave if we saw each other in town, but nothing more than that.' Mathers stopped, but cut across Rainer's next question. 'Oh, wait.'

'What?'

'I did see him. Just a . . . what, a few weeks ago. Where was that? Where?' Mathers patted his pockets, as though an answer were there. 'Lemme think for a second. I had the car, not the ute, so it must have been . . . a Tuesday. Definitely a Tuesday. I saw him out at that store – Jensen's Store, on the Derby Road.'

Rainer tried to hide the jolt.

'You saw him? Definitely Jeb? And definitely there?'

'Oh yeah, he hasn't changed much: maybe a bit paunchier than I remember. When you look like that, you kinda stand out. Big guy, bald, big shoulders. Yeah, it was him.' A sudden breeze caught Mathers' hair and shifted all of it sideways two centimetres. He slid the piece back into place with insouciance. 'Jeb was talking to the owner – I know that guy from the local business club, here in town. Uh . . . Lou. Yup. Lou Cassavette. Yeah, two peas in a pod, those.'

It was better than Rainer could have anticipated. A link – once removed – between Nathan Whittler and the victim.

'What were they talking about?'

'Oh, I only saw them in passing. I'd stopped for a long black and I was on my way out and back home; they were standing outside and yacking. I didn't catch what about. Is that important?'

Yeah, thought Rainer. *It really is.*

'Ever see them together before?'

Mathers became a little more cautious.

'Why?'

'Because I'm interested, Mr Mathers. Have you ever seen Jeb Whittler and Lou Cassavette together at any time?'

Mathers' eyes narrowed. It didn't strike Rainer that Mathers was dissembling; more that he'd suddenly realised he was sitting on a nugget of social gold. Mathers would bore his wife to death about it this evening, Rainer had no doubt. Without meeting Marlene, Rainer already felt a little sorry for her.

'Not that I recall. Both in the local business club, though. Possible they met there at some point. Can't say as I've noticed.'

'So, after you moved in, Mr Mathers, anything unusual happen?'

'How d'you mean, unusual?'

'Out of the ordinary?' Rainer leaned forward again. 'Find anything on the property that shouldn't be there; anyone visit that seemed out of place – that kind of thing?'

'Nope.' Mathers looked at his hands. 'You got me a little nervous now, son.'

'Oh, it's ancient history we're covering. Like I say, background.' Rainer gave his most reassuring smile. 'Nothing unusual after the sale?'

'Nope, we just moved in and started cleari— Wait, no, there was one thing.' Mathers prodded the air between them with one finger. 'We reported it to the cops as well. Yeah. Damn, I haven't thought about that in years. Spooked Marlene, I can tell you.'

'Oh?'

'So, a few days after we bought, we came over to take some measurements for the stables. Drainage trenches – real glamorous. As we arrive, there's a car coming down the driveway towards us. We pull over, thinking they're going to stop and talk, but no, she drives straight past. Never even looks. Woman, twenties, maybe thirty – pretty. Well, we go on up to the property, but there's no sign of breaking in;

nothing's missing. Anyways, we report it to the cops in case there's something we didn't notice and we need to claim insurance.'

'Did they ever get back to you?'

'They did, they certainly did. That's how come I remember it at all, really. It amazed us, to be honest. No offence, but where we were from, in the city, they wouldn't have given a rat's behind about that kind of thing. But yeah, they tracked her down in a day or so. I'd got some of the number plate and it was a blue VW Beetle, so I guess they found her from that. Apparently, she was an old buddy of Jeb's; didn't know he'd moved. No biggie. But we were sure impressed by your colleagues.'

Rainer spread his hands, as if that kind of anecdote were par for the course. '*Reassure and Protect*. We do exactly what it says on the tin.'

Chapter 29

'Mr Whittler.'

'Detective Russo.'

They'd played out the start of an interview five times already and it had an easy, comfortable cadence around it. Once again, Dana swept the formidably tidy tower of detritus into a bag she'd brought along. This time, her synapses fizzed with the connection between this neatness and the choice of knife. Physical proximity and tangibility of his sense of order supported her conviction that they were correct about him choosing the weapon.

She set a fresh water bottle before Nathan and received an almost imperceptible tilt of the head in acknowledgement. Once more, she tied a trucker's hitch in front of him with the string. This time, it worked.

'Is that a trucker's hitch you've just done, Detective?'

'It is indeed, Mr Whittler. Always fastens tight, zero slippage.' Her voice juddered noticeably as she said it. She had absolutely no intention of discussing how she knew about knots.

'Good choice. I took a book into the cave with me. Very useful: not only knots, but fastenings and other woodcraft.'

Dana put the bag down carefully by her foot. She was surprised by his relative chattiness. As if he'd reached some kind of accommodation with himself about how much he was prepared to share.

'I saw the clothes line you rigged up, Mr Whittler. Ingenious, to use the flysheet.'

'I needed to dry clothes in wet weather, and out of sight. Especially summer – the humidity next to the water was terrible. I had to have clothes drying all day and night to get them wearable. No breeze inside the cave, you see.'

Dana opened her file and circled some Pitman squiggles. 'I'd like to go back to 2004, if I may, Mr Whittler.'

The mood sharpened and cooled. 'Why, Detective?'

She paused, wanting to frame it exactly right. His explanation for leaving home might hint at motive for killing Cassavette, though she couldn't currently imagine how. At the very least, she needed to understand what kind of person he was becoming at that point: her perception was that the following fifteen years in a cave had merely refined that person.

'We need to build up a picture of why you left home. It's the reason you were in the cave, which in turn is the reason you were in Jensen's Store this morning.'

'I see.' Nathan's tone was determinedly neutral.

'Did you enjoy working at Pringle's?'

'Pringle's?' He seemed surprised she'd mentioned it. Perhaps that meant his employment was irrelevant to why he had left. Maybe he compartmentalised to such a degree that he didn't associate where he worked with leaving town.

'Yes, I suppose I did enjoy it, in a strange way. Mr Pringle was very kind to me. I've thought back at various times and realised I probably wasn't very good at my job. His other apprentices seemed to catch up and race ahead of me, somehow.' Nathan rubbed his palms together as he stared at the floor. 'I was diligent, but I don't think I was particularly good. Mr Pringle seemed to put up with that.'

Nathan had, she concluded, enough self-awareness to know exactly what Pringle had thought of him. It also tallied with Rainer's earlier interview. 'And he left you to it?'

'Yes, he did. I think he understood that was how I preferred it. My workstation was in a corner, tucked out of sight. None of the customers ever came down there. I could go a few hours without seeing anyone.'

It was out of her mouth before she realised how flippant she sounded. 'That was useful training.'

'Yes, yes, I suppose so. Although I didn't realise at the time, of course. I know the money was barely above minimum wage, but . . .' He shrugged and trailed off.

'Barely *above* minimum?' Rainer hadn't caught that titbit.

'Yes. I was on minimum originally. But that last year, Mr Pringle bumped it up by about ten per cent more than the award. I never told my family, obviously.'

The conversation was starting to steer the way she wanted. There was something about this family: some undercurrent.

'Why not?'

'I had to hand over ninety per cent to the family pot. We all did.' Nathan took a slow swig. Dana sensed he was trying to veer away from a particular road, hoping she wouldn't notice the junction. 'I needed the extra money for the camping equipment I was buying. I carried on paying the same amount into the family pot, and it didn't seem to occur to anyone to ask why I hadn't received a pay rise. One of the few benefits of low expectations, I suppose.'

On the one hand, he'd confirmed he was gradually building up the means of leaving – the equipment, the wherewithal – which sounded like long-term planning. Yet she was more convinced than ever that the precipitating incident they were all chasing lay inside the Whittler household. They couldn't interview the parents; Mike had talked to Jeb relatively briefly so far. She wanted to soften Nathan up a little.

'My colleague spoke to Mr Pringle earlier today. He seemed very nice. He was very happy to know that you're safe and well. Very happy.'

Nathan frowned. 'Oh, really? Oh, I hadn't . . . oh.'

'That surprises you?'

'Not . . . well, I hadn't thought he would think of me at all, to be honest. It's, well.'

Nathan dry-washed hand on hand and frowned again. He reached for the water bottle and gripped it tight. It wasn't computing for Nathan, this new data. Dana saw what that information did: the very notion that someone was thinking of him now, had him in their mind down the years, tilted Nathan off balance. The mere knowledge that someone thought well of him, cared: it was not a concept Nathan would have allowed himself. He wouldn't have considered that his absence left a hole for anyone. Perhaps he didn't want to imagine he'd caused unhappiness or pain. Or perhaps . . .

'Did you not think your family would miss you, when you left?'

'Miss me?'

His confusion made her look for a double meaning in her own question. His off-key responses had her constantly reappraising, reconfiguring where to go next. Nathan often took words literally. That, and the apparent OCD, made her think briefly about the spectrum and the possible need for a diagnosis before trial. If it came to that.

'I don't mean would they notice your physical absence. I mean, would they miss you emotionally, do you think?'

It was apparent from his delay that this wasn't something he'd considered. In fifteen years of solitude and reflection he clearly hadn't entertained this notion at all. Dana found it bizarre. How could he be so certain they were glad he was gone? Even if he was sure his parents hated him and wanted him gone: at some point, surely he'd consider the possibility that they missed him?

'I, that is, I . . . no. I don't think so, no. My parents would've . . . uh, they thought it was time for me to leave. Maybe, beyond time.' He paused, then threw in something else. 'Jeb would have been angry, though.'

Dana needed to pursue those two things carefully: why it was beyond time, and why Jeb would be angry. They meant something. They meant something significant.

'Your parents felt that twenty-three was old enough to move out, is that it?'

Nathan flinched before replying, and Dana realised that wasn't it.

'Uh, possibly. Most people have moved out by that age – university, new job, the military: some reason or other.'

He was misdirecting. She wanted to push it and push it fast, but she had to move at his pace: guide and goad. Driving on would also hasten the moment when she'd have to tell him that his parents were dead.

'But that isn't why, is it, Mr Whittler? There's a deeper reason than that.' Dana saw him wince, as if she'd leaned over to strike him. 'Regardless of your age, they felt 2004 was overdue for you to get out.' She pushed. 'Not so much leave as . . . *escape*?'

It was a hunch. If the parents thought his leaving was overdue, but Jeb would have been enraged by it, maybe the reason Nathan ran was not overly religious parents. She'd been inclined to assume his sudden departure was a rebellion against zealotry and imposed piety; now she was beginning to feel she might have been wrong.

'Escape, yes. It was, yes.' He was welling up, looking away to the corners. 'Horrible, horrible. I don't want to talk about it.'

But you have to, thought Dana. *I can't close this case without knowing why you ran.*

'You mentioned having to hand over nearly all your income, Mr Whittler. Was it a strict household?'

'Strict? Not . . . yes . . . I mean, not unusually, I don't think. My parents were quite religious, stern by modern standards. But not bad parents, really. Parents are, uh, very influential, don't you think?'

The question stabbed her. The pen stayed poised over the page, quivering. Dana caught her breath then took a moment to formulate an answer. Nathan hadn't asked what her own parents were like: he was too smart to be so direct. He'd fired from an angle; from a sniper's knoll. And hit.

'We can't always escape what they make us, that's true. But there's no reason we have to behave like them either. I try to take what I can from childhood, then move on. Don't you agree, Mr Whittler?'

'That's a noble aim, Detective. But no; I don't think that's possible. Their influence is in the marrow – literally. It can't be exorcised, can't be wished away. A large part of us is always shaped by what we experience as a child. I could never truly escape it.'

He looked straight at her: 'I don't think anyone can.'

She tried to swallow that down. It was impossible for Nathan to know about her life – impossible. And yet, and yet. He could infer it, sense it; understand enough from conversing with her to have some inkling. It made her fear she was that transparent with others: that they were discerning what she fought to hide.

'We do our best, though, don't we, Mr Whittler?'

'Oh yes, I think so, Detective. I mean, for men, fathers are the key, aren't they? We expect something more from them, somehow, purely because we share gender. We look to them for . . . values, example. Is it the same for girls with their mothers?'

No, she thought, *it isn't. But mothers can have a hideous, overbearing, dark impact. If you have no power, if what happens in your life is beyond your control.*

'Not really, no,' Dana replied. 'We're supposed to be close to our mothers, as you describe. But it doesn't always work out that way.'

'No, no,' he agreed. 'Sometimes, a big something comes along and rips all that to shreds. Leaves debris, really.'

Her silence would seem to him like assent. Which it was.

She needed to get away from this; could feel it unravelling her.

She had to switch the focus back on to Nathan's home life and what had made him run. They already had Jeb's take on it: he had seen a house of tight discipline, pared-down piety; a deliberate refusal to engage with the modern world. Jeb had heard no music: instead, quiet contemplation, the threat of cellars; a plethora of Bibles and strictures. Dana could picture such things – had lived them. She knew the iconography, the sounds, even the taste of the air. It chilled her to be wrenched backwards.

But Nathan hadn't seen that house: not quite as Jeb saw it. They'd witnessed the same things but had viewed them differently. She was close, but she wasn't quite nailing it. Nathan's answers were scattergun, deliberately imprecise: he dissembled when he turned the issue back on her. He was hiding something, able to hold back because he hadn't had to address it. She wasn't asking the right questions.

'At some point, Mr Whittler, I feel your family life took a turn for the worse. I feel sure of that. How old were you when that happened?'

'Eight, or maybe nine. About then.'

It was a hoarse whisper. She could feel the crackle in it, the giving way of the ice.

'What happened?'

Nathan shied away, turning his back. She thought about speaking, or even about reaching out, but decided against both. Nathan had his face buried in his hands. It felt like he was hiding. She understood that he had an acutely developed sense of shame, and not always for himself.

Eventually he sniffed then wiped his nose carelessly with a sleeve. His face was blotchy and he looked pale and drawn. She considered stopping the interview or calling the doctor, but Bill would lacerate her if she didn't keep going now. And, she felt, rightly.

Besides, Dana had an overwhelming need to know.

And Nathan had a latent need to tell.

'I . . . uh, okay. My brother, Jeb . . .'

Nathan stopped, blinked hard and swallowed. He reached for the cup with a shaking hand then changed his mind.

'Take your time, Mr Whittler.'

He nodded. 'Jeb was really big for his age. I mean, nearly two metres, and wide with it. He used to bully me a little, push me around. But, in reality, I was so small and young I didn't matter. He could shove me about quite easily, any time he wanted, so he didn't bother much.'

Nathan was staring at his reflection in the mirror, forearms resting on his knees. Again, that compulsive nail-draw down his fate line.

'Around that time, my parents became extra-quiet. I'm not sure I noticed everything at the time, except that one day I realised exactly what was going on.'

He stopped, looked to the floor and half coughed. She silently passed him a tissue, which he took without acknowledgement. He used it to wipe the snot and ignored the tears. He clutched the used tissue as he continued. Dana took short, silent breaths.

'My parents had been strict, yes. But fair. They had a code: respect the Bible, live simply, don't answer back. It was easy to follow, Detective. It chimed with my . . . with me. I didn't find it hard to stick to, so I wasn't in a heap of trouble. We'd argue about what was a suitable book, but other than that I was no problem to them. But Jeb? When he became a teenager, Jeb was a different story.

'When he got to sixteen he started pushing *them* around. Physically pushing them around. He argued with Father and locked him in the cellar. Literally – dragged him by the arm and hair and pushed him into our cellar. It was where we kept the root vegetables and the wood for the stove. Dark, damp, unhealthy; snakes and fear. And my father screamed. Claustrophobic, you see: I mean, he really screamed, like someone was chopping his limbs off. I'd never heard anything that bad before. An hour in there and he was begging. Jeb went down and told our father his fortune. That was all it took: we had a new boss.

'Jeb started to call the shots. Who went where, what we did. He could threaten Father with the cellar, and other things, and Father knew they weren't idle threats. Besides, Jeb had shown his power. It was that simple – all the prayer, all the authority of parenthood, dissolved when someone was big and brutal and violent and didn't care. Like that thing Mike Tyson said, Detective: *Everyone's got a plan until they get punched in the mouth.*

'And Jeb could threaten Father by threatening Mother. After all, Father was out all day and I was eight: she was at Jeb's mercy, and he had none. I had no choice; I had a new path in terms of discipline, orders and behaviour. A new master. A new father.'

Dana swallowed. Below the desk, finger and thumb tapped. She was horrified how many parallels there were between her life and Nathan's. Both were ruptured when they were eight. Both rattled and riddled by something they could barely comprehend. Both lives dominated by a quiet, resilient but directionless survival.

'Jeb began to change things. I liked some of them – a bit of pop music, some more TV. But it was only ever what Jeb mandated, only what Jeb allowed and could take away. Some of them I didn't like. Jeb took control of the bank accounts. Soon enough, they transferred all the property to his name. I was ten then, old enough to begin to understand what that meant. We were all Jeb's tenants now: at his beck and call.

'When I started high school I got a little release. Jeb never stopped me going, but he sneered at any education that wasn't practical. Useless, he called it. Empty. When he drank, he started hitting people. Things. Anything in his zone. It got uglier and uglier. He started having girls over from the city – his party nights. My parents and I had to go to the barn and sleep among the machinery – he wouldn't have us in the house. Shivering, silent; water from a trough. We never spoke of the implications, Detective. We barely spoke at all: we all felt the shame, and it didn't need spelling out.'

Nathan stopped, slurped at the water with a needy, raspy breath, spilling some of it. Dana wondered whether to speak or wait for him to resume. But it became clear he needed a prompt, for there to be another voice in the room. Some counterpoint to the sound of his own desperation.

'There was never any rebellion? No thoughts of escape?'

'Not really. Jeb could smash any of us to a paste, any old time. My parents were not the adversarial type, Detective. Nor was I. We were raised compliant – not so much submissive as accepting. There's a subtle difference. Our meekness was a practical survival instinct, an acceptance of the consequences. Jeb had the property, the money, the only car. We were isolated socially, physically. We were terrified; we'd seen what he could do and how easy it was to do it. That was the overriding thing – his cruelty was easy for him, a default. Sometimes I harboured ideas of sneaking up on him when he was asleep, slamming into his head with a shovel. But really, it was an empty dream – I lacked the guts and I knew it would go wrong. Dreaming it made me feel weaker: it emphasised that I would never do it.'

Classic abusive behaviour, thought Dana. The threats, the isolation, the destruction of self. Almost everything by implication; it rarely needed to be carried out. A very real but utterly intangible danger – one others couldn't see, chose to ignore or wouldn't care to understand.

'Didn't you acquire a car of your own? A Toyota? Couldn't you escape in that?'

Nathan thought for a moment, temporarily perplexed.

'Ah, no. That thing. That was much later. A scam by Jeb; my name on the forms, but I never even saw the car. He had some con going; insurance, I think.'

'I see. Sorry.' Dana cursed herself for interrupting the flow – she should have stayed silent.

Nathan sat back in his chair and regarded his hands. When he was struggling with what to reveal he seemed to shrink back to this child-like body language. Dana wondered when that impulse had emerged and felt a connection to her own finger-and-thumb reflex.

'I . . . uh, maybe I shouldn't be talking about this.' Nathan's voice was almost a whisper.

She shuddered inside. She couldn't let him stop – not now. Her interruption had given him the option.

'Why are you reluctant, Mr Whittler?'

He shook his head.

'I mean,' she continued, 'that you have something you've held within for a very long time. I respect that; understand that. As you appreciate. But I also know that some things have a natural timing; there's a reason they reach for the light and a reason you should let them.'

He shook his head sadly. She could feel revelation drifting from her grasp.

'As things stand, Mr Whittler, you have something inside you that you want me to know. You want me to understand it; that matters to you, and for a very particular reason. You know that I can put information together. You know I can comprehend. More than that, I can *understand*. So I think that, while you're nervous about the telling, you actually want me to know.'

She paused to see if she was having any impact. There was no sign of it.

'The telling doesn't have to be precise or perfect, Mr Whittler. It simply has to communicate what you wish me to understand. That's all.'

He swallowed hard, then nodded. Dana tried to hide her relief. Nathan resumed, almost reverential.

'He made me get a job. He wanted money, and Father's wages weren't enough. Jeb was working construction a little; dealing drugs on the side. Lots of building buddies wanted some stuff for the weekend – Jeb made himself indispensable. And then, about a year before I left, it got much worse. Oh, God.'

Nathan's limbs suddenly flailed, as though slapping away an invisible force. She feared he'd fall to the ground. Gradually, his shaking arms came under control and he settled again, his voice continuing to quiver as he stared at the wall.

'Each Saturday, Jeb would tell my parents after lunch that it was "nap time". I was twenty-three, Detective. A small, weak, pummelled, ashamed twenty-three. He was way bigger than all of us. My father was average height but skinny; my mother was tiny. Jeb was full-size: bigger than any of your colleagues. He barked, "Nap time," and they'd all shuffle off up the stairs. Jeb didn't need to tell me to stay where I was – one look was enough.'

She'd guessed this morning that the crucial issue would lie with Nathan's parents, but now, clearly, it was something about Jeb. Dana wished she had more on Jeb. Mike had started things and Rainer was chasing more background, but that wouldn't help her right now.

'They'd come back down around dark. They wouldn't have made a sound up there. I had no clue what they were doing. I only knew that nap time meant the three of them went upstairs and came back a few hours later. I was too scared of Jeb to go looking for answers.'

He reached for the cup without turning around. Dana slid the handle into his fingers and he took a swig, more to give his breathing some order than to assuage thirst.

'This went on for months. Months. I had no clue what it was about. Now I know, I wonder if I'd ever have been able to stop it. I don't think so. Just finding out about it nearly got . . . well, finding out was the worst thing I could have done.

'One day Jeb called nap time and sent our parents upstairs. But this time he didn't go with them. I must have frowned, or looked puzzled. He started smiling and told me he'd show me something I'd never forget.

'I was confused, Detective. I didn't understand. Whatever it was had been private between the three of them. None of them ever spoke about it or referred to it. I knew I wasn't allowed to ask anything. There was this big secret the three of them held, and now I was supposed to be a part of it?

'Something in me was certain I shouldn't have that knowledge. Maybe I thought that, if they were so silent up there, it couldn't be a good thing. Jeb's idea of fun wasn't mine. It usually ended with me hurting and him laughing. I couldn't see how this would be any different.'

Dana scribbled Pitman without once taking her eyes off Nathan. The air conditioning hummed.

'I thought it was a trick. I thought he'd get me upstairs and lock me in a cupboard or something. I told him it was a trick, and he looked at me funny. No trick, he said. Science.

'That jolted me. I wasn't expecting that word to be coming from him. Jeb knew nothing about science. I didn't think what he did for work involved science.'

Nathan put down the cup and the used tissue. He squirmed.

'Then he got mad and grabbed at my arm. I clutched at the staircase, but he was way too strong. He could still drag me around like a little teddy bear. After he slapped me I gave in and he pulled me up the stairs by the collar. Nothing I could do. Our parents' room was at the end of the landing. The door was slightly open and I could tell the curtains had been drawn. It was the middle of the day. I wanted to run, but Jeb was behind me with his hands on my shoulders. His fingers dug in – he knew exactly where the nerves were and he liked making me spasm like that.

'Closer, closer, closer: until we were right outside the door. Even as an adult, I never went in my parents' room: I always knocked and waited and they'd open the door a sliver to talk to me. Yet here I was, with Jeb telling me to push it open. I touched the handle but I was too scared. Jeb thumped on my wrist and the door shuddered open.

'At first, all I saw were crosses, statues of Jesus. Dozens of them: maybe half of all the icons in the house were in their room. Across every surface, crowded on every wall – Jesus and God, and the idea that this place was holy, safe and pure. It proved to be the opposite of that. I've never got that image out of my head, Detective. Never.'

Me neither, thought Dana. *That contrast never fades; it simply bites.*

'Inside, Father was sitting in an armchair. One of those tall, upright ones; butterfly chairs, I think they're called. His hands were tight on the arms of the chair – rigid. Terrified. I could see it in his eyes. He stared at me, and up at Jeb, and he shook his head slightly. Just a little. Jeb told him to shut up and he dropped his eyes.

'I looked across to Mother. She was lying on the bed, eyes closed, her arms across her stomach, like she'd died. I could barely see her chest rise and fall. Utter silence. Jeb marshalled me to the side of the room, next to a radiator. He walked into the centre of the room, took a glance at each of them in turn. He put a hand in his pocket, turned to me and said, "Look what I can do."

'I wanted to run. I felt so wretched. I could feel the pee running down my leg, hot on my skin. It was so . . . personal. Whatever they were doing, so personal. I didn't get it. I didn't comprehend. It never occurred to me that only one of them was playing. It wouldn't, would it, Detective?'

Nathan looked up at her with wet, horrified eyes. Dana shook her head silently.

'Jeb moved over to Father, who flinched. The movement made Jeb smile. Flinching always made him smile. He slid Father's shirt up past the elbow and Father started shaking. His feet lifted and he had to concentrate to put them back down again: like when the dentist hits a nerve. He'd wet himself, too. I didn't know what was going on but I could sense the pain. It was so apparent – the humiliation. I could see a tear roll down his cheek. He didn't want this, but he couldn't stop it. He wasn't in charge.

'Jeb took a needle out of his pocket. A hypodermic. It shone in the lamplight. I remember the glint made the liquid look like metal. He put it quite carefully into Father's arm, then pushed the plunger without even looking. He'd done it so often before, I suppose. Jeb was facing me. I must have been wide-eyed, fascinated; everything and nothing at once.

'When the liquid went in, Father kind of sagged. He lost the tension in his muscles, flopped down in the chair. His head fell sideways but he carried on staring at me, without blinking. At me, Christ, *at me*. Like I was causing this; like it was my fault and not Jeb's. Or maybe, like I could stop it. But he surely knew I couldn't do that. There was nothing I could do, except be an audience for Jeb.

'Jeb said I'd never seen Pop like that, had I? Father looked like one of those tranquilised animals on nature programmes: he was just a body, a bag of skin with no one in it. He looked . . . dead, Detective.

'That's what I thought. That Jeb had killed Father. Right there, in front of me. Jeb noticed, must have read my mind. Jeb told me he wasn't dead. He was . . . more helpful. That's how he put it, Detective: *more helpful*. As if Father wanted this, was trying to assist Jeb somehow.

'Jeb moved across to Mother. I wanted to run. Don't know where. Towards Jeb and knock the needle out of his hand, maybe. Or away, out of the door and find someone to tell. Or something. Or not be there any more. Be any place but that, looking at anything but that. He held Mother's hand when the needle went in. She never liked needles. I didn't understand why she wasn't shouting, fighting. She just lay there. Lay there while it happened.

'The silence deepened. It went from no sound at all to something thicker, stronger. I don't know how to describe it. Like the air was so full of despair, no sound could get in. Jeb nodded to himself, like he'd done well. It was hideous. It was so ugly, and so wrong. I didn't get exactly what he'd done, but I knew it was wrong. So why wasn't I shouting? Why wasn't I running? Why wasn't I doing anything? I was so weak, Detective. I'd never understood what rooted to the spot meant until then. You could have set me on fire and I still wouldn't have moved a muscle.

'Jeb turned back and tapped Father's cheek with a finger. Then he glanced at me and said, "Watch this." He slapped so hard, Father's head rocked to the other side and clouted the chair. You could hear the slap, then the thud. But like I said, Father was gone. He wasn't in there any more, I was sure of it. He dribbled a bit. "Ooh," Jeb said, "better tidy you up, Marty, don't want you to lose your dignity."

'Jeb opened a drawer behind him. I couldn't see what he was doing. I should have run then, Detective. It was my chance. I could have been down the stairs – I might have got away. I might have run to a neighbour and called for help. But I didn't. I was pathetic. I could only see the moment, only do what I was told. How could I go? I watched Jeb fish out what was in the drawer.

'Clothes, Detective. Silly clothes. A red nose and a clown's hat. He put them on Father. He tweaked the nose and made a honking noise. He laughed. He got some cosmetics and drew rosy cheeks and a sad, bloody mouth. He thought it was hilarious. He told him to dance; dance and amuse us. He asked where Father's little car was. Jeb turned to me. He asked me, "You see what your old man really is? He's a clown," he said. "He's nothing."

'I could see a tear on Father's face. Jeb was too busy sniggering to notice. I think Jeb was drunk – he was almost doubled up laughing at the sight of this sad, frozen old clown. The tear moved so slowly. I'll never forget the agonising slowness: off his cheek, then it splodged on to his shirt. Nothing else on his face moved. Just the tear.

'I was screaming. One of those dream screams where no sound was coming out. Only my throat wrenching, clawing at itself. All I could produce was a little whimper. It made Jeb laugh harder.

'He turned to Mother. He raised an eyebrow, as though he was daring me to intervene. Instead, he pointed to the door. "Go to your room," he said. I didn't. I stood where I was, wondering why no sound was coming out when I was screaming so hard. He shouted for me to go to my room – "*You don't get to see this; it's for grown-ups.*"

'I only moved when he stepped forward and raised his hand. I felt my bowels give way and I bolted. He was still chuckling when he closed the door.'

Nathan stopped to wipe the snot. He held his fists to his ears. Dana poured his water for him, even touching the bottle cap afterwards. She wanted him to understand she was taking care of his needs.

Her mind was racing with what she needed to ask next. This story, this . . . whatever this was: it would need verification. The substance Jeb was using, assuming this was all true, would be long gone: the parents had been buried over a decade ago. Maybe there was some remnant of it in the old Whittler house. They'd need a detailed forensic examination. For now, she needed to coax more details.

'This happened every weekend, Mr Whittler?' She'd dropped her voice to match his. She prayed the microphone was picking it up.

'Yes, every Saturday. A little ritual. Once I knew what was going on – or some of it, at least – I could detect the changes in my parents. The way they tensed up, closed off more, as the week progressed. The relief, the sense of utter release, every Sunday. They were allowed to go to church, and that day they seemed almost . . . okay.'

'But they never told anyone?'

'They couldn't.' Nathan took another swig; his shaking hand betrayed him and, without noticing, he dribbled a little on to the floor.

'Couldn't? Because Jeb had such a hold on them?'

'Worse than that, Detective. Much worse. Jeb didn't leave things like that to chance. He, uh. Oh.'

Nathan gagged on the thought of saying this aloud. She resisted the temptation to prompt.

'He started, uh, taking photos. Of them. Now I knew what was happening, I'd be sent to my room when they had nap time but I'd sneak a look at the corridor. There were flashes, Detective. Little spasms of light every now and then, in amongst Jeb's chuckling.'

'Wouldn't that incriminate him, to be doing that?'

'No, it wouldn't. My brother was, whatever else I thought of him, a clever person. He would take photos of them in horrid, sexual positions. Doing things to each other. Things they'd never do. Things they'd rather die than do willingly. He showed me a few, told me about the worst ones. We'd sit on the porch: he'd drink and boast and I'd try not to vomit. He'd be laughing and joshing me with an elbow.

My parents. Our parents. The stuff he had them doing when they had no choice, no will. It was grotesque. Using . . . objects. Things. I can't tell you half of it. Won't. But he had those photos and he would have used them if they'd tried telling anyone.'

Dana attempted to think it through. The blackmail would only work if the two people in such photos were demonstrably Martin and Pamela Whittler. But if the photos showed that, wouldn't they also show that the pair were drugged, helpless?

'But still, the photos would damn him, too? Or maybe he'd be in them?'

'No, Detective. He was very careful. He was proud of it. Said it was his plan for other people, now that he'd refined it. He took photos from clever angles – they were recognisably my parents but you never saw their eyes. He took photos including birthmarks. The pictures were obviously taken in their bedroom and were them, but you couldn't tell the state they were in.'

Yes, she thought, that would work. Perhaps Jeb was smart about not being visible in reflections or showing his shadow. Then he could claim he wasn't even there, that his parents were alone and took the photos themselves. At any rate, it would succeed because Jeb would never have to show them to anyone. Their power was in their potential; the mere thought of their circulation was part of the bullying, the intimidation, the control.

'Did you ever learn what drug he was using?'

'Insulin, Detective. He got especially drunk one night and told me. He was getting someone to steal insulin from the hospital, giving our parents something like an induced coma. He told me he started off with small doses, only making them drowsy and floppy. My brother could beat them both to a pulp without getting out of breath: making them sit for a needle was easy. He gradually upped it until he had a dosage that left them like that for a few hours.'

'My God, that's awful. That you had to witness that. I'm so sorry.'

'Thank you, Detective. It was . . . well, it became part of life. Part of all our lives. Jeb did as he pleased and we were terrified. He had control of all the bank accounts, had all the property signed over to him. If he was in a bad mood, our parents weren't allowed to leave the house. I don't even know why he hated them so much, or even if he did. I think Jeb liked pushing people around, and that was an easy way to practise it. He did it because it was convenient. He did it because he could.'

Dana was frantically recalibrating: she could never have predicted such a thing. But it was an opportunity, an open door she had to use.

'After you knew about it, and after you knew what the substance was, did anything change?'

She'd tried to frame it right; without judging Nathan. She was relieved when he took it that way.

'Well, he broke my arm. He started talking about maybe doing me that way, about finding out what my limit was. I think he was getting a little bored with my parents, running out of ideas. I said the first time he did that to me I'd tell the police. I'd run as soon as I was able.

'It was an empty threat, Detective. We both knew it. I'd never make it to the front door, let alone outside. He was faster, twice the size and he liked hurting things. He took me up into my parents' bedroom, past their comatose forms. He unlocked the French windows, dragged me on to the balcony and threw me straight off it. Just chucked me over the parapet. I had no chance. I landed shoulder first. I was lucky it wasn't worse. Or unlucky. I could never decide which.

'In the hospital, he said we'd been working on the roof, fixing broken tiles. He said I'd taken off the safety rope to reach a water bottle. He was very good as the anxious brother who sort of blamed himself. Impressed the nurses. He knew how to talk to nurses. On the way home, he told me next time it would be head first, so he might get me paralysed without using the insulin. Wouldn't that be a blast, he said. Wasn't a difficult lesson to learn: and he'd made me learn it in front of our parents. The threat was never death, Detective; the threat always involved me staying alive, but helpless.'

She nodded. Extreme interrogation techniques usually involved implied or future pain, not reality. To talk in excruciating detail about how a finger snapped under pliers was more terrifying, and more effective, than cutting off that finger. The threat of being a frozen victim, with his brother's lack of mercy, was the worst thing Nathan could have imagined. And Jeb had known it.

'And this continued, after the broken arm?'

Nathan had reached a point where crying neither hindered him nor bothered him. He spoke through the tears.

'Yes. He'd become less interested in it by then, I'd thought. My parents only had "nap time" occasionally. He varied it: kept them off balance. One month nothing, then maybe two days in a row. He wanted them in a permanent state of agitation. He wanted their silence, and their money.'

It was an obvious question and she needed to ask it.

'What happened just before you left, Mr Whittler? What made you decide to run?'

Nathan didn't speak for some time. He started a couple of times but halted mid-breath. He looked up at the ceiling and away into the corner. And he looked at his own reflection, as though for the first time. She could see the sweep of his vision: across his unkempt hair, over his drained and terrified features, down to his tense grip on the water bottle.

'He did it to me, Detective. He froze me.'

From what she now knew of Jeb, she suspected he wouldn't have been able to resist. Nathan was compliant now – he'd have been a pushover back then. And Jeb would have become bored with his parents:

he'd like novelty in his bullying. There would be a certain bizarre pride, she felt, in his ability to think up new ways to scare, to control.

'I . . . I was asleep in a chair. Late at night. The needle was in before I'd even begun to wake. By the time I . . . he'd plunged it, and I was still waking. I felt . . . hmm. I felt cold, actually. Cold as death. No pain. Not actually distressed in any physical sense. Like an anaesthetic. Like floating. The distress was all in here.' He tapped his forehead. 'The fear was what Jeb might do.'

In the silence that followed Dana made a decision. She looked across to the mirror and *felt* Bill's approval for what she did next.

'It's okay, Mr Whittler. It's okay. We don't need to know more than that. We don't need to.'

His face got nearer to a genuine smile, and nearer to peace, than she'd seen it.

'Thank you, Detective. Thank you. I . . . it's . . . you know. Raw.'

It was the first time they'd both looked straight at each other without one of them flinching and avoiding it. It lasted maybe three seconds.

'Perhaps . . . perhaps, Detective, I *would* like my parents to know I'm okay, after all. If you could let them know I . . . I can't explain everything. They might still . . . but if they knew I was okay.'

Dana swallowed.

'I'm sorry, Mr Whittler, I'm afraid that's not possible. You see . . . in 2007 . . . a car accident. Both of them. Instantly. I'm so sorry.'

It felt as though her words were echoing around the room: an aftershock of disaster. Nathan couldn't grasp them well enough. He looked perplexed for several seconds. Then a wash of comprehension swept over him as he dropped the water bottle. He buckled, fell undone, opened up at the seams. His knuckle went to his mouth as he began weeping. As Dana watched, blood started to flow from his hand, dripping off his wrist on to the floor.

Chapter 30

Bill watched through the mirror as Dana silently wrapped a handkerchief around Nathan Whittler's fist. She made sure never to touch his fingers. Not a word between them, and a conscious effort to avoid further eye contact. When she'd made a crude bandage, they both stepped back and held the two-metre space that felt like their natural distance.

Doc Butler was called in to deal with the teeth wounds on Nathan's hand; they weren't deep but, given the papery texture of his skin, they were still bleeding significantly.

Bill's fingers tapped a rhythm on the wall. He took a moment to work out how he was going to deliver bad news. Doc Butler paused at the doorway.

'Lucky I was here, clearing up all that crappy paperwork you have me do,' Doc Butler said as he watched Nathan being taken to the medical room.

'Yeah, I create lots of pointless forms for exactly that purpose.' Bill gave a shrug. 'We've already had Whittler in the Lecter Theatre on a ten-minute watch, but I'd like you to give him a full assessment. He's in jail, his home's been desecrated, he's chief suspect for murder; he's just found out his parents are long dead and he didn't even know it. Practically Suicide 101.'

Doc Butler headed off to find proper bandages and antiseptic. Bill entered Interview One. Dana was now exactly where she'd been when she'd called a halt. She stared at the far wall, shell-shocked.

'Hey. Might not feel like it right now, but that was top work.' Bill slumped into the chair. It looked strange to Dana to see anyone else sitting there, captured by that light. She wondered if it would now permanently seem odd; maybe Nathan's image would always appear when she entered the room.

Bill regarded her carefully; she could feel his gaze.

'This is killing you, doing this, isn't it?' he asked.

She shook her head and started fussing with her notes and pen. On any other day, no, it would be okay. On this Day, it was a high-wire act.

Bill reached out slowly and simply laid his hand on top of the papers. 'Dana? Isn't it? I can get Mikey to take it from here, if you need me to.'

She shivered physically at the thought of Nathan being anyone else's. And, she realised, it wasn't only for her sake: it was for his. Nathan couldn't do this without her. He couldn't get this far into his own fears without her sitting opposite. Making the case might ultimately be possible by other means, but if she could keep going it would build a stronger one.

'No, it's okay. Okay. Really. Thanks, Bill. I get it, but really, it's okay.'

Bill considered her. He could pull rank and insist, but he trusted her willingness to drop back if she felt the case needed it.

'Stu's about to finish shift,' he said, 'so I've asked McGregor to lead a search team at the old Whittler place at dawn tomorrow. He wasn't too impressed – look for small vials of tasteless, colourless liquid, on a property of twelve hectares.'

Dana could feel her batteries draining by the second. She was convinced any evidence was long gone, from both the farm and the parents' bodies. It was possible Jeb had continued with the practice and had some insulin stored elsewhere.

'Assuming it's there at all. Jeb doesn't live at the farm any more. Luce said it has new owners – some equestrian place. Jeb's apartment is over on Queen Street, I believe.'

'Yeah, we got an officer inside his building a couple of minutes ago and there's no sign of life. Warrant will take longer, but at least we've secured the place. Lucy says Jeb's back here again, demanding to see his brother. More belligerent this time, which, as we now know, is his default setting.'

'He can't see Nathan. We need to keep them well apart for now.'

'You think Jeb's given up freezing people?'

'Maybe. More likely his pathology has moved on.' Dana thought it would spiral. 'Getting his kicks maliciously toying with people some other way.'

'Banking? Internet provider?'

She gave a tired smile. 'Something like that.'

'I could give Jeb to Mikey again when he gets here. Mikey has a rapport from earlier and he unravelled Spencer Lynch today; might be worth a go.'

Dana tapped her pen against her teeth. 'Yes, maybe. Hmm. No. Actually, no. I think Jeb's the type who isn't going to like being faced by a woman. He'll overestimate himself against me. If Mikey went in a second time, Jeb would watch his step.'

'Okay. I'll have Mikey through the mirror, in case we need to turn it into a two-hander. And a uniform, in case Jeb doesn't play nice.'

'Deal. At least we know why Whittler ran, and why then.'

'Yeah, one episode of being frozen alive and at the whim of a psychopath would probably be enough.'

'I'd had some crazy hope he would have left because of Lou

Cassavette. You know – some kind of connection or incident we're not aware of?' She knew Cassavette had lived in the city until recently and had no discernible reason for being anywhere near Carlton. All the same, she'd hoped for some bizarre linkage, something they could never have spotted on their own.

'I still can't fit the two of them together,' she continued. 'They appear to have never met, or been within cooee of each other, until 5 a.m. today. All the forensics say it was an opportunist crime, but robbery isn't the motive and Whittler's never been violent before. Quite the opposite – a passive and compliant victim. It still doesn't make sense.'

Bill was about to reply when there was a knock and Lucy glanced around the door.

'Hey, Dana. Boss. Mr Jeb Whittler is still in reception, wanting to see his brother. In an ever-more charmless kind of way, too.'

Bill scratched his chin. 'Put him in Interview Three, with a uniform outside. Full – and I mean full, Luce – security check before entry. Especially for needles. Tell Whittler a detective will be with him shortly.'

'Boss.'

Bill turned back to Dana at the click of the door. 'So . . . where are we? I think we have a perspective on Whittler's life before the cave and we understand his life in the cave. We know what the motivation was for entering Jensen's Store this morning. We have a pretty good handle on how damaged Whittler's been his entire life and how that happened. Not bad for' – he checked his watch – 'under twelve hours.'

Dana nodded dutifully but her mind was reaching. 'Only a few hours left before he's gifted a lawyer. We still have no motive. We have nothing to connect Nathan Whittler to Lou Cassavette.'

'Maybe there is no motive, Dana.' He leaned forward. 'Maybe you want there to be, but it doesn't exist.'

She pondered that, gave it due weight. Bill didn't say such things in a vacuum.

'You think I'm wishing some gallant reason for Whittler's actions? Something that doesn't make it petulant or spiteful or vicious, or simply desperation to get past Cassavette and out the door?'

'Yup. You're looking for the mythical orphan in danger, the nun that needs saving – some altruistic heroism you want Whittler to have shown. At the very least, a morally comprehensible reason for killing.'

Bill put both palms on the table.

'He's an unhappy, isolated person who's had fifteen years to brood. He's damaged. He's seen brutality rewarded and being successful for much of his life. He's an inveterate thief, who has no actual moral problem with stealing each month for decades, no matter what he claims. He wants out of a store he chose to burgle and the owner's in the way. Maybe his OCD made him take the middle knife, maybe not. But he did use the knife, he did find the heart with the first and only stab, and he did kill Cassavette.'

Bill paused and dropped half an octave. 'And I would really, really, like a confession.'

There was no smile at the end of it. Bill simply stood up and left, a consoling tap on her shoulder as he passed.

She sat for some minutes, considering. Bill was right. She'd hoped for something better for Nathan Whittler . . . *from* Nathan Whittler. She'd wanted one single reason that made the killing less callous and more understandable.

Bill had pulled her up short, and rightly so. That, she thought, is why he's the boss. And why she never could be, never *should* be. The ability to cut through like that – to see the straight line, deliver bad news in such a temperate way: she didn't have those skills.

He was right, she concluded. Motive didn't really matter, when all was said and done. Whittler's defence could argue the fine detail – it was really dark; maybe it was more of a scuffle than the forensics suggested; perhaps Cassavette kinda fell on to the blade. The jury would convict anyway. There was no construct she could see that would be any kind of mitigation or benign explanation. In her mind, Nathan Whittler was guilty and all she had to do was calculate how to eke out a confession.

Before she set foot in a room with Jeb Whittler, Dana wanted to bring Mike up to speed. He'd taken a break after writing up his discussion with Jeb and now sat slurping coffee. Dana's office felt claustrophobic. She looked at her watch and set herself an hour to leave this place, come what may. Her knee was starting to really grind – it needed a warm bath. She grabbed at the nebuliser in her pocket, in case a panic attack was imminent. Placing a timescale on the working day's end seemed to have calmed her jagging nerves a little. Father Timms had been right. Everyone around her seemed to be wiser than her today.

'Is that even possible?' Mike was shaking his head after hearing Nathan's story. 'I'm not . . . don't get me wrong, I believe him. It's just . . . well, I would have thought it would be impossible to be that accurate with the correct dosage.'

'I'd have thought so, too. Maybe Luce could look into that.' Mike scribbled a note. 'We have to take it seriously, unless or until we can prove otherwise. My vague understanding is that the impact of the same dosage each time varies – according to time of day, what they'd eaten, their weight, and so on, as well as blood sugar level.'

'Maybe that's why he did it after lunch on a Saturday – he felt more confident about those details, able to control them better. He could dictate what they ate beforehand, for example. Still, you'd think he'd get it wrong sometimes, wouldn't you?'

'Absolutely. He probably did. I'm betting he kept some kind of antidote close at hand. There's something doctors use for blood sugar emergencies, I think. If Jeb was stealing insulin, he could probably steal the antidote, too. He must've had a few close shaves he never mentioned to his brother. It's Russian Roulette, basically.'

'Certainly is. But with other people's lives, not his own.'

'Did he strike you that way when you saw him?'

Mike considered carefully, unsure that his own reading of Jeb was good enough in light of this revelation. Perhaps he'd held too benign a view.

'Well, unless someone's behaving outlandishly, they wouldn't strike you that way. Because that particular behaviour is off the charts. But if you're asking do I think he's capable? Maybe. He has some streaks in him of total authoritarianism: as he said himself, "My way or the highway." I thought when he spoke about discipline and punishment he was only talking about his parents inflicting it on him and his brother. Now I'm convinced he was talking about himself. He used the words "me" and "I" a lot: I thought he was reliving being on the receiving end. But maybe he was talking about dishing it out. My bad, not picking it up at the time.'

'I don't know what kind of mental damage it would do to Whittler, seeing that.' Dana pictured the regularity of it, the drip-feed of horror and control. 'The insulin went on for nearly twelve months before Whittler left home. Plus, the years of bullying and domination that preceded it. That kind of abusive behaviour and imagery usually leads to some numbing, some habituation.'

In moments like these she was convinced her guilt and her pain were carved across her features. She was always amazed that they apparently weren't. Parents and pain, parents and humiliation, parents and guilt, years of drenching misery, feeling constantly off balance and waiting for the air to chill: she and Nathan had a disturbing amount in common.

The pain in her knee spiked.

'Yeah, maybe it's less about the trauma at the time . . .' Mike held his hands open, as if his statement explained itself, but Dana frowned. Mike had to expand the point, when usually he wouldn't need to: it confirmed his view that she was tiring badly.

'I meant,' he continued, 'as you say, he'd try to compartmentalise it. He wouldn't deal with it fully, he'd run and hide from it. His modus operandi, right? But out there, in the cave year after year, he'd surely have to come back to it again and again. That's when he'd process it: when he's isolated, with no professional help, turning it over in his mind. You can come to some pretty hideous conclusions that way.'

Mike had made a good observation, she thought: the impact of the freezings would be in the long term. There was no point trying to work out how Nathan felt about those things while he was at home; the key was how it had made him feel recently. She was guessing the chief emotion was humiliation. An ongoing humiliation that he'd counteracted by removing himself and hiding – Nathan had an acute sense of shame and this would weigh heavily. He would feel that he'd been feeble, that he'd failed, that he'd let down his parents; above all, he'd been weak and supine. And now he knew he could never gain their forgiveness. It was a dark, potentially fatal mix.

She asked Mike to wait while she checked with Custody that they had a uniform watching through the glass of the Lecter Theatre. She was told they had; Doc Butler would begin a psych evaluation in six minutes' time.

Mollified – or at least believing that Nathan couldn't take his own life right now – she turned back to Mike.

'So, how do you expect big brother to behave this time?'

Mike shifted in his seat. 'Jeb was fine with me earlier. But he was fishing then; looking for a way in and coming off as Mr Reasonable. I just saw him waiting in reception and he's busting – all bets are off. He must be worried we've talked to Whittler enough to get the insulin story out of him; or he thinks he needs to see Whittler and threaten him into silence about it. Not wishing to white-knight or anything, but we could do a two-hander on him?'

'Yes, Bill suggested that. I'm not against it, but I'd rather keep it in reserve, or for a third run. If what we've just heard is correct, Jeb's the worst kind of bully. He'll be complacent against someone he regards as too delicate to undo him. That might be a way in.'

Mike wasn't convinced. Maybe Jeb would become loose-lipped and give something away, or he might feel manipulated or angry that he'd let something slip. If he became aggressive, Dana would be in the firing line.

'Look: amateur risk assessment. According to his brother – and he's seen it first hand – Jeb is a psychotic wingnut who can and does explode whenever things don't go his way. He relishes pain and control. Could turn ugly if he feels he's losing. He's built like a . . . well, built pretty big. You hit that panic button fast if you're unsure. Don't take any risks.'

'With this knee? Everywhere with stairs is a risk. I'm like a Dalek.' She dropped her smile. 'I hear you. I'll be a good girl, promise.'

Mike could see her reasoning: Jeb might well talk more freely if he was trying to push Dana around. But it was sticking her hand in a lion's mouth, hoping for a reward.

Rainer knocked on the door and stood rigidly at the threshold.

'Rainer, you can come in. I'm only talking to Mikey.'

Mike pouted. 'Yet I cherish every moment of our speaking, m'lady. I'm slighted. I'm getting a chocolate bar as comfort food for my battered soul and I'm not offering to buy you one. So there.'

She grinned and shook her head as Rainer sat.

'Ah, creative types and their theatrical egos. Sorry, Rainer. No adult should have to witness such things. What have you found out about big brother?'

Rainer opened a pristine clipboard, like a student on the first day of the academic year.

'You asked me to focus on financial and legal. Well, it seems all the bank accounts and property deeds for the family transferred to Jeb in 1990. Jeb was plenty old enough by then – nineteen. The lawyer I spoke to said it was dressed up as an early transfer to minimise tax issues. He was uneasy about it, but said it was all perfectly legal and watertight.'

'Uneasy because?'

'Well, he knew the family a little and found it odd that Nathan had been cut out entirely. I mean, this effectively ended any claim Nathan had over the family assets, so it was a bit of a coup for Jeb.' Rainer flicked to the second page. 'Also, he found the family atmosphere creepy, he said. Couldn't put a finger on it: only that something was wrong.'

'Well, he was spot on with that, though maybe not how he thought. It put all the money into one pair of hands: another reason for the brothers' friction. Anything else?'

Rainer checked his notes again, although she had no doubt he knew exactly what was written there. 'In 2005 Jeb used the farm as collateral for a business loan. He was renting scaffolding to small building firms, then expanded into steel-frame buildings, which is his main business now.'

'Hmm . . . he started that business soon after Whittler left.'

Rainer shrugged. 'By local reputation, Jeb's a fairly straight shooter who's been remarkably successful in facing down local unions. Seems he doesn't get the usual kind of intimidation they hand out at other building sites.'

'Uh-huh. And no evidence of any financial or legal transactions with Lou Cassavette?'

'No. I double-checked: but no, not as such. However . . .'

'Go on, spill it before you burst.'

'Lucy sent me to the old farm, where the Whittlers used to live? It's an equestrian centre now and the new owners never met the Whittler parents – they bought direct from Jeb. But the owner said he saw Jeb Whittler a few weeks ago, at Jensen's Store. Chatting with Lou Cassavette. "Two peas in a pod," he said. Didn't hear what they were talking about, but he said they probably knew each other from the business club.'

Dana sat back.

'So Jeb knows the victim, and he's recently been to the crime scene. Wow.'

It presented a quandary. When, or even if, should she bring out that knowledge when she interviewed Jeb? Was it a trump card she should hold back? Maybe it would be better to play it while Jeb was off guard.

'That's a real coup, Rainer, well done. Could you follow up with the business club?'

'Already tried. They're closed today – repainting. The secretary's hiking somewhere in the national park. I'm on duty tomorrow so I can chase any further details then: there's a meeting Saturday evening.'

Dana glanced at the photo montage of Jeb that Lucy had emailed. Jeb at a charity function, Jeb meeting a politician, Jeb at a conference. You could dress the man in a tailored evening suit, or jeans and sweater: whichever, he was huge and overbearing. She started to reconsider Mikey's idea of a two-hander.

'Good, thanks, Rainer. What time does your shift end?'

'Oh, not till eight.'

'Okay, please help Luce with her follow-up, especially this insulin angle. If there's a medical reason that claim isn't possible, or ridiculously impractical to do, I need to know as quickly as possible. And you might have to tidy up some details when Luce leaves. She's pretty punctual.'

'Boss.'

When Rainer closed the door behind him Dana took a deep breath and checked her watch. Fifty-two minutes. In fifty-two minutes' time, she was walking out the door and home, no matter what. Dana had already broken the bargain she had with herself about this Day. She was supposed to be giving all options full airtime, really considering what her mind wanted for her. Instead, she was cheating: staying somewhere that made that kind of soul-baring impossible. It had cost her several panic attacks, and she had a constant feeling of slipping below the waterline, fighting for air. She couldn't afford to break this second deal as well: she wouldn't be able to take it.

She signalled to Mike as she went towards his office and he walked down the corridor ahead of her. She could hear him talking in low tones with the uniform. It was already established Jeb was a potential risk: she didn't need to hear it again in Mike's briefing to the officer.

At the door to Interview Three she nodded to Mike and stepped into the room.

Chapter 31

Jeb Whittler controlled a corner of Interview Three: he cast a hefty gloom. His frame was deep and imposing, predatory. Jeb had a head where the skull shape was easily distinguishable.

'Mr Whittler? Please, have a seat.' She indicated the chair with an open palm.

He took two giant steps towards her. Everything about him seemed to suck up the space.

'Where's Nate? I demand to see my brother.' The voice rumbled off every surface like a freight train.

Dana took two breaths while they glared at each other. His eyes were a deep brown, practically black.

'Mr Whittler? Please, have a seat.' The same intonation, the same hand motion.

Jeb sighed theatrically and swamped the chair.

'I was here before and your boss steamed me off. Not falling for that again. I've been here this time for' – he checked his watch ostentatiously; she saw the pearl glint – 'twenty-eight minutes. I want to see my brother. Right now.' He pressed his palms flat on the table, as though he could squash it by flexing a wrist.

Dana sat and waited a beat before replying. 'Hmm. Mike Francis is my colleague, not my boss. I'm sorry you've had to wait for' – she looked at her own watch – 'twenty-one minutes, Mr Whittler. We have several other things to do this afternoon.'

Jeb scowled. 'So do I, missy. I haven't seen my brother in fifteen years. I've been interstate all week: I have work to do. Where's Nate?' His neck muscles flexed against a white collar. The shirt looked creamily expensive. He had a boxer's neck; thick and strong.

'He's having a cup of tea, Mr Whittler. He's comfortable. We've asked you in to—'

'Nate. I want to speak to my brother.' Jeb slapped the table. 'He needs family.'

When she didn't jump to attention he recalibrated and flashed a charmless, rapacious grin. Looking her up and down as though everything about her was wanting, he waved a giant paw dismissively. 'If you can't authorise it, find someone who will.'

Jeb's glowering face wore deep, noirish shadows whenever he leaned in. Below the desk, Dana carefully slid her pen between her fingers as a potential weapon and surreptitiously checked the holstered spray canister on her right side. Her voice was calm and tempered.

'To explain, Mr Whittler. When the police require you to come to the station, it's because we have some questions for you. It's not so that you can demand things of us. The way' – her raised hand stopped his sentence mid-breath – 'this works – in fact, the only way it *can* work – is for you to answer those questions honestly and fully. There is, Mr Whittler, no other game in town.'

He sat back and smiled to himself. It was ugly. He glanced at the mirror and ran his hand over his polished scalp.

'Who's your superior officer?'

Dana held her nerve. 'I don't have a *superior* officer, Mr Whittler. I have a senior officer who'll be happy to speak to you when we're ready. And not before.'

Jeb's full-on grin had manic, icy zeal. 'Fine. Ask your questions.'

He folded his arms so that she'd see the bicep swell, the slap-you-into-next-week forearms. She could picture him swiping someone into a wall, watching them crumble to the floor. Someone he'd claim to love.

Jeb leaned in, tapping a car key on the table.

'Do you have a first name, Detective?'

She recognised the technique. Own the room, control the tempo.

'Everyone has a first name, Mr Whittler.' She looked straight at him. 'Even dogs.'

He chuckled; gravel through a cement mixer. 'What should I call you, then? Rover?'

'You can call me Detective.'

He pocketed the keys and shook his head. 'Ah, you should call me Jeb.'

'I'll stick with Mr Whittler, thank you.'

He snorted. 'Yeah, I bet little Nate insisted on being called Mr Whittler, right? Am I right? Thought so.' He withdrew a cocktail stick from an inside pocket and began to clean his nails with it. 'Still a self-important little prick, then. Always was. Always Mr Serious.' He arched an eyebrow. 'Needed a car jack up him since he was a snotty little brat.'

'The closeness of your relationship is deeply heart-warming. You suggested earlier that I should ask my questions. Shall we proceed with that?'

Jeb yawned and shrugged at the same time.

'I'll be needing your full, non-grooming attention for those questions, Mr Whittler.'

He sighed, flicked the cocktail stick into a shadowy corner. He folded his arms and puffed his cheeks.

'I'm at your command. Detective.'

Dana opened her file, even though she knew exactly what she was going to ask, and the sequence. Jeb made out that he relished confrontation, but she could see he wasn't used to being challenged.

'You mentioned to my . . . *colleague* . . . that you own a construction company. Steel frames, is that right?'

Jeb looked away dismissively. 'You know there's such a thing as the internet, right? You can look up my business any old time you like. This is bullshit. Let me see Nate.'

'Is that your only business, or do you have fingers in any other pies?'

He could see she was delving but wasn't sure where it was leading. He chewed his cheek.

'One or two. I co-own a gym in Earlville. Always looking for the right kind of opportunity. That's business. I don't get a guaranteed pay cheque each month, unlike some . . . I have to *earn* my money.'

'Do you know, or have you ever met, Lou Cassavette?'

'Lou? What's he got to do with this?'

It was a vague hunch; a detail she'd seen in the transcript of Mike's interview with Megan Cassavette. It was something that had nagged at her when she read it. Rainer's work had established the two had met, but she was taking a punt on a closer connection between them.

'Answer the question, please.'

'What's . . . ? He doesn't know Nate. Why are you asking about him?'

Dana gave him an implacable stare that showed she could wait all day.

'Urgh, this is bullshit. I met Lou a couple of times this year. We talked vaguely about me investing in his piss-ant little shop.'

Jeb had to know it was Lou who'd been murdered, she felt: it had been on the news all day, even if no names had been released. There was enough detail for someone who knew Lou to work out it was him and it was the only murder in the state this week.

'The fool,' Jeb continued with a sneer, 'bought the place freehold and tied up most of his cash when he did it. Meant he had a failure of a shop but a possible asset. When I went there I could see potential for tearing the dump down and building housing: it comes with its own forest. But the local planning geniuses soon banjaxed that. End of sports. I've met Lou for maybe an hour in my entire life. Why?'

Dana wrote slowly, to the background of his belligerent, fuming indignation. She wanted him off balance like this; as they'd suspected, Jeb would play fast and loose when he wasn't in control. She felt it was significant that he hadn't acknowledged he knew Lou was dead. There was an obvious reason why he might hide it: and he had been at the crime scene just two weeks earlier. Dana chose to keep her powder dry. Time to switch.

'Your brother went missing in 2004, is that correct?'

Jeb shrugged.

'Sounds about right, yeah.'

It wasn't something he'd forget. Dana didn't like the fake insouciance.

'About right, or absolutely accurate? You were there, Mr Whittler.'

'He'd have been around . . . twenty-one, twenty-two; so yeah.'

'Again: you were there at the time, Mr Whittler. May 3, 2004.' She glanced down at the notes before confirming the date.

The subtle implication of evidential weight made Jeb glance at the paperwork and pause before answering. He swallowed and shuffled his weight.

'Whatever. Around then. It's a long time ago. Why would I remember a specific date?'

'Because it's the specific date when your only sibling vanished, not to be seen again for fifteen years. Did you report him missing to the authorities?'

Jeb leaned forward and swept the table in front of him with the palm of his hand. Ostensibly cleaning it; actually marking out an arc of territory. 'Don't insult my intelligence. You've checked, so you know I didn't.'

'Why not?'

'I, uh, don't believe in wasting the taxpayer's money, Detective.' He smirked to himself. 'Nate chose to go; no need to have the police running around. Besides, my family are very private people. We don't like opening our lives up to all-comers.'

'Did you look for him?'

Jeb shot his cuffs. 'Yeah, I tried his usual haunts. Both of 'em. Turns out he wasn't in the library or the park. He had no friends to ask.'

'And then you stopped looking?'

He leaned forward, sensing an advantage. '*Au contraire*, Detective. I hired a private investigator.'

'And what did the PI find?'

'That he could charge a thousand and locate nothing. And then he found he wanted to give half of it back. We came to an arrangement.' He let the insinuation hang in the air and absent-mindedly clasped a knuckle with the other hand. It looked natural, subconscious. Habitual.

'Look, Detective, Nate took off for his own reasons and didn't want to be found. So in the end I left him to it. He knew where we were. We didn't move house or anything. He could have picked up the phone, or walked through the door, any time he liked. Why don't you ask him why he left and where he went?'

'I have, Mr Whittler. He has an interesting story. Perhaps you could help to verify some of the details?'

Jeb sat back, understanding that this was the crux of the conversation. 'Well, we've established what a helpful person I am.'

'We certainly have.'

Dana glanced towards her notes.

'How had you and your brother been getting along in the lead-up to his disappearance?'

He was, she guessed, wondering how much she knew; exactly what Nathan might have spilled and whether Jeb could be digging a hole for himself. If she knew all of it, maybe he needed legal advice. On the other hand, she was asking perfectly reasonable and neutral questions. If she knew little or nothing, he'd only open up her suspicions by suddenly reaching for a lawyer.

'Okay. As brothers go. You've met him. We're different people, Nate and I; different eras. He needed, uh, steering. They all did. My parents wouldn't say boo to a goose. Nothing got done unless I made it happen.'

'I see. So you're very much the driver of the family's life, is that so?'

'I was. My parents died after Nate left; car accident. But until those things, yeah. I was the one with the energy, ambition.' When he wasn't speaking his clenched jaw betrayed the tension.

'I understand. So it's true to say that nothing significant went on in the family without your say-so, or your own action?'

Jeb's eyes narrowed. He could see he was being pulled down an alleyway.

'What's Nate said? He's a bullshitter. You know that, right?'

She ignored him. 'You controlled the family finances in 2004?'

'Yeah. Yeah, I did. So what? My parents were hopeless with money. Nate was a low-achiever, contributed next to nothing. Someone had to make sure the bills were paid on time.'

'Quite so. Especially when you'd had full power of attorney granted in 1990. Your brother was only ten then?'

'It was a sensible, lawful arrangement. Tax efficient, too. Business people have to think of those things, Detective, unlike public servants. I assume you've got a copy of the agreement. You'll have seen it was witnessed by the bank manager himself.'

'Oh yes, it's a legal document. No question.'

'And? There is an "and", isn't there, Detective?'

She took a slow breath. Time to launch.

'Your brother alleges that, on a number of occasions, you injected your parents with insulin. To induce either coma or paralysis.'

She looked straight at him, wondering what Mike was making of this from the viewing room. Such an accusation should have brought incredulity from Jeb; shocked denial. Instead, it brought a *felinisation* of his features. He seemed to be calculating how much she understood. Or, more importantly, could prove.

Dana continued. 'He alleges that you embezzled your parents' money. He alleges that you bullied and controlled them, and him, over many years. He alleges that you broke his arm and threatened to kill him if he ever spoke about your insulin habits.'

She could see Jeb struggling to retain control. He focused on a corner of the room and dropped the volume.

'He says a lot of things, Detective. No doubt he's given you the concrete evidence to back it all up.'

She finished the accusations. 'He says that's why he ran in 2004: because you were going to end up killing him.'

Again, the casual stroke of the knuckle. Jeb simmered for a second, maybe considering whether he could get to her before anyone could burst in and stop him. She looked at him evenly. She could fall backwards and hit the panic button in half a second. But he might need only one punch to deform her face for ever. She made that exact calculation.

'That's some story, Detective.' His voice was quiet now, unnerving.

'We're looking into the evidence, Mr Whittler. What do you say to those statements?'

He separated his hands, clasped one knee as he crossed his legs.

'Hah, look. Nate always had an imagination. Apparently, he still does. That's, uh, fanciful. Ludicrous. Insulin? I don't even know if that's physically possible. Neither do you.' Jeb leaned forward and half his face disappeared in shadow. 'Nate always had thought bubbles coming out of his head. Never speech bubbles. If you catch my drift.'

'That sounds like contempt.'

'He's my little brother, Detective. We're linked in blood. But yeah, he was never going to amount to much until he learned to talk to people.' He raised a finger, as though this were simply a point of order. 'I mean, you're in a people business, aren't you? Wouldn't get far without those skills.'

Dana collected herself, aware of the station gossip from Nathan's arrival this morning: some felt her lack of informants, 'street smarts' and intel were apparently proof that she didn't have those skills and thus wouldn't get far.

'I meet people in particular circumstances. Maybe your brother would have, or develop, the skills for a particular job. They seemed to like him at Pringle's Furniture, wouldn't you say?'

Jeb leaned his forearms on the table and scoffed. 'Pringle's? Wow, that place. Oh, I'm sure. Twenty-three years old and still on minimum wage? Yeah, I bet he was employee of the month. He took two weeks to make a chest of drawers, for God's sake. Big whoop. Old man Pringle sold those for a fortune – saw the gullible hordes coming all the way up the highway.' He squeezed his hands together. '*Ooh, hand-made, crafted, built to last*: bullshit. What a huckster, and what a con.'

Dana noticed that Jeb remembered Nathan's exact age when it suited him. She wrote something he couldn't comprehend, in Pitman, then ticked it off, as if it were something he was bound to say. 'That sounds more like admiration, Mr Whittler.'

'Well, now, I admire the business model in some ways. Big profit margin, that's true. But he was using Nate, ripping him off.'

'And big brother was out to protect him, right?'

Jeb sat back suddenly. A sneering grin came across his face. 'You don't have any siblings, do you, Detective? Yeah? No? Thought not. I can tell. You don't get the connection – you don't comprehend it. You think brothers are school buddies that live in the same house. You don't get it. Brothers is different. Brothers is special.' He put his palms flat on the table again and his eyes fell into shadow. 'I want to see little Nate now, Detective.'

His counter was predictable: try to strike a personal nerve. She'd seen it coming. 'Are you denying the allegations I've just put to you?'

'Allegations? They're a bunch of laughable dreams. Nate probably read a book or ate some funny mushrooms. Overactive imagination. I don't know, you tell me.'

He tried a hollow laugh but it came out like a cough. He was rattled, she thought. Rattled, because he did all those things. She wasn't one for making rapid assumptions of guilt but her gut instinct had never been stronger.

Jeb felt compelled to continue. 'What would make a grown man come up with childish crap like that? Yes, Detective, I categorically deny every idiotic claim you've just made. Clear enough for you?'

'Crystal, thank you.'

Dana could hear him attempt to control his breathing. While she was convinced Nathan's accusations were true, there seemed scant chance of proving it unless Jeb was going to crumble. The parents' bodies would be decomposed; there would be no witnesses except Nathan. Forensics were a long shot.

'I'll see my brother now, then.'

She put her hand on her belt, lightly touching the spray canister. 'That isn't possible at the moment, Mr Whittler. If I get an opportunity, I'll mention that you're here.'

'You'll *mention*? What the hell does that mean?'

'Exactly what it says, Mr Whittler. I'm very precise with my language: it's a blessing and a curse.' She paused. 'As you pointed out earlier, your brother is an adult and can make his own decisions. I've had to tell him that his parents are dead; he'd been unaware of that fact. I think he has quite enough to deal with at present.'

It got to him. She could see it. Jeb ran his hand across his scalp and looked away to the mirror.

'You had to . . . what? He didn't know?' Jeb shook his head. 'Where the hell's he been? It was in the city newspapers, not just local. He must've been a long way away when it happened.'

Dana didn't answer. *Yes*, she thought, *he kinda was.*

Jeb spluttered on. 'Well, that's . . . that's exactly why he needs his brother. Time like this. News like this.'

'What he needs is medical attention, which he's receiving for some minor cuts. He needs some time alone to think, and then he needs to speak to me again.'

She stood up and gathered her files. 'When I think he's up to dealing with you, and if he agrees, you'll be able to see him. You're welcome to wait in the reception area if you wish.'

Jeb sat back again and extended his legs under the table. He was now off balance: all the aggression and bluster had won him nothing. 'I bet you love this, huh? Love acting like you own people.'

She walked to the door, watching his shadow rather than him, and took hold of the handle.

'Hmmm. As your brother has stated himself, I have his best interests at heart.'

She opened the door and nodded at the corner of the room. 'Don't forget to pick up your litter before you go, Mr Whittler. You can wait in reception or leave the station. Up to you. Good afternoon.'

Chapter 32

Earlville Mercy was a regional institution. Started way-back-when by some nuns, it had gradually morphed into a secular spine for the area. Other public bodies were mistrusted, abused or ignored; but Earlville was proud to have the area's public hospital. Old or young, rich or poor, postcode irrelevant – Earlville Mercy took them all: one of the few levellers uniting the region.

The original building had been a cottage hospital, but that elegant sandstone edifice was now the visitor reception and held several rooms of communications equipment. Above the main doorway the carving told of *mercy for all*. The words floated serenely between a unicorn and a dragon, as if to signify that such an outcome was pure fantasy. It was a facade, in every sense.

Beyond the main wing, units and wards had been added as temporary capacity that everyone knew would become permanent. Like much of the region, any part built before the Second World War was subtle, balanced and showed local craftsmanship in stone and plaster. Anything constructed after the war was timber or clinker-brick: thrown up by the cheapest-bid supplier, to the lowest cost.

Rainer had tracked down the incident mentioned by Dan Mathers.

From the original report, he'd uncovered that Natalie Brewer was the woman who'd skulked around the Whittler farm just after it was sold. It was no doubt routine back then, but with the benefit of hindsight, her presence at that place and that time now seemed significant. At the very least, she apparently knew the Jeb Whittler of old and Dana was looking for potential validation of the insulin story.

Natalie was a nurse who'd flipped mainly between pre-natal, diabetes and renal clinics around the state over the past twenty years. A call to the state's nursing board showed Natalie's return to Earlville two years ago, after over a decade in the city. Rainer was noticing that the town had a strange pull on its former residents, despite its lack of beauty or whimsical charm. The tug was deeper and more heartfelt than simply low property prices: they slid back to Earlville in later life as though the rest of the world were too much to bear, and they'd take familiarity over absolutely anything else.

They found a table in a corner of the canteen area, which Rainer was surprised to find appeared to be closing down for the night. Five o'clock on a Friday afternoon. In another corner three doctors laughed raucously at their own jokes, desperately stealing glimpses at the one nurse at their table to see who was impressing.

Natalie had recently downshifted from ER to the Stoma unit. Now she was in her forties, Emergency was too much hassle. Because of what it did, it was at the forefront of hospital politics. The peak times were chaotic, challenging and, despite the trauma, it was fun. But the quieter moments – when adrenaline junkies had too much time and too little that was urgent enough – became the setting for petty squabbles. Arguments about shifts, about perceived slights, about who was screwing who; she found the rumour and innuendo both exhausting and pathetic. So she'd switched to running Stoma – more regular hours, a smaller team; patients who were grateful and, by and large, stoically courteous. Something about a physical opening in the body that shouldn't be there – and the equipment around it – made people humble and accepting. Hard for patients to be on their high horse, when they needed someone to show them how to empty a colostomy bag.

'What do the night shift do?' Rainer asked, nodding towards a shutter that squealed as it closed access to the refrigerated goods.

Natalie was intelligent but somehow wearied by her own life. Rainer speculated she'd made some poor decisions and had never quite escaped the consequences. She had a sparkling awareness, ill matched to her pallid skin and enduring fatigue.

'Oh, there's dozens of machines around the place, Officer. If you work shifts, what you really need are healthy, nutritionally balanced meals to help you cope with the body clock. So what they offer you are sugar-loaded fats.' She eye-rolled. 'Go figure.'

Rainer smiled. 'Please call me Rainer. So, as I said on the phone, we're interested in Jeb Whittler, specifically in the time around his brother's disappearance, and again when he sold the farm. Let's start with how you met Jeb.'

Natalie put her chin into a cupped hand and sighed. He could tell it was not going to be a happy reminiscence.

'Urgh, mainly by being an idiot. This is nearly twenty years ago, mind you. I was a stupid little cow back then. Young, dumb, and full of . . . crap. Any sense I have now was learned the hard way. So I was a perky little nurse, thinking that since I was saving life and limb, I should be treated royally by all and sundry. If I met that version of me now, I'd end up slapping the little madam. You get the picture. I won't bore you with how I became that kind of person, but I was.'

She stopped suddenly, as though the memory was saturated by loss. Just as abruptly, she resumed. 'I'd met Jeb occasionally at parties. He was always very popular, but I could never work out why. I mean, he's an odd looker and lacks charm. Have you seen him?'

Rainer grimaced. 'Mainly on web pages or camera, not for real. Not a face that sells calendars, is it?'

Natalie smiled but kept her tinge of ingrained sadness. 'Agreed. But at that age, you take your cues from everyone else, and they all looked so happy to see him. That mystery intrigued me, I suppose: I mistook it for enigmatic charisma. Ha. Gullible little fool.'

The two staff who'd closed the food area now drifted away, each too engrossed in their phones even to bid farewell to each other. Rainer always found hospitals brutally impersonal, despite their work being deeply intimate.

'Anyway, we started going out, and at first it was okay. Then I began to realise that he was popular because he was the party connection, the supplier. Now it all made sense – everyone whooped when he arrived because of what he brought with him. By then, though, he assumed I was his girlfriend and therefore his property. He's that type of person. The arm around the shoulder, but the fingers dig into the collar bone? The silent volcano? I'd spot it a mile off now, but at the time I didn't realise until too late. He thought he owned me, and I thought he did, too.'

'Was he ever violent towards you?' Rainer had seen footage of Jeb being interviewed by Mike, and got the impression of a simmering anger.

Natalie paused to spit out some gum into the wrapping. She looked around for a waste bin that wasn't there, then shrugged and simply held the wrapper in her hand.

'Not . . . immediately, no. I mean, yes, but . . . ah crap, sorry. Look, Jeb was huge, compared to me. At that age I was this tall but only half as wide, if you can imagine. It felt like Jeb could put his hand on my head and press, and the ground would swallow me up. He could snap any bone in my body; I felt like a matchstick. So there was always this, uh, implied threat. He didn't have to shake his fist or tell me what he might do. Didn't need to be said. It was always there; off our shoulders, all the time. Over time the shadow became real, but it all spiralled so slowly I barely noticed. Each bit seemed inevitable from the previous bit; normal, somehow.'

She was visibly shaken. Rainer nodded.

'Other than that implied threat, how would you characterise the relationship?'

'How would I characterise it? Well, it was a one-way street. I'd be at his beck and call because I was scared of him, and he'd ignore me whenever it suited. I had to wait for his telephone call, whether it came or not. Woe betide me if he tested that and I failed to answer. He made plenty of money from the dealing, so he spent a fair bit bringing down, um, *escorts* from the city. He had a highly pornified brain, and the cash to live it out. Does that paint a picture?'

'Very much so. We're say, a year before Nathan disappears. That would be 2003 or so. What do you recall from then?'

Natalie squirmed in her chair. It seemed to Rainer that part of her discomfort was having to admit how much Jeb had controlled her.

'Some time before his little brother went missing I made a mistake. Can't recall exactly when. Uh, maybe December of that year? Don't quote me on that. Jeb kept bugging me about *acquiring* stuff for him, and he wasn't going to keep taking no for an answer. At first he wanted Valium, Temazepam, that kind of thing. He kept pushing – what drugs I could get, what they did, how they might be useful to him. He wanted something: no point dating a nurse unless he was getting some product. I told him about insulin, about how patients froze if they were given a certain dosage. I thought he'd find it funny. Jesus – he knew all about it. It was stomach-churning, how matter-of-fact he was. But he simply told me – ordered me – to get some.'

Rainer thought about interrupting to ask about protocols and security – how she actually got the insulin. But he felt the mechanics of the theft weren't the key issue. Dana and Mike wanted to know what was done, not how.

'I'm not proud of it, Officer. Rainer, sorry. Not proud at all. Ashamed, in fact. It was simply the lesser of two evils. By asking me for it he made me a potential problem if we split up, so there was that future threat as well as the current one. It was easier to get hold of insulin illegally than face the consequences of refusing him. I was weak, I was thinking self-preservation. Didn't even feel like a choice.'

'How often did you do this, Natalie?'

She looked off towards the garden that separated the canteen from the back of Intensive Care.

'Look, Natalie. We're not interested in prosecuting the possible theft of some insulin nearly twenty years ago. Your job isn't at risk here. But it's very important to us to get your impression of what happened around that insulin, and what Jeb was like at that time.'

Natalie hesitated and closed her eyes.

'He wanted to tell me what he was doing with it – as if it was some funny anecdote from being on holiday. I'd already guessed.' She turned and looked at him. 'It was vile. I begged him not to speak about it. At least – here was me, being a total coward – at least he wasn't doing it to me. But it would surely only be a matter of time. I knew enough about how his mind worked to understand it was coming.'

'And what did he say he was doing?'

She rubbed the side of her face. 'His parents. He was doing his parents. Freezing them, then doing all sorts of weird crap with them. Taking porno pictures, playing dress-up. Humiliating them, I suppose. Being Jeb, but to a whole new level. Like I said, it was only a matter of time before he tried someone else. Me, or his brother, or both.

'After, I don't know, eight or nine months of this, I made plans to escape from Jeb. By then I had bruises on my throat, bits of hair missing from my scalp; classic signs of escalation. Always my fault, of course. Something I'd *made him do*, naturally. People noticed – they gave me this whimpering look, as if I was some kind of run-over kitten they wouldn't cross the road to help. I was terrified, you see: scared to leave, scared to stay. I'm sure you've seen other women in that kind of plight. It was the sort of thing I never thought would happen to me, until it happened to me. Until I was that victim; I was that trapped little bird in his closed fist.'

Rainer passed her the water bottle and she took a deep swig. Her hand still shook.

'I'm sorry, Natalie, I don't mean this to be difficult, but we need to bottom out some things. Were you there when Nathan left?'

She shook her head. 'I assumed he was still there when I ran. I moved interstate, all in one night when I thought Jeb was away. A friend of my sister had an apartment across the border. She was going travelling, wanted a house-sitter for six months. I dropped a letter at the farm gate and scrammed. Hoped to God that Jeb didn't follow me, track me down. He could have, easily: I wasn't hidden that well. I got lucky. Turns out that was the night after Nate ran, too. So I guess everyone was bailing on Jeb at the same time.'

Rainer frowned. 'How do you know it was the night after Nathan left?'

'I had some friends I'd asked to keep an eye on Jeb after I went: you know, see if he was sniffing around the old apartment, asking after me, and so on. I gave myself way too much credit. I was only a scaredy-cat to play with when Jeb couldn't buy company. He couldn't have cared less that I was gone. But anyway, one of those friends said later that Jeb had been riding around that day looking for his brother, putting out the word.'

'So Jeb wasn't worried about you telling tales out of school?'

'Apparently not. He knew I was terrified of him. I imagine his ego thought that would always stick; that I'd never tell, and he was always safe. I imagine that's how his mind still works.'

Rainer thought about it. Everything tallied with Nathan's interview – everything. There was no way Natalie and Nathan could have co-ordinated; the pictures fitted because they were the same pictures.

'So you'd escaped. Why go back months later, a few days after Jeb had sold the farm?'

Natalie scratched at the table's surface.

'That friend who was keeping an eye out for me? Worked in real estate. Told me Jeb was selling. I was sure Jeb still had some of the last insulin I stole. He wasn't using as much in those last months before I went, so he probably still had some on the farm. Or maybe, old packaging lying around. I couldn't risk it, Rainer. That stuff comes in packets with reference numbers on the side – it's traceable. I could still have lost my job, my career. I heard Jeb had shot through and moved out in a hurry. Thought he might have left behind something incriminating – well, deadly for me, anyway. My friend said there were a few days before the new owners arrived. I went back when I knew Jeb wasn't there, had a check around.'

'Find anything?'

'Two packets, and some used syringes in the rubbish. I threw some of the other rubbish around, made it look like animals got into the bags. Burned everything incriminating. You said you didn't need to know . . .'

'We don't, no.' Rainer glanced at his notes, trying to think what Dana would ask. He turned to face Natalie again.

'Final question, Natalie. Are you okay? Is there something we can do to make you feel safer?'

The question buckled her: part surprise, part overwhelmed by the humanity of it.

'Oh. Oh, Jesus. Um, no. Thanks. No. Well, you could shoot Jeb, that would be real handy. But no, not really. I've been back two years and I've never even seen him across the street. I'm uh, older and wiser now. Haven't been drawn into that sort of garbage in a very long time.' She collected herself. 'But thank you, anyway. I mean it – thank you.'

Chapter 33

Mike was waiting outside the door; the uniform was standing sentry, ready to escort Jeb Whittler back to reception. Dana raised an eyebrow at Mike and they started walking towards her office. Her pulse was vivid; she felt a rush of heat and relief.

'There you go; isn't he quite something?' asked Mike. 'Now that's a man who could stab someone in the darkness. And he's been to the store. And we know that he knew Lou.'

'Yes, all that, Mikey. Plus, after talking to him I'm finding it easy to accept what was said about him: the bullying, the control, the insulin. All of it. He gave off that . . . danger. In waves.'

People like Jeb Whittler generally didn't faze Dana. They were a known quantity: a threat whose main pathways were easy to spot. Costlier were the insidious, the undermining, the covertly political; the ones who presented two very different faces when it suited them. In the confines of an interview room she could pick them out. In the real world, she found it tough.

'He didn't mention knowing Lou was dead,' said Mike. 'He must know, right?'

'Yes,' agreed Dana. 'Unless he's avoided the news. The radio reports said it was Jensen's Store; one man dead. Jeb has to make that calculation. He would avoid talking about it if he was involved, of course.'

A corridor light was flickering; it felt like a stab behind her eyes.

'To be fair,' said Mike, 'there's a number of reasons he might avoid mentioning that. You think he was there? You think his brother is covering for him? Or is Jeb doing the covering?'

'Don't know.' She shrugged. 'But Jeb's curious enough to stick around. I have nothing to hold him on right now, but he won't go far. He'll be lurking around trying to find out more, which buys us a little time. Although you said you thought he has a source here?'

'Yup. Peripheral, though. Not well placed. A good source would know we haven't charged Nathan Whittler with anything.'

They passed Lucy on the way to the office. Dana could see she had been viewing a silent feed from Interview Three. It was common practice within the unit: a standard safety measure, no matter who was involved, or how harmless they were assumed to be. Lucy looked troubled.

In the office, Dana sat and massaged her kneecap. 'For all that, I don't know that we're any further on. Jeb flinched at the allegations, and he didn't have a ready or persuasive response. But all we've got is hearsay. So we've proved nothing.'

Mike leaned against the wall. 'Indeedy. But your gut instinct?'

'My instinct won't stand up to prosecutors, Mikey, let alone a trial. Jeb genuinely didn't know what happened to his little brother when he ran.'

She thought for a moment about the process. A sibling goes missing – what would be the first steps?

'Jeb knew he'd gone off somewhere, but the effort to track him down was a cover. If he'd really wanted to find his brother, he would have called us on day one. Hiring a PI is a fig-leaf; it's a sop in case anyone asks. Like offering a reward: it looks like something major but it really isn't helping. If I didn't know Whittler was alive and kicking, I'd be asking Jeb and thinking murder.'

'He really had no idea that his brother didn't know about the parents. You shook him when you said that.'

Dana's finger and thumb twitched. She wondered how many minutes were left in her Day.

She shook her head. 'I don't know if he's rattled that Whittler didn't know, or angry that his little brother has stayed alive and out of his reach. He'd have expected Whittler to come crawling back, unable to cope with the real world.'

Mike couldn't work out which part of Dana's characteristic finger-twitching was the backdraught of Jeb, and which part was the underlying tension she'd shown all day.

'Having watched them both,' he said, 'I'd have bet on the latter. Jeb wants everyone within reach and scared – any other scenario annoys him. Whittler coming back would have been swiftly followed by Jeb offing him and burying him on the farm. Turns out running and hiding saved his little brother's life.'

'Yes, yes it did, and he knows it, too, I'm sure. Feels it deep down. That notion infected everything he did from that moment on.' She checked the drawer for nebulisers. 'Any further news on that intelligence between Lou Cassavette and the Alvarez family?'

'Yeah, no, that looks like a dead end. It's true that Lou knew the Alvarez boys, grew up alongside them, shared the same accountant. But Kaspar's minions haven't found anything to connect them in a criminal sense. No intel on money laundering or protection, or anything. No evidence they're in touch.'

Lucy poked her head around the doorframe. 'Need an update?'

'What do you have, Luce?'

'So, I've looked into this whole insulin thing. Which, by the way, is totally screwed up. Anyway, it seems it is technically possible, but immensely inadvisable. The body's chemical reaction to *exactly* the right dosage is as Whittler described. So theoretically, it's possible to do that, and then I suppose, in theory, do it on more than one occasion.'

Something in the back of Dana's mind said she'd heard of such a thing before. 'But since this isn't happening all over the nation, there are some big problems, no?'

'*Précisément, chérie*. So, the first problem is getting the dosage right. I mean, it's a very fine line between right and totally wrong. Get it totally wrong and they can die. Blood sugar's a constantly moving target. Even if you knew the required dosage now, it might be potentially fatal an hour from now. I'm assuming Jeb had controlled their diet and circumstances before injecting them. That would help, but it would only turn it from near impossible to pretty near impossible. Basically, Jeb got incredibly lucky to identify the correct dosage, then incredibly lucky again that the same dosage didn't produce a different outcome the next time. When I say "different outcome" I mean of course, serious illness or death.'

Mike gave Dana a sidelong glance. 'Like we said, Russian Roulette.'

'Which was probably part of the appeal for him,' Dana mused. 'I bet Jeb didn't get it right every time – sometimes overcooked it, sometimes left them partially mobile. Of course, under-cooking was fine. He could do what he liked anyway; having to control two people acting like drugged kittens wouldn't be a stretch. So the window of "correct dosage" was wider than, for example, a doctor would deem acceptable.'

She shivered at the thought that Nathan had been subjected to that.

'What else, Luce?'

'I was just going to add on that point: Jeb would never be able to take them to hospital, would he? I mean, if they were in diabetic coma and wouldn't wake up, he couldn't allow a doctor to see them. They'd be in a diabetic coma, but clearly not diabetic. The doctor would twig and Jeb would be prime suspect.'

'Good point. I hadn't thought that part through.' The gamble was bigger than she'd first calculated: Jeb was playing with his parents' lives but, in addition to that, he couldn't ask for help if anything went wrong.

Lucy beamed. 'Second problem is the cumulative effect – like anything where you continually whack the human body to an extreme, especially when the extreme is unhealthy. In the longer term, the human body starts to break down. It would be like bingeing, or burning: something the body can't keep trying to cope with. Jeb apparently did this regularly. The nurse I spoke to said the victims' systems would be under severe stress. The organs, especially – prone to collapse.'

Dana was doing a quick calculation based on Nathan's evidence of frequency. The irony was that the Whittler parents were – on one measure – two of the luckiest people on the planet.

'Third,' continued Lucy, 'you asked if there was some wonder drug that could bring them back from the brink? There is, sort of. It's called Glucagon. It's used in ERs, and diabetics often carry it for a one-off emergency. It restores blood sugar levels, and fast.'

'Ah,' said Dana, 'so if he mis-cooks, he can remedy that with the antidote.'

Lucy nodded. 'All the same, it's not perfect. It only acts temporarily, it's an imperfect science, and it has some side effects. In other words, if you're an untrained psycho jabbing a restorative into a comatose person, you're not doing it right. Not accurate enough, not controlled enough, and no way to monitor if you're getting it right. So, again, their bodies are put under immense strain. Jeb got very lucky, constantly.'

'Jesus,' said Mike, shaking his head, 'it was a wonder they were still alive when Whittler left. Jeb had no idea what he was doing.'

'And he seemingly couldn't care less about that,' replied Dana. 'Especially once he had that power of attorney and the property, the parents would gradually feel like disposable toys to him.'

She thought about after Nathan had left. Jeb getting bored with only two helpless victims; maybe knowing that he was pushing his luck each time; eager to move on with a new phase of life, and having the money he needed to do it.

'Makes me think their car accident might be no such thing,' she continued. 'Maybe they were killed by freezing and Jeb put them in a car and rolled them down a cliff.'

'Yeah, or faced with endless abuse and no respite, they deliberately . . .' Mike left it unfinished as Dana blanched.

'Ah,' said Lucy. 'Once again I can assist in a way that's almost spookily clever. I've had the estimable Rainer following all the detail on that car crash. It looks absolutely . . . uh, "benign" is the wrong word. Legit: that's the word. Icy evening, a corner. There was a truck driver coming the other way, had to slam on the brakes. He thinks the car driver would have fought the skid all the way: car found a small gap between two trees, then down into the ravine. Not really suspicious' – she glanced at Dana – 'but the digging isn't over.'

'Notwithstanding all that, Luce, it still doesn't sit well with me. I mean, of course it is possible to go into an icy corner too quickly and come a cropper. But equally, it's possible for the driver to plan it.'

Dana could feel the judder in her voice as she recollected this Day twelve months ago: staring at a tree while the engine purred. The calculations of speed and trajectory; the need for the impact to be on the driver's side; the assessment of where the debris might fly and who it could strike; the imagined faces of the emergency services and her role in their subsequent PTSD; the will and testament sitting on her kitchen table that morning; the anticipation of what colleagues might say. She knew how the Whittler parents would have prepared: what they would anticipate, how it would sit in their guts. She could guess that they held hands as the car left the tarmac. Dana could see it all.

'I don't like the convenience of it. The parents' death frees up Jeb nicely, doesn't it, at precisely the time he wants autonomy? Or, their death is the only way for the parents to escape because the whole insulin story is true? Either way, I want some more details around it. I don't like the idea of Jeb getting away with anything.'

She was about to ask another question when the phone intervened.

'Hey, Rainer. Your ears must be burning. Okay. Yes, push through.'

She grabbed a pen and scratched Pitman speedily for a couple of minutes. Mike and Lucy played rock, paper, scissors. Lucy remained unbeaten.

'Uh-huh. Oh, really? Yes, certainly, as long as it's not needed in court it won't be public: that's all we can offer.' She sat back. 'Thanks. Good sleuthing, Rainer, Lucy would be proud.'

She replaced the receiver. Lucy leaned forward expectantly.

'What will make me proud? What did my protégé-stroke-minion do?'

'He just verified the insulin story. When Rainer went out to the Whittler farm earlier, the new owner told him someone was sniffing around the place a day or two after Jeb shot through. They reported it, and it was investigated and the woman identified. She claimed she was an old friend who hadn't realised Jeb had moved. Rainer got the initial report and followed up. Turns out, it's a little more complex than that. She's Natalie Brewer, former girlfriend of Jeb's. She was a nurse at Earlville Mercy at the time. She'd told Jeb about the whole coma thing, never thinking he'd actually try it. He already knew of it. He muscled her into stealing some – not hard to picture that – and he started on his parents.

'She made a statement just now at Earlville Mercy. Rainer will email the statement and the interview in about an hour. That places Jeb right in the spotlight, capable of doing exactly what Nathan said he'd been doing. Makes a little more sense now. No doubt Natalie procured the insulin and the . . .'

'Glucagon.'

'. . . yes, what you just said. Might have got the needles for him, too. Apparently when she heard Jeb had sold up and left she went there looking for the extra packs she figured he hadn't used, because they might be traceable back to her.'

'So we know for sure why Whittler ran, and we can prove it,' said Mike.

Dana nodded, almost ecstatic that, however outlandish it had seemed, everything Nathan Whittler had said was true.

The phone rang again.

'Dana Russo.' She paused, and the others could hear a tinny microcosm of Bill's voice.

'Is he okay? . . . All right, yes. Sure. The doc's fine with that? Uh-huh. I think we' – she glanced at her watch – 'we can do that, yes. I'll see him in Interview One in ten. Thank you.'

She put the phone down and took a deep breath.

'Whittler okay?' asked Lucy.

'Yes. Well, sort of.' Dana was distracted, trying to race ahead even as she ran out of petrol. 'I mean, he passed the psych test and he's bandaged up. So, all good there.'

Mike frowned. 'So what's up?'

'They say Whittler has asked to talk.'

Chapter 34

It was unusual for Dana to arrive first. For the first time today, Nathan was setting the agenda and the timings. Dana didn't feel she could delay: he might change his mind and decide to wait for legal advice. It was hard to escape the notion that this was still a window that might slam shut at any moment. But alongside that was an uncomfortable sense that she wasn't controlling and shaping what now took place.

She frantically read back through her notes, trying to make sure she could slip from fact to fable, number to date, speculation to concrete, without breaking stride. She wanted to be able to interpret everything Nathan said without disturbing his flow. If she screwed it up and let the momentum fail, they probably wouldn't get another chance. Nathan's faith in her was genuine, but fragile.

Dana was aware that he was considered vulnerable. She guessed that his defence lawyer – when they arrived, and if they were worth their salt – would claim he was in no fit state. She knew better; as did Nathan himself. They both understood, after hours facing each other across the table, what Nathan could deal with and what was beyond him. They both knew Dana wasn't pushing him into anything. The trust that stemmed from that was precisely why he was now seemingly prepared to talk. This was the pay-off for the patience, the empathy, the politeness. The humanity.

Nathan came in and she experienced the novelty of his shadow falling across hers before sweeping away. She hadn't had to pay attention to his stride before. It was a shuffle. Nathan was embarrassed to be here: not only in this room under these circumstances, but to exist at all. She poured his water while he tapped his fingers together. When he moved his gaze from shoe to table, he was able to see her touch the bottle cap for him.

'How are your hands, Mr Whittler?'

He examined them, as though for the first time. She would have called his skin pale, but against the dazzling white of fresh bandages she could see some ravages of sun and wind. His hands were locked in a crabby half-grip.

'Oh, good, thank you, Detective. The doctor was very efficient. Self-inflicted, so . . . I can hardly complain.'

'I'm sorry we had to tell you something that led to that.'

'Yes. Well, I'm glad to know. I . . . missed that information. Sometimes I would acquire a newspaper. Always an old one, though: the ones they kept out the back for return later. Useful insulation. Emergency toilet paper. Crosswords. But I didn't read anything like that. No. Thank you, Detective.'

It had occurred to her that Nathan might very quickly pass through the shock and feel his parents had escaped to a better place – free at last of Jeb and his sick little hobbies.

'I think, Mr Whittler,' she began, 'we've reached the time where we talk about this morning. Specifically, what happened in Jensen's Store before dawn.'

'Oh?' Nathan raised his eyebrow, staring at the floor.

Dana thought for a moment. She could phrase the next question strategically, to make it seem inevitable that he should then talk about Lou Cassavette.

'Is there anything else you'd like to discuss before we talk about this morning?'

Nathan sat back and puffed his cheeks. He held his hands together in his lap; he looked as if he were clasped in invisible handcuffs. His body language resembled that of the condemned.

'I can't . . . no, I can't think of anything. The insulin? You've satisfied yourself on that score, Detective? I sensed you had reservations of some kind.'

'It was quite a lot to take in, Mr Whittler. It needed verification, research. Yes, we have, thank you. We contacted someone, and we have a statement from them.'

Nathan nodded slowly, trying to pull back a specific detail.

'Ah, probably . . . Natalie? Yes. I only met her a couple of times. Nice girl, pretty. Terrified of Jeb, of course. Like all of us. Still, all that's in the past now.'

Nathan blinked and a tear escaped. Dana pretended not to notice.

'Any crime investigation I undertake, Mr Whittler, is a search for the truth. Innocence, guilt, or anything in between: that's a matter for lawyers and courts. My job is veracity, integrity and evidence. Whatever we say here, about this morning, is simply one more piece of evidence.'

Nathan frowned at his bandaged hands.

'Well, of course. But it might be compelling, mightn't it? I mean, if I confess.'

Much of her discussions with Bill during the day had been, obliquely, about how Nathan's potential confession would sit. Hence the concerns she'd had about not tiring him out, about showing due concern for his welfare. If he sat here and admitted killing Lou

Cassavette, she needed it to be on terms that couldn't be attacked by a defence lawyer. Nathan was rested, supported, had overtly refused legal help and had been treated well: all that added weight to any admission. All the same, she wanted to minimise any pressure he might impose on himself.

'Hmm. People often think confessions are the be-all and end-all, but they seldom are. For example, sometimes people confess when they're nowhere near the crime in question. They might want attention, they might need help, they might be fantasists. Any confession, by anyone, is never more than another brick in the wall – it has to be corroborated, just as much as a witness statement.'

'I see. Yes, I can see that. But thinking from the other end, Detective, if I had done something wrong, why would I confess?'

It was a logical question. Dana hadn't yet come at him with killer forensics, for example, or CCTV coverage of the killing. He didn't know what she had or didn't have; perhaps, strategically, it would make sense for Nathan to simply wait and see what she could throw. But he didn't seem inclined to follow that path.

'Well, each to their own, Mr Whittler. But in my experience there are three main reasons why people confess to what they've done. Firstly, they may simply consider it part of a longer process and set little store by it. In that sense, it doesn't matter to them if they confess or not: it's simply another minute of the interview. Or secondly, they seek to gain an advantage from it. They believe they can either influence future processes or they can gain favour. Or thirdly, they think they'll feel better for having done so.'

Nathan snorted. 'Good for the soul, or something?'

Dana didn't consider herself an expert on what was good for the soul. Others decided that – seldom well, in her experience. No: confession was only good for the soul when the torment of *not* confessing was even greater. It was a judgement call; a balance. It was perfectly possible, she knew, to carry a guilty conscience for the rest of your life without it ever quite breaking you. The vice tightens every day; but you never quite snap. As Nathan had said earlier, *everything can be survived, if you go about it right.*

'Everyone's soul is different, Mr Whittler. I won't presume to know the state of yours. But didn't you run through this very scenario while you were sitting in your cell? That you'd be sitting in front of me, at this kind of moment?'

Nathan nodded. 'Yes, I did. Imagined it every which way. But now, when you actually ask me . . .' He ran to a halt and squeezed his hands together. A small bloom of blood pulsed against the bandage.

She gave him a minute. A long, silent minute where she made sure not to move a muscle. The only thing in motion was Nathan's mind: whirling and twisting, predicting consequence, mulling angles and options.

'I'm glad you understand what sort of person Jeb was,' he said, 'and what sort of home I grew up in. The iconography in the house, the threat; the dread in my anticipation of each day. I was permanently waiting for the dam to burst. I think – no, I'm *certain* – you understand that feeling, Detective. Am I wrong?'

Another response that could be given to defence counsel and thus to the world, but she couldn't avoid making it. Nathan needed the last little shove.

'You're entirely correct, Mr Whittler.'

'I've been considering and, hmm . . .' Nathan nodded to himself.

'And?'

'And I think that, now you understand why I ran and lived in a cave, you can understand why this morning happened. It might make sense now in a way it wouldn't have, earlier.'

It jolted her assumptions to learn that Nathan also had a plan. There had been polite inquiries she'd had to parry, there had been questions she'd answered to gain trust and find common ground, but she hadn't detected a strategy behind them. But apparently Nathan had prioritised and put the crucial information into a preferred sequence, just like she had. It was something she'd semi-comprehended, but hadn't truly appreciated. Not every reluctant answer, glance to the floor, hesitation or obfuscation was involuntary: some of it was conscious.

Nathan would confess now, because he was certain Dana could process and contextualise: she had the prerequisite data. *Clever*, she thought. *Clever Nathan.*

'I see. Well, I'm happy to talk about this, Mr Whittler. But I really must suggest to you once again to have a lawyer beside you at this time. We're about to discuss something that has profound legal implications for you. A lawyer would be able to advise you: I cannot. It's your own free choice, but that would be my advice at this point.'

'Uh, I've thought about that, too. No lawyers. I don't really trust them, to be honest. But more than that, I think what I have to say is fairly self-explanatory. So I don't really see how a lawyer would help. But thank you, Detective Russo. I appreciate that.'

'Very well. I'll try to keep my interventions to a minimum. In your own time, and in your own words, please, Mr Whittler.'

'Okay. So. I'd visited Jensen's plenty of times before. It's the nearest walkable store. It'll be in the journal, Detective, of course. But I hadn't been there for a while. I went recently at dusk – trying to see their process for the alarm. I hide in the undergrowth when I reconnaissance. The tree ferns, the mulberry: you can get within twenty metres of that store and no one has a clue you're there. It helps to watch them closing up, you see: you can infer what their alarm system is like.

'I was . . . well, surprised at what I saw, in that particular reconnaissance. Rattled. I thought about never returning there – placing it off limits. Perhaps it was too risky, perhaps the stakes had become too high because of those changes. Even though it was handy and I knew the layout, and it was all so convenient, by my standards. But I thought it through later; I believed I'd set it all in context and worked out how I was going to deal with things. At least, I thought I had.

'Since I'd scoped it out last, it seemed they'd added some security. A couple of the lights had changed on the corners, and I thought there might be motion detectors. But other than that I didn't know there'd been any changes.

'I've told you about the trick with the window locks. I'd picked a window right in the middle of that store front. I thought if any windows were going to be opened in daytime and then closed at night it would be the ones next to the coffee corner. They might open those. But the main ones at the front middle? Stores don't open those up. Flies, dust on the produce – that sort of thing. They usually like to keep them closed and crank up the air conditioning. Besides, this time of year they probably wouldn't be opening any windows much. So I was fairly happy that no one would have discovered the trick with the lock.

'It was my own fault I hadn't visited the place the previous week. I got caught in a rainstorm and I had a bit of a cold. I'm not feeble, Detective: I can live with a cold. But when you don't live in a building, colds go down to your chest. I had a wheezy cough for several days and I couldn't risk going out like that. Then I had to wait another couple of nights, because there was no cloud cover and it was a full moon. Out there, a full moon is practically daylight.

'So what I'm saying is; I never intended to be there this morning. If I'd gone when I'd intended, I'd never have . . . well, perhaps I wouldn't be here now. And if I'd known about what the owner . . . well, if I'd fully realised, then of course I would never have gone. I'd spent years being careful, avoiding . . . all that. I should have had more information, ought to have done it all the previous week. Just so you know. I was a little off my game. It was slightly outside my comfort zone. So maybe I wasn't at, you know, full capacity or something. Not enough, uh, *due diligence*, on my part.'

Dana had a picture: she thought it was accurate because it fitted everything she knew – *felt* – about Nathan. He would sit among dripping ferns for hours, peering through the fronds at Jensen's. Knowing that one mistake – one worker staying late, one missed camera – could bring his time in the cave to an end. And that would be crushing.

'I like Jensen's because they have so many things in wire baskets and bins. When it's displayed haphazardly like that, it's easier to acquire stock without anyone noticing. And they have a lot of batteries. Always well supplied with batteries.

'I like that store as well because I don't have to canoe down the lake to start the trip. Everything's more complicated with the canoe. At night, you can hit tree roots, and so on. You have to moor it some place you'll find it, but others won't. And going from the mooring through the woods takes you nearer to people, for longer. So Jensen's was a good store to go to generally, but not . . . then. Not recently. But I got there without a problem, about 4 a.m. or so. Dead of night. And I waited for an hour and nothing moved.

'Everything went okay at first. I threw a couple of small branches at the corner of the store. It was to test the lights: they might be motion-sensitive themselves, or they might have motion sensors for an alarm on them. If they're alarm sensors, you often get a tiny red-light flash for half a second. Alarm companies sometimes think that's not a problem but in total darkness you can see that quite easily. Nothing. The branches, if anyone found them, would look like debris from the wind. Which they were – I picked them up off the forest floor, so they had the right kind of natural break at the base, and so on. No one would know the security had been tested.

'Because I'd checked in my journal, I knew where the electrics box was – under the eaves by the side door. It has one of those Allen-key locks: I had the right tool and in a few seconds I'd switched off the electrics. Alarms have back-up batteries, but often people don't replace dud ones. I intended to switch the electric back on when I left: everyone's used to minor outages these days and I'm sure it never feels suspicious. I waited another minute in the shadows to be sure the coast was clear.

'I opened the window and went back to the bushes and watched. But I couldn't see any movement inside. I gave it a few minutes and then climbed in. So far, so easy, Detective: plastic bags on my boots, and the windowsill. I started filling the rucksack. They'd moved some things since my last visit and I started going up and down aisles, trying to find what I wanted. It was a bit of a pain, so I set the rucksack down near the window and walked along the aisles. I knew the cameras were on the main checkout, and the storage room; the aisles weren't on film.

'As I put some toothpaste in my pocket I thought I heard a noise. The window was still open, and sound carries in the forest. It might have been something out in the woods. I stood and waited. I'd about convinced myself I was imagining it, when I heard it again. A little squeak, like someone's shoe on the flooring.'

Nathan was staring at the middle distance: a spot in the air between his knee and the wall. Dana couldn't have sworn that Nathan even knew she was there at that moment. He was back in the darkness of the store, gathering for winter and about to make the decisions that would change his life for ever.

'My first mistake, as I've said, was not enough reconnaissance. I should have known more about, well, the changes at the store. I should have been better prepared. My fault, my responsibility, I know. But my second mistake was right then. The moment I heard the squeak I should have grabbed my rucksack and run. I might have done it. If I'd made it into the undergrowth, I'd be difficult to find at night. I move quite well in that terrain. I should have gone through the window and away.

'But I didn't, Detective. Fool that I was, I stood in the darkness and waited to hear it again. Strange how we do that – con ourselves that we haven't heard or seen something. Then we expect to see or hear the exact same thing again, for verification. When we know, in our instinctive selves, that we don't need to. We don't trust ourselves and our capabilities – we keep looking for something else as a double-check.

'So I stood and waited. It was very dark, Detective. There was a glimmer of orange light from the main road but it was several hundred metres away. All it gave was the vague outline of silhouettes: it didn't actually illuminate anything. I had a torch, but of course now I couldn't use it again without giving my position away. I heard the squeak again. It might have been a rodent outside. Or the refrigerator – they make quite a lot of noise, the older ones. But something told me it was a person.

'It was only the second time I'd been caught with someone else in the store I'm visiting. The other time, I'd hidden until I could leave unseen. I'm very careful, Detective. I didn't want any trouble. I wanted to be in and out, unhindered. But since I was sure no one knew I was even in these places, it had never occurred to me that someone might be hiding in the store for precisely this moment. I mean, why would they? Why hide in a store when you have no idea you've been burgled, in case you get burgled again?

'If only I'd known more about Jensen's Store, of course. If I'd done more surveillance I would have understood more about what was going on in that store. I'd never have gone near it if I'd known.'

The self-recrimination brought him to a halt. At first, Dana assumed he was simply collecting himself, gathering. But he sat back with his eyes closed and she began to worry that he might clam up just as he reached the decisive moment.

'Mr Whittler, are you okay?'

He shook his head slowly, as if he had a migraine and couldn't bear to move. He kept his eyes shut.

'This is very difficult, Detective. I was . . . I was ashamed of the stealing, as you know. It was humiliating. But this . . . this is on a different level. This is . . . just awful. What played out.'

She thought about what might get him over the line.

'Mr Whittler, what took place in the store this morning has happened. It's done. Neither you nor I can do anything to change what has occurred. It will not magically get worse – or better – for you telling about it. Your words can't change anything inside that store. But they can change your future.'

She glanced at him for her own reassurance. He gave her nothing.

'Your words, Mr Whittler: they can change what life you lead and how you feel about it. Your life is about to swing away from the cave, from your solitude. I'm sorry about that. But it's vital for you – for your wellbeing – that you make some effort to control your new direction.'

Dana thought she'd blown it. She thought it was too pompous, too portentous. He seemed to sit and hum to himself for a minute, while the tape spooled on. His eyes danced behind his eyelids and it came to her that he might be running through the memory of those events. Perhaps he was, even now at this late stage, picking and choosing: charting an explanation that would fit the evidence, yet exonerate him. Or perhaps, he was summoning courage.

'So I was there, Detective. In Jensen's, with a man who shouldn't have been there at all. Shouldn't have been anywhere near. I was in it, and I had a problem. I had no idea where he was, but if he'd been hiding and watching he'd know from my earlier torchlight where I'd been. I couldn't be far from the last spot before I turned off the torch. He knew for sure: I knew nothing for certain. He had the drop on me.

'What I wanted was to get back to the window. My eyes started to adjust and I could see – down the aisle – the vague outline of the window. There seemed nothing between me and it. But I thought he'd realise that: that the window was my only way out, and that if he stayed near it I was trapped. I figured he'd be smart enough to get that. I tried circling around the back of the store so I could check which aisle he was hiding in.

'Twice, I bumped into something. It really was that dark. I didn't make much noise, but enough to tell him I was well away from the window. I couldn't see where I was going, and he had me pinned. He didn't have to go anywhere, or make a sound, or bump into anything. The day would only get lighter. If he had to stay like that for three hours, he could. I needed to get out now, or I was caught.

'So I was surprised when he did move. Just a little, from the end of one aisle to the end of another. I suppose he wanted to be as close as possible to the window, but still hidden. I happened to be crossing another aisle and caught his outline for a second.'

Nathan paused, swallowed.

'His silhouette against dark grey. It sent a shudder, Detective. As you can imagine, a hot shudder. My insides did the same nauseous flip they always did.

'I waited. He waited. I don't know how long. But the light was beginning to change. Still darkness, but behind me and towards him it was starting to look dark purple instead of jet black. He clearly wasn't moving. It was up to me.

'I made a decision. I would need a weapon of some kind. I never carried anything like that, Detective. The very idea – repulsive. So I had nothing on me. I was finger-searching the shelves, trying to find something without tipping everything over. Not that it would have mattered, now that I think about it. I'd have been better off using the torch. But I didn't: not at that point.

'The inevitable happened and I knocked some packets of something on to the floor. They landed with a dull kind of thud. Sugar or flour, or something like that. And he laughed. He actually laughed. My plight was funny. He found my distress funny. I shuddered again. And something in me switched. Old, familiar feelings; a fear I'd hidden away was resurfacing. I'd thought I was past it, but instead it started to cloud my judgement.

'Now, I was going to use the torch. It was stupid to fumble around in the darkness. He knew I was here, knew where I was and where I needed to go. Suddenly, I wasn't prepared to take it any more. I wasn't going to have my life torn off me again, Detective. It wasn't fair the first time, and it wouldn't be fair now. I wanted to be left alone, and now I wouldn't be. It would be like it was before; like the thing I'd run from; like the thing I couldn't take.

'I flicked on the torch and found a set of kitchen knives. I could open the packet with my gloves on; it wasn't too fiddly. I tore open the packaging and got a knife in my grip. The middle one, naturally. I felt a bit more in control, then; proactive. Then, torch off.

'I don't know that I felt any braver, Detective, but I felt a little more decisive. Adrenaline, probably. I imagined that I could actually come out even from the encounter. He might back off if he knew I was waving this thing around. He might think me a danger, especially if I was behaving as wildly and desperately as I felt. He could, I hoped, step back and consider I wasn't worth the hassle. Part of me knew that would never happen, but all the same. Sometimes, you hope, don't you?

'I didn't think it was worth delaying. It would start getting light, and I felt this adrenaline might be the only advantage I had. I wasn't going to win a fair fight, Detective, I already knew that. I never could.

But I had the knife, and maybe he had nothing. Perhaps he thought he could swat me away, deal with me through fear and surprise. So I called out. Said I only wanted to get out through the window and I'd never come back. And I had a knife.

'He chuckled. A low, back-of-the-throat chuckle. Like he'd seen something quirky at the end of the news – something like that. He wasn't scared: I wasn't intimidating him. Of course I wasn't. In my heart of hearts, I already knew that. In fact, it probably made him come and get me.

'Suddenly I could hear steps. Tentative at first, then stronger. I was fumbling for the torch – I thought I might blind him with the beam and be able to get past. I saw his silhouette flash past the window. It terrified me. I thought, this is it – this is my chance, now he's moved. I knew roughly where the window was: I could make out the edges of the glass now. Dawn was coming.

'I don't know how he did it, Detective. How he knew where I was. If he did. Maybe he was as shocked as me. But we collided. I felt our chests hit. I felt a flicker of his hand, or his finger, brush my face. He was that close: he was in front. Now he knew where I was, I had no chance of escaping. It was over. Everything was over. Fifteen years, and my life was falling away again. All the life I built; it went to pieces in three seconds – the time it took for him to bump me, reach out for me. And for the knife to go in.

'I had no idea, Detective. No real idea. I knew he was near and in front, but he might've backed off and been two metres away. I held the knife tight and shoved it into the darkness. Just wanted him to go away, or maybe get hurt enough to back off. I didn't know I'd struck anything until I felt my knuckle against his clothing. Maybe the gloves . . . it'd gone in so clean, so fast, so sharp. I never would have believed it. The knife was jammed into him, and it went through like I was stabbing water.

'He tipped towards me and we sort of tumbled over. I got him to the ground, on his back, I think. Something fell on the floor. So I groped around his chest, trying for the knife. He didn't make a sound. Nothing . . . then there was a light on my face.'

Nathan stopped. Red-faced, sweating, his hands cupped, and shivering in the warmth of the room. He shook his head while Dana sat silently.

'Why did he have to be there, Detective? Why did he have to be there?'

The room felt heavy; the air refused to budge. Dana tried to control her breathing, tried to think. What she asked now would be crucial at trial; she couldn't afford to blow any holes in the case. She needed to ask questions that clarified, gave Nathan no way to back down from this confession.

And yet her internal radar was firing to wake the dead. Something in the back of her mind was screaming. She thought it might be her own imminent nervous collapse, chiming through at exactly the wrong moment. But no, it was worse than that. So much worse.

She thought back to what Nathan had said earlier in the interview: about his confession needing context. She'd taken it at face value – that she needed to know what sort of person he was, the privations that had shaped him, the way he'd built a life in solitude, his fear of return. All of that. All of that would shape her feelings about why he'd killed.

But perhaps she'd been wrong.

Something tiny, a seed of an idea, took root in the recesses of Dana's mind. It began to move, slipping forward and then finding momentum. Faster, closer, gaining credence, accelerating: it gathered and pushed and then exploded into her consciousness. She frowned. It wasn't, couldn't be.

Yes.

Yes, it was.

Monstrous and grotesque but, quite suddenly, she was certain she was right. Never more certain in her life.

She'd been stupid. Colossally, unforgivably stupid. It was entirely her own fault. She'd stopped seeing Lou Cassavette. She'd committed the cardinal sin of ceasing to really see him. He was a victim and a human being, with all the complexities that implied. But instead of truly observing that, she'd turned him into data. He'd become instead the focal point on a whiteboard diagram; a name; a set of bank accounts and telephone records; a husband to a faithless wife; a failing businessman; someone who'd married up.

Lou Cassavette had saved her life this morning, by dying. This is how she'd repaid him.

In all that information, she'd forgotten – or never bothered – to take a really good look at Lou Cassavette. Her glance at the scene, lifting the sheet while the 'twins' held the stretcher, had been cursory. Unprofessional. Dumb.

In the darkness, in silhouette, in desperation, in the shadow of fifteen years of solitary brooding: Lou Cassavette would look exactly like Jeb Whittler.

Nathan believed he'd killed his brother. He still believed it now.

She hesitated, unsure how to approach it. The confession was fine – it was detailed, it was coherent; it tallied with all the forensics she'd seen and all the things they already knew. It would stand up. There was no doubting that Nathan had done it. Except, he didn't quite know what he'd done. He thought it was fratricide.

'What happened when the officers discovered you, Mr Whittler? Can you tell me in exact detail, please.'

Nathan looked perplexed. Presumably he was expecting follow-up about the killing, not its aftermath. Perhaps, she thought, he was wondering why she was being so pedantic about the actions of the officers.

'Uh, their torchlight was in my face. Totally blinding, Detective, after all that darkness. All I could see was white, and green blotches. I fell back a little, away from his body. Their torches bobbed and I realised they were coming towards me. They grabbed my arms and dragged me on my backside around the corner to the next aisle. Then I was on my stomach and handcuffed behind my back.

'I was having trouble breathing. The after-effects, I suppose, but I was wheezing. One of the officers leaned in and asked if I was okay. I nodded, and I think his torch was near enough that he understood. The other officer had stepped away somewhere and was talking into his radio. They'd need "everyone", I think he said. And he started talking about forensics, and searches, and detectives. But I was tuning it out, to be honest. I think I was in shock, and all I could hear was a rushing sound, like being under a waterfall. Everything looked and felt artificial, untouchable; happening to someone else. I was bewildered, and hurt, and appalled.'

Nathan stopped, as though unsure Dana would still believe him, or still respect him, if he went ahead with his next statement.

'And relieved, Detective. Relieved he was gone. At last. I'd forgotten to be worried about him, out in the cave. Took a while, but I'd learned to tune him out entirely. That was where the real peace came from, Detective, the real serenity. Knowing that if I remained careful, Jeb would never find me. Knowing I'd got away, and I'd never have to face him. I thought, if he was finally gone, then maybe my parents would be pleased, too. Maybe they'd forgive my weakness for all those years. But at least I'd never have to worry about Jeb again. When I'd spied him at Jensen's a few weeks ago, walking to his car, I'd been rattled, I admit. The memories came flooding back and I'd considered never going there again. Just for the peace of mind that would bring. But then, later, that struck me as stupid. He was just shopping, surely, just in the neighbourhood. It never occurred to me he'd bought the store, let alone that he'd be there in the night. Sheer chance, but I'd found him. And ended it. At least I'd ended it. And for that, I was relieved.'

Dana put down her pen. Deep breaths wouldn't come. Her pulse was too skittish, and this mattered too much.

'Mr Whittler, I need you to look straight at me, please. I need you to understand this.'

He struggled. He tried once and couldn't do it. He swallowed and collected himself, and at the second time of asking he could look her in the eye.

'Mr Whittler, Jeb was not at that store. I met him fifteen minutes ago. The man you killed was not Jeb. It was Lou Cassavette, the store owner.'

Nathan was shaking his head.

'No, no. It was definitely Jeb. I'd know, Detective. I'd know him anywhere. My own brother. It was him. You've . . . there's a mistake. You must have made a mistake.'

'I'm afraid not. Your brother is alive and well, and was at this station until a few minutes ago. Mr Lou Cassavette is in the morgue.'

Dana would never forget that scream. She'd hear it in the night for years; echoes of it ripping through her mind. It sounded like her own pain. It tore itself from Nathan's body, primeval and bereft. She couldn't bear to look and turned away, reluctant to face the mirror as Nathan howled into his hands. She lifted a hand to the observers to warn them all to keep out. Nathan needed his terror, his shame, to remain between them.

She waited him out. She sat silently through his tears, through his scratching at his own face until it bled, through his shaking. She waited it all out. Because while he didn't need a witness, he still needed a human being there for . . . validation. She could do that, and did.

After perhaps twenty minutes Nathan was empty to the core. She reached forward and, for the first time that day, touched his skin. Her fingers rested lightly on his forearm as he wept into his sleeve. He looked up and blinked.

'I'm so sorry, Mr Whittler. I understand; I get why you mistook one for the other. In darkness, I'd have done the same. I understand: the jury will, too.'

She flushed at how unprofessional that was; but how necessary. She'd ride it out with Bill if she needed to. Nathan had to have something to hold on to. It might save his life.

She stood wearily. She must get out now. Not only from this room but from the station. From people. The Day was closing her throat.

As she opened the door Nathan called out to her.

'Detective?'

She turned. He was wiping his eyes with a fist.

'Thank you for, for helping me through this. For your compassion. Thank you, Dana.'

Her own name had never pierced her like that. She could barely push out an answer ahead of a sob.

'You're welcome, Nathan.'

Chapter 35

No one entered the women's bathroom after her. Lucy, she assumed, had gone home before the confession. Neither Mike nor Bill came in to check on her. Dana took two hits from the nebuliser then wiped her face with a tissue. Even by her standards, she felt she looked awful. The Day, and the events, had dragged life from her and left a shattered, sallow figure in its place.

Now the adrenaline surge from the confession was ebbing from her, fear and anxiety took over. In some ways, it felt the same: a rising heartbeat, restless movements from her eyes, a frantic need to rush and finish anything and everything at once. But the adrenal boost was a positive thing – it was a wish to achieve, a desire to complete. Whereas what was infecting her thoughts right now was relentlessly, almost comfortingly, negative – a need to avoid, a wish to hide, a craving to run.

She could hear their low mutter of conversation outside the door. She took a deep breath: better to get this done as fast as possible and get the hell out. Checking her watch, Dana noted there were twenty minutes before Father Timms expected her text. She wanted to keep that appointment. The corridor felt brighter, less claustrophobic.

'Hey. Is that everything you need today, boss?' She tried to sound perky and upbeat but the sentence lacked conviction.

'More than enough, more than enough. And twelve hours to spare before the lawyers get to him. Whittler's back in the Lecter Theatre; doc's going to give him a fairly hefty sedative. He seemed remarkably calm when we walked him back' – Bill looked to Mike, who nodded in agreement – 'so hopefully he'll be better tomorrow.'

Dana leaned against the wall. 'Okay. Maybe confession was good for the soul, after all.' She paused. It was, surely, the opposite of what she'd always believed. 'Sorry about that last bit, Bill. The jury'll hear that.'

The lead detective's assertion that mistaking one person for another was 'entirely understandable' was rash, to say the least. It was fodder for a downgrade of the charges and ammunition for clemency requests. A defence lawyer would suggest it was further evidence the death was partly accidental, akin to a bar fight where someone gets concussed in a fall. They'd spin it as the police having known that all along, and trying to push Nathan. She'd said it from basic decency. She wouldn't blame Bill if he was livid.

Bill raised a hand. 'Not a problem. In the context of the whole set of interviews, it's another piece of rapport. Works in our favour in some ways – someone as obviously concerned for his welfare is less likely to be seen as applying undue pressure. It's fine.'

She was unconvinced. There would be fallout, she didn't doubt that, but she also knew Bill would stand foursquare behind her.

Dana understood how Nathan could mistake Lou for Jeb in the dark, amid his rising panic. He would have been jolted badly by having seen Jeb a few weeks before – the first sighting in fifteen years, and a brutal recoil back to the darkest days and the insulin. But she hadn't had time to process why Nathan hadn't become aware of who was dead. Surely there had been some point where someone had mentioned Lou?

'He didn't know it was Lou,' she pointed out. 'I don't mean at the time; I mean all day. How is that possible?'

Bill shrugged. 'Well, Whittler never saw the body in daylight, or any light. He was dragged away in absolute darkness and held in the next aisle. He would have been put in the patrol car by uniform long before daylight, and they only turned on the store lights after they were sure Lou was dead – they needed to switch on the electric supply first. By then, the scene was filling up with people and Whittler was hunkered down in a car with tinted windows, and no direct view inside the store. Those guys never talk when they're bringing suspects in, except to tell them to shut up. So no, he wouldn't have known who he stabbed.'

Mike chimed in. 'Yeah, and since he was never charged until now, except for the burglaries, we probably never spoke the name Lou Cassavette in front of him. We weren't going to quiz him about the stabbing until we had enough ammunition. Don't forget, we were building up to that final discussion all day. Whittler was so sure – and ashamed – that he'd killed Jeb that he never questioned us about who he killed. So no, he'd have no way of knowing. But it never actually occurred to me that he *didn't* know.'

It made a crude kind of sense. Nathan had been focused on directing the discussion his way, giving Dana the background to understand why he'd killed. That kind of approach also precluded talking about the stabbing until the latest possible point. In fact, both Dana and Nathan had been working on the same strategy – for different reasons – without the other realising it. Both schemes precluded mentioning Lou Cassavette until the final moments.

Dana could feel the last of her energy slipping away.

Mike opened his arms and they hugged. She was crap at hugging; her arms hung around in the littoral next to Mike's shape, never quite getting there. Bill shook his head, as though he never expected her to get better at it.

Bill tilted his head. 'Now go home, sleep long, and we'll sort out the details in the morning.'

She nodded wearily and sloped off.

Passing reception, she wished Miriam goodnight. The lights were dimmed for the evening; Miriam's glasses reflected the fidgeting blue screensaver as she read her paperback and waved absent-mindedly. Dana had hoped there would be a message from Lucy, but there was nothing.

As the reception doors swooshed open she felt a blast of cold air. It was a relief to her skin, if not her psyche.

Her shoes clacked on the pavement as she ducked down a long path known as Deadman's Alley. It was the quickest route between work and home: the alley where, decades ago, they used to store bodies before cremation. The remains of the original Carlton ice house and morgue were now a mound of temporary seating overlooking the sports oval. In summer, cicadas screeched all evening along here; now, it was silent.

The cold made her fingers tingle. She started to feel less stooped and less drained with every step away from people and towards the sanctuary of home. Poor Nathan, she thought: *his* sanctuary is no more, and he lost it all without even ridding himself of Jeb. And poor Lou Cassavette: simply trying to protect his failing investment.

It shook her that she still thought about Nathan far more than she did about Lou. It remained the Whittler case to her, not the Cassavette case. Thinking more about the killer than the victim was surely the act of a callous, selfish person. She had no doubt about that at all.

Home was a narrow terrace of clapboard, in sharp relief under the streetlight she'd paid the council to have right outside. A *gunshot house*, they used to call them; the corridor and stairs ran the length of one side of the home, each room off it to the right. Once inside, she snapped all the door locks and did a sweep of the ground floor by torchlight. Reminded by Nathan's explanation of the window-lock routine, she tested every one on the ground floor.

Only then did she put her gun away in the lockable metal cupboard, take off her coat and turn on a light. She switched on the kettle and texted Father Timms.

Home. Got a confession from the suspect. Thank you.

The answer came in seconds; she'd seen Timms' ham-fisted, chubby-fingered efforts at texting and was surprised by his speed.

Call if you feel you need to. Or should. Stay safe.

The clock said there were six and a half hours of the Day left. She wondered if this feeling of exhaustion would help her through it: perhaps she'd quickly fall asleep and drift through to morning. Or maybe her mind would push through the tiredness: drag her to a new place where she was too fatigued to think straight. She'd never done the Day this way: it worried her that she had no knowledge to draw upon.

Home was the counterpoint; the place where she didn't have to work, in any sense. Here, she could simply be; without constantly having to intuit what people were thinking, what they meant behind what they said, what effect she was having on them. People were continually, relentlessly exhausting. Home was where none of that had to matter.

It hadn't always been this way; in fact, until she was an adult the reverse had applied. School, the library, outdoors – anywhere was safer, easier and less chilling than home. The library was the place where the books were, and her mother wasn't: that was the point and the appeal of it. It was when her childhood self stepped through the front door of the house that her fears began to solidify, when the pit of her stomach twisted and her legs buckled. It had taken her until the age of twenty-five to begin inverting her life – until then, the mere sight of home could make her choke on thin air.

She'd set the tea by the side of her chair when the telephone rang. She frowned. About six people knew her mobile number; maybe three knew her landline. She half hoped it was some hapless telesales person she could rip into without conscience.

'Hello?'

'It's Luce. Hope you don't mind. This a bad time?'

Lucy had a honeyed tone down a landline. Like a long-loved radio voice, it sounded different to how the speaker looked. She sounded velvet and gold.

'Uh, no. No, that's fine.' Dana was flustered. Lucy wasn't quite inside her home, but was – sort of. It was a strange sensation that she'd never expected to face. 'Did you hear we got Nathan for it?'

'Yeah, Mikey sent me an email.' There was a clatter, as if Lucy was moving around in a kitchen. 'Mistook him for Jeb?'

Dana sank into her armchair but sat rigidly forward, a polite guest in her own house. 'Apparently so. Nathan had seen Jeb briefly a couple of weeks before, so he was in the front of Nathan's mind. Lou and Jeb had an identical silhouette: baldness, the bulk, the shoulders, the shape of the head. I remember now – Rainer said someone had called them "two peas in a pod".'

'Plus, he'd been fixating on Jeb for fifteen years in that cave. Anyone who looked quite like Jeb was going to *be* Jeb, in his eyes.'

That was a good point, Dana thought. Nathan hadn't seen Jeb for a decade and a half; then a brief glimpse from a distance a few weeks ago. He'd still have been guessing a little at how Jeb had aged. Anyone with a pretty good similarity and a shiny bald head might be moulded by Nathan's mind into an older Jeb. Plus, the feeling of being trapped – of having your future controlled by someone else – would have come flooding back in the store. It was the feeling Jeb had engendered for years at home: then a sinister muscle-memory in the dark for Nathan, shaping his other senses accordingly.

'Look, I wanted to apologise.'

Dana was perplexed. 'What for?'

'For bailing on you, just near the end. I felt like I left the team to finish the job. Sorry 'bout that.'

There was something beyond her apology, but Dana couldn't work out what it was. 'No need, Luce. I know you're, uh, pretty prompt. No need to be sorry about it.'

Another clatter and the ping of a microwave. Dana strained to imagine the setting: maybe a one-bed apartment with clean, straight lines, or perhaps a cottage with sloping ceilings and wide floorboards. She had no source material to work with.

'It's just' – Lucy paused – 'that I could see you were getting pretty anxious. Not about Whittler – you were always going to get your man there. I mean generally. What it took from you today. I mean. Ah, crap. I mean *specifically* today.'

'Don't get you, Luce.' Dana had grabbed the arm of the chair with her free hand, her knuckles white.

'It's probably nothing, but . . . I'm one of those sad sacks that keeps a diary. Well, a journal, really. I flick back to what I was doing the same day last year, and so on. Trying to spot some progress in my life. Anyway, I'd noticed that the last two years you've been very adamant about having this day off. This exact day. So I thought maybe you found it tough working on this day. And then when we spoke – in the bathroom? I could tell you didn't want to talk about it much, but . . .'

A silence caused by Dana fighting back a tear.

'Ah, sorry,' Lucy continued above the clack of spoon on saucepan. 'None of my business, I know. I dunno. Thought that's what it was.'

'No, no, you're right.' Dana had her hand raised in placation, irrespective of Lucy's ability to see it. 'Yes, it's a weird kind of commemoration.'

There was no more extraneous noise from Lucy's end. Whatever she'd been doing, she'd stopped.

'You don't have to—'

'No, let me, Luce. I have to. Want to.'

'Okay.'

This time Dana did sink back in the chair, felt it settle about her shoulders. She focused on the strips of light spearing through a louvre blind on to the carpet.

'Most of today, one way or another, I've been talking with Nathan about family. It kept coming up. I mean, each time I thought I was talking about something else we ended up mentioning our mother or father, or his brother. Always, back to family.'

'Yeah, sometimes it feels like the world is going to fixate on a topic, no matter what you do.'

'Exactly. And it was a quandary. Because, as I kept telling Nathan, everything I said in those interviews goes to defence counsel. They can discuss it in open court, they can quiz me on it. It was deeply personal. Deeply. I don't want that sort of stuff in the public domain. And it might undermine the case – if I'm that sympathetic, did I really believe he'd done it? Did I con him into confessing by being his pal? Don't I think it's manslaughter, a mistake in the dark? I ended up saying that at the end, as it turns out. But all day, I kept trying to steer him away from my family.'

Dana switched off the table lamp. The only light was the muted orange shards spearing in through the louvres.

'But?'

'But I needed to have a rapport with him. It would be what undid him, convince him to tell. And it did. But there was this *quid pro quo* all day: I had to give, to get. He knew it; I knew it. So I spent half the time talking about things that I normally keep stuffed away in a safe place.'

A safe place so buried that skilled professionals could get nowhere near it; but which held its own weight, its own gravity, within her.

'And today, of all days,' asked Lucy, 'it was especially raw? That's a heap of bad luck at once.'

'Tell me about it. Bloody kid of Mikey's – if not for him, I might have been secondary and not lead.'

Lucy laughed. 'Yeah, little bugger had eaten two tubs of ice cream in the night. Not appendicitis after all, just gluttony.'

'Is that what it was? Crap. And God, I didn't even ask Mikey about it. Bill nagged me and I still wiped it. Bad Dana.'

Lucy was silent. Then:

'So today's date is special because . . . ?'

Her gentle way of pulling Dana back on track. Dana liked being led this way, by this person. Her grip on the arm of the chair relaxed without her realising.

'Like I said before, it's an anniversary. Two, in fact. They're twenty years apart but totally connected. I struggle to deal with . . . ah, not explaining myself very well. Sorry, Luce. I need to— Jesus. I've explained this to I don't know how many shrinks and counsellors: I should be word perfect by now.'

There was a moment before Lucy replied.

'No need to be word perfect. Take the pressure off. Just say how it started.'

'You're right. Okay.' Deep breath. 'So, we lived near Carlton when I was a little kid. My mother worked at the church – St Vincent's, a short way down the road from here. Dad was a road engineer for the council. My mother' – another deep breath – 'didn't like that I was an only child. She had this vision of . . . I don't know, of a brood. Of a clutch of little kids trailing after her like ducklings, raised on her religion and absorbing her version of wisdom. I spoiled it – came out being strangled by the umbilical. The damage . . . well, she couldn't have any more, and that was my fault.'

'She sounds charming,' said Lucy drily.

'You haven't heard the half of it. I'll spare you years of detail. So we lived out of Carlton, on the Gazette road. Near the abattoir – you could smell the stench in a westerly. I don't think Dad liked it, but my mother seemed to think it reminded us all of mortality. Which was apparently a good thing.'

Dana could hear the edge in her voice and tried to rein it in.

'My dad had heart problems all his life. From before I was born, in fact.' She gave a watery smile to the darkness as she recalled his face. 'Anyway, as far back as I could remember, he had to have his heart pills nearby. He used to tap his pocket without even thinking, to double-check. It was a reflex. Like me with those nebulisers, I suppose.'

She wondered if Lucy had even noticed that. The silence suggested she had.

'So, one day my mother had gone to the church for organ practice – a new hymn the preacher wanted to introduce.' Dana could still feel the way her shoulder blades eased when she heard her mother's car backing out on to the road. The clunk-scrape as it cleared the gutter; the slight squeal as it pulled away. She could recall that day now; rippling shadows as she ran around the tree, blowing soap bubbles that nestled on her arm.

'She and Dad had been arguing about making me a treehouse. I was only eight. We had an old poinciana at the bottom of the garden: must have been twenty years old, even then. Wizened, crooked; a pair of sagging branches that looked like helping hands, cupping you into the foliage – it looked like the trees in children's books, the ones that kick-started an adventure. It was deep summer – that explosion of crimson that poincianas do: delicate shade, fallen blossom on the grass like a field of poppies. Dad wanted to build a small treehouse for me, but Mother said it was an indulgence – I'd grow out of it soon enough and I wasn't to be encouraged. Those were her exact words.'

The resentment billowed again, like smoke from a petrol fire. The rising fear in her throat made her stop for a second. Dana looked around anxiously for a nebuliser, fearing another attack exactly when she needed to be composed. Gulps of air somehow helped.

'Sorry. Bit panicky.'

'I can tell. All good. Take whatever time you need.'

'With Mother out for a while, Dad winked at me and pulled some wood out from behind the shed. He must have reckoned on getting so far into it before she returned, she'd have to go along with it. So he started sawing, and hammering, and measuring. I was the little girl holding the nails and clapping occasionally.'

Dana could no longer tell for sure what was memory and what was reading reports, listening to neighbours, and her own dreaming. Decades of overthinking had melted ideas, memories, notions; second-hand views and second-rate psychiatry. But she sensed once again the sun on her skin, the muscles in her face as she smiled, the buzz of insects and a distant harvester.

'It's hellish hot. I know that now, but I didn't really notice at the time, because I'm sitting in the shade and not working. There's no air, no breeze. Suddenly, Dad drops to his knees and on to his side. He's lying on those scarlet blossoms, clutching his shoulder. I think he's hurt his arm, because that's what he's looking at. Except he isn't: he's looking for his pills. The heart pills. He croaks at me to get his pills. By his bed, in the brown bottle.

'I run. I probably wasn't quick but it felt like I ran like the wind. Up the stairs, into their room. I know which side of the bed is his and I grab the bottle. I'm on my way down the stairs, daring to take them two at a time, when it hits me.

Dad needs some water.

'I stop at the bottom of the stairs. Maybe I can – but no, he always takes them with a glass of water. I've come to believe that the water is part of the pills; that they can't work without it. He'll be angry if I only take out the pills. He's hurting; he needs his little girl to bring the water so the pills will work.

'I go to the kitchen and drag a chair to the bench. Up on to the bench, on my knees. I swing open the cupboard and take a tumbler. Crawl across to the tap and fill the glass, pretty full. I climb down on to the chair and then to the floor. Put the tablets into the pocket on the front of my dress. I need both hands for the water. Can't drop it.

'When I come outside again the sunlight hurts my eyes. The heat smacks me. I start down the path, as fast as I can without dropping any. He needs the pills *and* the water. I know this.

'As I get near him I can see Mother bent over him. She's screaming his name, over and over. I'm right next to her before she notices. Her hair is over her face, her eyes are wet. She's . . . angry. Angry and desperate.

' "His pills!" she shouts. "His pills!" I'm shaking now. I hold out the water to her and she gets this strange look. She knocks the glass away into the bushes. "Where are the pills?" she screams.

'I take them out of my pocket. She snatches them off me. She pours some of them straight into his throat. I don't understand. That won't work, I want to say. But something about her makes me shut up. Now she's shaking him. Slapping him. Screaming again.

'When she lets go of him he falls back, hard, on to the patio. His head bounces. I can still hear it – the big thud, and the little secondary one. She looks at me and, eight as I am, it feels . . . terrifying. I take a step back, wanting to run but scared she'll catch me. She's a monster now. I can't stop shaking. She wants to know why I didn't bring the pills quicker, why I didn't run.

'I whisper: *Because he has to take them with water.*

'She looks down, and everything is very, very quiet. When she looks up, Mother's eyes are narrow, like a cat's.

' "You killed him," she says to me. "You scheming, evil little bitch." She dropped her voice, I could barely hear it. "You . . . *Jezebel.* Child of the devil. Murderer." '

There was silence at the other end. Dana snapped herself back from twenty-five years ago and wondered if the phone was dead, if Lucy had run, if . . . she had no idea what.

'Jesus Christ, Dana. I'm so sorry. That's . . . I don't even know what that is. You've carried that for so long.'

Lucy struck a nerve with the one word. *Carried*. It was exactly that; a burden Dana could never shake, a perpetual weight permeating everything she said, or did, or thought. Everything, poisoned by her mother's words. All that came after was caused by that moment. Everything she did or didn't do, tried or failed, was or could never be: rooted in those few seconds of summer.

Her hand was shaking, her vision beginning to swim.

'Carried? Yes, yes, that's . . . that's part of the battle, Luce. That's how my life changed. When you're eight and your father dies, you think your life's over. But everything was just beginning. My mother went from anger to cold brutality – like that switch was always there, within her. It all got . . . it got really dark, brutal.

'I could never doubt that she blamed me. She wanted a reason for Dad's death, and she wanted that reason to be me. She needed it to be me. And she needed me to have something *wrong*. Something hideous inside me, but somehow fixable if she pushed her own warped faith far enough. That way, she would have some control of consequence: as if she couldn't be a victim herself, if she created one in me. The physical abuse, the mental torture, the emotional iciness: she kept trying to exorcise a demon in me that wasn't there.

'It took me years to escape it; to physically get out of there. Because the people I should have been able to run to; they turned away, or gave up, or – incredible to me – indulged her and helped her. That thing they say to kids in trouble – *tell someone*. Well, I did, and it just got worse. Because young kids don't always know who they can trust, so they guess. I guessed wrong: oh, so wrong.

'The Day just brings it all screaming back. I bluff through every

Day: have done for years. I kid myself I'm managing it, but really I'm hanging by my fingertips. Working a murder on this Day? It's too much, it's a tidal wave. Turns out, I should have stood down.

'The second anniversary I mentioned? That was twenty years later. Twenty, to the day. That was . . . Jesus, I can't talk about it, Luce. Not now. It was worse. Much worse than the first anniversary. Much worse. Terrible. Sorry.'

Dana was about to choke; to howl like Nathan.

'I . . . I have to go, Luce. Thanks. For calling. Listening. Thanks.' She wanted to throw the phone down, but couldn't.

'Thank you for telling me. I, uh, I feel very close to you tonight, Dana. Sleep tight.'

It was so intimate, so quietly powerful, it cut through Dana totally.

'G'night, Luce.'

'Night.'

The phone found its cradle at the third attempt. She hadn't talked about it all for maybe four years – Father Timms had been the last to hear it. She understood saying it out loud gave it a new resonance, an echo bouncing back and shimmering through her.

She'd told Nathan, effectively, that he should confess because it was good for his conscience, and because it gave him some semblance of control over his future. It had worked; Nathan had seen the sense in it.

Dana didn't. It was a monstrous lie.

She glanced at the clock. Six hours and twelve minutes of the Day to go.

Dana didn't think she was going to make it.